The Ship in the Sand

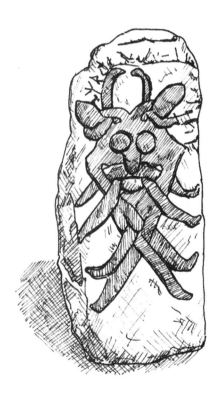

Published by the Navillus Press
1958 Onyx Street
Eugene, Oregon 97403

www.oregonhiking.com

Front cover and spine: Viking Age chess pieces in the British Museum. *Back cover and frontispiece:* Stone carving at the Moesgaard Viking Museum in Århus, Denmark. *Back cover:* The Oseberg ship at the Vikingskipsmuseet in Oslo, Norway.

This book is a work of fiction. Significant historical personages in this book (English kings, Viking leaders, Danish celebrities, Hollywood stars, and the like) are based on actual historical descriptions. All other characters are strictly products of the author's imagination. An Author's Note at the end of the book includes information about historical details.

THE SHIP IN THE SAND

By
WILLIAM L. SULLIVAN

ILLUSTRATIONS BY
KAREN SORENSEN SULLIVAN

NAVILLUS PRESS
EUGENE, OREGON

FOR MY EXCHANGE GRANDSON HOLGER,
AND OTHER DANISH FRIENDS

4

CHAPTER 1
JELLING, DENMARK, 958

She blinked in confusion, trying to focus on the ravens. Two large black birds were circling above her. Was she dead? Only in Asgard, the home of the Norse gods, would you expect to see Huginn and Muninn — Thought and Memory.

Odin's birds traded places, cawing as they stole thoughts and planted new ones like barleycorns. Somewhere from the darkness came a deep, echoing laugh that might even have been the one-eyed god himself.

But then there was the familiar, earthy scent of garden herbs, steeping in hot water. An old, bony hand took the steaming bowl from her even as she slumped to the ground in a cloud of light linen.

"Are you all right, child?"

The man's voice was a growl in a language she hardly knew.

She rubbed her eyes with the backs of her hands. Where was she? Before, she had been —

Or had that been a dream, already fading, all but gone? Her memories were as jumbled as if she had been hit on the head, but nothing seemed to hurt.

The hall was huge and dark, lit only by a flickering central hearth and a murky ceiling smoke hole. Long axes clanked on stone as two giants in helmets and chain mail lifted her to her feet.

"The girl collapsed," one of them grunted. "We'll take her away."

"No." It was the old man, with a gray beard and silver chains, propped up by heaps of furs in an elaborately carved wooden bed. He held the bowl in his shaking hand. "She — she was helping. I felt something."

The soldiers released the girl and stepped back into the shadows.

5

"Who are you?" The old man's eyes were cloudy, troubled, weary. What could she answer? She looked down at herself and shook her head. Her linen shift hung straight from a very young girl's thin hips. Her arms were narrow and white. She felt as if her mind had been emptied of everything except a hidden wish, trapped behind a dozen doors.

Her young body, however, felt wonderfully alive. It seemed to know what it was doing. She smiled, pulled her long ash-blond hair behind her ears, and used her linen sleeve to dab the sweat from the man's brow.

The old man relaxed. When his eyelids fluttered, she nearly gasped aloud. She had seen through the lids to the darkness of Niflheim beyond.

Did he know he was dying? Had he already seen his fetch, the spirit that would lead him to other side? She took the bowl from his hand, dipped some bread in the broth, and held it to his lips. He breathed in, his eyes now closed, and took a half step back from the land of the dead.

"Yes," he murmured.

Suddenly two large doors swung open at the far end of the hall. An entourage of nobles and dignitaries walked in, whispering in earnest tones. The sight of all these men and women made the girl wonder where she was. This was clearly some sort of Viking hall, but these people's clothes, speech, and mannerisms all seemed new. So much jewelry and colored cloth! The men wore short hair, or none at all! The Norse they spoke slid from their lips like song — slippery waves of words.

If ever the girl had seen a queen before, the majestic woman at the front of this crowd was surely one. Her golden hair, tied up in a single thick braid, hung over a dark blue cloak amid silver keys and gold clasps. An even row of teeth shone between remarkably wide lips. Was she smiling or gritting? She seemed about to take a bite. Instinctively the girl fell back and dropped to one knee.

The queen swept up past the hearth and towered at the foot of the bed. "Ah, Gorm, my love. And how have you been managing with my little English elf?"

Gorm closed one eye, a slow wink. "A smart one."

The queen laughed, her wide mouth both beautiful and alarming.

6

"I'll admit the girl has a cunning way with herbs. Although she can't be more than ten winters old."

"Who?" Gorm pressed out the word from wrinkled lips.

"Lifu," the queen replied. "Her name is Lifu, although that is almost all I know about her. Harald's crew brought her back from England as one of the many hostages last week. Then we learned that her family in Oxford is dead. There's no ransom, so I took her on as a thrall."

"Eyes," the old king said. "Pretty."

"You think so?" The queen lifted the girl's chin with a finger. "One is blue and one is green. I suppose anything that makes a man look twice can be called beauty. Plenty of mystery in this one. Can't speak a word of Norse."

Lifu — for apparently that was her name — blinked in surprise. Couldn't she speak Norse? Then how could she understand them?

At this point the queen suddenly switched to another language. Some of the words rhymed with Norse, but everything else was different. Incredibly, the girl understood it perfectly.

"Lifu," the queen said, "Fetch a pitcher of fresh water from the well by the old temple."

"Yes, my lady," Lifu heard herself reply in English. She bowed and took a jug from beside the bed.

The queen looked out imperiously at the crowd. "And as for the rest of you — honored guests, noble jarls, rival kings, ambassadors, warlocks, and vultures — you can see for yourself that King Gorm of Denmark is still fighting battles. Now that my son Harald has returned from his travels, Gorm and I have much to discuss with him in private."

The old king grumbled, "Leave us."

A powerfully built young man of perhaps twenty winters, evidently Prince Harald, crossed his brawny arms over a chest plate of gilt armor. "We will call you back if there is any news you need to hear. Guards too — wait outside. Tonight there will be meat and ale for all in the long hall." His light brown hair and beard were short and finely groomed. Hawk-like eyes glared from beneath a thick brow. His mouth was as wide as his mother's, but when he stretched it into the same voracious grin, he exposed a front tooth that was a startling blue-black. If that tooth had been damaged in a fight, Harald's grin suggested that the man responsible was dead.

Lifu retreated with the others, afraid and confused. Outside she blinked at the bright gray sky. She felt lost and alone. Why on earth had the gods sent her here?

Then she remembered the jug in her hands. She was supposed to fetch water from a well by an old temple. At least this was a manageable goal. Around her was a city of wood and thatch, with horses, wagons, and people. But there was also one large hill, with dirt so fresh that grass had only just started to take hold. She decided to climb it for a look around. She needed to get her bearings in this strange new world.

The hill was only a little taller than the largest of the halls, but she caught her breath at the view from the top. She had expected to see the ocean, or perhaps a mountain capped with snow. But that would be Norway. Had she once lived in that wilder, rockier land to the north? Here the horizon in all directions blended from a patchwork of green farm fields to wooded dales and gently rolling hills. Herds of reddish cattle grazed peacefully. Men with horses plowed rich brown earth. This was Denmark, and for some reason she was here as an English slave.

Something smelled wrong.

The stench seemed to be coming from behind an enclosure of rough planks near the top of the mound. She found a gate, peered inside, and gave a start. The decaying head of a goat stared back at her from atop a pole. A raven hopped from one horn to the other. The bird pecked at a ghastly eye socket and cawed.

The ravens of Odin! She remembered them circling in her dream. Surely that was a clue. She would have to use her wits to find out more.

The queen had told her to go to an old temple, but this altar was obviously new. In fact, now that she considered it, the entire hill was not natural, but rather a freshly built mound. Perhaps a grave mound for an important person? Perhaps even for a king who had seen his fetch?

On the far side of the mound she noticed two rows of standing stones. The rows converged to a point, as if to outline the prow of a gigantic ship. She thought the fallen stones near the front might be the remnants of a temple. And in fact, when she ran down the hill, she found a well beside the stones. She filled the jug and returned to the king's hall.

Soldiers were guarding the hall's door. Lifu hesitated, unsure

8

whether to ask the guards for permission to enter. Would they understand her? Even if they did, would they bar her way? She decided to wait, as inconspicuous as any small girl with a water jug. Eventually the guards were distracted by a lady in a clingy dress riding a horse — something that even Lifu found shocking.

Lifu slipped into the hall's shadows like a swallow returning to its nest. It was so dark inside that she stopped, afraid that she would stumble and break her jug. While she waited for her eyes to grow accustomed to the dark, her sensitive young ears began to make out

voices speaking in the lilting Norse of the Danes.

"You yourself called them vultures!" Prince Harald's voice was the angriest, and the easiest to overhear. "You invited all the realm's enemies here so they could divide up my inheritance."

"No, I asked them here so I could keep my eye on them." The queen lowered her voice. This time when she spoke, Lifu caught only the words "friends" and "distance."

The prince scoffed. "I've seen the other Danish kings strolling about the streets of Jelling as if they already owned it. Each of them dreams of uniting the islands with the mainland under his own hand. That is our danger."

"Have you seen so little of the world in your travels?" the queen asked loftily. "Both Sweden and Norway are united, with fleets of warships we cannot match. To the south, Emperor Otto's lands stretch to a distant sea at Rome. His Frankish armies are Christian, and believe it is their duty to convert or slaughter people of other religions. This is the real danger. It is why, during your father's illness, I have been in Hedeby, rebuilding the ancient Danevirke, our wall to the south."

"Really, Mother? Is that why you were in the south? I've heard you've been meeting with the Slavic jarls of Pomerania."

"Of course I have. An alliance with the Slavs would help secure our common border to the south against the Franks."

The prince countered, "Wouldn't it be wiser to unite Denmark, so we can stand together against threats from all sides?"

For a moment the queen and her son glared at each other. Then she suggested, "Let's ask your father which strategy he would prefer."

The queen sat on the edge of the bed and lowered her voice. Lifu crept closer so that she could hear. The queen held the old man's bony hand. "Gorm my love, what do you recommend? Defending our border against the Frankish empire, or attacking our fellow Danes?"

The old king's eyelids had sagged. But now he opened his mouth. For a moment his labored breaths merely blew the white whiskers of his mustache back and forth. Then he swallowed and spoke. "Do not argue, my wife and son. You are both right. I am too old to wield a sword. But I fear the time may have come for Holger to be drawn from its scabbard once again."

"Your ceremonial sword?" Harald asked doubtfully. "Is that old thing even useful as a weapon?" He took a bedraggled leather sheath down from the stave wall above the king's bedstead. When he slid the sword out, even Lifu could see the gleam of steel that was still shiny. Had she seen that blade before? One of the doors blocking her memories opened a crack.

"Oh yes," the king whispered. "Holger is not its real name."

"If it's not Holger, then what is it?" the prince asked.

"Cursed." The queen held up her hand, as if to ward off evil. "Do not be tempted to use it. At our wedding your father was gifted this sword by an Arab emissary from the Caliphate of Cordoba. But I fear it was forged somewhere else, long ago, for a darker purpose."

"Why do you say that?" The prince examined the blade. "Damascened layers. Excellent work. With some sort of engraved pattern."

"It wins battles, Thyra," the king admonished his wife. The exertion left him coughing. Then, more quietly, he said, "You know as well was I that Holger secured the kingdom in my youth."

"At a cost. It is a heartless thing, this sword. Everyone loves you better since you set it aside."

"Perhaps so," the old king sighed. "Still, it is a sword of fate, merely sleeping. One day Holger will awaken to save Denmark in her hour of need."

"May that day never come." The queen shook her head.

Meanwhile, the prince was turning the sword in the firelight, marveling at the ancient markings. "There are runes." Even Lifu could see them.

As if pushed from behind, Lifu stumbled forward. She held out the jug and stammered in English, "Here is the water you asked me to bring, my lady."

Harald flashed the sword up to the ready. "How much did you overhear, spy?"

"Harald!" his mother objected. "She's an English slave. She doesn't speak Norse."

"Intruders should die." Harald stepped forward to swing. Lifu cowered in terror.

The queen caught his arm. "Don't you hear yourself? That's the sword talking. Lifu brought water, just as I asked. She's not a spy. She can't understand our Norse."

Harald lowered the sword. His bushy eyebrows were knit in thought.

"Hang the sword back on the wall," the queen said.

"No. Keep it." The king slowly closed one eye. Was this another wink, and if so, what did it mean? "Perhaps, Harald, you will choose to bury Holger with me when I die. Or perhaps you will use it."

The silence in the hall was as thick as the smoke from the hearth. At length the queen drew herself up, her hands on her hips. "My husband and I need to speak alone. Harald, escort this girl on your way out."

The prince strapped the leather scabbard about his waist. "I'll kill her when we're outside."

In response his mother recited a verse from the skalds, the court poets:

The boy who breaks
A tiny tree
Will never taste
Its foretold fruit.

Without reply, Harald turned to go. He held out his hands, herding Lifu before him as if she were a sheep. Unlike a sheep, however, Lifu had understood that she was almost certainly being led to slaughter. Her ten-year-old legs wanted to run, to dash through the city's dirt streets and hide. But she knew the prince's men would probably find her. And the barleycorn of an idea in her mind had already sprouted a more complicated plan.

In the hall's doorway Harald caught her by the arm. He pulled her around the edge of the mound to the old temple of fallen stones. There he pinned her leg against the ground with his foot and drew the sword.

Lifu brushed her hair casually aside and said in Norse, "I can tell you the real name of your sword."

Harald stopped, the sword over his head. "What?"

"That sword you're waving around. Its true name isn't Holger."

"You speak Norse after all?" Harald lowered the sword a bit. "Then you *are* a spy."

"I could be."

"You have a strange accent. How did you learn Norse in Mercia? And why does my mother think you only speak English?"

She dodged his questions. "Aren't you going to ask how I know the name of your sword?"

"I don't ask slaves. I command them. Speak."

"The sword's name is written on the side of the blade. Look at the runes for yourself. It says *Fenris*."

"But that's the name of the wolf god." Harald frowned at the markings. Everyone knew Fenris, the evil demon destined to devour the world at Ragnarök. He looked to Lifu warily. "How is it that you read runes? This is not the skill of a slave. Are you a witch?"

Lifu stood and straightened her linen dress. "I am Lifu, the heiress of an estate at Oxford. If you kill me, you will prove that your mother is right about the sword. If you set the sword aside I can offer you something of great value to a future king."

"You have nothing of value to me."

12

"Are you sure?" She lifted an eyebrow. "I have surprised you twice in as many moments. Who is stronger? You, or an old sword with too many names?"

Harald weighed the sword in his hand. Then he set it on a fallen stone beside him. The hilt remained just inches from his grasp. "What is your offer, Lifu of Oxford?"

"To serve you. You asked if I was a spy. Let me be yours. Every king needs eyes and ears in unexpected halls. You are surrounded by rivals. You suspect even the queen may have plans of her own."

"And in return, am I supposed to spare your life?"

"No, that is not payment enough," Lifu said, giving her blond hair a shake.

"What?" Harald laughed at her. "Would you also have a ring from my hand? Perhaps my smallest ring would fit on your big toe."

"No ring," Lifu said. "But one day I would like to have what is rightfully mine. An estate in England."

Harald's smile vanished.

Lifu asked, "Or do Vikings not honor such rights?"

"Nowhere do slaves or little girls have such rights." Harald paused. "Even the rights of free men were seldom respected by the Vikings of the sagas." Those men had been banished to Iceland generations ago by his namesake, Harald Fairhair of Norway. He lifted his head. "Danes are different. We respect honor."

"Even when you are raiding England?"

"The eastern half of England is called the Danelaw for good reason. There, as here, law speakers are elected to recite the laws and hear grievances. Juries, not kings, decide guilt. In your half of England, where the king and the laws are weak, rival warriors do as they please. The weaker ones sometimes ask the Danes to help settle their scores, promising us treasure and slaves."

"Is that why your men killed my family?"

"Your parents were killed by the English duke who called us in. The west of England is a lawless, dangerous place." Harald shook his head. "Are you sure you would want to go back there?"

Lifu bit her lip. She wasn't sure. "Will you let me live and serve you?"

"You are full of surprises, little Lifu. I've never met a slave who dares to talk to me in such a tone. I might yet kill you. I haven't decided.

But in the meantime you have made me curious to learn what fruit you foretell."

She jumped up and kissed his hand.

He shook her loose. "Do you swear loyalty to me? By all the gods?"

She thought a moment. "Yes, I swear it."

Harald picked up the sword and slid it into its scabbard. "I wonder if, like this blade, you have more than one sharp edge." He tapped the hilt. "Are you Fenris, the destroyer, or Holger, the rescuer?"

Fear fluttered in her heart like the beating of a raven's wings. "Will you bury Fenris with your father?"

Harald turned, eyeing the grave mound. An opening at its base, framed with timbers, tunneled into its dark depths. A cold wind, gray with the smoke of evening hearth fires, shivered across the mound's fresh grass.

CHAPTER 2
JELLING, DENMARK, 1940

Julius worried about the planes he had seen in the distance — big, droning cargo ships, low on the horizon. But he didn't want anything to spoil this picnic with his fiancée Mette and her parents. It was a beautiful April day, and they had spread a blanket with a wicker basket and cups of beer in a field of wildflowers beside the whitewashed stone tower of a Danish country church.

Mette's mother Kirstin had prepared an astonishing array of little sandwiches on square slices of buttered pumpernickel bread — Tilsit cheese, liver paste, pickled cucumbers, sliced eggs, blue cheese, and pickled herring. For Julius's sake she had left out the ham and bacon. Finally, over coffee, she had taken out an envelope.

"Look what I found at the back of a drawer." Kirstin slid a dozen old black-and-white photographs out of the envelope. "It seems I've catalogued everthing except our own family's history." The first of the photographs showed Kirstin as a girl in upstate New York. She was happily holding hands with her Norwegian mother and her American father, a Cornell professor with a mischievous grin. The next picture was of a Viking ship being excavated from a hill on a Norwegian farm.

Mette shared a glance with Julius, knowing what was coming. Her mother had once been one of world's leading archeologists, and had inspired Mette to take up the same profession. Even now, the National Museum in Copenhagen was so dominated by men that her only path to a position had been to vastly outmatch them in skill, knowledge, and tact. Her mother had once done the same thing in Oslo, but without tact, which was perhaps why she had brought the photographs. Mette wondered why her mother felt the need to challenge her, especially here, at Mette's excavation in Jelling.

Mette's mother had always looked like a woman who should be in charge. Her tall white forehead suggested intellect. Her flashing eyes meant business. Even at the age of sixty-seven, in a calf-length floral dress at a picnic, Kirstin Andersen sat on a handkerchief on a field stone as if this were her throne.

Mette, on the other hand, had struggled with curly brown hair that made her look like a hopscotch schoolgirl. Hats could tame the mane, but when she took them off the remaining curls sprang out on all sides like a fright wig. Today she had taken her usual approach and pulled her hair back fiercely from her face with a wide hair band.

She also lacked her mother's domineering gaze. Mette's left eye aimed just slightly to the right of center — something Julius said he particularly admired. You didn't notice the faint misalignment at first, Julius said, "But the beauty of it is that everyone has to look at you twice."

Mette made up for all of this by dressing as professionally as she could. The dark blue jacket she wore over her white blouse could have been a man's suit coat, with three-quarter-length sleeves and double-wide lapels. The matching skirt started out business-like at the waist, but then curved with a feminine flare. Sitting in the grass with her legs folded to one side, the skirt's hem exposed her knees.

Julius found it difficult to focus on the photographs rather than on Mette's bared knees. He had been engaged to her for three months, but she insisted they couldn't marry until fall because of her work. Julius kept telling her, in different ways, that he was ready now.

At twenty-eight, Julius was one of the most eligible bachelors in all of Copenhagen. His parents owned three piers in the downtown harbor. They had given him one to see what he might do. Julius had surprised everyone by closing the docks and building a row of waterfront apartments. In fact, that was how he had become acquainted with Mette. Her parents had bought one of Julius' third-floor apartments.

Mette was still a little unsure about the young, wealthy, blue-eyed landlord. She was five years older than Julius, but in some ways he seemed even younger. Julius wore a pencil mustache and black hair slicked back to one side in the style of Clark Gable. In fact, Julius looked so much like the famous Hollywood actor that people sometimes stopped him on the street. What Mette particularly liked was his derring-do. Any wealthy young man might gamble successfully on an apartment complex, but he was the only one she could imagine who would take her for a ride over the Øresund to Sweden in a Fokker monoplane. And it wasn't just a World War I relic, but rather a sporty production model from 1931. When the elder Gustmeyers wanted to buy a new family car — a Bentley, and not some Volkswagen — Julius had offered to take Mette on the ferry to England to pick it up in person at a factory outside London. Of course she had said no. A trip like that without benefit of marriage would have damaged her reputation at the museum. Still, the thought of Julius driving that elegant taxicab of a car alone across France and Germany in the tense political atmosphere of 1938 had made her heart speed.

For the picnic Julius had dressed in dapper linen slacks and a white sport coat. He stretched out on the edge of the blanket, tipped a straw boater to shade his eyes, and squeezed Mette's hand. They pretended to pay attention to the photographs.

Mette had always wished she could travel, and not just to conferences in Berlin or vacations in Norway. Julius made that dream seem probable. Mette had grown up as the good, stay-at-home daughter, a counterbalance to her wandering younger brother Lars. Instead of going to college Lars had shipped on as a crew hand on their father's freighter. When Magnus later traded the ship for a Danish fishing trawler, Lars had stayed on in America. Even there, rather than settle near relatives in upstate New York, he had drifted as far as possible across the continent to Oregon. In the latest of his infrequent letters Lars reported that he was enrolled in college after all — but instead of studying something practical he was in journalism, drawing political cartoons of Hitler and Mussolini as drum majorettes.

"Here, Mette. This is where I first met your father." Kirstin Andersen tapped a picture of a fenced excavation. The ribs of a Viking burial ship protruded from a pit at the top of a hill. "Tønsberg, Norway, in the summer of 1904." A younger version of herself, without the wrinkles or the confidence, confronted the camera with a small black hat, a puffy-sleeved blouse, and a voluminous skirt that concealed all but the pointed toes of her shoes. Dour gentlemen stood on either side with mustaches, derby hats, and watch chains.

"At first I thought Magnus was gruff and coarse," Kirstin admitted, pointing to a worker at the back of the picture. The man squinted warily beneath a sailor's cap as he leaned on a shovel.

"And I thought you were a bookish prude," Magnus Andersen said, stroking his mustache to hide a smile. "Turns out I was half right."

Kirstin looked up sharply. "Which half?"

Magnus sat cross-legged on the grass like a troll with a bushy red beard and broad shoulders. He took a briar pipe and a pouch of tobacco from his jacket pocket and began pressing shag into the bowl. "Those were dangerous times in Norway."

"More dangerous than now?" Mette asked.

Magnus replied with a long, low, grumbling "*Joda!*"

Although some of Magnus' words still had a Norwegian sharpness to them, he had mastered the pronunciation of "*joda*" perfectly. It was a contradictory Danish assent, along the lines of "Oh yes it was!" or "You better believe it!" While whittling at sea or mending nets in harbor, Danish sailors rumbled the word as sonorously as moaning foghorns.

Magnus lit the pipe, sucking puffs with one eye closed. "That was the year Norway won its independence from Sweden. More dangerous yet, women won the right to vote."

Kirstin rolled her eyes.

"I'm afraid I agree with Mette," Julius said, although he knew that he risked spoiling the picnic's mood. "A shadow has fallen across Europe."

Magnus grumbled again. "Oh, I don't know. It's been six months since the Germans invaded Poland. They got what they wanted."

"But the French and the British have spent the winter mobilizing for war." Mette set down her coffee. She glanced from her fiancé to her parents. "War is coming to Europe. That's the real reason the government sent me here to excavate at Jelling."

Kirstin raised her eyebrows. "The decision didn't come from the National Museum?"

Mette shook her head so slightly that the curls behind her headband hardly moved. She lowered her voice, although they were alone. Everyone else on the excavation had gone into the village for lunch at an inn.

"Our instructions may even have come from the king himself. Not as a show of force. As a demonstration of pride."

Her mother nodded. "I had wondered, why Jelling? Why now?"

Mette continued, "Denmark has the oldest monarchy in the world. We've lost a few wars, but have never been conquered, not in a thousand years. That's why the National Museum is excavating the burial mound of the first Danish king, Gorm the Old. To remind people."

Julius sat up, his ears perked. The sky was empty, but once again he heard the drone of a distant motor. He knew airplanes by their engines. And this one was definitely wrong.

"Let's pack up." Julius stood, frowning.

"Why? What is it?" Kirstin looked alarmed.

"I'm not sure." Julius walked to the gravel road between the grave mound and the church. He opened the door of the black Bentley and turned on the radio.

By then they could hear a voice from the direction of the village. "Miss Andersen! Miss Andersen!" Mette's assistant Henrik, a middle-aged man with a bow tie, was running toward them past the church.

The radio crackled to life first. ". . . expecting a statement from the king. A crowd has gathered here at the Amalienborg palace, stunned, uncertain, afraid."

"Miss Andersen?" Henrik stopped to catch his breath, leaning against a large rune-inscribed stone in the church cemetery. By then they had all gathered around the open door of the Bentley. Even Henrik watched silently. His eyes were wide and white, as if the crackling device in the car were not a radio, but a bomb.

"His Royal Highness, King Christian the Tenth, is stepping out onto the balcony in full dress uniform, complete with sash, medals, and plumed hat. He scans the crowd, touches his mustache, and then leans to the microphone. Ladies and gentleman, I give you His Majesty the King of Denmark."

The voice from the radio was not strong.

"This morning at 4:20 a.m.," the king said, "Military forces of the German Reich disembarked from a warship in Copenhagen. Other German troops have landed at sites throughout Denmark and Norway. In view of the Reich's overwhelming military advantage, the Danish government has decided, under protest, that our defensive forces should lay down their weapons, and that the population should refrain from resisting the occupying troops."

"What!" Magnus balled his fists. "We surrendered without firing a shot?"

19

"Shots were fired," Henrik said. "Although only a few. It was too sudden."

The king's voice continued, "Under these conditions, so serious for our fatherland, I call upon everyone, in the cities and in the countryside, to demonstrate dignity and the utmost correct behavior, because every ill-considered action or utterance can have the most serious consequences."

Mette marveled, "Is this really our king? The descendant of Gorm the Old?"

The voice on the radio sounded weary. "God save us all. God protect Denmark."

There was no applause. Even the radio commentator was silent.

"We have been asleep," Mette said quietly.

"Then this is just a bad dream?" Julius wondered.

"What about Sweden?" Kirstin asked.

Henrik shook his head. "The Swedes declared neutrality. The Germans left them alone."

Magnus banged his fist on the car's hood. "Well, they won't take Norway so easily. Beyond Oslo are a thousand miles of fjords and mountains, all the way to the Arctic. Even the Wehrmacht can't drive across that in a morning."

"But Denmark is so small they can." Mette had been watching the road that crossed the fields from the broad valley at Vejle.

A car was coming their way. It was a shiny black sedan, longer and lower than Julius' Bentley, and with more chrome. It didn't pause in the village. Instead it motored directly toward them, as if drawn by the rune stone before the old church.

"A Mercedes," Julius said.

Snapping above the fenders of its front wheels were two flags.

Red flags with black, broken crosses.

Swastikas.

Mette narrowed her eyes. Then it was true. In the space of a single April morning, a millennium of monarchs had fallen to the Nazis' "thousand-year" Reich.

CHAPTER 3
JELLING, 970

A dozen years had passed since King Harald Bluetooth had buried his father Gorm beneath the mound in the rolling farmlands of central Jutland. Now many of the same courtiers, soldiers, and dignitaries had returned to Jelling, this time to lay Gorm's wife Thyra to rest nearby.

Thyra's English slave Lifu had been left with the unenviable task of keeping the deceased queen's two grandchildren out of mischief until the bonfire at dusk.

Gunhild, at eleven, could already hold her head high like a princess, but she could just as easily take off running after a herd of goats like an impish girl. Her younger brother Svein was nothing if not trouble. Every stick he found — every spoon and fern — became a weapon in his hands. He would thrust and parry at anything that moved, grunting like a fierce, high-pitched dwarf. He had yet to start the growth spurt that might turn him into a genuine warrior, but he was large for his age. In fact he had been so large at birth that he had killed his mother, the original Gunhild. King Harald had later remarried a Slavic queen, Tove, who had neither time nor patience for the offspring of Harald's earlier marriage.

"Do you want your fortunes told?" Lifu asked casually, just as the two children were about to escape into a dining hall in search of treats. At once she had their attention.

"You can do that? Svein asked skeptically, lowering the twig he had used as an ax against a rebellious cobweb.

Gunhild looked askance at Lifu. "Can you really write runes?" Lifu had been her grandmother's thrall. Could she have been a witch as well?

"Yes." Lifu stared intently at the children, knowing they might be

21

unsettled to see that one of her eyes was green and the other blue. "Would you like me to show you how?"

Svein exchanged a conspiratorial glance with his sister. Telling fortunes was a dark art. "Ooh!" he said. "Sure."

Gunhild feigned a lack of interest. "Maybe."

"Then follow me." Lifu looked both ways to make sure they were unwatched. Then she crooked a finger. "I know a woodworker's hut where we can find books." She ducked into a side street and began crouching along alleyways.

Close behind, Gunhild asked, "Books? You mean like the priests from Frankia use? I've seen those."

In a less enthusiastic tone Svein added, "Papa lets some of the *Skiring* priests come into Denmark. Mostly people kill them."

"No, not Christian books," Lifu whispered. "Those are merely stacks of leaves. Norse books are actually made of *book*, the wood of the beech tree. They're real books."

She led them to the lower part of the village, near the forest, where the huts had wattle walls instead of staves. In an empty back yard Lifu found what she wanted: a workplace where carpenters had used adzes to chisel water troughs from beech logs. The sweet smell of the new wood was strong. She gathered a handful of white, foot-long splinters and crouched away, hurrying to a spot she knew just inside the woods.

Lightning and age had ravaged a great oak tree until it was little more than a hollow stump with a few green leaves. Inside was a mossy circle of duff where she had spent many an afternoon preparing her herbs, practicing her incantations, and trying to remember her other life, before she had awakened as Lifu.

She sat cross-legged at the back of this small, shadowy cavern. The children hesitated at the entrance.

"Come inside. You have to carve your own book or it won't have any meaning. This is a place I've found that works." She held out one of the long splinters of beech wood.

Svein took the wood and stepped inside. "We have to carve them? With what?"

Lifu reached under the hem of her gray woolen tunic and withdrew a knife with a sharp three-inch blade.

"Ooh!" Svein exclaimed. "You're allowed to carry that?"

"I do." She turned the knife to offer him the handle. "You'll need

22

to whittle staves the size of your finger, with square ends and a clean flat side."

The boy hefted the knife in his hand.

Lifu offered a splinter of wood to Gunhild. "I'm afraid you'll have to take turns with the knife."

"No." The girl reached under the gold-embroidered hem of her blue linen tunic. "I have my own."

Her brother goggled at the elegant five-inch blade she revealed. "You never told —" and then, open-mouthed, "How come you get to carry a knife and I don't?"

"You're only eight. This is Denmark, not the wilds of Mercia." Gunhild had planned her comment to carom off the boy and sting Lifu. Gunhild took the piece of wood and began shaving the edges. "You'll get a knife after your ninth winter. If you live that long."

"And why wouldn't I?"

Gunhild rolled her eyes. "Yesterday you jumped off a roof and tried to ride a cow."

Lifu asked, "Is that the fortune you want to know from Odin? How and when you will die?"

The children were quiet. They hadn't thought much about death until recently. They had just seen their beloved, too-generous grandmother Thyra being carried stiff and white into the dark tunnel of her own grave mound.

Lifu began snapping the beech splinters into three-inch lengths. "It's the question most people ask. But Odin's tricky. He traded his own right eye for knowledge. His ravens bring him news of everything that happens. He knows the past and sees the future. Still, if you ask him about your death, his answer is always the same."

"What does he answer?" Svein looked serious.

"He says, 'Yes.'" Lifu smiled slightly. "Odin knows everyone will die. Even the gods, someday. What matters is what you do with the life you have. Ask him about that if you want a useful fortune."

Gunhild pulled back her hair. "And we have to ask on book staves?"

"A fresh set each time. The nicer you make them, the clearer the answer. Whittling gives you time to think about your question." Lifu traded her rectangular staves for the longer splinters the children had been carving. "Here, work on these. We'll need sixteen."

For a while they all worked in silence. Outside, through a gap in the forest boughs, Lifu could see the afternoon shadows lengthening. Birds began to call, early singers in the evening choir. Harald's men would be sealing the entrance to Thyra's grave mound with boulders by now. Lifu had at least another hour before she was to bring the children to the bonfire.

"Why so many?" Svein whined, tossing another finished stave on a pile. He stabbed Lifu's knife into the ground.

She pulled the blade from the duff and cleaned it with her finger. "Because there are sixteen runes in the futhark alphabet. Each has its own sound, name, and power. The first letter has the sound *fff*. Its name is *Fe*."

"Its name is cattle?" Svein screwed up his face. "Where's the power in that?"

"Cattle are wealth. *Fe* stands for all kinds of riches. I'll show you." Lifu took a blank stave and used the point of her knife to carve a single straight line in the middle, against the grain. "*Fe* is the only rune with two arms standing up on the right." She showed them the finished letter: ᚠ

"That's wealth?" Svein asked doubtfully.

"Don't be dense," Gunhild chided. "It merely stands for wealth."

"Exactly," Lifu said. "Runes can stand for more than one thing. Ideas as well as sounds. My name, for example, starts with the sound *lll*. Here is its rune." She took a new stave, carved a vertical line as before, but this time added just one arm hanging down from the top: ᛚ

"It can mean Lifu, but its true name is *Logr*."

"A lake?" Svein howled. "Your name begins with a stupid rune."

Lifu drew herself up. "*Logr* also means ocean. It surrounds Denmark. The ocean has the power to crush entire navies."

"What about my name?" Suddenly shy, Gunhild blushed.

"Yours starts with the sound *g*, so we use the rune named —" Lifu paused. The most common name was *Kaun*, a burning ulcer. Sickness. Death.

"Named what?"

"Named *Korn*. It has a single arm up to the right." Lifu showed her the carving: ᚴ

"Corn?" Gunhild mused. "That doesn't start with the same sound as my name."

"Not quite, but *k* and *g* are close. With only sixteen runes you sometimes have to make do."

"Corn is grain," Gunhild added thoughtfully. "I suppose it stands for food."

"And health. Prosperity. Peace." Lifu didn't enjoy lying, but she could do it convincingly.

The young princess studied the carved character. "I like it."

Svein interrupted. "What about my name?"

"Svein starts with the sound *sss*." Lifu carved a zigzag of three short lines: ᛋ "Your rune is named *Sol*, the sun."

"Strong and bright," Svein said proudly.

"And blinding."

Without further comment Lifu set about carving the rest of the futhark alphabet. She named the runes out loud as she went, a singsong verse:

> F is fe, for cattle and wealth
> U is ur, for iron and rain
> TH is Thorn, for Thor's power
> A is As, for the wisdom of Odin's clan
> R is Rad, for wheels and journeys
> K is Corn, for health
> H is Hail, when winter becomes spring
> N is Need, for troubled times
> I is Ice, for the frost giants
> Á is the Auer ox, for stubbornness
> S is Sol, for the sun
> T is Tyr, god of war
> B is Birch, the tree of purity
> M is Man, tool of the gods
> L is Lake, the world ocean
> And Y is Yggdrasil, the yew of doom

When Lifu had finished she arranged the sixteen staves in four stacks of four. "Now it's time for your fortunes. Have you decided what questions you want to ask?"

"We get more than one question?" Gunhild asked.

"Two apiece. But be warned that Odin's answers aren't always clear."

"Me first," Svein said.

"All right."

"I want to know when I'll get my own sword," Svein announced. He wrinkled his brow and added, "And if I'll be king of everything."

"Everything?" Lifu asked. "Russia, Byzantium, the whole world?"

The boy hedged. "Just the parts where Danes live, I guess."

"The North, then. And half of England. Very well." Lifu picked up two blank staves. "I'll write 'king' on one and 'blade' on the other."

"Will Odin understand?"

Lifu smiled. "He already knows. We just need a way for him to answer."

"Will he write back?"

Lifu laughed. "No. We'll drop the entire book at once to see how the staves land."

"Oh." Svein sounded uncertain.

Lifu turned to Gunhild. "And what about you? What does a princess want to know?"

The girl reddened. With her pale skin, she blushed easily. "Who will I marry? And will I be happy?"

Lifu thought: Of course. She is eleven. But even such tired questions can give the gods a chance to reveal unexpected fates.

"I'll write 'man' and 'peace.' Is that OK?"

The girl bit her lip. "I suppose."

Outside, the sun had just set behind the forest. A nearly full moon, white as a winter snowfield, glinted through the lowest oak boughs. A cold wind swirled into the deepening shadows of the hollow stump.

Lifu gathered their book in both hands and held it over her head. She spoke in a strange low voice, as if she had become someone else.

> Nine long nights you hung
> In Yggdrasil, a tree no one knows,
> Spiked by your spear,
> Swayed by the wind.
> This price you paid
> To read these runes.

26

Lifu opened her hands, releasing a cascade of bright staves. The wood chips tumbled as they fell, seemingly in slow motion. Then they danced on the duff, made their decisions, and finally lay still.

Some were overlapped. Many were upside down. A few had sprung from the moss and lay by themselves.

Svein reached out.

"Don't touch them!" Lifu's voice was sharp.

"What do they say?" Gunhild asked. "Can you read Odin's answer?"

Lifu bent to inspect the staves, squinting to make out the carved letters in the dim light. "Here is *Sol*, the sun rune, close to the one marked 'blade.' I'm afraid young Svein will get his sword sooner than he should."

"Yes!" the boy exclaimed. "What else?"

Lifu turned over a few of the chips. "I wonder where your 'king' stave is?" For an instant she caught her breath. "Oh! Here it is. Upside down, very close to the blade."

"What does that mean?"

"You'll get your wish. One day you will be king of the Danes."

"Hurray! I knew it."

But Lifu's look had darkened.

Gunhild asked, "What's wrong?"

"Nothing of importance now."

The princess hurried on to ask, "What does the book say about me?"

Lifu flipped a stave. "Your *Korn* rune bounced all the way over here, next to 'man,' purity, and wealth."

"That sounds good."

"No doubt about it, your husband will be rich and handsome. But I'm afraid the book suggests he lives far away."

Gunhild smiled. "Maybe that will be for the best."

The distant tone of a lur-horn sounded across the dusky fields. At once the children turned, as if it were the voice of their grandmother herself, calling them home.

Lifu quickly gathered the fallen staves. "We need to get back to the town." She was glad that the children had been distracted before they could think to ask about the two other important staves of their books.

"That was fun!" Svein said.

"Can we do it again sometime, Lifu?" Gunhild asked.

"This set of staves can only be used once," she replied, tucking them away in a pocket. "But I have other games and stories I could share, if you like."

"Oh, yes!"

"We'll ask father!"

Lifu put away her knife and herded the children outside. They skipped ahead of her all the way back.

* * *

After delivering the children to the royal entourage, Lifu was tempted to slip away into the night. What was the meaning of the mountain of firewood that soldiers had piled amidst the fallen stones of the ancient temple? There were rumors that Thyra's slaves would be freed when the bonfire was lit. The dowager queen had promised as much. But other tongues warned that her slaves would accompany her to Niflheim through the flames.

A hand caught Lifu's wrist. She turned, frightened.

It was Grady. "Stay. Trust Thyra."

An Irish silversmith, Grady had also served the queen as a thrall. He spoke Norse, but ground his R's like a Gael.

"Thyra is dead." Lifu tried to pull her arm away, but Grady's grip might as well have been a vise.

The smith's beard was short and his face ruddy from his years at the forge, so it was hard to tell how much older he was than Lifu. He smiled, wrinkling amber eyes and exposing a handsome row of white teeth. "She asked us to stand together among the nobles with our heads held high."

Grady released his grip. The first flames of the bonfire began licking up into the twilight.

Lifu rubbed her wrist. Her heart was beating like the tread of running feet. But she stayed by Grady's side.

The growing fire sparked and flickered, illuminating a strange circle of faces: young and old, rich and poor, noble and slave. No one seemed at ease with this mixture of castes, a strange break with tradition. The great grave mound where King Gorm the Old had been buried with his ceremonial sword twelve summers ago rose to one side, black against the glowing mauve horizon. On the opposite side of the bonfire was Queen Thyra's grave, a mound exactly as tall and wide as her husband's.

King Harald Bluetooth had been talking with his two excited children while his aloof wife Tove looked on. Now he clapped the children on their shoulders, turned, and climbed atop one of the stones. He raised his hands and grinned, revealing the dark tooth that had won him his name.

"Danes! Friends! All of you who loved Queen Thyra!" The king's voice was as clear as the call of a lur-horn. "Know that I agree with you. Our gathering here tonight is both sad and strange. For three days the realm has mourned my mother, the wise and beautiful Gift of Denmark. This afternoon I helped the jarls of the kingdom launch her on the voyage to Valhalla in the traditional manner of great royalty, with all the food and clothes she will need. Now she rests in her own hill, near her husband."

So far this had mostly been the sort of speech Lifu expected. But now the king looked down and cleared his throat. He scratched his beard, as if searching for words. When he spoke again, his voice cracked with emotion.

"The truth is, my mother did not entirely believe in that tradition."

The nobles in the firelight glanced to each other. Thyra's slaves, in their gray tunics on the other side of the bonfire, watched warily.

"On her sickbed my mother told me many things," Harald continued, looking up. "She doubted that we will go to Valhalla when we die. If that hall must house the dead of all time, she said, it would be a crowded place, with too many scoundrels, fools, and killers to make the feasting fun."

Lifu stifled a gasp. Others around the firelit circle chuckled or shook their heads.

Harald sighed. "She said death is a mystery. And for all she knew, it may be simply death."

A voice from the crowd called, "These words are blasphemy against the gods!"

"They are the words of my mother, Queen Thyra, the Gift of Denmark," Harald countered. "She made me promise that I would hold this gathering tonight, after her traditional burial. Children and slaves were not allowed at that earlier ceremony. But Thyra wanted everyone she loved to have a chance to say goodbye. Including my children, Gunhild and Svein." Harald held out a hand toward the young princess and prince.

29

Then the king nodded to the men and women in gray tunics on the far side of the fire. "And Thyra's personal thralls."

Harald thought a moment before continuing. "As you know, my mother spent many winters in Hedeby, the market town on our southern border. She oversaw the reconstruction of the Danevirke, our wall against the Franks. She forged alliances, sometimes in secret. But she also claimed to have learned much about the mysteries of the world at the slave market square. The traders there had instructions to save for her the most cunning, knowledgeable slaves. Over the years she bought two dozen for her court — men and women who might have been great scholars, wizards, or artisans in their own lands. They served her as servants do. But she also encouraged them to develop their skills and share their knowledge. Eventually, she told me, she came to love them almost as family."

Aware that this was a dangerous thing to say before his jarls, Harald narrowed his eyes at the faces in the firelight. "Has no one here met a slave whom you secretly believed deserved to be free?"

No one spoke. The bonfire settled, sending a column of jerking red sparks up toward the night's first stars.

Harald commanded, "Grady of Ireland, step forward."

Lifu felt the smith beside her shrinking back. This time she was the one who caught his wrist. She whispered, "Head high, like a noble!"

The smith swallowed hard. Then he stepped out from the crowd. Seeing him there in the firelight Lifu realized that he did not look like an Irish slave. He dressed as a Dane. He had cut his reddish hair like a Dane. He even held his shoulders like a free man.

Harald scrutinized the slave more closely. "My mother asked that you tell us your story. And then, that you tell us what you think of death."

"Of death?" Grady stammered.

The king rolled his finger in the air. "First, tell us your story."

"Forgive me, Your Royal Highness." Grady ground out his R's as he bowed. "I am a humble blacksmith from the west of Ireland, captured by Norwegian Vikings at the age of twenty."

"That was before the Norwegians submitted to me as king?"

"Yes, Your Highness. The raiders had stolen so much silver that I trained as a silversmith at their camp in the Orkney Islands. After three winters my owner ran out of silver. He sent me to Hedeby to be sold. Thankfully, it was Queen Thyra who bought me."

"My mother wore the finest silver jewelry the North has ever seen," Harald said. "We buried her with some of it. Was it your work?"

"Yes, Your Highness."

Harald considered this a minute. "And what do you think happens when a person dies?"

Grady's nervous stammer returned. "I — I'm no longer sure, Your Highness."

"No longer? Explain yourself."

The smith swallowed. "Well, I was raised a Christian in Ireland. The priests there say that if you believe in their god — a single god, but with three forms, and a son who died but didn't — oh, it's complicated, Your Highness."

"We've heard this. I asked about death."

"Sorry, Your Highness. If you believe in the Christian god, then the priests say you will grow wings when you die. You will live happily forever in the clouds."

Around the circle of faces, eyebrows raised doubtfully as the listeners considered this tale.

"And if you don't believe in their god, like Thyra?" Harald asked.

"Then you live forever in agony, deep below the ground in caves of burning rock and sulfurous fumes." Suddenly Grady caught himself. "But no, Your Highness, I don't believe Queen Thyra could be in a place like that. I don't know what happens after death."

The king stroked his long beard. "You speak well, Grady the silversmith. What would you do if you were free? Return to Ireland?"

"Oh!" The smith caught his breath. "No, not Ireland, Your Highness. I feel at home in Denmark now. I have my trade here and my reputation."

"Yes, but what if you were free?"

"If I were free, Your Highness, I think I might like to spend a winter afoot. I'd travel south where they say it doesn't snow. The leader of the Christian church lives there. I would like to ask this man some questions before I return to my forge."

The king nodded. "Go, Grady of Denmark. You are free."

The silversmith clapped his hand to his mouth. He turned and hugged the first person he saw — Lifu. Then he pushed his way through the crowd and ran into the night, whooping.

The king leaned back, laughing so hard that everyone soon joined in. When he finally dried his eyes with his sleeve he called out, "Bulbul! That's a name you don't hear every day. Is there a Bulbul here tonight?"

A bald man with a tunic of brightly colored quilt patches edged to the front of the circle. "My name is Bulbul, Your Highness."

"Bulbul," the king repeated. "Why have I not seen you before? Were you my mother's jester?"

"No, Your Highness. I was her tailor. Clothes may seem a public art, but the artists who make them are rarely on display." He shrugged apologetically. "I may have overdressed."

"Yes. But my mother always dressed to her advantage." The king waved him forward. "Step out, Bulbul the tailor. My mother asked that you too tell your story. What manner of name is Bulbul?"

"It is Turkish, Your Highness."

"Turkish? Where do these people live? Who is their king?"

"The Turks have no king, Your Highness, but rather many clans," Bulbul answered cautiously. "They live in a vast treeless desert east of Byzantium. To cross this land requires three weeks on a fast horse or two months with a camel."

"A camel? What manner of beast is that?"

The tailor held out his hands, but seemed unable to draw a suitable picture in the air. "It is a pack animal the size of a horse, but slower and meaner and less thirsty."

"For a tailor, you seem familiar with pack animals."

"I am, Your Highness. I grew up in a clan of traders, leading caravans of camels on the Silk Road from Samarkand to Persia. One night we camped by the Caspian Sea to water the camels. In the morning half a dozen Viking ships beached nearby. There was no point trying to fight against three hundred well-armed Russian Swedes. To their credit, the Swedes killed no one, but they confiscated half our cargo and took three of us young men as slaves."

"Have the Swedes sailed so far?" Harald mused. "Even to the deserts beyond Byzantium?"

"Yes, Your Highness. I had to row for four months to reach Sweden. We used sails for the first week to cross the Caspian Sea. Then we rowed against the current of the Volga River, which is longer than any river in the North, or even in Frankia. At its headwaters we rolled the ships on logs for ten miles over forested hills to reach a different river that flowed north to the Baltic."

The king nodded. Everyone knew the story of Rus, the Swedish Viking who had founded a kingdom on a river beyond the Baltic Sea, and had named his realm *Russia*. Nor was Harald surprised that the Swedes had brought back slaves from those lands. The Norse word *slave* had been taken from the word *Slav*. What interested him was that the Swedes had traveled so far to raid a desert caravan.

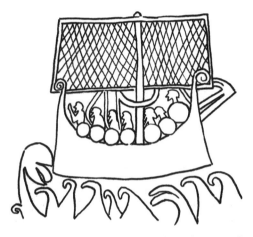

"What cargo did your camels carry that the Swedes found so valuable?"

Bulbul grinned with stained, uneven, dangerous teeth. "Silk, Your Highness. Silk and porcelain from China."

"Describe these things."

Bulbul tilted his head. "Porcelain, Your Highness, is an exceedingly strong, light pottery. It is so thin that you can see light through it. It is baked not merely from clay, but from the powder of ground bones."

Around the circle, women raised their eyebrows and men stroked their beards in marvel.

"As for the silk, Your Highness," Bulbul continued, looking dreamily up toward the stars, "Silk is a cloth fit for gods. Light as a whisper yet strong as canvas and shiny as gold. It is woven in China, a kingdom at the end of the Earth. Silk is made from the cobwebs of caterpillars."

A voice from the crowd shouted, "He lies! These things can't be true."

The king studied the tailor. "Do you lie?"

Bulbul met the king's gaze. "No, Your Highness. I tell the truth. That is why Queen Thyra bought me. That, and the very nice clothes I had learned to sew."

"Very well, Bulbul the truth teller. Tell us what happens to people when they die."

Bulbul's shoulders sagged, as if his body had deflated within his colorful clothes. "It is hard to know the truth about such things, Your Highness. But my clan believes the truth was discovered long ago by Gotama."

"A god?"

"No, Your Highness, Gotama was a prince in India. The people there believe that when you die your spirit is reborn somewhere else, perhaps as a person, perhaps as an animal. You usually don't remember your former lives. But if you have led an evil life, killing people, you will not be celebrated in Valhalla, where Vikings imagine they will wake up again each morning to kill again. Instead your spirit will be reborn as a lesser animal — a dog, or even an ant. On the other hand, if you live a good life of peace and honesty and kindness, you will be reborn as a nobler person. Perhaps even as a prince."

"I see." Harald humphed. "So this Prince Gotama thought he had done well. He was proud to lack the skills of a warrior."

Bulbul's hands rose before him, as if he were struggling once again to describe something as difficult as a camel. "Not exactly, Your Highness. Gotama realized that most of our lives are about suffering — birth, illness, and death. If you are reborn endlessly, it is an eternal cycle of pain. Gotama sat under a tree and thought about this for a very long time, much as Odin spent many days hanging in a tree in search of wisdom. Finally Prince Gotama saw the answer. In that moment he became the Buddha, the enlightened one."

The king humphed again. "What was his answer?"

"That good deeds are important, but they are not enough. To escape the cycle of suffering, you must clear your mind of emotions. Then your spirit can enter the eternal happiness of Nirvana."

"Nirvana? Is this a place like Valhalla? Or is it the Christian version, with winged people in clouds?"

"It is neither, Your Highness. Nirvana is not a place at all. There are no wings or swords. Nirvana is a state of mind where pure spirits merge with the consciousness of the Earth."

Harald shook his head. "These are strange words for strange ideas. Still, you and Grady have both told entertaining tales. You have given us much to think about. Evidently that was my mother's intention, asking us to meet here tonight. The world is a bigger place than Denmark. And there are mysteries that cannot be known by the living."

The bonfire had burned to embers. A last flame licked the night. The king's gaze swept the circle of silent faces, dim in the reddish glow of the coals. His eyes stopped at Lifu.

"All of Queen Thyra's slaves are hereby freed," Harald announced, "Except for the one who answers to me. Now go back to your homes, all of you, men and women, noble and common. And let us remember Queen Thyra, Denmark's Gift."

The crowd slowly dispersed. Some people talked, others muttered, and a few laughed.

Thyra's former slaves were in especially high spirits. They resolved to drink a cask of ale in celebration. But Lifu stayed behind, waiting. She had served as Harald's spy, so her future was unclear. She told herself: Head high, like a noble.

Eventually the king noticed her, alone by the glowing firepit. He ordered his retinue to wait, and asked his wife Tove to take the children to their beds. Then he signaled for Lifu to approach.

"Lifu, my little English spy." Harald smiled with half his mouth, considering her. "Who have you really served all this time, my mother or me?"

"Both." Lifu had never called the king *Your Highness*. Despite everything, she wasn't going to start now. "You wouldn't listen when your mother gave you advice. Ironically, you believed a spy who told you the same things."

Harald's half-smile vanished. "That's not true."

"Isn't it? Thyra always wanted an alliance with the Pomeranian Slavs. You wound up marrying their princess."

"I did that for reasons of my own."

Lifu continued, "What about building the wall at Hedeby? And the ring-forts with standing armies? You resisted all these plans until I warned you that Thyra might undertake them on her own."

He shook his head. "You give yourself too much credit, spy. Are you forgetting that my mother told me never to attack, yet I defeated four kings?"

This time it was Lifu who shook her head. "They attacked *you*. Thyra knew they would. That's why she had you build the forts, to surprise them with strength. One year the King of Norway was able to raid and burn Aarhus. The next year, when he came back to do it again, you crushed him with a fleet from a fort. Suddenly you became king of Norway too."

"That is how my mother would tell the story, I suppose." Harald looked at the embers of the fire and sighed. "I'll miss her strategy. And her kindness. I wonder if she really is in Valhalla, or one of those other places."

"Without her, you won't need a spy."

"No." Harald changed the subject. "The children say you taught them magic today. Is that wise, reading their fortunes?"

"I —" Lifu stammered. "I thought a king's children should know how to read."

"What did you tell them?"

"I told Gunhild that she might marry a wealthy, handsome man who lives far away. I predicted Svein would be king one day."

"Is that all?" Harald demanded. "The boy said there was more."

"Svein wanted a sword," Lifu added cautiously. "I said he would get a blade sooner than he should."

"What does that mean?" Harald glanced to the starless space where Gorm's burial mound blocked the sky. "You're still afraid of Fenris, aren't you?"

"Yes."

"Why?"

Lifu shook her head. She really didn't know why she wanted Gorm's old sword to remain forever in a tomb. "Perhaps because Thyra disliked it too."

Harald admitted, "I haven't told Svein about the sword yet."

"Don't."

Harald scoffed. "What kind of slave are you, ordering a king?"

She didn't have an answer. Harald didn't need another slave. Anything she said now might spell her doom.

"I'm thinking of moving the court to Hedeby," Harald said, suddenly switching subjects yet again.

Lifu's voice was scarcely a whisper. "That's what Thyra suggested."

"And she was right. Jelling is too far from the ocean. I need a port where I can build warships and trade. Hedeby is on the Baltic, but has an easy portage to the North Sea that saves three days of sailing around the Skaw. It will be a better place for the children, too. More exposure to the world."

The king looked at Lifu from the side. "Could you teach them English?"

"Gunhild and Svein?" she asked, surprised. "In Hedeby? Yes, I'd like that."

"Good. That's settled, then." The king nodded and turned to go. But then he looked back. "Of course their teacher shouldn't be a slave. And I'd prefer that she were married. Have you thought of a husband?"

Lifu gasped. "Not really."

"You have no preference at all?"

She had to say something. The first words out of her mouth were, "I suppose I've always been fond of smiths." Why did this seem so true?

Harald smiled. "I've been thinking of minting my own coins in Hedeby. When that Irish silversmith comes back from Rome — if he comes back — I'll put him to work where you can spy on him."

Before she could think of a reply the king had walked away.

Alone again, Lifu tried to calm the rapid beating of her heart. She was going to be freed from her thralldom. But then perhaps she was going to be married?

She would also be tasked with teaching the king's children, a challenge with dangers of its own.

She reached into her pocket and took out the beech staves. The first one, face up, was *Logr*. The worrisome ocean. The rune for Lifu. It had fallen face up in the middle of the pile that afternoon, just as it always seemed to do. Her fate seemed always to be caught up in the middle of things.

She began tossing the staves one at a time into the coals. Each one darkened and smoked before flaring.

The last stave out of her pocket was blank — until she turned it over. And then, of course, it was Gunhild's rune, the *Kaun*. Why, Lifu wondered, were the good always doomed before their time?

CHAPTER 4
JELLING, 1940

The black Mercedes with swastika flags eased to a stop by the churchyard wall, fifty feet behind Julius' Bentley. Two German soldiers with dark green helmets opened the front doors. Lugers in hand, they eyed the archeologists.

Mette stood there in shock. A moment ago her family had been picnicking and Denmark had been free.

One soldier nodded, seemingly satisfied. He opened the rear side door and snapped to attention, clicking the heels of his shiny jackboots.

The man who stepped out wore a civilian fedora, a brown necktie, and a tan, calf-length trenchcoat. He took off a pair of spectacles and smiled. He had a hooked nose and puffy, blood-shot cheeks.

"Frau Professor Andersen! I expected to find you here. But the elder Frau Professor as well? This is indeed an honor." Suddenly he caught himself and switched from German to accented English. "Forgive me. If I recall, your family has an American background."

"Professor Wedel?" Mette recognized the Viennese professor she had met at conferences in Berlin and Stockholm. A well-regarded author of medieval studies, he hadn't seemed interested in politics. He had once asked her out for drinks to discuss runology, and she had nearly said yes.

"I am known as Colonel Wedel, for the moment." He stepped forward, holding out his hand to shake.

Mette crossed her arms indignantly. "What in God's name are you doing here?"

He blinked, taken aback. "I've come to see your excavation."

"Not just you. The German army. Denmark isn't at war. Why on earth would you invade?"

"Invade?" The professor looked a little hurt. "We're here for your protection. Haven't you heard?' The British were planning to set up bases all through Norway and Jutland. They've already stationed a quarter million men along the border in France. The German Reich has come to stand by your side."

Julius spoke up. "We heard the Danish King on the radio, talking about surrender."

"Nonsense." Wedel waved this aside. "Your King is still king. Your parliament and police will continue as before, with guidance. Once the British leave the Continent and agree to peace, Denmark won't need the help of German troops."

Magnus's English wasn't perfect, but he had understood enough. He smiled broadly and spoke in Danish, "We will dance on the graves of you bastards."

Colonel Wedel smiled back. "I knew you would understand." He cleaned his spectacles with a cloth, put them back on, and continued in a more business-like tone. "Now, about my visit here. Our Führer, Adolf Hitler, is extremely interested in Nordic history. He wanted the State Secret Police here at the Jelling excavation on Day One."

Mette asked, "You're a colonel with the *Gestapo?*"

Wedel chuckled. "Quite a rank for a history professor, isn't it? The chief advantage of the Gestapo is that we don't have to wear uniforms. My assignment is to bring back the Sword of Empire. If I'm not mistaken, you did the original research on that subject."

"Actually," Mette said, tilting her head, "That would be my mother, the elder Frau Professor."

Kirstin flushed. "It was just a theory. One of the sagas suggested that Harald Fairhair was aided in his conquest of Norway by a dragon with the power to build empires. At first I thought it might be the ship we unearthed at Oseberg." Mette's mother had become so enthused by her subject that she began talking faster. "But then we realized that the Oseberg ship burial had been robbed early in the Viking Age. What had the thieves taken? A dragon can be a metaphor for many things. Why not a sword?"

Magnus added in accented English, "It was not only your theory, Kirstin. We heard the story from an old woman at Oseberg."

"Oral histories are often true," she replied defensively.

The colonel asked, "Did you find a sword in the Oseberg burial?"

"No. But Danish kings started winning victory after victory shortly after the site was robbed, about 940 AD. They obviously didn't have the Oseberg ship, but perhaps they had found its sword?"

The colonel's eyes gleamed. "And how about here in Jelling? Have you found a sword?"

Kirstin looked to her daughter.

"No." Mette shook her head, inadvertently bouncing her curls. "We've learned a lot, though."

"No sword. We may have to excavate elsewhere as well. The Reich's historians have a theory of their own." Wedel stroked his mustache. "For today, however, I'll have you give me a tour, to show me your findings."

"Professor Wedel," Mette said coldly, "I am not your subordinate."

"Not as Professor Wedel, no." He spoke a few words in German to the soldiers by the car. The men raised their Lugers. Wedel smiled. "But as a Gestapo colonel I have a different authority. You see, we don't want to meddle in most Danish affairs, but Hitler is very keen on Germanic symbology. I've been assigned to oversee the National Museum's work. Technically that makes you my employee. Still, I'd rather we kept on with our old relationship as friends."

"Friends," Mette repeated doubtfully.

"Yes. I've always admired your research on runes." The colonel pointed to a large carved boulder beside the church. "Let's start here, in the middle of things, at Harald Bluetooth's famous rune stone."

Mette bit her lip and looked to Julius. He gave a small shrug, as if to say she might as well do what the colonel said. The way Julius pressed his lips together, however, suggested that they would talk about their own plans later.

"All right, Colonel," Mette sighed. "A friendly tour at gunpoint." She marched stiffly across the churchyard to a carved granite boulder the size and shape of a haystack. "The inscription begins on the far side."

As soon as the colonel had followed her behind the stone he grabbed her by the elbow. "Mette!" he whispered fiercely. "I'm not a Nazi. It's me, your friend Franz. I begged for this assignment so they wouldn't send some military idiot. The German army has no business in Denmark. Hitler's an obsessed fool. I'm here to help you."

"With a car full of armed soldiers?"

"I have to play that role. I'm afraid one of them understands our English." He let go of her arm, put a hand on his stomach, and grimaced. "Damned ulcer."

Mette studied him skeptically. His stomach was growling as if it were a car trying to start. For a professor of medieval studies, Franz Wedel had made quite an effort not to show how much stress he was under.

"How about Danish?" she asked.

"What?"

"Do your guards understand Danish?"

He waved a hand disparagingly. "That's a dialect no proper German understands."

Mette flushed, her sympathy dimming. "Danish is not a dialect of German. It's as different as English. That's why my father felt safe calling you a bastard."

The colonel looked tired. "I didn't catch every word, but I got the idea. Look, I know how awkward this is. But it's also an opportunity. Berlin is willing to provide a lot of money for research. We just have to humor them by finding some artifacts, a few mysterious old Germanic clues. If we refuse to lead the excavation the Wehrmacht will be here next week with bulldozers."

Mette shivered. She didn't trust Franz Wedel, but what he had said about the Army bulldozers might actually be true. The Reich might well be willing to destroy the foundation stones of Danish history in their quest for Germanic knickknacks.

"Work with me, Mette." Franz held out his hand again to shake. His stomach growled. He smiled painfully. "I'll help you if you help me."

She hesitated. "I'm not sure."

"Neither am I. I'm just trying to make the best of a bad situation." He held his hand out further. "Please, Mette. For the sake of your research."

She put her hand in his. He clasped and shook it eagerly. "Excellent. Let's get started."

"How do you propose to start, Professor Wedel?"

"Franz. You simply have to call me Franz. And I was serious about starting with the tour. How do I know how to help if I don't know what you've found so far?"

Mette looked past the boulder to the people by the cars. She was relieved to see that the German soldiers had put away their weapons and were instead admiring the Bentley, with Julius pointing out the car's features in fluent German. Her fiancé obviously had a knack for defusing tension.

Meanwhile, Franz had begun running his fingers along the stone's four rows of incised runes. The stick-shaped letters were framed by an intricately knotted, decorative snake. "You know, this is the first time I've seen Harald Bluetooth's monument in person. The runes look like sixteen-sign Futhark. Can you read them?"

Mette pulled his hand away. "Please don't touch. This is one of the clearest inscriptions left in Old Norse. It says, *King Harald had this kumble built for his father Gorm and his mother Thyra.*"

"Kumble? Is that an old word for a rune stone?"

"More than that. A kumble is an entire memorial complex." Mette relaxed a bit, talking about her area of expertise.

"You didn't translate the last line," Franz pointed out.

"It may have been carved later. The runes read, *Harald won all of Denmark —*"

Mette walked around the stone to where the inscription continued on a surface with an elaborate four-legged beast. "*— and Norway —*"

She continued to the final side of the triangular boulder, where a crucified Jesus battled a tangle of snakes. "*— and made the Danes Christian.*"

Franz nodded. "That does sound like a postscript. If I recall, Harald Bluetooth didn't turn away from the Norse gods until late in his reign."

"And his kumble reflects that."

"How so?"

She pointed to a thirty-foot-tall circular hill behind the church. "Harald built a grave mound for his father in the old style, on top of a smaller mound from the Bronze Age."

"So Jelling was already a sacred site?"

"Exactly. The original mound stood at the point of two huge, curved lines of standing stones. Most have been moved, but in Harald's day they would have formed the outline of a gigantic ship."

"Was an actual Viking ship buried here?"

"No, but the stone outline is the largest in history, five hundred feet from stem to stern. When Harald's mother died he built a second mound that covered part of the ship's stones."

"I assume the burial mounds have been excavated."

"Many times. A previous excavation found a grave chamber lined with boards, but we're the first to find bones and grave goods."

"Why is that?"

"Because of the church." Mette nodded toward the whitewashed bell tower.

"Of course. Harald must have built this church when he converted."

"Not this one exactly. The stone church was built in the 1300s. But you're right, it's on the site of Harald's original church from 985 AD.

That one was built of wooden staves. We assume that Harald dug up his heathen parents and had them reburied inside, in ground that was holy to the Christians."

"So that's where you've been excavating, inside?"

"I suppose you'll order me to show you."

"I'd prefer to ask. May I?"

Silently she walked to the church door and unlocked it with a heavy iron key. Beyond the whitewashed foyer the church opened up into a hall with wooden pews. A five-foot model of a fully-rigged ship hung from the brightly colored rafter beams of the ceiling. Gilt cherubs decorated a wooden pulpit to one side. Chalkboards along the walls had the white numbers of hymns. But at the front of the church, beside the altar, plank railings fenced off a rectangular pit.

"Did you find Harald's parents?" Franz asked quietly.

"Not Thyra, but probably Gorm. A man in his fifties with gout. And no, there wasn't a sword with him."

"Then what kind of grave goods did you find?"

"A few fragments of iron and pottery. The grave appears to have been looted at a very early date. But the thieves missed something important."

She took a small glass jar from behind the altar. Inside was a square chip of age-blackened wood, perhaps three inches long.

"What is it?" Franz asked.

"A book."

"What?

"A piece of beech wood. This is the sort of chip that would have been carved with runes for fortune telling. Or for a curse. Or as a claim."

Franz turned the jar to the light of a stained glass window. "Yes, I see it now. They've carved the same zigzag thunderbolt used by the Nazis' SS troops."

"It's the sun-rune, for the letter S. It could stand for anything that starts with that sound."

"Perhaps someone's name?"

"Perhaps."

Franz turned over the jar and drew in his breath. "A Nazi swastika!"

Mette took back the jar. "Don't be absurd. It's just the sun-cross. It means the same thing as the S-rune. It's been used since ancient times to represent the sun, or Odin."

Franz whispered, "A stormtrooper S and a swastika. We're getting close."

"What are you talking about?"

"The holy grail of the Third Reich's historians."

"It's just a wood chip with a rune. We haven't found anything surprising in Gorm's tomb."

"Yes, what we're looking for isn't here. It's somewhere else. Don't you see the pattern? As soon as an important monarch is buried, someone else steals the sword of power. They can't resist the chance to build their own empire."

Mette shook her head. "We don't know what was stolen or where it was taken."

"No?" Professor Wedel gave her a sidelong smile. "Follow the empires. Who defeated Harald Bluetooth?"

"His son Svein. In a sea battle by Hedeby in 985 AD."

"Exactly. The same year as Gorm's burial. And the victor was Svein — a name that starts with an S. That's why we need to finish up here and move our operations to the ships we've found in the sand at Hedeby. How much more time do you need here in Jelling?"

"A week, at least." She paused. Hedeby had been Svein's capital. "Why haven't I heard about these ships?"

"Because Hedeby is in Germany now. The Germans call it Haithabu. Last winter a fisherman from Schleswig complained about getting his net stuck in the sandy shallows there. He brought in a carved piece of planking that might date to the 980s. Aerial photos show the outlines of what may be half a dozen ships. Want to come see?"

She did, but she worried about the war. If she traveled to Germany she might be seen as a traitor to Denmark. "Who would be in charge of excavating these ships?"

"You, of course. I'm just a history professor." Franz spread his hands. "You can close up the dig here in Jelling, keeping everything safe. Then you lead a Danish expedition to Hedeby. You can even tell the Danish newspapers you're invading Germany, retaking the ancient Danish capital. All paid for by the Reich."

"What do you get out of it, Wedel?"

"My name is Franz."

"Franz, then. What's in it for the Gestapo?"

He shrugged. "Hitler wants a sword. We all want to unearth a piece of Norse history. And to be honest, Germany doesn't have the manpower to take on a new archeological project right now. We're —" he rolled his hand in the air. "— in the midst of something big."

"Invading Scandinavia?"

"Bigger than that."

"The world?

"Smaller."

Mette puzzled over this. "What if I said no?

Franz smiled sadly. "You won't say no."

* * *

That evening Mette and Julius climbed the grassy mound to the south of the church to watch the shadows lengthen, and to talk. Julius stopped short at the hill's rim. "I didn't know there was a crater on top."

Mette nodded. "That's the work of Harald Bluetooth. When he dug up his father's grave he left a pit that filled with water."

"Not a very careful archeologist."

"Later diggers weren't much better," Mette said. "In 1704 the Danish king had a ditch dug to drain the pond. Water kept coming out. By 1820 the local farmers decided to dig deeper to find the source of the spring. Instead they chopped up the planks of Gorm's old grave chamber."

"Did they find anything?"

She shook her head. "Neither did Frederik the Seventh. He had workers tunnel in from the side in 1861. We were more scientific, but didn't really have much luck here in Jelling."

"You found Gorm."

"I suppose." They watched swallows spiral about the church tower in the yard below. "Professor Wedel thinks if we excavate at Hedeby we'll find the Seventh Wonder of the Viking World."

Julius took her hand. "Do you want to go to Hedeby?"

She laced her fingers into his, one by one. "No, because it's farther away from you. Yes, because Wedel might be right. No, because of the war. Yes, because he says I'd be in charge. No, because I don't trust him."

"And yes, because Colonel Wedel isn't really giving you a choice." Julius squeezed her hand. "You should do it. You've always dreamed of a ship excavation like this."

"That's true."

"Then go. But you'll have to promise to visit me in Copenhagen as often as you can. I won't be able to risk going to Germany."

She looked at him, alarmed. "Do they know your family is Jewish?"

"They'll find out. Last November the Nazis burned synagogues and smashed Jewish shop windows all through Germany. Rumors from Poland say they've rounded up thousands of Jews and put them on trains. No one knows where they're going, but I don't think they're coming back."

"They wouldn't do that in Denmark, would they? The Jewish community is so small. And you're Danes."

Julius sighed. "I need to get back to Copenhagen to find out what's going on. I'm worried about my parents."

Mette pulled him closer. She pressed her head against his shoulder. "Maybe we shouldn't wait to get married."

"Mette!" Julius coughed in surprise. "You were the one who wanted things settled first."

"I know, but —" she bit her lip. Her eyes began to tear. "I'm afraid."

He put his arms around her. "Never do anything out of fear. The greatest Danish Vikings have always stood their ground and stayed strong. We'll come through even this."

"Do you promise?"

In reply, he kissed her on the lips.

CHAPTER 5
HEDEBY, 971

When spring came again Lifu moved her "school" for King Harald's children to one of the watchtowers beside Hedeby's south gate.

Most of a year had passed since Lifu had traveled with the king's vast court entourage — first by wagon and then by ship — to this polyglot trading town on Denmark's southern border. Harald expanded Thyra's old halls, hiring craftsmen to decorate posts with writhing beasts, colorful runes, and gilt knots. Lifu and most of the queen's other former slaves slept in the same wattle-walled buildings as before, one for men and the one for women, although now the buildings were renamed the Free Retainers' Halls and the walls were painted with bright patterns. She sometimes thought of Grady, the Irish silversmith who had rushed off to Rome. She wondered if he remembered her too,

and the kiss he had given her when he won his freedom.

The winter had been so cold that the salt fjord beyond the harbor had frozen. Men on bone skates had dared to pole across the ice two miles to the low island where Harald's jarls had their military outpost. There they told tales and drank mead in the long dark evenings by the hearth fires of their icicle-eaved boat sheds.

Lifu had been assigned to spend an hour after breakfast each day teaching English to the thirteen-year-old princess Gunhild and her ten-year-old brother Svein. Lifu took her work seriously, studying and planning so that their sessions beside the fire of the otherwise empty feast hall were entertaining. She often let the lessons range afield to topics she thought a future king or queen might need — history, legends, the stars, other cultures.

At the end of the week-long feasts for Yule, the king gifted Lifu a roll of beautiful red linen so that she could sew herself a dress befitting a royal tutor. Gunhild received the first key that she was allowed to pin on her dress, a token of her coming adulthood. The key fit an ivory box that contained some of the elegant silver jewelry that Grady, the Irish smith, had once fashioned for her grandmother. Svein, to Lifu's dismay, was granted his first metal sword. To be sure, it was only a half-length blade with the uninspiring name of Dogbane, but the boy flailed it so dangerously at the Yule feast that his father assigned him an additional hour's weapon practice each afternoon with a jarl tutor.

When the last of the snow had melted and the beech trees were tinged with green buds, Harald Bluetooth and his jarls sailed out of Hedeby with fifty ships to check that the fleets in each of the realm's five ring-forts had weathered the winter well.

Lifu, too, had felt the magic of spring. The urge was strong to escape the dark, smoky halls of Hedeby. Of course she was bound by her daily task, and would not be allowed to risk taking the king's children beyond the town's mile-wide semicircular palisade. But the watchtower was a close second choice. Two of these plank-roofed huts perched atop the palisade's twenty-foot-tall earth berm, flanking the massive, iron-hinged south gate. The soldiers on guard duty used only one of the buildings, so Lifu commandeered the other each morning for her lessons.

The staves in the walls had been spaced to allow lookouts to aim weapons through the cracks, so there was plenty of light. The smooth dirt floor made an adequate slate for drawing runes or figures. On chilly mornings she built a small fire in the middle of the floor and pulled up benches.

Through the slots on the little classroom's north wall the view extended across a sheep pasture to the town's jumbled rooftops of yellow straw and dark planks. The distant sails and mast spires of the harbor shimmered dream-like through the haze of arching smoke plumes.

To the east, the wall's slots overlooked the curve of the palisade itself, the easternmost section of the great Danevirke wall that crossed all of Jutland to the Eider River and the North Sea. The top of the grassy embankment was so wide that soldiers could march five abreast, protected by a stockade of sharpened logs.

To the south were the forests of Frankia, home to highwaymen and patrols of strange, German-speaking troops.

But it was the view to the west that often interrupted English lessons. The slots there faced the gate. Gunhild and Svein always jumped up to watch when the guards winched open the heavy, creaking doors. Sometimes the visitor turned out to be merely a sleepy drover with a herd of cattle. But it could also be an entire cavalry troop in glinting chain mail, or a caravan of merchant wagons from distant lands.

You never knew who — or what — might knock on Hedeby's back door.

"Today," Lifu announced in English that spring morning, "The two of you have learned enough of my language that we can start to memorize an English poem."

Svein groaned. "Aw, those poem stories go on forever."

Lifu laughed tolerantly. The poem she had in mind was in fact more than three thousand verses long. It had taken her a month to learn it by heart. She didn't expect the children to master more than a few dozen lines each. But she felt that understanding the skill of the skalds should be part of every prince's training. And this particular story had a moral the boy needed to note. Lifu had prepared a few tricks to win over Svein and his teenage sister.

"This poem is about battling monsters," she said, loosening the drawstring of a woolen bag. "And it is sung to the music of an English harp."

The children watched in surprise as she withdrew a shiny wooden instrument from the bag. She strummed an eerie chord from its six

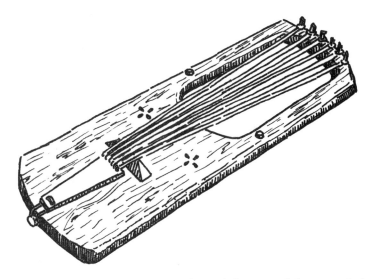

strings. Inlaid patterns of mother-of-pearl decorated the rounded rect-angular box.

"It's beautiful!" Gunhild marveled. "Where did you find such a treasure in Hedeby?"

"I told your father we need music for your poetry instruction. He hired an English craftsman to build a harp in the proper style. Here, you try." She handed the harp to Gunhild.

The girl and her brother took turns strumming the melancholy six-note chord.

"Is that all it does?" Svein asked.

"That's how you start." Lifu took the harp and demonstrated. "If you strum just three of the six strings you get different chords. And if you pluck the strings one at a time you can play entire melodies. It takes time to learn things like that. For now we'll just strum. The idea is to accompany every stressed word in the song with music, four beats per line."

"Do you always sing poems in England?" Gunhild asked.

"Usually."

"Even women?"

"Especially women. Girls start to learn at your age."

Svein objected, "Girls can't sing about battles with monsters."

"You think not? Let me show you." Lifu strummed the harp and began,

Listen! I'll tell you a tale from the days
When Danes fought dragons of dread and fire.

She handed the harp to Svein. "Go ahead. You try." She helped the boy rehearse the English words of the first two lines until he managed to repeat them, strumming the harp on the accented syllables.

Gunhild, who had been watching jealously, then took the harp and sang the two lines straight off.

"Every skald who sings this poem can change it," Lifu explained, "But you have to use the same rune-sound two or three times in each verse. In the second line it's the 'd' sound that you hear in dread, dragons, and Danes."

Gunhild nodded. "Our skalds rhyme the same way."

"Who's the poem about?" Svein asked.

"A Danish king named Hrothgar. He built a great hall where his warriors could feast and drink mead."

"Hrothgar?" Svein wrinkled his brow. "Never heard of him."

"It was hundreds of years ago," Lifu admitted, "And some of the characters might be made up."

Gunhild looked thoughtful. "Why would the English sing about ancient kings in Denmark?"

Lifu had to pause to think. "Nostalgia, I suppose. Originally the English lived in Denmark, you know. Back then the Danes lived in Sweden. When the Danes invaded Jutland they drove out the English. There were three English tribes back then, the Jutes, the Angles, and the Saxons."

"Didn't the English fight?" Svein asked.

"I don't know. Mostly I think they got in their ships and sailed overseas."

"Cowards," Svein scoffed.

"Or bold adventurers. It depends on your point of view. Rome had just withdrawn its legions from the province of Britannia, so the island was easy prey for the Anglo-Saxons. They plundered and burned the cities and slaughtered the people."

Gunhild put her hands on her hips. "How can the English complain about Viking immigrants? The English are the barbarians."

"Or plucky opportunists. Again, it depends on who tells the story. But English poets still think of Denmark as a beautiful lost land, and of those days as an age of heroes. Now, getting back to the song —" Lifu strummed the harp.

> A monster of the march by the name of Grendel
> Hated the harp-songs in Hrothgar's hall.
> By night when men napped, Grendel grabbed thirty
> And carried their corpses to gobble in his lair.

Now Lifu had the children's full attention.

"What did this monster look like?" Gunhild asked.

"The poem doesn't say. But it suggests that Grendel's race may once have been men."

"Why didn't the warriors just kill the monster?" Svein put in. "Thirty men would have thirty swords."

Lifu shook her head. "Grendel was protected by a powerful curse from the gods. No weapon could bite him. Grendel was invulnerable to the steel of warriors."

As soon as Lifu spoke these words, she heard them echoing back from her lost memories. Did King Gorm's buried sword Fenris have a similar power, and a similar curse?

Mechanically she added the words, "The curse that had made Grendel victorious also made him evil, gradually turning him into a monster."

Lifu stared at a slice of sky beyond a wall slot, as if in a trance. Odin had sent her here for a purpose, and now she was beginning to remember it. Her hand fell from the harp's strings. A stumbling, discordant note hung in the air.

"Lifu?" Gunhild asked. "Are you all right?"

Svein complained, "The poem can't end like that. Someone has to defeat the monster. Who's the hero?"

"Beowulf," Lifu said, quickly shaking her head to clear her thoughts. "The hero is a Geatish prince named Beowulf from southern Sweden."

"Beowulf? That's a strange name," Gunhild mused.

"No, it's clever," Lifu countered. "It means 'bee wolf.' English poets use that term to describe a bear without saying the word 'bear'. Beowulf was the strongest of men, with hands like a bear's. He offered to sleep in Hrothgar's hall and fight Grendel bare-handed."

Both children laughed. "With his bear hands!"

"That night the prince and the demon battled in the dark hall. They wrestled, smashing benches. Finally Beowulf ripped Grendel's arm off at the shoulder." Lifu strummed the harp.

> The weird monster wailed, and away he fled
> To his home in the marsh to be mourned
> by his mother.

"The next day Hrothgar rewarded Beowulf with gifts of gold and a great feast." Lifu lowered her voice. "But that very same night Grendel's mother, an even more terrible monster, returned to the hall to avenge her son's death."

Svein's eyes widened. He swallowed.

"When darkness fell and Hrothgar's men were sleeping off their mead in the hall, Grendel's mother crashed through the door and began killing them with her claws and her teeth. She ate some on the spot. She dragged the bodies of others back to her swamp to eat later. The next morning the bloody track left by Grendel's mother was easy to see, but only Beowulf was brave enough to follow it. He tracked the blood to a black lake full of snakes. He knew Grendel's mother must live down there. He held his breath, dived in, and swam down until he found her in an underwater cave. Again Beowulf battled, and again his own sword was useless. But the monster's hoard of treasure included a sword stolen from the giants. Beowulf thought that blade

might be immune to curses meant for men. He swung the huge sword two-handed and cut off the monster's head. Then he swam back to the surface with his grisly trophy, twice a hero."

Both children had listened to the tale open-mouthed. Gunhild recovered her composure first. She shrugged and said lightly, "Two monsters. You said there'd be a dragon."

"And there is. A fire-breathing dragon attacks Beowulf's home later in the story." Lifu plucked the harp's strings slowly, one at a time. "What do you say? Shall we learn the song of Beowulf? We'll each take parts so you won't have to memorize too much. Then we'll perform it for your father and the queen at the midsummer night's festival."

The children glanced at each other, excited and frightened by the prospect of singing an English saga in front of the royal court.

Before either of them could answer, however, a creaking of iron caught their attention. Instantly the children forgot everything else. They pressed close to the slots between the wall staves, straining to see what new marvel might emerge from the wilds of the Frankish realms.

Lifu sighed and put her harp away in its woolen bag. The hour for their English lesson was over anyway. Tomorrow they could talk about performing Beowulf. She had set the hook deep enough, however, that she was confident she would land her two young fish.

"It's just more priests," Svein grumbled, disappointed by the bald monks entering the gate.

"But they're accompanied by a guard of Norse soldiers," Gunhild pointed out. "They've come a long way, from the looks of their gear. Hey, I think I recognize that man with the red beard. Wasn't he one of grandmother's old slaves?"

At once Lifu was at the window slot, watching the men below. One of the soldiers was in fact Grady. Her heart beat in her throat. The Irish silversmith sat up straight on his short horse, a spear in one hand and a scabbard at his side. He wore the acorn-shaped helmet of a warrior, but he had no other armor and his purple cloak was threadbare. His amber eyes looked older and his face even ruddier than before. Would he remember kissing her at Queen Thyra's bonfire?

"Class is dismissed," Lifu announced. She hurried out of the watchtower so abruptly that the children looked at each other in surprise.

CHAPTER 6
JELLING AND HEDEBY, 1940

Every evening the radio brought astonishing war news. During the days, Mette's archeological team had to work to finish their excavation of King Gorm's grave in Jelling. But after dark, they huddled around the inn's radio.

On the day Denmark fell, Colonel Wedel had hinted that "something bigger" was in the works. Mette would never have believed it possible that in May, just thirty days after the Wehrmacht had occupied Denmark and Norway, a much larger German force would storm across the borders of Holland, Belgium, and Luxembourg toward France. Unlike the "soft" invasion of Denmark, this was a full-scale blitzkrieg, with waves of droning bombers, strafing fighter planes, and rumbling panzer tanks. The Reich had ignored the heavily fortified Maginot Line on the French border with Germany, and instead had raced through the Low Countries, ignoring their neutrality. Already half a million French and British troops were stumbling backwards towards the English Channel.

No one was coming to Denmark's aid.

Telephone calls from Jelling to Copenhagen were wildly expensive, and possible only from a desk in the local post office, but Mette placed two that month. Her call to the director of the National Museum confirmed that Colonel Wedel of the Gestapo had indeed been given oversight of their operations, with a seemingly limitless budget. Mette could take all twenty of her staff people from Jelling to Hedeby. The National Museum would send an additional dozen engineers from Copenhagen with expertise in building drydock coffer dams for the shipwrecks in Hedeby's harbor.

Mette's second telephone call was to her fiancé. Julius answered on the tenth ring, out of breath. "Gustmeyer here."

"Julius, it's me. Are you all right?"

"Mette! It's so good to hear your voice." His laugh was a sigh of relief.

"Then you made it home OK?"

"Yes, although the Bentley blew a tire when I drove off the ferry at Korsør. Your father says those steel ramps are too sharp. The tire had already worn through the tread, but the shop in Korsør wouldn't sell us a new one. Saving rubber for the war effort, I guess. We had to patch it and limp back as best we could."

This relatively mundane news lessened Mette's tension. "And your parents are safe?"

"Oh, yes. Most things are frighteningly normal. The King has taken to riding his horse around Copenhagen each afternoon to calm people's nerves. Oh, we've been told to black out the city at night by painting our windows or using heavy drapes. Apparently the Germans want to protect us from night raids by the dreaded British RAF."

She could almost hear his wry smile. "I think the Royal Air Force is busy elsewhere."

"Do you suppose?"

Again, the wry tone she loved. "I miss you, Julius."

"And I miss you so much it hurts. Are you really going to an excavation in Germany?"

"I'm afraid so. We leave in a few days."

A woman's voice broke onto the line. "Two and a half minutes." They only had thirty seconds left!

"Are you sure you're all right?" Mette blurted. "They haven't made you wear a yellow star or something?"

"No, nothing like that." He hesitated. "Although we did hide the synagogue's Torah and candelabras in a basement, just as a precaution. The newspapers say other congregations are doing the same thing. They say there are 7,400 Jews in Denmark."

"How did they get that number?" Mette asked.

"Apparently from the Germans."

"Oh!"

"Three minutes," the operator announced. "Please end your call."

Frantic, Mette said, "I won't be able to make international calls from Germany, but we can write."

"How?" Julius cried. "To what address?"

"In care of the city museum in Schleswig!"

The line went dead.

* * *

Looking casual in his tan trenchcoat and fedora, Colonel Franz Wedel checked all twenty passports of Mette's Danish team, carefully gluing a stamped and signed visa into each. He had ordered a modern bus for the archeologists and two canvas-covered Army trucks for their equipment. As they drove south through Jutland, Wedel walked down the aisle of the bus, chatting with them in English. Soon he was able to remember everyone's name.

After two hours the colonel asked the bus driver to stop in Åbenrå, the last Danish town before the border. He had the driver park the bus in the center of town, beside a cobblestone square lined with half-timbered shops and cafes. Then he held out his hand toward the tables on the sidewalk.

"Lunchtime for my honored colleagues. Please, order whatever you like, courtesy of the Führer."

The colonel's largesse was clearly intended to put them at ease about cooperating with the Gestapo. Mette noticed that many in her team accepted this VIP treatment with smiles. Martina, the too-pretty cataloguer who sketched artifacts, batted her eyes flirtatiously at the colonel. Claus, the preservation specialist with a Santa-like white beard, ordered cod and white potatoes as if he had earned it. But Mette's second-in-command, the bow-tied Henrik, frowned skeptically, ordering only a light snack. And although the two university interns, Asger and Eskil, ordered full seafood dinners, they dared to make silly faces at the colonel behind his back.

After lunch, when the bus stopped at the border, the colonel switched to German. "English is not so popular here," he told Mette.

"My German is rusty," Mette warned him. "Some of the others can't speak more than a few words."

"I know. Don't worry. Your translator here is the curator of the Schleswig museum. He's a German who speaks Danish."

Mette raised her eyebrows. "There are such people?"

"The Reich is linguistically rich, Frau Professor."

The highway curved around a low hill and began following the shore of Schleswig fjord, a broad inlet that gradually narrowed toward the distant ships, cranes, and steeples of Schleswig itself.

"Hedeby is over there, on the south shore." The colonel pointed across the fjord to a flat landscape of farms and forests. "The old harbor is too shallow for modern ships, but Vikings only needed a foot or two of water."

"It doesn't look safe to me," Mette commented.

"What do you mean?"

"A Danish king might have allowed craftsmen to build a trading center on land like that, but Viking jarls always preferred an island for their warships. Towns need land access, but they were usually defended by a naval camp on an island nearby."

"No sign of that here."

"Maybe we'll find it."

The bus and the two Army trucks rumbled along the brick streets of Schleswig toward the arched steel roof of a train station on the edge of the oldest part of the city. Two blocks later they parked at the foot of a small wooded hill beside a long brick building with arched windows. Metal letters bolted above the red-and-white striped entry doors read *Schleswiger Stadtmuseum.*

"Welcome to your new headquarters," the colonel announced in German, opening the bus door. Then he reached to the steering wheel and sounded the horn four times: *dah-dit-dah-dah.*

The entire Danish team had time to gather on the sidewalk before one of the entry doors finally opened. A small, elderly man with a bushy white mustache peered out at them uncertainly. He wore the red cap and uniform of a train conductor from a previous century. The jacket sagged on his stooped shoulders.

"Herr Matthiasen!" the colonel said loudly, evidently because the old man was hard of hearing. "These are the archeologists we talked about!"

"*Jawohl, Herr Oberst Wedel. Danke,*" the man mumbled back.

Wedel spoke to Mette. "Frau Professor Anderson, may I introduce Herr Matthiasen, curator of the local museum."

They studied each other for a moment in silence.

Matthiasen chewed on his mustache.

Mette sighed, fearing already that professional collaboration might be difficult with this uncommunicative man.

"Herr Matthiasen," she said, "You don't really speak Danish, do you?"

The little man drew himself up. *"Joda!"*

He pronounced this strangely typical, affirmative Danish denial with such authentic conviction that all twenty of the Danes on the archeological team couldn't help but laugh.

"Where did you learn Danish?" Mette asked.

"Here at home. Handy as a secret code, huh?" Matthiasen winked. Apparently he wasn't hard of hearing at all — at least not in this language. "Before Bismarck whupped the Danes in 1864 this was Slesvig, not Schleswig. Some of us old-timers still stick to the old ways, although they've mostly put us in museums by now." He pushed open the other door, grumbling. "Well, come on in and see the rest of the relics. I'll show you your rooms later."

While the archeologists filed inside, Colonel Wedel called over their heads to Mette, "Go ahead. I'll see that the drivers unload your gear."

The first high-ceilinged room was devoted entirely to trains. There were old railway signs, a wooden passenger car converted to cabinets, and a clunky old steam engine.

Mette's assistant Henrik asked the curator, "Was this building a train station? The brick arches actually seem older than that."

"You're right," Matthiasen said. "It was built in the 1700s as a stable for the carriages of the local duke. After the war in 1864 the duke donated it to the railway. The Prussians used it as a machine shop for sixty years. Then they turned it into a museum."

Claus, the expert on preserving wood, asked, "So most of your artifacts are relatively recent?"

"That's why we're so enthused about your excavation at Hedeby," the curator said. "Our Viking-age collection is quite small. Oh, we've got one small rune stone. And the school classes always want to see our mummy, an old woman thrown into a bog, probably as a criminal. The acid in the water tanned her skin to leather. But what we really need is a Viking ship. Then our museum would be famous."

Henrik nodded toward the big cast-iron engine. "Until then your centerpiece is a locomotive?"

Matthiasen apparently did not notice Henrik's disparaging tone. "The Iron Dane," he said proudly. "She was the first steam locomotive built in Denmark. Prussian engineers said it was a waste of metal. They call her the Iron Cow. But I've taken the whole thing apart and put it back together. I bet her pistons would still pump if she had enough steam."

"Will we have enough space to work here at the museum?" Mette asked, getting back to business.

Matthiasen tipped back his conductor's cap and scratched his thinning gray hair. "We're already crowded. The colonel says you'll build workshops and dormitories and everything out there at Hedeby. Until then you can stay at the manor and take a train out to the site."

"There's a rail line to Hedeby?"

"Almost. They run a little commuter train twice a day from the Schleswig station as far as the old factory at Gammeltop, a kilometer or so south. We'll have to catch it at 7:45 in the morning. You'll want to get up early."

Martina, the fashion-conscious illustrator, asked, "We're staying in a manor house?"

"I'm afraid we've only opened twelve bedrooms of the duke's old place, so some of you will have to double up or sleep on sofas." The curator waved for them to follow. "Come on, I'll show you."

He led them through two more exhibit rooms, past the rune stone and the mummy, to a garage where Colonel Wedel was overseeing the unloading of equipment from the Army trucks.

"How was the tour?" the colonel asked. Without waiting for a reply he added, "We left your luggage up on the front step. Dinner's at seven. See you then."

Behind the museum a gravel lane switchbacked up through a forested park to what looked like a stone castle, with a spire atop a green copper turret.

"I have to say I'm impressed with the duke's hospitality," Mette said. "We'll have to thank him."

"He's not here," Matthiasen grumbled. "Carl and Brigitte Sakse-Gottorp abandoned the place last month. Moved permanently to their winter home in Portugal."

"They left the country?"

"I guess so."

Mette asked quietly, "Are they Jewish?"

"No, but she once ran for mayor as a socialist, so she had been on the Nazis' blacklist. The family had mixed feelings anyway. The dukes of Schleswig had been under the Danish crown until the war of '64. The last straw was when the German Navy decided to base a U-boat in Schleswig and draft the duke as captain."

The old curator stopped to stretch his back. Then he opened the massive oak front door of the manor.

Mette stepped inside. For a moment she simply stood there, marveling at the entry hall's brass chandelier, balustraded staircase, and tapestries. The herringbone parquet of the wooden floor creaked.

She shook her head. "Why are we being allowed to stay here?"

Matthiasen took off his conductor's cap. "The government confiscated the duke's property. They told the museum to take care of it. Someday I guess we'll restore everything for an exhibit. In the meantime the colonel ordered us to set you up here and treat you like royalty."

"Why? We're just archeologists."

Matthiasen shrugged. "You don't question the Gestapo." He waved the others in with his cap. "Bring your bags upstairs. Bedrooms are to the left and right. Take your pick. There's no maid service, so keep things tidy. And don't damage the furniture. It's all property of the museum."

When Mette brought her own suitcase inside, Matthiasen motioned her to one side. "You'll be staying on the first floor, in the ducal suite." He led the way through a parlor to a wood-paneled study and an adjacent bedroom with a canopy bed. Leaded windows looked out through a gap in the forest to the harbor and the fjord beyond.

"I can't stay here," Mette objected. "This is where the duke and duchess lived."

"Don't get used to luxury," Matthiasen said, snorting. "The quarters they're planning at Hedeby will be barracks."

"And how are twenty archeologists supposed to build something like that? Colonel Wedel said he didn't have any manpower to spare."

"Maybe he didn't last week, but he does now."

"What do you mean?"

"Prisoners of war. Trainloads are coming back from the western front. You're getting eighty."

Mette sat down on her suitcase. She didn't like the idea of using prisoners for their work. Would they be English or French? Perhaps they would be relieved to be working with Danes, and not in armament factories.

"I simply do not understand the importance of this excavation to the Reich."

"A Viking ship," Matthiasen said. "Maybe a sword. Some good science. Don't you think that's enough?"

"Maybe."

But when Mette looked into the old curator's gray eyes, she could tell that he didn't believe it either.

* * *

That night Mette sat down to write at the duke's desk.

Dearest Julius,

I am sending you two letters in separate envelopes. The next one will be about the weather, the excellent Schleswig museum, and the beautiful manor where we are staying. This first one is a test to see if our mail is being censored. Please write back soon to let me know what you receive.

Professor Wedel is supplying us with eighty prisoners of war to build workshops, dormitories, and an airstrip at Hedeby. Of course I'm excited by the scale of the project, but I'm also a little alarmed.

Our liaison here is a German citizen of Danish heritage named Matthiasen. After dinner he took me aside and asked if any of the people on our team had Jewish ancestors — even a great-great-grandfather. I said I didn't know. The racial purity laws here are getting stricter. Full-blooded Jews were taken away by the police years ago. People with any Jewish ancestry had to wear six-pointed Stars of David. But now they have disappeared too. They are supposed to be safe in detention centers, but no one knows where they are, or if the Jews are even really alive.

Although there are no Jews in Schleswig now, park benches still have signs, "For Aryans Only." What scares me most is that Matthiasen says the post office has a chart showing who is allowed to marry whom. Aryans can marry Aryans and Jews could theoretically marry Jews, but mixed marriages are illegal in Germany.

Mette stopped and bit her lip. It wasn't religion that gave her pause about Julius. He was so much younger than her, and handsome enough to turn the heads of prettier girls. Mette had been hurt before. Eight years ago at the university she had accepted a ring from a happy-go-lucky medical student named Peder. Like Julius, he had said he admired her seriousness — her career ambitions. But then Peder had run off with a young barmaid. When Mette's brother Lars had suddenly left for America, she had felt abandoned yet again. Since then a nervous inner voice had warned her to be cautious with love. She sighed and put her pen back to paper.

I'm afraid that there will be a knock on the door one night and you will disappear. Please, fly your plane to Sweden. Wait out the war in a neutral country. Go now, my love. We will be married when the storm passes and the sun shines again.

Your Mette

CHAPTER 7
HEDEBY, 971

By the time Lifu had scrambled down the wooden steps from the watchtower, she was having second thoughts. The troop of monks and guards — including the Irish smith Grady — had already passed by. She could hardly run after them on the road into town, waving to catch Grady's attention as if she were a besotted milkmaid. The man knew her only as one of Thyra's former slaves. He had undoubtedly forgotten kissing her at the queen's memorial bonfire. She had simply been the first girl he had happened to see in his euphoria after winning his freedom. Certainly he knew nothing of King Harald's advice that she take a husband. Even the king had probably forgotten suggesting the silversmith as a candidate. In the past half year an entire imaginary romance had grown in her mind from that seed.

"Lifu?" Svein had started climbing down the watchtower stairs with a bag. "You forgot your harp."

Svein's older sister smirked. "I think our English teacher fancies that guard with the red beard."

"I do not." Lifu raised her chin and went to take the harp. Leaving the king's children alone had been foolish. She was expected to accompany them back to their halls. "It's just that Grady spent the winter visiting the emperor in Rome. Don't you recall, at your grandmother's funeral? Grady was the one who wanted to ask the leader of the Christians some questions."

"Oh, him," Gunhild said. "I wonder what stories he'll tell?"

"Come along, we'll find out." Lifu led them on the street into the city. Unlike Harald's ring forts, Hedeby had not been laid out with the geometric precision of a military base. Even the main road zigzagged around buildings and branched confusingly. A bumpy pavement of poles had been laid crosswise to keep down the mud. Although horse hooves had evened the logs somewhat, wagon wheels still thumped so violently that passengers usually got out to walk. Here and there, smelly ditches drained effluent from latrines out to tidewater. When Lifu finally caught up with the monks' wagon, it was already followed by a motley parade of curious children, dogs, drunks, and slaves. At the sandy plaza between the harbor and the immense royal longhouses, armed guards in chain mail held back the riffraff. But they nodded deferentially to the young prince and princess, allowing them and their tutor to pass.

Lifu paused beside the helmeted silversmith as he untied a bundle from a packhorse.

"Welcome back to Denmark, Grady."

He looked up, momentarily confused. "Oh, Thyra's spy. We have business with Harald Bluetooth. Is he in Hedeby?"

Grady's matter-of-fact tone made her heart sink. "Yes," she said, copying his cold tone. "The king returned last week from a month's progress with the fleet."

"Good. Tell him a delegation from Rome requests an audience." Grady returned to his work, untying ropes.

Lifu gritted her teeth and walked on toward the hall.

Gunhild asked brightly, "Were you really grandmother's spy?"

"Not exactly," Lifu said, her teeth still clenched.

CHAPTER 7 ~ 971

"Then what were you?"

"Her handmaid."

Gunhild cocked her head, swinging a light brown braid. "I want a handmaid like that someday."

Gunhild and Svein brushed past the guards at the door and ran across the hall to King Harald and Queen Tove. The king and queen were standing beside a table, discussing wooden ship models with a dozen boatwrights.

"Papa!" Gunhild hugged the king's arm. "Thank you for the English harp."

Svein added, "Lifu's teaching us a scary English poem about monsters and dragons."

"Beowulf?" The king asked.

"That's right!" Gunhild replied, surprised. Then she blushed. "We want to sing it for you on midsummer's night."

Queen Tove raised her head. Her hair was a shiny black and her Slavic accent thick. "A girl? Reciting poetry?"

"It's in English, my Queen," Lifu explained. "They do things differently."

Harald chuckled, exposing his blackened front tooth. "Perhaps you kids will put my skalds out of a job."

"Then we can?" Gunhild asked.

"We'll see." The king squinted to Lifu. "Is this why you've let the children interrupt?"

"Not entirely." Lifu still refused to call him 'Your Highness,' perhaps to remind him that she had once served as more than just a tutor. "Do you remember Grady, your mother's Irish silversmith?"

The king frowned, remembering. "I freed him, and he ran off to the sunny south."

"Well he's back, with a delegation of priests from Rome. They're outside, and request an audience."

"Interesting." Harald motioned for the boatwrights to leave. "We can talk about ship designs later. Let's see what our doubting Christian smith has brought back to Denmark with him."

The king signaled to the guards at the door. Then he and the queen sat in their thrones behind the table. Lifu and the children retreated to a bench in the shadows where they could watch.

A minute later Grady appeared in the bright light of the doorway, followed by the three soldiers and five monks. Grady and the soldiers doffed their metal helmets and knelt before the royal couple. Behind them the monks bowed awkwardly, aiming the bald circles of their tonsures at the king. Lifu found it disturbing that four of them kept their hands in the loose sleeves of their brown robes. What were they hiding? The fifth monk held a large leather satchel.

"Grady the smith," Harald said, "Have you been liking your freedom?"

The Irishman grinned, bristling his red beard. "Aye, Your Highness. Italy is a far sight different from your realm. Rome is a city of stone, a hundred times bigger than Hedeby, with palm trees and wine and olives. Still, it is good to be home."

"Did you find the leader of the Christian church?"

"I did, Your Highness. Pope John the Twelfth put me to work in his artisans' shop. They had more gold there than I'd seen in my life. I was able to teach his craftsmen a thing or two about working with silver, though. When I left, the pope gave me this ring."

Grady held out his hand. A slim gold band gleamed above his hairy knuckles.

"A reward I'm sure was well earned. Then I assume you have resolved your doubts about the Christian god. Have you been baptized?"

Grady frowned. "I was baptized as a boy in Ireland, Your Highness. They like doing it in Rome, and it reassures them about foreigners, so I took their bath. But my doubts remain."

"Then why have you brought me a wagonload of priests?" The king's voice held a hint of anger. "Who are these people?"

Grady's voice wavered. "They are monks dedicated to the order of Saint Benedict, Your Highness. They are originally from Ireland. Monks like them are venturing out across all of Europe, trying to found churches. These five were determined to come to Denmark. I was going their way, and I speak Irish, so they took me on as translator and guide. They also hired three Norwegian soldiers of the Papal Guard for protection. It is safer to travel in a group."

"Norwegians?" Harald ignored the monks and turned instead to the three kneeling soldiers. "How did you come to Rome? Rise, tell me your names."

The three men who stood up to face the king did not look like Norwegians. Their faces were dark and wrinkled. Their long hair and beards were streaked with gray. Their legs seemed short, while their shoulders and arms bulged with muscles. These were obviously men who would be dangerous in a wrestling match.

"I am Bjorgulf of Horthaland, Your Highness," the man in the middle said. Despite his swarthy features, his voice had the unmistakable echo of Norway's western fjords. "My comrades Hrolf and Hergil and I sailed for treasure seven winters ago on one of the three ships of Egil the Bold."

Harald stroked his beard. "I have heard of Egil. He was one who never returned. Egil left Norway before I ruled there. Perhaps you know I have since banned this kind of Viking raid?"

"Your laws came too late for us, Your Highness. Egil had us sail south through the English Channel. All the towns there were already plundered, or else too well defended for our three ships to attack successfully. We stopped only to take sheep and wine from isolated farms. The winds were with us, so we kept sailing around Spain and through the stony gates to the Roman Sea. Malaga looked weak and rich. We stormed into the harbor, trusting to good luck. But the caliphate's sultan had hidden six ships behind a cliff. We fought bravely. Egil fell with an arrow in his ear. Only seven of us survived."

On the bench next to Lifu, Svein gasped. "Ooh!"

The king gave his son a reproachful glance. "Continue your tale, Bjorgulf. I assume you became Muslim slaves?"

The grizzled Viking nodded. "We learned enough Arabic to repeat that Allah is the one god and that Mohammed is his prophet. We rowed as oarsmen on the sultan's ships for three years. Two of our number died from poor food and disease. One was whipped and thrown overboard for spitting at the watchman's back. Then our ship was surprised by the fleet of Emperor Otto at Barcelona. Our legs were chained. We were naked. We couldn't fight."

"Did you want to fight on behalf of your Muslim slave masters?"

Bjorgulf looked up at the hall's painted rafters, considering. "It seems foolish now, Your Highness, but we did attempt to resist. Nonetheless, we soon became Roman slaves. For the next two years we baked roof tiles at a factory in Ostia, the port city for Rome. Another from our group died there, crazy in the head. And then one day a Swedish Viking from Russia happened to be passing through on his way to see Pope John. He heard us speaking Norse and convinced the officials that we would be of more use as soldiers in the Papal Guard."

Harald raised an eyebrow. "Why would the Pope want Norse soldiers in his retinue?"

"All of the Pope's private guardsmen are Norse. He values the skill and courage of Vikings."

"And I suspect he doesn't trust his own countrymen," Harald added.

"Perhaps not, Your Highness." Bjorgulf grunted. "This spring our commander asked for volunteers to accompany priests on a mission to Denmark. We three jumped at the chance to complete our long voyage. Although it is true that we had to return merely on horses, instead of by ship."

"Your adventures have proved your worth, Bjorgulf," Harald said. "I need men like you on my ships. Would you three rather stay here and serve me, or go home to your kinsmen in Horthaland?"

The three soldiers discussed these options quietly for a moment. Then Bjorgulf spoke for them.

"Both, Your Highness, if it is permitted. We are eager to see our kinsmen in Norway, and to discover who is still alive. But they are farmers, and we are not. In the fall we would like to return and serve you."

"Agreed." Harald tapped the table with his fist. "A trading ship leaves for Norway next week. Sail with it as my retainers. For the summer, consider yourselves on furlough."

The three Vikings mumbled their thanks and withdrew.

"Now Grady," the king said, raising his voice, "What am I supposed to do with your priests?"

The smith cleared his throat. "They have brought gifts, Your Highness."

Svein whispered, "I knew it!"

His sister shushed him. "Gifts aren't for children."

"Sometimes they are."

Grady spoke to the monks in Irish, a language no one else understood. Then the monk with the satchel stepped forward. He opened the flap and withdrew a leather scroll. Grady unrolled it on the table, revealing dozens of silver coins attached with wires. The leather itself had been inscribed with meandering black lines. Some of the outlined areas were blue, while others were green or the natural brown of the leather. The coins had been attached only to the green areas.

"What is this?" Harald demanded.

"A map of the world, Your Highness," Grady explained. "The blue around the edges is the World Ocean. Christian lands are green, and other realms are brown."

"Fascinating." The king leaned over the map. The queen and the others in the hall peered with interest as well. "This large island must be England. And Bjorgulf's voyage would have taken him here, around the gates of Spain to Italy. The brown area across the sea must be Africa. But what's this over here?" The king pointed to a brown region in the east.

"Arabia, Your Highness. Beyond it is Persia, and then India."

"Where is China? I remember Bulbul the Turk talking about a distant land of silk."

Grady shook his head. "I don't know, Your Highness."

"Denmark is certainly drawn wrong. The Pope obviously doesn't know much about us. And why are the silver coins only in green areas? We have lots of silver in my realm, and most of it comes from Persia. Both of them are brown."

"This is a coin collection, Your Highness," Grady explained. "Silver denari have been attached to the map everywhere that coins are minted by Christian kings. See, here's a coin with the face of King Edgar in England, and one from Aethelstan before him. The Holy Roman Empire has dozens of such kings. Along the edge of the map are coins minted by the Roman emperors themselves — Otto and Charlemagne, going all the way back to Constantine."

Harald tapped the brown islands of Denmark. "This reminds me. Why don't we mint our own coins here in Hedeby? You're a silversmith, Grady. Could you do that?"

"I think so, Your Highness. I'd forge an iron stamp with the pattern backwards. Then we'd weigh out chunks of silver, heat them a little, and smash them flat. Of course I'd need a workshop."

"I'll expand the workshop you used under Queen Thyra." Harald ran his finger over the silver coins on the map's edge. "Kings mint coins like this for more than one reason. If people trust that the king is fair, they don't need scales to weigh out silver for purchases. That's convenient, of course. But each coin is also a subtle reminder of the king's name and face. This summer I want to start paying my soldiers with coins instead of hack silver."

"Very well, Your Highness."

Harald eyed the monk's satchel. "Is this map all that you have brought me from Rome?"

"No, Your Highness." Grady took the satchel and removed a wooden box. "Pope John also sent you this second gift."

"As well he should," Harald said. "A handful of silver sewn to a hide is hardly payment for feeding five of his holy men."

Grady set the box on the table. "I designed the silver hinges and clasp, Your Highness."

The lid was a checkerboard of light and dark wooden squares. The king lifted it and frowned at the contents of the box.

"A chess set? A *wooden* chess set?"

"The game is as popular in Rome as here, Your Highness. Although some of the pieces are different there."

"This is no treasure for a king." Harald stood the pieces on the table disparagingly — a robed queen carved of white wood, a bearded king on a throne of polished dark wood, and a pair of horsemen. Harald examined the next piece more carefully. It was a man standing between two wheels.

"A charioteer?"

"A rook, Your Highness. I'm told the Persian word for chariot is *rukh*. We more often depict the rook as a fortress or a warrior."

"And what is this?" Harald studied the carved figure of a robed man. The man's right hand held a spiral-headed staff, while his left hand raised two fingers as if to cast a spell.

"A bishop, Your Highness," Grady explained. "He's a sort of duke among priests. Bishops report directly to Rome. As a chess piece he takes the place of our elephant. A bishop can move diagonally as far as you want."

Harald turned the piece in his hand. "Are real bishops so powerful?"

"Powerful and wealthy, Your Highness. Unlike the shamans and witches of our gods, bishops can levy a religion tax, build castles, and hire armies in the Pope's name."

"I see." Harald's expression darkened. "Then these are ominous presents, this leather map and wooden game. The Pope did not intend to give us treasure. Instead he has sent a subtle threat."

Grady looked confused. "I don't understand, Your Highness."

"My mother Thyra would have been able to interpret these gifts." Harald turned his gaze to the bench in the shadows. "Isn't that true, Lifu? You were her confidante."

Lifu shivered with foreboding. "I think so. The map could be seen as a kind of chessboard."

"Exactly. The Pope has shown us that Denmark is confronted by silver pieces — dozens of Christian kings. And what of the game box, Lifu?"

"It contains a different warning. New pieces are in play. The Pope has bishops and charioteers. Armies that move by land."

Svein piped up. "Just kill the priests. That'll send the Pope a message."

Lifu added quietly, "It would also give him the excuse he needs for war."

Although the five monks in the hall did not understand Norse, the conversation's somber turn made them exchange nervous glances.

Lost in thought, Harald had begun placing chess pieces on the map — black bishops in Frankia, a white king in England, and a wall of chariots around Rome. Then he picked up two of the Viking ship models that the carpenters had left on the table. He placed one ship in the North Sea and the other in the Baltic, flanking the tiny, poorly drawn islands of Denmark.

"What do these monks want?" Harald looked up at Grady. "Ask

them in their own language."

The smith spoke with the monks for several minutes in the lilting, guttural tongue of Ireland. Then he turned to Harald. "The Benedictine monks want to buy a house here in Hedeby where people can watch their rituals."

"They have silver?"

"Yes, Your Highness. They've also brought farm tools and seeds. They want to buy farm land near the town walls. They call their project a monastery. They intend to grow grains and herbs. They had wanted to grow grapes for wine, but I've explained that this is not possible in our climate. Instead they will brew ale."

Harald chuckled and the guards in the hall laughed. "Will we have to take their holy bath before we can join them for a horn of ale?"

Grady translated this jest, and wound up discussing it with the monks for a surprisingly long time. Finally he said, "Anyone can drink their ale, but only those who are baptized can join them in the purification ritual that they claim allows people to grow wings and fly to Heaven when they die."

"What is this ritual?"

The smith hesitated. "I have seen it in Rome, Your Highness. Christians gather in a church to drink the blood and eat the flesh of Jesus."

"What!" Harald sat back in his throne. "Surely this is a *kenning* — a metaphor, as in our poems."

"No, Your Highness. They insist it is the literal truth. A miracle allows Christians to eat their god."

"They glorify cannibalism? How could such a barbaric creed spread so far?"

Grady shrugged. "This is why I have decided to stay true to Odin."

Harald let out a long, weary breath. Now he spoke directly to the monks, although he knew they couldn't understand. "What on earth am I to do with you? Your beliefs are strange, but the forces behind you seem too powerful for Denmark to resist forever. Should I follow the example of the English kings, and keep your bishops at bay by claiming to be Christian? I've been to England. Many of the people there still follow the old gods. Or will you someday convince me that your god is right?"

The king shook his head. "The ways of gods are mysterious

indeed." He took a white bishop from the leather map and studied the carved figure's pious gaze. The he tossed it into the box. "Enough of this! We can't kill the monks, and we can't send them back. Both of those choices are asking for trouble. I suppose I'll allow them to buy a house and a farm. Grady, you're the only one who understands them. Put them up for the time being in your silver shop. Maybe they can even help you make some sample coins."

"You want me to house them in the workshop, Your Highness?" Grady was taken aback. "I left that hut empty. I would need bedding and food and —"

"Lifu can organize all of that for you," the king interrupted. "She tutors my children in the morning but has afternoons free for my other commands. Or is that too much to ask?"

"Yes," Lifu said, jumping to her feet, her thoughts in turmoil. "I mean, no! Yes, I can help with Grady's housekeeping." Apparently the king had not forgotten his plan to throw her together with a possible husband. How was she going to explain this to Grady?

Harald tossed the rest of the chess pieces back in the box. Then he handed the box to Grady. "Keep this toy for now, Grady. Our game with Pope John has only begun. Next winter I'll send him my own delegation, along with one of his priests, to prove that they are alive. And I'll give him a gift crafted by the smith who once served in the Pope's own workshops."

"A present, Your Highness? Made by me?"

The king smiled. "A chess set like this, but ten thousand times more valuable. Carved from the ivory of unicorns."

"Narwhal horns!" Grady exclaimed. He knew that unicorns did not exist, but the northern seas did have whale-like creatures with a single long horn. Norse traders had convinced gullible southerners that narwhal horns actually came from unicorns.

"I'll send Pope John a threat of my own," Harald said. "The chess set I have in mind will have new Danish pieces more dangerous than bishops."

He winked to Lifu. "I wonder if the two of you can conjure such a prize?"

CHAPTER 8
COPENHAGEN, 1940

Julius sat by the open dormer window of his apartment overlooking Copenhagen's harbor, writing by the dim glow of a blackened bulb. A crescent moon reflected in broken shimmers on a strip of water between the shadows of ships and the silhouettes of steeples. Denmark's capital, a city of half a million, had gone dark. Although he could see no one, Julius knew that people were peering out from behind thick curtains — fearful, worried, and angry.

> Dearest Mette:
>
> Thank you for your letter describing the beautiful weather and the interesting city museum in Schleswig. Dare I admit that your dispassionate tone scared me more than anything I have read in these past weeks? Then I remembered that you are writing from the German Reich.
>
> And so I am replying with two different letters, as a test. The other letter begins with the weather, goes on at length about how much I miss you, and begs you to come home at least briefly for the weekend after midsummer's night.
>
> In this letter I'll explain a bit more about the reason for my request. We're planning a costume party with a Viking theme. I'm coming as Leif the Lucky, and your father as Holger Danske!

Julius paused, chewing uncertainly on the cap of his pen. Had he given away too much? If censors really were checking the mail, a Dane would suspect a double meaning in these disguises. But would a German? Leif the Lucky's father had been banished from Scandinavia. Leif himself had fled to Greenland, and then to America. Would Mette understand?

Holger Danske, of course, wasn't a real person at all. According to an ancient legend, he was a mighty warrior who had helped the early kings of Denmark conquer the North. His deed accomplished, Holger had been cast under a spell that put him to sleep for a thousand years. A century ago a Danish king had commissioned a sculptor to carve a stone statue of Holger Danske for the casement vaults of Elsinore's Kronborg Castle. With his sword across his lap and his bearded head bowed, the giant warrior sleeps away the ages in a stone chair in the fortress' basement.

But every Dane knows the statue in Elsinore is not the real Holger Danske. According to legend, the real Viking warrior will wake up to save Denmark in her hour of need.

As yet there was little public support for an underground movement to fight the Nazi occupation of Denmark. The Germans were too powerful. King Christian X and the Danish government thought they could better protect Danes if they did not resign their positions, instead offering the Nazis a more subtle form of resistance.

But a small underground group had already formed. Eventually the Danish resistance would announce its name: Holger Danske.

Julius licked the tip of his pen and continued writing.

> My darling! When we last spoke you asked me twice if I was safe. I think you worried that there would be a knock on my door in the middle of the night.
>
> That knock came last night. Just after eleven o'clock a very nice Danish policeman appeared at my apartment. He was extremely apologetic. He had come from the airport at Kastrup, where I keep my Fokker. The Germans, he told me, have requisitioned all private aircraft. In most cases they'll pay a nominal rental fee. But the Reich is unable to make payments to non-Aryans.
>
> The plane is gone. Visas are impossible. The world is shrinking.
>
> In your letter you wrote that you probably would not be allowed to leave your work for the first month or two. Please be here for the costume party. You might come as Thyra, Denmark's Gift. I miss you, Mette. I will always love you.
>
> — Your Julius

* * *

It was only 7:10 in the morning, but the sun had already been up for hours when the twenty Danish archeologists carried their suitcases down the park road to the Schleswig train station. This was the longest day of the year, the name day of St. Hans. If they had been home in Denmark they would have been preparing for the festivities of midsummer's night. But here there was little for them to celebrate. After a month in the ducal manor they were moving to barracks built by Polish prisoners of war.

The thousands of French and British soldiers captured while trying to escape the rout at Dunkirk had not been sent to Hedeby. This part of the Reich had been deemed too close to England and France. To discourage thoughts of escape, POWs from the western front had been relegated to factories in the industrial east at Breslau, on the Polish border. Meanwhile, the Luftwaffe was bombing English cities and airfields from London to York, softening up the island for a choice: Sue for peace, or submit to a blitzkrieg invasion.

Only Herr Matthiasen seemed in a good mood. The museum curator had worn his old conductor's uniform, with a black-billed cap and ostentatious gold epaulets. "I served thirty years with the *Reichsbahn,*" he proudly confided to Mette, "So I still have some clout with the railroad baggage handlers."

As it turned out, the station's baggage handlers were busy elsewhere, but Matthiasen did manage to commandeer a couple of German soldiers to help stow the archeologists' suitcases on the commuter train's two passenger cars. Strangely, half a dozen boxcars and a pair of flatcars loaded with pipe had been coupled to the back of the train. As Mette passed by on the platform, she heard voices crying out from one of the boxcars. Although she couldn't understand what they were saying, the tone sounded Slavic.

"Henrik," Mette whispered to her assistant, a man who wore a bow tie even for the June solstice, when the weather was sure to be warm, "I think those cars have more Polish prisoners."

"Really?" Henrik looked alarmed. "We have more than we need already."

A German official on the platform blew a whistle, waving for passengers to get on board. The locomotive at the head of the train belched a cloud of black coal smoke. Although the engine had parked just outside the station's arched roof, a mist of soot blew back into the hall, speckling Mette's light jacket and making her blink. She climbed the step and chose a seat by herself so she could think.

The locomotive rumbled, releasing a roar of steam. Car couplings clanked tight, a rapid cadence of steel the length of the train. The snorts of steam came faster, and the station platform began scrolling past Mette's window. First came a switching yard where the tracks split, curving off in three different directions. Then they chugged past the warehouses and docks of the harbor. Schleswig's submarine happened to be in port. The white insignia "U271" gleamed from the ship's conning tower. A red swastika banner waved at her prow. Then the train curved away from the fjord and left the city behind, puffing rhythmically through fields of green barley and yellow sunflowers.

During the past two months Mette had spent a lot of time on these train trips thinking about Julius, wishing she could go home. Finally she had won permission for a three-day vacation to Copenhagen. A week from now she would rush into the arms of her fiancé. She would also learn the truth about how he and her parents were faring. Evidently half their letters had been confiscated. The remainder had arrived with the flaps slit open by censors. Still, disturbing clues had leaked through. Why had Julius and her father both specifically asked her to be there next weekend? It also appeared that Julius no longer owned an airplane. Had it been taken by the Germans? Would they demand his car or his apartment next? A network of hate seemed to be closing in around Denmark's Jewish community. If only Julius had thought to escape earlier! He could have stayed in England when he went to pick up the Bentley. She should have gone with him. They could have traveled to America to live with her brother Lars. Or was running away not the answer?

After twenty minutes the train slowed, clanking on old, uneven rails into the village of Gammeltorp. Storks roosted in stick nests atop the thatched roofs of brick houses. The square, seemingly unfinished steeple of a church rose across the street from a half-timbered shed that served as the rail line's end station. Weeds had overgrown the tracks ahead, where the line curved through the locked wire gate of an old factory.

Colonel Wedel had met the train with an uncovered truck for their luggage. He tipped his fedora apologetically. "I was only able to bring one truck this morning. We're saving on fuel. Still, I could take some of you if you're willing to sit on suitcases in back."

After Matthiasen had translated this, Claus sniffed. "The walk will do us good." He threw his duffel onto the truck bed.

Meanwhile the muffled sound of foreign voices had been growing from the boxcars at the back of the train. Fists began pounding in unison on the sliding wooden doors.

"What about the prisoners of war?" Mette asked the colonel in German. "You can't keep them locked up like animals. We're running an excavation, not a concentration camp."

"Oh, those cars aren't for us," the colonel explained. "The new workers will be accommodated at the Gammeltorp factory. It's being reopened."

"What kind of factory is it?" Mette asked.

"A bicycle factory. It's always been a bicycle factory, hasn't it, Herr Matthiasen?"

"It has been," the museum curator admitted.

"Bicycles? In wartime?" Mette noticed that a group of German men were in fact unlocking the wire gates. They waved the train forward.

Colonel Wedel took off his spectacles and began polishing them with a handkerchief. "With gasoline rationed and private cars in short supply, bicycles for the civilian population are an essential part of the wartime economy."

"I thought everyone had the 'people's car,' the Volkswagen."

Wedel waved his spectacles. "Oh, thousands of people bought subscriptions for the 'beetle', as the Führer nicknamed it, but only a few were actually produced. The assembly lines at Wolfsburg have all switched to military vehicles."

"Then who is using Hitler's famous freeways?" she asked. "The military?"

"Don't be such a skeptic, Mette. Building the *Autobahn* put millions of men to work when Germany needed it. Times have changed." He got in the truck and patted the empty passenger seat. "Sure I can't give you a lift?"

She shook her head. After the colonel's truck had driven off, the locomotive chugged a great cloud of steam and clanked forward, its wheels screeching on the rusty rails of the curve. Mette could see soldiers with rifles standing by the track in the old factory's yard.

"Bicycles," she mused.

"They should have given us bicycles when we got here a month ago," Henrik put in. He joined the others walking toward their work site a kilometer away.

The gravel road to Hedeby, between a dairy farm and a beech forest, was not unpleasant in June, when the long northern days brought out a rush of wildflowers and chattering birds. The forest ended, however, in a field of stumps, where the POW workers had started clearing ground for an airstrip. Mette had argued that they truly did not need a landing field, but Colonel Wedel had insisted, saying that it was mostly for show. The runway might only be used once, he said, when the Führer came to see what treasures they had unearthed.

Beyond the future airstrip, the road jogged briefly to the right, dodging through a gap in the grassy dike that had once been the Viking city's outer wall. Mette could imagine the stockade and entry gates that must have been here. It would be an interesting place to excavate, she thought, although the roadcut had damaged the site.

The field just inside the wall had apparently been a pasture even in Viking times. Mette had agreed to have their tent camp set up there. The eighty Polish POWs lived in two rows of white canvas tents. Two much larger tents housed the kitchen and mess hall.

The camp's first permanent structure — and this was not Mette's choice — had been a water tower over a pumphouse and a well. With its conical tin roof, the sixty-foot tower looked as incongruous in the camp as a rocket ship. The second building to be constructed was a washhouse with bathrooms, shower stalls, and laundry sinks. A wood-fired boiler provided hot water. Mette had to admit this was practical.

The latest addition to the camp was a long one-story wooden structure for everyone except the POWs who had built it. The main entrance, in the middle of the building, opened onto a large room that could be used for meetings or social activities. Long hallways to the left and right had doors to bunkrooms, offices, and workrooms. A few days earlier, Colonel Wedel and his ten German soldiers had moved into the east wing. Now that the west wing was finished, it was time for the Danish archeologists and engineers to settle in.

After the luxury of the ducal manor, their new quarters seemed spartan. The floors were planks. Bare studs lined the uninsulated shiplap walls. The nine-paned windows opened stiffly and had no curtains. Pull chains turned on light bulbs dangling from ceilings. Only a few rooms had pot-bellied stoves for heat.

Mette and Henrik shared a relatively large office at the far end of the west wing. They each had private bedrooms, just large enough for a cot and a chair. Everyone else had to stay in rooms with four bunks.

Unpacking gear and nailing up shelves for storage took most of that morning. Their work was finally interrupted by the clanging of a ladle on an empty oil drum, the signal that the POWs were ready to serve lunch. Mette and the others crossed the field to the mess tent. There they lined up under the yellowish glow of canvas.

It seemed to Mette that no matter what ingredients the POWs were given their cuisine always turned out Polish. Today they dished up a watery stew of beef, cabbage, and potatoes, with a crust of bread on the side. The chicory coffee resembled real coffee only in that it was hot and black, but she had gotten used to it. There wasn't enough seating for everyone at once, so the POWs had to eat later in two additional shifts. The tables and benches were the wobbly kind of pipe-and-plank furniture rented for German beer festivals. Straw had been spread on the ground between tables to cover mud left from May rains.

As usual the Danes sat on one side of the tent while the German soldiers clustered by themselves on the other. Colonel Wedel kept trying to bridge that gap, with little success. Today he sat opposite Mette and struck up a conversation.

"That coin you found shows we're getting closer, Mette. It also proves you were right to try test plots all over the townsite."

"Test plots are the usual way to start an excavation," she replied. "Besides, we had to do something while we wait for the shipwrecks in the bay."

The Viking ships were still underwater. The National Museum's engineers had rented a barge with a pile driver that was hammering steel plates into the muddy sand, but it might take several months before they completed a large circular coffer dam, sealed it, and pumped out the seawater. Only then would the archeologists be able to dig out and preserve the remains of the old ships.

"The ships in the sand are still our best hope," Wedel said, dipping bread in his soup. "But now I'm wondering if we might not find a sword in the townsite itself. The coin proves we're looking at the right time period. It's got Harald Bluetooth written all over it."

The colonel smiled at his own joke. The small silver coin, originally worth just a quarter of a denar, had the words "HARALD+REX" written in a circle around a bearded head with a crown. The obverse side showed a Viking ship with a reefed sail.

Mette was more cautious. "Yes, but it's in Latin, without runes, and includes a Christian cross. That suggests it was minted near the end of Harald's reign, after he had accepted Christianity. Isn't this sword you imagine supposed to be pagan?"

Wedel frowned. "I still sense we're closing in. Can I come look at the test plots this afternoon?"

She sighed. "Of course, Colonel."

"Franz."

"Of course, Franz."

* * *

That afternoon Mette walked Colonel Wedel to the five places she had chosen for trial excavations. The most productive site, in terms of the quantity of artifacts, was a ditch that must once have been a latrine.

"People throw away amazing things in outhouses," she said, kneeling by the strings that marked off square meters. "Broken dishes, glassware, buttons, chicken bones. Garbage pits and latrines tell the story of a civilization."

"But no one throws away silver," Colonel Wedel pointed out.

"Not on purpose, no."

The second test site they visited was in a patch of willow brush that Mette thought might have been the edge of the bay in Viking times. A crew of POWs was still clearing the brush, so there was little to see.

The third and fourth sample digs had both hit dark-stained soil where wood had rotted.

"I think these sites were houses. They're just fifty meters apart, but very different."

"In what way?" the Colonel asked.

She pointed to a series of brown rectangles. "These are the remains of staves. Split logs make for a very sturdy wall, but it's hard to build. This must have been the hall of an important person."

"Harald Bluetooth?"

"More likely a jarl, this far from the harbor. Now look over here." She walked to the other test excavation. A much thinner brown line ran diagonally across the meter-square hole. "This would have been a wattle wall. It's just a row of sticks with interwoven branches, plastered with mud. Walls like this are much quicker to build, but not as strong. Probably a peasant's home or a craftsman's shop."

"Where did you find the coin?"

"Where we least expected it." Mette walked with him to the final test plot. "I chose this spot on a hunch. It's in the middle of everything, right between the harbor and the first houses, but the only thing here appeared to be packed dirt. Perhaps it was a public square. Usually you don't find much in open areas like that. If somebody drops something valuable here, someone else is likely to pick it up."

"Then what about the coin?"

Mette stepped down into the square pit and ran her finger along a thin black layer in the wall. "Thirty centimeters down we found a stratum of charcoal. The coin was the only artifact in it."

"Peculiar." The colonel examined the black line. "Maybe a house was here after all, and it burned down?"

"The fire area appears to be circular, and it's only two meters across."

"A fire pit? In a public square? Were they burning witches?"

Mette couldn't help but smile. "Danes do have a tradition of burning witches on midsummer's night. People build bonfires and dress scarecrows in black rags to look like witches."

"Sounds gruesome. And horribly medieval."

"I suppose so. The strange thing is that Vikings honored witches. I'm quite sure they didn't burn them. Criminals were thrown into bogs, not fire pits."

"Then where did the tradition come from? On midsummer's night people in parts of Germany build bonfires too, but not for witches. They jump through the flames to scare away the ghosts of the past year."

"I wonder if that was the tradition in Harald Bluetooth's time?"

The colonel considered this. "And maybe someone dropped a coin when they jumped?"

* * *

That evening, on the longest day of the year, the sky kept glowing a dark blue long after the sun had sliced into the horizon above Schleswig fjord. At ten o'clock Mette was still at her desk, writing reports and drawing maps by the light of the window.

Henrik opened the door. "Your presence is requested at the volleyball court, Madame Director."

She looked up. "Volleyball?"

Her assistant merely crooked his finger and smiled. Sharing a small office had brought them closer over the past months. Henrik might be older than her, but he was so unfailingly attentive that she had begun to look at him with approval.

Mette set down her pencil and followed. The volleyball court had been the Polish prisoners' idea. One day they had strung a rope between posts in the storage yard and challenged the Danes to a game. The Danzig team had proven hard to beat. But no one would be playing volleyball after the POWs' nine o'clock curfew.

As soon as Mette saw light flickering on the storage tents, she knew a different game was afoot. When she walked up to the bonfire and put her hands on her hips, the entire crew of Danish archeologists and engineers applauded.

Claus offered her a bottle of Tuborg beer. "Any demons you'd like to burn, Mette?"

"Maybe a few," she admitted, accepting the bottle with a sigh. Her team had worked hard and deserved a break, especially on midsummer's night.

The Danes had built a fire with the scrap ends of lumber. Somehow they had found two cases of Danish beer and several bottles of Aalborg akvavit. These refreshments had been set up on a plank as a makeshift bar. People sat on folding chairs, talking and drinking.

"Tonight I think we're all wishing we were home," Mette said.

"I'll drink to that." Martina lifted a shot glass and winked. The illustrator was always a little flirty, but tonight seemed especially incautious.

Eskil and Asger, the university interns, were poking the fire with sticks to send up sparks.

Henrik raised his glass to Mette. "You actually get to go home in a few days. Aren't you worried about leaving me in charge? Look what terrors I have allowed."

"I'm more worried about what I'll find in Copenhagen." Her words left the group somber.

Claus ran his hand through his long white beard. "I hear they're compiling lists of Jews." He didn't look at Mette, but she flushed anyway. Her engagement to Julius was no secret.

Claus added, "They aren't requiring Jewish people to wear yellow stars yet. If they do, lots of people say they'll wear them too, for solidarity."

"Even the king!" Martina laughed.

"Really? Mette asked. She was surprised that Christian the Tenth would have that kind of courage, although she had heard that he rode his horse through the streets each day without a bodyguard.

"Maybe not the king," Claus admitted. "But lots of people. Lots."

Eskil scoffed, "Don't ex-
pect heroism from Danes. Denmark fell like a tin soldier. The BBC says Winston Churchill is calling us 'Hitler's canary.'"

One of the engineers asked, "How do you listen to English radio programs?"

Eskil shrugged. "Maybe I don't."

Henrik poured himself another akvavit. "What about this new resistance group everyone's whispering about?" Mette's assistant seemed uncharacteristically casual about such a dangerous topic. "They're probably just disgruntled Communists. I heard someone has already suggested a name — Holger Danske."

Mette choked on her beer. "But that's an imaginary hero."

"Maybe it's an imaginary group," Claus said, staring into the fire. There were already more coals than flames.

"*Hallo! Achtung!*" The sound of German voices made everyone freeze. Two young soldiers, returning late from the washrooms, had spotted the bonfire and marched to confront them. "We have blackout orders! Fires are *verboten!*"

No one moved.

The second soldier switched to English. "Don't you know about the blackout?"

"Yes," Mette replied, "But the sky's not dark yet. This is midsummer's night. It's a Danish holiday. Don't you like festivals?"

"Holiday or not, you should put out the fire," the first soldier said, now also in English.

"We are," Claus said. "We're watching to make absolutely sure it goes out." He held up a bottle. "Care to join us for an akvavit while we wait?"

The soldiers glanced at each other. The second one ventured, "What is this 'akvavit'?"

"The water of life, my friend." Claus poured two shots and handed them over. "Danish schnapps. Not for the faint of heart."

The second soldier sniffed the clear liquid suspiciously, but the first one downed the shot in one go. He gasped with his hands at his throat, comically mimicking strangulation.

Finally everyone could laugh.

"You're young for German soldiers," Mette observed. "What are your names?"

The one who had merely sniffed his drink pointed to the other. "He's Richard. I'm Ernst. But we're not Germans."

Richard added with a wry laugh, "We're not really even soldiers."

Claus cocked his head. "You're not?"

"We're Austrians. Four of us here are from Vienna. We're students from Professor Wedel's art history class."

Ernst added, "The other soldiers are plumbers and carpenters. They speak Polish and know what they're doing. We're just trying to stay out of trouble."

Eskil, the Danish university student, nodded appreciatively. "That's what I call a loyal professor. A man who keeps his students away from the front lines."

"If you're students of art history," Mette said, "Maybe you could help us with the excavation."

Richard brightened. "That would be great. Sentry duty is boring. Professor Wedel promised us more excitement than we've seen so far."

Martina winked at him. "How about if you try lighting my fire?"

The young soldier blushed. "Pardon?"

Claus explained, "It's a Danish tradition. People tell witches to go home if they've had too much to drink."

"That's not true," Martina pouted. "I'm just trying to make friends."

"Where I come from, the tradition is more about jumping through fire," Richard said. "It's supposed to scare away ghosts."

"Show me, honey boy."

The soldier set down his glass. Then he took a running start and leaped across the firepit's embers. "See? No more ghosts."

"Let me check." Martina waved him closer.

Henrik held the young soldier back. "Don't go there, son."

Meanwhile Ernst had stood up, as if at attention. The dying fire cast a red glow across the polished black leather of his uniform's straps and boots.

"I'm afraid there really is a ghost in my family." The young soldier stared into the fire. "It haunts my uncles and my parents." He held his shot glass out before him. "My family's ghost is alcohol. I don't dare drink your schnapps." He poured the liquid onto the coals. At once, flames leapt up. Undaunted, he crouched, swung his arms, and broad-jumped forward.

Jumping with both feet was a dangerous move. Ernst landed awkwardly at the far edge of the coals. For a moment, whirling his arms for balance, it seemed he might fall. But he caught himself and took a deep breath, wiping his brow.

Mette was the first to applaud.

CHAPTER 9
HEDEBY, 971

When it came time for their morning English lesson on the longest day of the year, Svein vanished. Lifu and Gunhild started looking for the young prince at his favorite haunt, the harbor.

A low mist still blanketed Hedeby, leaving rows of seagulls perched on the thatch rooftops of ghost houses lost in the mist. Before Lifu saw the ships she heard them, gently clunking and creaking at their moorings. She and the princess walked out the longest of the rickety, wood-planked piers. The walkway had been transformed by the fog into Bifrost, the god's legendary bridge through the clouds.

Gunhild sat down at the end of the dock, swinging her legs as she looked out into the great unknown beyond. Wavelets lapped at the crooked pilings. The damp air smelled of tar and fish. Birds cried above the unseen fjord.

Lifu knew they weren't going to find Svein that morning. He would already be off with the older boys, planning mischief for midsummer's night. And there was no need to rehearse Gunhild's part for the Beowulf recital — the princess had learned it perfectly. Instead Lifu sat on the edge of the dock beside her and asked, "What are you thinking?"

"Oh, I don't know." She looked down at her feet. "About how I don't want things to change. And yet I do."

The girl was thirteen, a delicate age that teetered between the innocent freedom of childhood and the tempting terrors of the adult world. Already Gunhild had grown to what would probably be her full height, an inch taller than Lifu. That winter she had begun to fill out her thin frame with the shape of the woman she would become.

"Are you thinking about the future I predicted at Jelling? That you would marry a wealthy man from far away?"

"Hardly!" Her haughty tone told Lifu that she was right. Then, as if to prove Lifu wrong, the princess talked about something else. "There's going to be a surprise at the feast tonight."

"I know. Your father's going to give everyone a silver coin. Grady and I have been minting them for weeks."

"Not just that." Gunhild's cheek dimpled with a smile. "There'll be a surprise for you too. A secret about your husband."

Lifu wrinkled her brow. She had already discovered a number of things she had not expected about Grady, the Irish silversmith. Most of them were the sort of quirks that women learn to tolerate. She wasn't sure she wanted more surprises.

For a while Lifu and the princess stared out across the water in silence. As the morning sun burned through the fog a dim outline of the far shore began to emerge.

At length Gunhild asked, "How did you manage to get Grady? Did my father arrange things?"

Lifu hid a smile. She had been right about the princess's thoughts after all. Gunhild was old enough that it wouldn't hurt for her to hear successful stories — and cautionary tales — about the business of love.

"The king helped," Lifu admitted. "My parents were murdered in Oxford, you know, so Harald has been kind enough to keep an eye out for me. A year ago he asked me what kind of man I'd like to marry. All I could think to say was 'a smith.'"

"That's what you wanted? A smith?"

"Smiths are strong. Craftsmen are not to be disparaged."

"I suppose. And of course you were already so old."

Lifu bit her tongue. At twenty-four she was hardly a spinster, but she must seem old to a girl of thirteen.

Gunhild asked, "What was it like, that first night when Grady came back from Rome?" The fact that she blushed made the true nature of her question clear.

"Well," Lifu began, "The king suggested that I help Grady move back into his old workshop, so that was a start. I'd had my eye on Grady for some time. I liked his looks well enough, but he hadn't yet given me a second glance. It didn't help that I also had to fit five monks into the shop that night. And then it turned out the place was a wreck. Grady had sold his tools to another blacksmith before he left. Thieves had stripped the rest of the house bare. The hut wasn't fit for a pig."

"What did you do?"

"I sent Grady to buy back his tools and any housewares he could find. I put three of the monks to work fixing the wattle walls. It looked like a herd of cattle had torn gaps in the sticks. The other two monks went with me to fetch food, a kettle, and some old sleeping furs from the Retainers' Hall. I figured my first task was to fill stomachs, so I made a big barley cheese soup with lots of herbs."

"You know a lot about herbs," Gunhild commented. "Did you mix in a love potion?"

"Food *is* a love potion, especially for men who have just walked a thousand miles. The monks had taken a vow never to marry, so they just prayed, ate, and prayed some more. I gave them some cow hides and told them to sleep. Meanwhile Grady ate his fill and started heading toward the bedding I had prepared. But I blocked his way. I told him, 'These sheepskins are clean. When did you last bathe?'"

The princess covered her mouth with her hand. "What did he say to that?"

"Something about the public baths in Rome. But that was ages ago. He smelled like a shepherd after winter. I ordered him to take off his clothes and get in the water trough."

"You didn't!"

"Oh, at first he objected that he didn't take orders from women, but I reminded him that my housekeeping assignment came from Harald Bluetooth himself. Eventually Grady got in the trough, grumbling. Immediately I threw in his purple tunic and started scrubbing it with soap."

"While he was right there, naked?"

"Oh, yes. I'd also made sure that the clasp on my shoulder strap came loose, so my dress was sort of hanging open in front."

"Lifu!" the princess gasped.

Lifu shrugged, "That was the whole idea, wasn't it? To get his attention? By the time I got around to scrubbing Grady's back, his thing was poking out of the water like the handle of Thor's hammer. The rest was easy, even with the monks praying as loud as they could."

Gunhild clapped both hands over her ears.

Lifu squinted up at the sun, now rising above the town. The morning's fog was gone. "Let's get you back to the halls. I think that's enough of a lesson for today."

* * *

When the call of lur-horns echoed through the streets Lifu was still finishing her preparations for the midsummer night's feast. She and Grady were to be honored guests, seated just behind the jarls. She had started getting ready a week ago, collecting the fresh green leaves of woad, the mustard that grows wild along the Danevirke. The leaves had to be crushed, chopped, and fermented in a sealed pot. The resulting yellowish-green goo resembled pond scum, but when she daubed it above her eyes it gave the lids an enchanting blue shadow. Next came kohl — an Egyptian trick, blending blackest charcoal with oil to outline her eyes. Finally she crushed a handful of wild blackberries. The juice looked purple, but it blushed rosily when she smeared it on her cheekbones and kissed it to her lips.

"Lifu?" Grady called from the workshop door. "Are you coming or not?"

She pinned her yellow braids up as a crown above her ears, studied herself one last time in the little silver mirror, and strode out to meet the world. This would be her first feast day as a free woman with a man by her side.

"Thor's thunder!" the smith said, admiring her. His gaze rose from

93

her bare feet to the curves of her pleated white dress, drawn tight by a crimson sash. "You are a sight for Valhalla."

"This is no evening for Thor," she replied, her chin high. "Midsummer's night belongs to women's deities — Freya and Frigga."

"You're telling me this is Frey-day, and not Thor's day?"

"Exactly." Lifu was pleased to see that Grady had trimmed his red beard. He wore a black leather vest over a loose white shirt that was open at the collar, exposing just enough fine, curly hair that a woman might easily imagine running her hands across that broad, muscular chest.

"You'll fit right in among the goddesses," Grady said. "Now come on, Brother Michael is waiting for us."

Grady put on a red felt hat before heading out into the street.

"Where'd you get that?" Lifu demanded.

"What?"

"That hat."

"From Rome. Square hats are very popular with fashionable people there."

"Well, I think it looks silly."

He rolled his eyes. "Come on."

All along the street the corners of houses had been decorated with birch boughs, turning the city into a magical forest of shivering green leaves. The five monks were indeed waiting for them outside the small stave house they had converted to a church by nailing a wooden cross on the gable.

"Ah! Grady, you've come at last." The tallest of the monks, Brother Michael, had learned an impressive amount of Norse in just two months, no doubt because of the help he'd received from his Irish kinsman, the smith. "We almost drank the ale without you."

"Four barrels!" Grady marveled. The monks had hitched two ponies to their wagon to haul the load.

"It is a small gift for our neighbors on their holiday." Michael's Gaelic accent was a brook tumbling over sharp pebbles.

None of the monks had dressed up. They were barefoot, wearing their usual brown robes with hoods and loose sleeves. No one wore shoes on midsummer's night, but Lifu realized she had never seen the monks any other way. They must have walked the entire route from Rome, even across the Alps, without so much as sandals.

94

The lur-horns sounded again, this time followed by the beat of drums.

Brother Michael clicked his tongue to the ponies. They flicked their ears and leaned into the traces. The heavily loaded wagon began thumping along the pole-paved street. Crowds of merrymakers joined from side streets until the thoroughfare became a parade of bobbing heads and laughter.

At the edge of town the ponies shied. A curtain of flames was rising ahead where the road crossed the pasture to the South Gate. Someone had put a row of burning firewood directly across the road.

"What does this mean?" Brother Michael asked, frowning.

"It's part of the festival," Grady explained. "On midsummer's night you're supposed to jump through fire to scare away ghosts. It's a kind of purification."

The people in the crowd were giggling and whooping as they hopped across the flames to the festival field.

"Not for horses," Brother Michael said solemnly. "Or for Christians either. We will go a different way."

"But we'll meet later, right?" Grady asked.

"Yes, as agreed." The monks led the ponies off the road, cutting across the pasture. Meanwhile, Lifu and Grady jumped through the flames, following the crowd.

Red-and-white pennants marked off the festival grounds, a five-acre field bounded by the road and the Danevirke's wall. Tables along the base of the grassy dike had been reserved for the king, his helmsmen, and their families. Rows of tables and benches — enough for six hundred people! — filled the sides of the field. An area in front of the king's table had been left open for performances. Gigantic poles marked the four corners of this grassy stage. Each pole was an entire fir tree, hewn to white wood for eighty feet, but with a spire of green limbs at the top. Just below each of these green treetops, a spar supported two circular wreaths. And suspended inside each wreath was a brightly colored egg — the symbol of Freya's fertility. Beyond the stage were a series of firepits where five butchered oxen and forty whole pigs had been roasting for most of a day.

Lifu and Grady had some trouble finding an empty bench. Although they had been told to sit between the jarls and the wealthiest towns-people, no specific table had been reserved for them, and the people there were suspicious of former slaves. Eventually they squeezed in amongst the jarls' children, some of whom recognized Lifu as a tutor from the royal hall.

"A toast!" someone cried, and soon voices everywhere echoed the call.

Grady had to nudge Lifu with his elbow. "Isn't that your job?"

"Oh! Of course." Women were supposed to bring their men the first drink at a feast. Lifu had never been in that position before. She stood up and made her way among a throng of women to vats by the ox pit, where horns were being distributed as quickly as they could be scooped full of mead. Carrying the honey wine back without spilling it proved to be a challenge.

Eventually the king stood up and the crowd hushed. Lifu had to crane her neck to see over the heads of the jarls' wives. Harald Bluetooth seldom wore his gold crown, but he had it on tonight. More remarkably, he had plaited his beard into four braids — perhaps to hide the streaks of gray among the brown.

At his side, Queen Tove wore a bizarre headdress instead of a crown. Resembling a birch bark basket, the contraption stood nearly two feet tall. She was able to keep it on her head only because of straps under her chin. Lifu assumed this must be some Slavic custom from Pomerania. She had to admit that the white of the bark set off Tove's long black hair. The queen had left her hair unfletted, so it cascaded over her shoulders.

"A toast!" the king called again, raising his oversize, gold-mounted horn. "To the people of Denmark, and to my subjects in Norway! May we always be strong, stay united, and live free."

A cheer rose up from the crowd, the roar of a giant beast. "Hail Harald" some shouted, and soon the entire throng was chanting, "Hail Harald! Hail Harald!"

As the king drank from his horn, Lifu couldn't help but think that this was a man at the peak of his power. Was no one else worried about what might come next, after the peak had passed?

Harald smiled at the crowd, revealing a dark tooth in the armor of his wide grin. He held up his hands until the roar had quieted. "Our first toast was of mead, as is Freya's due. But you may also want to try the ale that is a gift of the Christian monks of Hedeby. Let the feast of midsummer's night begin. We'll have pipes and dancers while you eat. And when you think you are satisfied with the generosity of your king, the drums will beat to show you that there is more to come."

After this somewhat mysterious pronouncement, the king set down his horn and clapped his hands. At once a dozen young men with flutes leapt onto the grassy stage, followed by a dozen girls in red bodices and white skirts. While the boys piped the girls twirled, spinning their braids and whirling their skirts like wheels.

For the next hour Lifu arduously made her way back and forth from their table to the ox pit, fetching plates of meat or horns of ale. She wasn't particularly hungry herself, but Grady ate like a starving man.

The evening sun was casting long shadows when the dancers stopped and the drums began to beat in unison. This time when the king stood up and raised his hands for silence, Lifu noticed that the table before him held four leather bags, arranged like a row of cabbages.

"The feast of midsummer's night is an evening when a king shows his generosity." His voice was strong enough that it reached even to those on the farthest benches. "Yes, there will still be taxes due in the fall. Everyone must save up a share of summer's harvest to pay for the warriors and ships that keep our realm safe. But now, on the night when summer begins, it is my turn to reward my subjects."

Harald opened a bag, scooped up a handful of silver, and let the coins clink back through his fingers.

A sigh of wonder breathed through the crowd.

"In the past two months," the king continued, "I have secretly had my smith forge six hundred silver coins, enough for every free man, woman, and child in the city. Tonight the helmsmen of my six fleets will distribute them as my gift to you."

For a while the crowd was too surprised to react. Giving money to commoners, simply for their loyalty, was not something a Danish king had ever done. But as the helmsmen began making their way along the benches of the crowd, pressing one coin into each pair of outstretched hands, the cheers began again, "Hail Harald!"

The clamor was so great that no one could hear what the king said next. He had to hold his hands in the air for quite a while before the names "Grady" and "Lifu" carried far enough for them to hear. The king was motioning for them to step forward.

"Come on, then," Grady said, standing up.

"To the king's table?" Lifu asked, amazed. "You knew about this?"

In reply the smith took her hand and led her through the crowd to the stage. In front of the king's table Grady removed his red hat. They bowed.

"This is my silversmith, Grady, and his woman, Lifu," the king announced loudly. "Tell them, Grady, what they are receiving from their king."

Grady turned around to face the crowd. "They're quarter denari," he said, crumpling the square hat nervously in his hands.

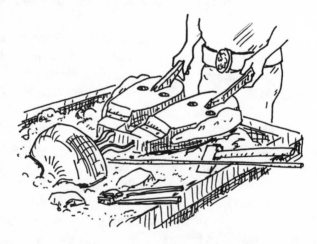

Voices called from the crowd, "What?" and "Speak up, man!"

"You're each getting a quarter of a denar!" Grady shouted. "The standard silver coins of Rome or London are heavier and thicker, but each of these should be enough to buy two chickens. Twenty of them would pay for a sheep." He stopped and looked down at his hands.

The king added, "The silver has been weighed out carefully, so you don't need scales." He lowered his voice. "Go on, silversmith. Tell them what's on their coins."

Grady cleared his throat. "The front of each coin shows our king and his name."

Lifu whispered, "In Latin."

"Oh, it's written in Latin because Roman lettering is understood throughout the world." He added more quietly, "Even in Denmark, most people can't read runes."

"Why is there a Christian cross?" the king demanded.

For the first time, Grady smiled. "Is the cross really Christian, Your Highness? It looks like the sun sign of Odin to me. Could be either."

The king nodded. "And the ship on the back? I think that is not your work."

"No, Your Highness." Grady put his arm around Lifu's shoulders. "Both the ship and your likeness were drawn by Lifu, the teacher of your children."

She smiled nervously. The king had liked her drawings so much that she had begun designing the ivory chessmen he wanted. She had already carved a helmsman and a berserker from wax to use as models before attempting to cut valuable ivory.

Meanwhile the six jarls had returned with their leather bags empty. Lifu was more than ready to return to her seat, but Grady held her firmly by the shoulder. "Wait," he whispered.

"These coins are your reward for loyalty," the king announced to the crowd, "But the smith who forged them deserves a reward as well. I asked what he wanted. He replied with an unusual request. Grady the smith has asked to marry his woman Lifu."

The crowd laughed appreciatively. Lifu blushed so deeply that the blackberry tint on her cheeks looked pale. Grady squeezed her shoulder and asked, "Is that all right, Lifu?"

She stammered, "Well yes, but why in front of the whole town?"

Even the king chuckled at this. "Grady was raised in Ireland, a Christian land with different customs. Here, any man and woman who live together for three months are considered married. If either says 'I divorce you' three times, they are divorced. Freya is our goddess of love, and midsummer's night is her festival, but she does not rule over marriage. The Christian god apparently does. Grady admits he has doubts about Christianity, but he is fond of their marriage ritual. Brother Michael, step forward."

The king motioned to the monk who had been waiting to one side. "Denmark is not a Christian land, but show us how your god oversees marriage."

The next few minutes were a blur in Lifu's memory. While the crowd watched curiously, the priest read something in Latin from the leaves of a leather-bound book. In awkward Norse, Brother Michael asked them questions about honoring and obeying. Lifu came to her senses only when Grady took out his gold ring — the ring he had received from the hand of Pope John in Rome — and slipped it onto the fourth finger of her left hand. The ring should have been far too big for her. Grady's fingers were sausages compared to hers!

"But — how can it fit my hand?"

"I'm a smith, my love."

A voice said, "You may kiss the bride," and suddenly Lifu was being kissed passionately in front of all Hedeby.

The king laughed and the crowd cheered. This part of the ritual everyone understood.

"I think Freya would approve," the king said. He raised his voice to the crowd. "May generous kings and gods of love watch over you in the seasons to come. And now you may go to your homes. Although my jarls may choose to stay, share another horn of mead, and hear a tale from some unlikely skalds."

Grady squeezed Lifu one more time. "Good luck with the unlikely skalds." Then he retreated to a bench.

While most of crowd dispersed and the jarls refilled their horns, Lifu quickly prepared the king's two children for their performance of Beowulf. By then even Queen Tove had left with her retinue, balancing her birch headdress with haughty poise. Gunhild and Svein were not her children.

The warriors who remained on the benches around the stage were a tough crew with scars, scraggly beards, and iron arm bands. They eyed Lifu doubtfully as she adjusted the English harp.

When the strings were in tune Lifu handed the harp to Gunhild, spoke a few encouraging words to the nervous young prince, and walked to the side of the stage. There she beat the great drum three times.

After the drumbeats Gunhild struck a mournful chord on the harp. Then she nudged Svein with her elbow.

"Listen!" the boy said, his voice as high and clear as a girl's. "And I'll tell you a tale from the days when Danes fought dragons of dread and fire."

Some of the brawny jarls snickered. Lifu silenced them with a beat of the drum. She nodded encouragingly to Gunhild.

The princess struck the harp again — the same mournful chord, but backwards, from high notes to low.

"*Hwaet!*" Svein announced, switching to English. Then he repeated the same two lines of poetry in the language of the Anglo-Saxons.

The jarls who had laughed glanced to each other uncertainly. One called out, "What is this?"

The king smiled. "It's English, Rolf. You've sailed with me to the Danelaw. Didn't you learn any English poetry?"

"Not much," the jarl admitted.

"Then pay attention. Maybe you'll learn a thing or two from my ten-winter-old son."

This earned Harald a round of laughter. He continued, "Lifu, the silversmith's wife, has been teaching my children English. They are going to sing us the poem of Beowulf."

"Sing a poem?" another jarl asked. "A girl?"

Lifu stepped forward to explain. "English poem-tales are sung by both men and women. England's laws may be primitive, and their kings chaotic, but their music is pretty good."

Unprompted, Gunhild gave the harp a defiant strum. She met the jarl's eye with a steady gaze.

Lifu continued, "The saga of Beowulf is too long to recite here, and there are few enough of you who understand English, so we've shortened it for you. We'll also explain the story in Norse along the way. Gunhild?"

The girl plucked the strings one at a time as she spoke. "The story of Beowulf is set in Denmark long ago, when a king named Hrothgar built a hall."

"Should we know this king?" a jarl asked.

Gunhild glared. "It was long ago."

"Svein?" Lifu prompted.

"Oh yes." The boy began telling his part of the story. "A jealous monster showed up. He was named Grendel. Each night he'd kill and eat some of the men in the hall. No one could stop him, because the monster had a spell, and swords didn't work on him. Then one day a prince named Beowulf arrived. He was so strong he ripped off Grendel's arm and killed him."

Gunhild plucked a three-note chord, "But the next night, Grendel's mother came to the hall, killing men in revenge. Beowulf tracked her to an underwater cave and killed her with a sword from the Giants."

Then she sang, strumming at each stressed English word.

> Our hero got many gifts from the king of the Danes —
> Gold for Grendel and a goblet for the mother.
> Then he sailed home across the strait, this son
>   of the Geats.
> There the king had been killed, so they
>   crowned Beowulf.

Lifu translated these lines while Gunhild gave the harp to Svein. Then the prince continued the song.

He ruled fifty winters, until one fall
A bad thief burrowed in a burial mound
And stole a cup from a dragon's hoard.

Svein had mixed up some of the words, but Lifu translated it anyway. Next it was Gunhild's turn to recite.

> Three centuries asleep, the snake awoke,
> And sniffing for his treasure, smelled the thief.
> That night he harrowed the homes of the Geats,
> Flattening farms with his fiery breath.

After a pause, Lifu prompted Svein, "Though old . . . "
The boy recited,

> Though old, Beowulf went out with his men.
> But at the barrow's mouth he bade them wait.
> This was his fight. Beowulf alone
> Went boldly to battle the beast in its den.

The princess took back the harp and continued,

> His blade wouldn't bite. Beowulf lay dying
> When Wiglaf, his kinsman, attacked the worm.
> And the king then killed it with a cut of his dirk.

Gunhild offered the harp to her brother, but the look of panic on his face told Lifu that the boy had forgotten the rest. She took the harp herself and finished the song.

> Woefully wounded, the warrior Beowulf
> Gave the treasure to Wiglaf and gave up his life.
> Wiglaf then became the king,
> And long the land was ruled by him.

Lifu gave a final strum. She and the children bowed.

Harald stood up, clapping his hands in the manner of English audiences. Although applause was new to most of the jarls, they gradually followed the king's example.

"Before we dismiss your English class," Harald said, sitting back down, "I have a question for our two young skalds. In your tale, is it true that Beowulf was not actually a Dane?"

Gunhild nodded. "The poem says he was a Geat, from what is now Sweden."

A jarl with a Swedish accent commented, "I have heard of this lost tribe. The Geats died out long ago, pressured by Swedes from the north and Danes from the south."

Harald touched his fingertips together, thinking. "Nonetheless, this prince came to the aid of Denmark. And what exactly was the horror that harrowed the Danes?"

"It was a monster," Svein replied. "Grendel was a monster."

"Is that all?" his father asked.

Lifu thought: What a question! She thrilled to see Gunhild slowly turning it over in her mind.

"I'm not sure," the young princess said, "But maybe the poet meant the monsters to stand for something else."

"They're monsters," Svein said. "You kill them."

"But swords didn't work against them. And they had hoards of treasure." Gunhild turned to her father. "I think the monsters in the poem were meant to represent greed and envy."

Harald Bluetooth nodded. "These may be the most difficult of all monsters to defeat." Then he waved his hand. "Bedtime for poets. Well done, Lifu. Take your lucky husband home."

* * *

Lifu had intended to escort the king's children to their hall, but they promptly vanished into the twilight. She couldn't blame them. There was too much excitement afoot on midsummer's night for anyone to respect bedtime. It also turned out that the monks' ponies had been so frightened by the festival that she and Grady had to spend half an hour helping the monks catch them. By the time the wagon was once again thumping along the town's main road, the blue glow on the horizon had become so dim that the birch boughs on the houses really did seem part of a ghostly forest.

They were just saying goodbye at the church when Gunhild ran up, breathless.

"Lifu! Brother Michael!" the princess exclaimed. "Svein and the other boys have a built a bonfire by the harbor. They've stolen something from your church."

"What did they take?" Lifu asked.

"I don't know. Some kind of Christian leaf."

Brother Michael exchanged a tight-lipped glance with the other monks. "You stay here and guard the church. I'll go see what they've done."

As Lifu, Grady, and Michael followed the princess toward the harbor, the girl talked almost nonstop.

"No one's supposed to have bonfires inside the city because of the fire danger, but the boys say they need to get rid of ghosts everywhere. They've been catching girls, holding them by the hands and legs, and tossing them across the fire. When they couldn't find any more girls they threw a dog and even a goat." She lowered her head. "I think the boys may have found something to drink."

When the street opened up onto the square by the harbor, Lifu could see the circle of boys — perhaps twenty of them, gathered around the flickering light of what must once have been a large bonfire, although it had now mostly burned down to coals. Svein was small for his age but he was a prince, so he seemed to be in charge. Most disturbing of all, Lifu noticed that he was wearing a scabbard with his half-length sword, Dogbane. No one was supposed to be armed on the night of Freya's festival.

"There's the priest!" one of the boys shouted. The others whooped, and Svein swaggered forward.

"What did you take from the church?" Lifu demanded.

"English class is over, woman," the prince said. He turned to Brother Michael. "I hear you Christians were the only ones who wouldn't jump over the flames on the way to the festival."

Michael pulled back his hood, but didn't answer.

"Aren't you worried about ghosts?" Svein asked. "People say your god is a ghost."

"God has three forms," the monk replied, his Irish accent thick. "One of them is the spirit inside the true believer."

Svein turned to his friends. "I told you. He's haunted." And then, to the monk, "I dare you to jump across our fire."

Michael crossed his arms. "No."

"Not even to save your book?" The prince motioned to a boy on the far side of the fire. The boy took a sheet of parchment from his shirt and held it over the flames.

"That book is the word of God," Michael said, his voice louder.

"Then jump over and get it. Someone might accidentally drop it in the fire."

Grady objected, "Stop this!"

"Shut up, smith." The prince drew his sword. "I could kill you, you know."

"Svein!" the princess cried. "Put the sword away."

Svein ignored her. He nodded toward the parchment. "What's written on that leaf, priest?"

"It is the start of God's book, the Bible. I have been translating it into Norse."

"What does it say in Norse?"

"It says, 'In the beginning God created the Heaven and the Earth.'"

"Drop it," Svein told the boy.

Before anyone could intervene the parchment fell into the flames. The sheet began blackening, but it did not immediately flare up. The smoke had the foul smell of burning flesh.

Svein turned to Brother Michael. "You Christians are cowards. You have no weapons. You know nothing of fighting. You're afraid to jump over a fire, even to save the book of your god."

The young prince spat at the monk's bare feet. "Christians know nothing of bravery."

Brother Michael took a deep breath and closed his eyes. He pressed the palms of his hands together.

"Yes, pray!" Svein laughed. "Pray to your god for a miracle. I've heard how little it helps."

Slowly the monk began walking forward. One deliberate step at a time, with his eyes still closed, he walked past the prince and into the fire.

Lifu gasped. She started to rush forward, but Grady held her back.

Brother Michael walked onward, his bare feet now entirely surrounded by red-hot coals. In the middle of the fire he slowly stooped to pick up the singed parchment. Flames licked around his robe. No one dared to breathe, much less to speak. In the flickering light, the boys' faces had become masks of awe and fear.

When Brother Michael stepped out from the far side of the fire pit, the ring of boys scattered to make way. Paying them no attention, the monk walked on, at the same solemn pace, through the darkness toward Hedeby's church.

CHAPTER 10
COPENHAGEN, 1940

For all her fears — about Julius, about the future — Mette found herself flushed with a heart-quickening feeling that seemed inexplicably like happiness. A week's vacation, traveling with just a light valise, to see her fiancé and her parents — yes, that was reason enough for elation. But her mood had begun only beyond the border.

Germany saved its dirtiest, oldest trains for the passenger run to Denmark. The intercity Hamburg-Copenhagen express rattled through the industrial wasteland north of Flensburg like a rusty washing machine on wheels. Broken windows, sooty walls, and dead trees clattered past, marchers to a borderland dirge. At Padborg, a train station without a village, the only things that were clean and bright were giant Nazi flags snapping black swastikas in squares of bloody red.

A conductor announced in German that all passengers would have to get out of the train and carry their bags through the gravel beside the track in order to walk through a checkpoint gate. There a Wehrmacht soldier with rifle and helmet squinted at Mette's passport and visa before waving her wordlessly on.

A few feet later a smiling blond man in a red Danish military uniform stamped her pass with a flourish. "*Velkommen hjem til Danmark, Frøken Andersen.*"

Welcome home!

"You're in the Danish army," Mette said, amazed. "Germany didn't really let our soldiers keep their jobs, did they?"

"*Joda!*" he replied. He held out his hand toward the open doors of the waiting Danish train.

The Danes had obviously put their finest passenger cars at the border, if only to thumb their noses at their German "protectors." Mette ran an admiring hand along the plush seatbacks, mahogany wood-work, and shiny brass luggage racks. After a small clank the wagon hushed forward through the countryside as if the unseen diesel engine had taken flight.

Outside, white wooden flagpoles stood at attention in front of every farmhouse, flying the kind of long red-and-white pennant that had once graced the topmasts of Danish sailing ships. Homes in villages flew the rectangular version that had become the world's first national banner centuries ago, a red field with a white cross — the flag named *Dannebrog*.

A red-capped attendant pushed a refreshment cart down the aisle, bottles and glasses tinkling like Christmas candle chimes. "Sandwiches? Pastries?"

Mette ordered a coffee with cream. The attendant accepted a *Reichsmark* note, but she gave change in solid crowns, minted with the mustachioed visage of King Christian X.

While drinking that powerful coffee, and listening to the murmur of her fellow Danish passengers, Mette looked out the window. The train miraculously lifted from the shore of a pebbly beach. The entire carriage swung over a field of red cattle and flew through the iron framework of the Lillebælt Bridge, leaving Jutland behind. A soft green stripe on the horizon ahead was Funen, the first and largest island of the Danish archipelago.

How could she not be happy? Despite everything that was going wrong in the world, Denmark would always be the last refuge of *hygge*, the comfort that comes with peace and fairness and caring for each other. Perhaps even the Nazis could not crush that spirit.

Mette held the little white ceramic coffee cup in both hands and breathed the dizzying spice of faraway sunlands. Danes had been travelers since Viking times. Anglo-Saxon historians — clerics writing centuries later — insisted that the heathen invaders had been violent men. But the actual archeological finds told a different story. Wherever the Danes had settled they had left evidence of farmers, traders, and craftsmen. Excavations revealed that the Danelaw, the eastern half of England, must in fact have been one of the most peaceable parts of the British Isles. The Danes had quietly paid taxes to Anglo-Saxon kings for a century, but they had also kept their own system of law and order. The Danelaw had relied on cooperation and honor. It had been a social democracy at a time when Europe was ravaged by despots who called themselves Christian.

Mette wondered how Danes could have become famous for both violence and *hygge*. Would the excavation at Hedeby, the Danish Vikings' capital, unearth an answer?

Mette unclasped her valise, opened a velvet pouch, and set a small, clumsily struck silver coin on the little window table. Next to the ancient coin was the modern one she had received in change with her coffee. HARALD REX and CHRISTIAN X. Almost exactly a thousand years separated the two Danish kings. Would both of their reigns end in disaster? Mette looked out the window and sighed. *Hygge* alone, it seemed, was not enough to save kingdoms.

* * *

When the train pulled underneath the great arched roof of the Copenhagen train station Mette was leaning her head out the window with unladylike enthusiasm, searching among the crowd of hats for a certain tan fedora. There! With his thin Clark Gable mustache, Julius looked stern and worried. Then he saw her waving and his whole expression changed to sunshine. A few moments later they were in each other's arms, scattering passersby as he spun her around off the ground. By the time they finally found words, they were nearly alone on the platform.

"I've missed you so much, Julius. Are you sure you're all right?"

"Better than might be expected, my dear. And how are you surviving in the *Vaterland?*"

Mette hurried past his question. "But our letters! Half of the ones I sent you didn't get past the censors."

"Mine too! You had the same idea? To write two kinds of letters?"

They both laughed. But then Mette's smile faded. "Is it safe to talk?"

Julius picked up her valise. "Within Denmark the censorship is more subtle." They walked into the cavernous waiting room. Loudspeakers echoed an unintelligible background babble.

"But the —" she caught herself and whispered, "The 'Chosen People.' The Jews. You're at risk. They stole your airplane."

Julius knit his brow. "That was a mistake. Private citizens aren't allowed to have aircraft for security reasons, but the Germans can't dictate how we're reimbursed. The same Danish policeman who showed up at my apartment last month came back later and apologized. He gave me a check for three thousand crowns."

"Oh! That's — surprisingly civilized." They had pushed through the big glass doors to the sidewalk. She asked, "Did you bring the Bentley?"

"The streetcar's easier in downtown traffic. I hope you don't mind?"

"No, in fact, let's walk. I've been cooped up on the train, and I only brought the one small bag."

"Excellent. Hungry?"

"Ravenous."

He took her hand. "First stop: the *pølsevogn* at Tivoli."

She followed him eagerly. Every child growing up in Copenhagen, and certainly every hungry university student, loved the city's little wheeled hot dog stands. The sausages themselves were ridiculously long and ridiculously red, but their seductive scent drifted through the streets for blocks. None of the booths was more beloved than the one halfway between the train station and City Hall, before the triumphal arch at the entrance to Tivoli Gardens.

Tivoli! What other capital city would jam an amusement park into the heart of downtown? Tivoli might have been been named for the gardens in Rome, but it had become a cabinet of curiositiies from the entire world, with diversions collected for the well-traveled Danes: a pagoda from China, a wood-railed roller coaster from Brooklyn, the

Arc de Triomphe from Paris — all mixed in amongst lakes, hidden garden paths, bandshells, restaurants, and theaters.

As Mette and Julius ate their hot dogs, she pointed. "Look! On the marquee. There you are!"

Julius glanced up at the theater sign and sputtered. The giant face of Clark Gable smiled moodily down at them beside the red plastic letters, "GONE WITH THE WIND — Winner, Best Picture!"

"I suppose we should go see it." Julius stroked his pencil mustache.

"Oh, let's do. Lars says he's from Oregon."

"Really? Your brother wrote about Clark Gable in one of his letters?"

Mette dabbed mustard from her cheek with a napkin. "I guess Gable was originally from Ohio or something, but he couldn't get any theater work there so he drifted out West. He worked as a logger on the Oregon Coast for a while. He was finally discovered after he got a job selling ties in Portland at a big department store. I think they called it Meier and Frank's."

"Sounds like a Jewish shop." Julius raised an eyebrow. "Who discovered him there?"

"A Portland theater manager named Josephine Dillon. She paid to get his teeth and his hair fixed. Gave him voice and acting lessons. Then she took him to Hollywood. They got married, although she was seventeen years older."

"Did that work out?"

"No. Gable's on his third wife by now." Mette blushed, suddenly embarrassed. Why had she blurted out such a stupid thing? Apparently her subconscious fears about their age difference had momentarily taken over her mouth. And now Julius was standing there tight-lipped.

Mette dropped her napkin into a trash can. "We're not like that. Marriage will work for us." She took his arm. "We've got all week to talk about it. Come on, I need to drop some things off at the National Museum."

The museum was on the way to their unspoken goal — either the garret room that Mette rented on Nyhavn, or perhaps the waterfront apartment complex a few blocks farther where Julius lived. But first their walking route took them across Rådhuspladsen, the city's largest plaza, dominated by the pointy square tower of City Hall. Buses, streetcars, newspaper stands, and a crowd of commuters lined the edges of the vast square. A flock of pigeons that rose up from the middle could have been snow in a shaken glass globe.

"Everything looks just the same," Mette marveled. "I don't see a single German uniform."

"They're all in there." Julius nodded toward a five-story stone building facing the square. "The Gestapo took over the old Shell Oil headquarters. You don't see their uniforms in Copenhagen, but rest assured, the Germans are seeing you."

Mette shivered and walked on. A block farther she spotted the first of the National Museum's banners. This one announced a new exhibition: "Gorm the Old: 1000 Years of Danish Monarchy."

Mette couldn't help but smile. The exhibit was obviously based on her work in Jelling. What's more, whoever had organized the exhibit had chosen a provocative title, poking fun at the Nazis' seven-year-old Reich.

Greeting visitors in the museum lobby, as always, was a full-size replica of Harald Bluetooth's famous rune stone. But this time Mette was surprised to see Harald himself standing to one side, resting his hand proudly on the massive plaster reproduction. A white-haired woman was fussing with the wax mannequin's royal ermine cloak. The woman looked up at Mette and gasped. "You're back!"

"Mom!" Mette exclaimed.

Kirstin Andersen gave her daughter a long hug. "We've been so proud of you. It's good to see you home."

"How did you —?" Mette gestured vaguely toward the mannequin, as if Harald might finish her sentence.

"How did I get a job as curator?" Kirstin gave a light shrug. "The Germans have been throwing so much money at research that I've been hired back. Our new Jelling exhibit is a huge hit. Please tell me you've brought something we can use from your excavation at Hedeby."

"Actually, I suppose I have. Julius?" She motioned for him to bring her valise to a counter. She unsnapped the clasps and hesitated. "Don't look," she told him. "These are women's things."

"You dug up women's things?" Julius asked, puzzled. But he looked aside.

"Even suitcases have layers." She rummaged beneath blouses and underwear before she withdrew a velvet bag and a packet of papers. "Here."

Kirstin quickly took a pair of white gloves from a pocket of her dress. "May I?"

Mette nodded.

Her mother carefully tipped the contents of the bag into her palm. When a silver coin slid out, she drew in her breath. "Harald Rex. Oh dear."

"What's wrong?"

"I've made his face too fat." Kirstin sighed. "I didn't have any contemporary images of Harald Bluetooth when I designed the wax model."

"Looks like the guy had a bony jaw," Julius said. "He's Hollywood material."

Kirstin gently turned the coin over. "And a ship on the obverse. This must be one of the first Danish coins ever minted. Where did you find it?"

"In a fire pit near the harbor," Mette said. "I've brought drawings of all the sites, with notes and sketches. The real work will begin when we can get at the sunken ships in the bay."

"How long will that take?" Kirstin asked.

"The engineers have to build a coffer dam and pump out the water. They've had setbacks." Mette frowned. "It will be at least a year."

"A year!" Julius exclaimed. "But I thought the two of us — you know — "

"I do know." Mette put her hand in his. Then she told her mother, "Take care of Harald's coin. Julius and I need to talk."

As soon as they were back outside, walking along the canal beside Christiansborg Castle, Julius fumed, "A year!"

"Hedeby's important." It sounded cold, and she regretted having to say it.

"So are we." Julius turned aside. He braced his arms on an iron railing and glared out at the canal's wavy reflection of castle spires.

She slid her arm around him, but he didn't move. "I didn't mean it that way."

"For God's sake, Mette, there's a war on. This is a time for decisions."

"Like getting married?"

"That too. But we also have to fight for what we believe in."

Mette felt a new fear. "What are you thinking?"

"I want to help the Allies."

"As a pilot?"

"I could, you know. The RAF would train me for their fighters. They need pilots."

"Because their own pilots are dying in the Battle of Britain. There must be something else you could do. And how would you get to England anyway?"

"Your father has a fishing boat." Julius lowered his voice. "He's with the resistance, Holger Danske."

Mette bit her lip. Then it was true: the underground movement was real. She had wondered, rereading Julius's letters, if he had been trying to warn her. Joining the resistance was even more dangerous than becoming an RAF pilot. Her father's pride sometimes made him reckless. Suddenly she feared that the war might cost her both her father and her fiancé.

"What is —" She dropped her voice to a whisper, "— What is Holger planning to do?"

"There's not much public support for blowing up train tracks or anything like that. So far the Germans have left us our police, our government, and our press. They've even backed off on their threats against Jews."

"Really? No yellow stars?"

"No." The tension in his shoulders relented a little. "The Danish Nazi party isn't even polling enough to win a seat in parliament. One of their fanatics set off a fire bomb in front of the Copenhagen synagogue, but the fire department put out the blaze and the Danish police arrested him. He's been sentenced to two years in prison, despite the Reich's objections."

Mette's heart lifted. The Danes' sense of cooperation and caring — their *hygge* — had won a skirmish after all. But Julius had avoided answering her question. She tried again.

"What is the resistance planning?"

"I don't know. Once a week your father steers his boat over to Sweden. He makes it look like he's out of gas or has engine trouble, but I think he's delivering information to be forwarded to the British embassy in Stockholm."

"What kind of information?"

"Troop movements? I'm not sure. But this week he wants to smuggle out passengers. Including me."

"You! This week! You're thinking of going to Sweden this week?"

"It's not just about me, Mette." He turned to face her. "They want me to persuade Niels Bohr to help the Allies."

She looked at him, baffled. "Niels Bohr, the physicist? They want you to smuggle a science professor out of Denmark? Why?"

"Bohr's mother is Jewish. He went to school with my parents. We may be able to convince him."

"Yes, but why? How on earth could a physicist help the Allies?"

"I'm not exactly sure. Maybe we'll find out tonight." He took her hands. "My parents and I have been invited to the Bohrs' house for dinner. I want you to come with us."

"I haven't even unpacked yet."

"I know it's hurried, but everything is speeding up. Can't you feel it? If Bohr agrees to go, your father will take him and me across on the first dark night with a fog. That's why I want to get married as soon as possible. Tomorrow, if we can."

Mette's head was spinning. "Let me —" she ran out of words.

"Don't you want to get married?"

"Yes, but —" She caught her breath. "You've given me so much to consider all at once. Let me take it one step at a time."

He stood back, uncertain. "So the first step would be what? Dinner tonight?"

She smiled, her eyes damp. Should she laugh or cry. "All right. Dinner tonight. With a physicist. Let's start there."

* * *

Mette worried about her clothes, partly to avoid worrying about everything else. After showering and washing her cantankerous hair she stood in her underwear before the small closet of her apartment and frowned. She had lots of professional-looking skirts and jackets, but not much for what was likely to be a fairly formal dinner, and nothing at all to wear for a wedding. Why did the thought of marrying Julius suddenly frighten her so much?

Finally she chose a flower-print dress, hoping it would look less casual at dinner when accessoried with white gloves, white pumps, and a white hat with a big round brim. While she tried on this outfit in front of her dresser mirror, she began trying on the different emotions Julius had awakened in her. She would have to choose one of those moods to wear tonight as well.

First she really was frightened, and not just by the prospect of marrying a man who was too young and too handsome to be trusted. If Julius fled to Sweden he might never come back, especially if he joined the Royal Air Force. That dark mood didn't go well with the cheery dress in the mirror. For a while she tried being happy and excited, thinking of weddings. She had been dating Julius a long time. He had been patient. Didn't that prove his loyalty? On the walk to her apartment Julius had assured her that the Nazis' ban on mixed marriages did not extend to Denmark. Danish law still treated people of all religions as equals. They could legally marry. But the thought that she might be sleeping in the same bed as Julius, perhaps as soon as tomorrow night, made her blush.

The red in her cheeks went perfectly with the white hat and the dress's white collar. Looking at herself in the mirror, she realized that her blush looked exactly like the flush of anger. Yes, anger or resentment. Where had that mood come from? She didn't have to look far. She remembered how shocked Julius had been when he learned at the museum that her excavation in Hedeby would keep her in Germany another year. Did he think so little of her career that he wanted her home at once, to be his wife? And then, in the next breath, he had announced that as soon as they were married, he himself planned to leave for a suicide mission in England. Did he care that he might leave her pregnant, or widowed, or both? Why were men so often blinded by their passions?

A buzzer on the wall interrupted her mental rant. Still red in the face, she pushed the intercom's button and demanded, "What is it?"

"Uh, Mette, it's me. Are you ready?" The voice from the little speaker was as scratchy as an old record, but obviously filled with concern. It was the sound of love.

She closed her eyes and took a deep breath.

The voice asked, "Mette? Are you all right?"

No, she thought.

"Yes," she said. "I'll be right down."

* * *

On the sidewalk Mette let herself be kissed, although she wasn't feeling quite in the spirit. The black Bentley purred at the edge of the cobblestone street, its eight cylinders idling. The front seat was empty. Julius' parents had chosen to sit in the back.

"Don't tell them about my going to Sweden," Julius warned.

"What? You haven't talked to your parents about leaving the country?"

"Shh!" Julius put a finger to his lips. He whispered, "It's safer for them if they don't know anything about the resistance."

Mette stiffened. Julius had never shushed her before. It also seemed dishonest not to tell parents that their only son would be taking such a risk. "Why do they think we're meeting with Niels Bohr? To chat about physics formulas?"

"Yes. My father likes that sort of thing. Come on, you'll see." Julius opened the car door for Mette.

Claudia and Jakob Gustmeyer leaned forward from the back seat, waving to her. "Hi!"

It was too late for Mette to do anything other than smile. She slid into the front seat, put her hat on her lap, and turned to hold out her gloved hand.

Fru Gustmeyer clasped it eagerly. "Frøken Andersen, this is such a pleasure, seeing you again." A slightly stocky matron in her mid-fifties, she wore a black dress with a black sequined pill hat. Dimples in her cheeks and a silver-haired fur wrap at her throat lessened the otherwise somber effect.

Herre Gustmeyer winked. "You look positively delicious, *frøken,* Our son is a lucky man." He wore a goatee in the style of the previous king. A bowler hat perched above a fringe of thinning white hair. His starched collar, silk tie, and black suit made Mette self-conscious about her casual, flower-print dress.

Julius got in the driver's seat and put the Bentley in gear. "Off to an evening with the Bohrs."

"Oh, Julius," his mother said, "Do swing by the old house to show your fiancée where Niels was born."

Julius sighed. "Mother, please. She and I have walked by it countless times. I've always refrained from pointing it out."

"Why?" Herre Gustmeyer objected. "You should take more pride in your family."

"All right." Julius turned at the canal by Christiansborg and waved toward a five-story stone building faced with Greek columns, directly across from the palace. "Here it is. The former Gustmeyer house."

Mette drew in her breath at the size and extravagance of the building. "Oh! I've always thought this was a bank. Why do you call it the Gustmeyer house?"

Jakob stoked his goatee, obviously pleased to tell the story. "A great-great-grandfather of mine, Frederick Gustmeyer, built the place as a general merchandise store, with living quarters upstairs. But then Denmark sided with Napoleon against the Germans. In the economic collapse after the war, Frederick lost everything. The house has had many owners since then."

"Interesting you should say it looks like a bank," Fru Gustmeyer put in. "The Adlers who own it now really are in finance. Niels' mother Ellen has been a major supporter of our synagogue's charities."

Mette asked, "Then you know Herre Bohr from the synagogue?"

Fru Gustmeyer frowned. "Not so much." She didn't elaborate. Mette was curious, but decided it wouldn't be polite to ask further, at least yet.

After driving past the house they motored along City Hall square and then a mile south toward the tall brick smokestack of the Carlsberg brewery. It was common knowledge that Niels Bohr, having won the Nobel prize, had been given the use of the Carlsberg mansion for his family and his Institute of Theoretical Physics. Years ago Mr. Carlsberg, the founder of the famous beer company, had decreed in his will that the Royal Academy of Sciences should choose a man or woman engaged in science, literature, or art to occupy the honorary residence.

Mette had imagined the beer magnate's estate would be a factory, so she was surprised when the entrance proved to be a boulevard through Italianate gardens with classical statues and cypresses. The faint, sweet smell of malt in the evening air suggested that somewhere there must be beer tanks and loading docks, but the three elegant stone buildings arranged in a U shape at the end of the lane looked more like a cardinal's Roman villa.

By the time they had parked the Bentley and stepped out, the famous physicist had come down the stone steps to greet them. He shook the Gustmeyers' hands warmly.

Niels Bohr looked young for his age, partly because of his boyishly puffy cheeks and partly because of the way he slicked his hair back from his tall forehead. Mette mused that his brown suit, starched collar, and tie might have come from the same tailor as Herre Gustmeyer's.

"Young Julius!" Bohr exclaimed, holding out his hand to shake. "You've grown into quite a man since I saw you last. We could use you on our local soccer squad."

"I wish I had your knack for ball sports," Julius admitted. "Allow me to introduce my fiancée, Mette Andersen."

"Charmed." He embarrassed Mette by kissing her glove. Then he added, "I imagine you are often confused with the National Museum archeologist of the same name?"

"Actually, that is me." Why couldn't people think she looked the part?

"Really? Well, this is an honor. Margrethe is still overseeing things in the kitchen. Could I offer you a short tour of the house before dinner?"

The entry room could have served as the lobby for a grand hotel, with gilt medallions and oil paintings on the paneled walls.

"The dining hall and our quarters are to the left," Bohr said. "Straight ahead, through the French doors, is a private garden. But most visitors want to see the institute's laboratory."

He led them through a door to the right. The high-ceilinged room beyond had blackboards filled with equations and diagrams. Bizarre glassware apparatuses stood on tables. A counter below the windows held sinks with beakers and coffee cups. Hanging like laundry from a wire across the side of the room were a series of strange photographs. The prints were mostly black, but with streaks and starbursts.

Herre Gustmeyer immediately went to admire the photographs. "Ah, cloud chamber images. This is where you are taking apart atoms, piece by piece?"

"Yes, it's a way to prove our theories to a doubting world," Bohr said.

Julius spoke with hesitation. "I don't want to sound ignorant, but how are atoms put together?"

"Our thinking has changed over the years," Bohr said, moving to a table with models made of sticks, balls, and wires. He held up a sphere of wire hoops that looked like a giant broken eggbeater. "In 1911, Ernest Rutherford proposed that atoms look like this, sort of like a solar system. The positively charged protons are here in the middle like the sun, while negatively charged electrons orbit around like planets. But it didn't explain the chemical properties of elements. The following year I suggested a more satisfactory variation."

Bohr held up a melon-sized ball of foam that had been cut away to reveal concentric spheres. "The electrons still orbit, but they're in layers with different energy levels. If an electron drops from one level to another it releases a specific amount of energy — a quantum of energy."

"And that is the quantum theory?" Julius asked.

"It used to be." Bohr set down the model. "Back in the '20s one of my assistants here was a brilliant young German, Werner Heisenberg. He developed quantum mechanics, a theory that is hard to explain. We now think of electrons in terms of probabilities instead of trajectories, although the quantums of energies between levels remain true. Basically, electrons at a certain energy level can be anywhere and nowhere at once, depending on how you look. Our friend Albert Einstein still thinks it's nonsense."

"But the theory works?" Julius asked.

"Oh yes, except a few years ago a fellow in Italy discovered neutrons. I had to adapt the whole model. Now we know that the nucleus of an atom is a ball of protons and neutrons, held together by a force that's very hard to break."

Mette's attention had wandered to a shelf of awards. "Do you keep your Nobel prize here?" She was curious to see one of the famous gold medals, stamped with the image of Alfred Nobel, the wealthy Swede who had invented dynamite and then, as penance, the prizes.

Bohr gave a small laugh. "Actually, my colleagues and I have got three of those medals now. They're right before your eyes."

Mette looked around. "I don't understand."

He pointed to a bottle of what looked like water. "When the Nazis arrived in Copenhagen we dissolved them in a mixture of hydrochloric and nitric acid. I suppose we overreacted. Eventually we'll precipitate the gold back out and have the medals restruck."

The door opened and a thin, middle-aged woman with bobbed hair announced, "Dinner's ready."

Herre Bohr introduced his wife Margrethe. Then the entire group crossed the entry hall to the dining room.

When Margrethe Bohr opened the double doors to the dining hall — another high-ceilinged room with wood-paneled walls and an electric chandelier — the cooking aroma was so wonderfully different from the Polish stews at the Hedeby excavation that Mette's knees went weak.

"It smells so delightfully —" she found the right word "—buttery."

Margrethe smiled. "It's the only way to cook flounder. But first the leek soup."

"More cream than leeks, I suspect," Niels added, chuckling. "There's a reason the Germans call Denmark the *Sahnefront*."

"The cream front?" Julius asked.

His father humphed. "A Wehrmacht posting here has both military and culinary advantages over assignments to Poland or Norway."

They took their seats at a too-long rectangular table, with Herre Bohr and Herre Gustmeyer at the far ends. A young maid in a starched apron brought in the soup, balancing three bowls at a time.

After everyone had ladled a while in relative silence, Herre Gustmeyer set down his spoon. "So what's this I hear, Niels, about the Germans bursting uranium atoms?"

Bohr raised his eyebrows. "You've been reading the academic papers?"

"Well, yours, anyway."

Julius looked earnest. "Then it's true?"

Mette said, "I thought atomic bonds were extremely powerful."

"And so they are," Bohr replied. "But a little over a year ago Otto Hahn took up my theoretical suggestion and bombarded some uranium with a stream of protons. Afterwards he detected a trace of barium, an element almost precisely half the atomic weight of uranium. He wondered if he had in fact split an atom."

"Your paper called it 'nuclear fission,'" Herre Gustmeyer added.

"Yes. I reported about the experiment at a conference in America just before the war broke out. I had some trouble convincing the physicists there at first because the energy released in Hahn's experiment was not quite what my model predicts for standard uranium 238." He pushed back the soup bowl and looked up into empty air. "When someone told me the exact quantum of the discrepancy I stood there as if struck by lightning. Suddenly I understood everything."

"What did you understand?" Julius asked.

"That Hahn hadn't split uranium 238 at all. It's too stable. He had split an impurity in the sample, the U-235 isotope!"

Herre Gustmeyer leaned back and laughed as if this were the greatest joke in the world. Mette and the others laughed too, although with less conviction.

At this point the maid brought in an enormous china platter filled with a browned flounder that must have weighed ten pounds. The huge flat fish, with two eyes still in place on the upper side, swam in a yellow sea of melted butter.

"I'm afraid you'll have to pass your plates," Fru Bohr apologized. "Niels, could you serve?"

"First, could I offer anyone free beer?"

"Free beer?" Julius asked.

Fru Bohr scolded her husband, "Niels, really. We also have water or wine."

The physicist stepped to a spigot on the wall and began filling glasses with foamy beer. "Yes, but this is the specific advantage of living in the Carlsberg mansion — a tap with a direct line to the adjacent brewery. Old Mr. Carlsberg, rest his soul, imagined it would inspire us to greater achievements. Who wants a glass?"

The men raised their hands. Julius asked, "Has the beer been effective for inspiration?"

"I suspect it lubricates celebration more than innovation." Bohr set three glasses on the table and returned to his post beside the fish platter. Meanwhile, the maid had returned with a large bowl of bright yellow curried rice, steaming with spices from India.

Fru Gustmeyer commented, "I see that you are still keeping a kosher kitchen."

Bohr paused, his knife in a slice of flounder. "By habit rather than conviction, Claudia."

"But you can't deny that you're Jewish, Niels," Fru Gustmeyer countered.

Bohr continued serving fish. "My father raised me as a Lutheran, complete with Christmas elves and Easter bunnies. As an adult I gave up such childish things. Before proposing to Margrethe I renounced my membership in the Danish Lutheran church. We were married in a civil ceremony. I like to think we've been living civilly ever since."

"Nonetheless," Fru Gustmeyer said, "If your mother is a Jew, you are too. You cannot renounce your heritage."

Herre Gustmeyer grumbled, "I'm afraid the Nazis see things the same way."

"A fact that merely demonstrates their lack of imagination." Bohr held the fish knife up like a baton. "We physicists have demonstrated that photons can be two things at once. If you look at them one way, they're particles. If you examine them from a different angle, they behave like waves. I see this as physical evidence of Kierkegaard's philosophy of complementarity."

Herre Gustmeyer frowned. "Wasn't Søren Kierkegaard a rather conventional Christian?"

"Yes, but his philosophy is still empirically valid. I believe it is possible for an atomic particle, or a man, or an entire country, to be two seemingly incompatible things at once. As Claudia says, I am Jewish. But I am also a devout atheist. Denmark has been swept up in war. But we are also at peace."

Julius sighed, staring at his plate. "If only everyone believed that."

For the rest of the dinner they spoke of lighter things — the birth of a hippopotamus at the nearby Copenhagen zoo, and how, during one of Niels' American lecture tours, he had autographed a program flier for a fan who turned out to be none other than the Swedish actress Greta Gustafson, popularly known as Greta Garbo.

After a dessert of *rødgrød med fløde* — a raspberry compote with cream — Herre Gustmeyer leaned back with brandy and a cigar while his wife and Fru Bohr discussed charity work over coffee.

Meanwhile Julius spoke quietly with Niels Bohr. "Could I have a word with you privately? Perhaps in the garden?"

"If you wish."

Mette said, "I'll come along."

"I'd rather you didn't, Mette," Julius whispered.

"I'd rather I did." She was tired of Julius' secrets.

The three of them slipped out through the French doors to a courtyard. A labyrinth of privet hedges and hollyhocks surrounded a birdbath in the garden's center.

"So what's on your mind, Julius?" Bohr asked, ignoring Mette for the moment.

"Herre Bohr," Julius began.

"Call me Niels."

"Yes. Well, the truth is, I was sent here tonight by Holger Danske, the Danish resistance."

"Really?" Bohr's eyebrows rose. "I thought that group was fictional."

"It's still quite small, but we are in contact with the British."

"Then you're taking quite a risk, young man. Why?"

"We fear for your safety here. The British want your help with a top-secret project. They want you to escape with me on a fishing boat to Sweden."

"And what is this top-secret British project?"

"An atomic bomb, sir. Only a few people in the resistance know of it. They use the code name *Fenris*."

"Fenris," Bohr mused. "An interesting alias. Wasn't that a Norse god?"

"A wolf god," Mette added darkly, "It's said that Fenris will bring about the end of the world."

Julius asked, "Is it possible to build a uranium bomb?"

"Technically, I suppose." Bohr ran a finger thoughtfully along his cheek. "The energy released by splitting one uranium atom would be enough to split several more, and so on. It could create a chain reaction."

"What would a bomb like that do?" Mette asked.

"It would release as much energy as you had fuel."

"More than dynamite?"

Bohr nodded. "Pound for pound, about a hundred million times more than dynamite."

For a moment Mette and Julius stood dumbstruck, pondering the scale of such a bomb's destruction. A targeted city — an entire country — the whole planet really might be at risk.

Bohr continued, "But the problem is getting enough of the right sort of fuel. Uranium is both uncommon and dangerously radioactive. And the only kind that splits easily is an even rarer isotope, U-235. You only find a few atoms at a time. It's all but impossible to separate it from the more common U-238. Securing a supply adequate for a bomb would take decades. All of the countries that could attempt it seem to be using their resources for conventional war."

Julius shook his head. "We have reason to believe that the Germans may be working on such a bomb."

"The Germans?" Bohr scoffed. "They won't get anywhere without Heisenberg. The Nazis have been trying to sideline him as a 'white Jew.' They're afraid he's polluting Aryan science because he's been hobnobbing with Einstein and me. No, from what I hear the Germans are working on uranium strictly as an energy source. They see it as a possible replacement for oil."

"Nonetheless, sir, the British want you," Julius persisted. "Come with me, as soon as possible. It will be safer."

"Safer!" Bohr shook his head. "Sneaking out through a naval blockade on a fishing boat with the Danish resistance? Anything in the world would be safer. Besides, I'm doing valuable work here at the institute. And Jews are not being persecuted in Denmark — at least no more than us atheists." He looked from Julius to Mette and back. "The two of you are young. This is no time to be running away from your country and risking your lives."

Bohr put his hand on Julius' shoulder. "And now, if you will excuse me, I need to attend to my other guests."

Bohr gave Julius' shoulder a squeeze and walked back toward the French doors.

Mette turned to follow him, but a firm grip caught her by the arm. Julius whispered, "Stay, Mette!"

She managed to control her anger until Bohr had closed the doors behind him. Then she shook her arm free and spoke through her teeth. "Let me go!"

"Stay a minute."

"I am not a dog that you can command to heel."

Julius drew back, flustered. "I didn't mean it that way, darling. We need to talk."

"All right, talk."

"That's better." He sighed. "Bohr is obviously not seeing the big picture. This will be a setback for the resistance. They'll have to convince him later. In the meantime, we need to move ahead with our plans."

"Our plans?" Mette put her hands on her hips. "Since when did you consult me in your decisions?"

"All along, I thought." He looked puzzled. "We've been over this before. Denmark is occupied. The British need help. If I can't bring them Bohr, I can still go myself."

"Didn't you hear Herre Bohr? He says the secret weapon isn't practical. And the occupation is not as bad as he'd thought. He said he'd overreacted by melting down his Nobel medals."

"Mette! The Nazis have overrun eight nations. Their armies have driven thousands into the sea at Dunkirk. Their air force is bombing London to rubble. They're preparing to invade England. If we lose England, we've lost the Continent."

Mette closed her eyes, steadying her breathing. "I know what you're feeling. The urge to go and fight is strong. But if you had listened to Bohr you would have heard what he was saying. You have obligations here — parents to care for and work to do. I too have a job, excavating a Viking city."

"I'm not asking you to give up your job, even when we're married."

She touched the engagement ring on her finger. "I'm just not sure anymore, Julius. Sometimes it takes more courage to stay and work for peace. Maybe the ones who rush off to die are the cowards."

"Is that what you think? That I'm a coward?"

Her heart felt as churned as the raspberry dessert they had eaten at dinner. Had she been swayed by her fiancé's blue Clark Gable eyes, slicked back hair, and mustache? Had she and Julius been in love, or had they been acting? He was going to leave her —all along her inner voice had warned that he would abandon her, just as Peder and Lars had walked away.

"What frightens me," Mette said, "is that you might be braver than I deserve."

"What are you saying?"

She tightened her lips. Then she twisted her engagement ring loose and slipped it into the pocket of his suit coat.

"Stop." Once again he caught her hand. "I'll stay."

A tear ran down her cheek as she shook her head. "I don't know, Julius. I just don't know."

Later they both remembered standing there, holding hands, unable to speak. In the labyrinth of the twilight garden, the war seemed to stretch ahead forever.

CHAPTER 11
HEDEBY, 977

As Lifu crept through the late summer woods toward a meeting with King Harald, silently following one of her secret paths, she began to sense that she was not alone. A distant snap of a branch, a thrash of brush — this clumsiness sounded more like a moose than Bluetooth. Why had he asked to meet her out here anyway, at the graveyard of the ancients?

She left her path and explored, curious. Along the way she noticed any number of woodland gifts that would bring her back in the months before winter — ripe red rose hips, the fruit for a tangy compote. Puffball mushrooms, still no bigger than her fingernail, but promising a musty stew. They peered from beneath the first fallen beech leaves like the white eyes of elves. And bees, their thighs fat with pollen. These were not from her own hives. Somewhere there would be a stump full of honey. Her apprentice, Vilbi, would be eager to find it.

Crack! Smash! Even a moose would not be this careless. Finally Lifu parted the leaves of an elderberry bush to glimpse a swordsman slashing through the forest as if it were a field of English attackers. Jarl Haakon? Vilbi's father was the renowned warrior who had been training Prince Svein for the past six years, ever since the boy had been given his first blade, Dogbane. Either the jarl was lost or he was heading for the old cemetery too. Stranger still, flitting like a shadow in the path he had hewn was the bald-topped head of Brother Michael. A Jesus monk and a Viking. Peculiar companions indeed!

Lifu fell in behind them, the shadow of a shadow. When the jarl cut his way out into the bright sunshine of the graveyard's grassy knoll the king was sitting on a granite boulder at the top, admiring the view across the blue of Schleswig's fjord. He turned and smiled, his dark tooth laughing at them from an unruly and prematurely gray beard.

"Excellent. You've all three come at once."

"Three?" Haakon turned in bewilderment. He straightened at the sight of the monk. "You! What are you doing here?"

Brother Michael shrugged. "You seemed to be going the right way, so I followed."

Haakon grunted. "Still," he grumbled to the king, "we are but two, Your Highness."

Harald held out his hand toward the forest, beckoning Lifu forward with a wave of two fingers. She stepped out from the leaves into the sun. In her leather dress and light brown hair she could have been a deer.

"What!" Haakon gasped. "The silversmith's wife?"

Brother Michael looked just as startled. "The medicine witch!"

"Actually, she's an English teacher," Harald said. "Come, Lifu, and join our council."

"What is the meaning of this?" Haakon demanded, forgetting for the moment to add the usual 'Your Highness.'

"Is there some evil afoot?" the monk asked.

"On the contrary, Denmark is at peace, so we have a season to amuse ourselves." He looked back across the bay, lost in thought. For that moment Lifu recognized him not as a king, but as an overgrown boy. She was glad that she had committed long ago to serve as his spy. In those early years she had been a confused girl, stumbling to discover what mysterious mission the gods had sent her to carry out. Her world had seemed to revolve around a cursed sword — Fenris? Or Holger? But then she had seen the weapon laid to rest with Harald's father Gorm, beneath a great burial mound at Jelling, and her mission had seemed simpler. There had been peace.

"Surely peace is a good thing," Brother Michael suggested.

Haakon grunted. "You wouldn't understand."

Harald nodded. "This summer I took the fleet looking for trouble, but didn't find much. We sailed to the five ring forts. Swung past the coasts of Pomerania and Sweden to remind our allies of their bond. Sailed up the coast of Norway, collecting tribute, and still had the men home in time to bring in the harvest. Meanwhile the fearsome wolf-Pope to the south and his mighty wolf-Emperor appear to be toothless pups. Or else they're sleeping down there, under the palms of Rome."

The king looked to the monk. "Which is it, do you think?"

Michael furrowed his brow. "Neither, I suspect."

"Really? It's been five winters since I sent a longship to deliver a gift with a threat as subtle as the Pope's. I gave back one of your monks, to prove you are still alive. A silver coin with my image, to add to Pope John's collection. And a chess set carved by Lifu here from the ivory of unicorns. Tell him, Lifu, what new pieces you devised."

"Berserkers, biting their shields. And helmsmen, at the prows of swift dragonships."

"Military novelties for which the Holy Roman Empire seems to have no response," Harald said. "England, Frankia, Rome — it's all in chaos."

"I wouldn't rely on it, King." Michael tilted his head. "A response may be coming. The Church is not hasty."

Harald waved the possibility off into the future. "In the meantime, let us prepare by practicing something I enjoyed as a boy in Jelling. We called it 'Capture the King.'"

Haakon's eyes lit up. "I know this game. It's both good training and good fun. All the young people get involved — everyone from twelve to eighteen. How many armies are you thinking, Your Highness?"

"Three. Stone, steel, and leather."

"Like the hand game," Haakon chuckled.

"We'll train for a month, each army with different weapons and a different strategy. Then we'll let them loose in the woods."

"Yes," Haakon said, "But who is the king they're all trying to capture?"

Harald tapped Haakon on the forehead. "Me. I'll wait here on this rock, surrounded by a last defense of adults."

The jarl leaned back and roared. "Wonderful!"

Brother Michael looked skeptical. "This game sounds dangerous for children."

"It can be, although the weapons are made of wood," Haakon said. "Risk improves the motivation for training."

Lifu asked, "Would girls be allowed to participate?"

"Why should they not?" Haakon cut her a sharp glance. "My daughter is the best sword handler her age in Hedeby. Although you might know her as a beekeeper, she is a shield maiden."

Harald added, "Each of the armies has different attractions, for young women as well as young men. The battles in this game can be as much about love as war. If you fill the woods with teenagers, romance is inevitable."

The monk coughed indignantly.

The king continued, "My own children are of an age when they need to make choices."

Lifu considered this new motive. It was true that Princess Gunhild was now a very marriageable eighteen. A promising, well-bred young Dane by the name of Palling had been brought from England's Danelaw for the summer, allegedly to brush up on the culture of the Motherland. Despite hints, Gunhild had so far managed to avoid him. Prince Svein, at sixteen, was in less need of a hurried match, but had been making clumsy advances toward Vilbi, Haakon's daughter. King Harald obviously knew that games were already afoot.

Brother Michael finally found words for his displeasure. "Sex is sin."

"Is it?" Harald mused. "Did you really grow up in Ireland without ever once going a-maying?"

The monk hedged. "Maying is discouraged. And it's only in May."

"In Denmark it's more of a harvest tradition. Before winter shuts things down you play a game, celebrate with a big feast, and choose a girl to keep out the chill."

Lifu held up her hands. "All right. I understand that you want a game. What I don't understand is why you have called the three of us here."

"That's right," Brother Michael agreed. "Why this secret meeting?"

Haakon pointed his thumbs to the commoners beside him. "And why, by all the gods, did you invite a monk and a housewife?"

Harald smiled just enough to show the tip of his blue tooth. "Because three armies need three commanders."

Michael was the first to object. "Priests do not command armies."

"First you claim to know nothing of sex, and now you say you know nothing of war." Harald fingered the gold hilt of the sword at his belt. "For our game I was thinking the stone army would be Norse, armed with shields and axes. Jarl Haakon would oversee it, although he might appoint a field commander. My son Svein could be a candidate."

Haakon nodded slowly, accepting this suggestion.

Harald continued, "To inspire rivalry, I had thought the steel army should be Christian, with swords and chain mail. You say, Michael, that such armies are not led by priests. But aren't they commissioned by bishops and popes? Without priests praying for victory, would Christian armies march to battle?"

The monk opened his mouth to object. When he spoke, however, he merely said, "I am just a monk. I know nothing of military matters."

"Haakon can find someone to help you train your troops. Your task would be their spiritual guidance. Isn't that why you were sent to Denmark?"

"Yes, but King, I fear you are mocking our religion. You might as well have the children in this rival army play the role of Ostrogoths."

"Have you made so few converts?" As the king spoke a distant bell began tolling. Although it was not a pretty sound — more the clank of an iron pot than the peal of a proper bell — the tone had carried a mile from the rooftop of Hedeby's small wooden church. Harald waited, counting ten chimes. Townspeople complained about the intrusion of this Christian clamor, but Harald himself found its predictability comforting. Even when the sun was hidden by clouds, everyone knew the time of day.

"Our monastery's ale is popular, King," Michael said, "But we have baptized only a few dozen souls to share holy communion."

"Then this is your chance to win soldiers for Christ. I give you permission to preach to the children in the steel army. And I think you have a candidate of your faith who could serve as their leader. Young Palling of England was raised as devout a Christian as you could wish." Harald lowered his voice. "Perhaps at the head of an army he would finally catch my daughter's eye."

"Armies of Christians and Norsemen," Lifu said. "None of this explains why you have asked me here."

"You're here to lead the third army, of course."

"But I know even less of war than Brother Michael!"

The king chuckled. "The third force in our game is an army of elves."

"Elves?" Lifu asked, amazed.

Haakon nodded his agreement with the king. "Traditionally, if there is a third army — a leather army — they are elves."

Harald asked her innocently, "Don't you believe in elves?"

Lifu dimly recalled an earlier time in Norway when there had been trolls — large, ugly creatures that pulled travelers from bridges or waylaid them in the mountains. Denmark was a calmer landscape, without the whitewater rivers and rugged peaks that attract monsters. Here the shadows were inhabited by smaller, less threatening imps. They had pointy shoes and big red stocking hats. Elves might sour your milk or dance your sheep astray, but they would never drown or steal your children.

"Yes," Lifu said. "I suppose I do believe in elves."

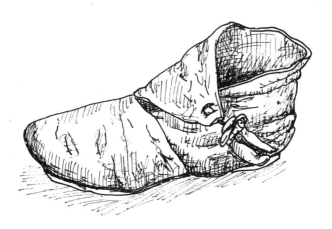

The blue tooth grinned once more. "Then you know more about war than you realize. The victor is not always the army with the biggest weapons or the boldest inspiration. Guile, cunning, and even treachery have their role. The elven army is the command for a spy."

Jarl Haakon and Brother Michael turned, studying Lifu cautiously from either side. She willed herself calm so her cheeks would not flush.

"A month from today," Harald announced, standing up from the granite tombstone, "The game will begin when the church strikes twelve. The winning army feasts in my royal hall. If no one captures the king by the time the church bell rings twice, I'll feast there by myself. Good luck to you, all three."

* * *

The forest hummed with the wingbeats of bees. The thirty girls and dozen boys who had followed Lifu out of Hedeby's west gate, joking and laughing about their new leather caps, gradually fell silent.

Beyond the hum, Lifu heard the pulse of fear in their hearts.

She stopped, still a stone's throw from the first of the beehives. She spoke in a low voice that matched the hum. "We are the smallest of the three armies, so we need allies. Fortunately, our base is defended by thousands of brave soldiers, and they are armed."

A small, scared voice asked, "What if they sting *us*?"

Vilbi knelt beside the young boy who had spoken. Although Vilbi was just sixteen, she was half a head taller than Lifu and far more muscular, having swung heavy swords with her father every day for years. Her leather cap hid all but a wisp of blond hair. Belts crossing her chest tied in place a suit of leather armor that managed to exploit the curves of her breasts and hips to good advantage.

Vilbi held the boy's hand. "Your cap will keep bees from getting caught in your hair. Roll down the cloth visor — like this — so they're not in your face. We've tied your collar and cuffs with twine so bees won't get inside your clothes. Above all, they don't like being trapped. Let them fly free."

"Ow!" Gunhild exclaimed.

"Were you stung?" Lifu asked.

The princess looked at her hand, turning it for closer inspection. "No, but a bee bumped against my skin."

"That's a message," Lifu explained. "A small warning, like a tap on your shield. The bees are saying, 'We see you. Are you friend or foe?'"

"How do they know the difference? Can you tell them I'm their new queen?"

"Tell them yourself. Show them that you're part of their family. We elves are as harmless as trees, and just as friendly."

"Never swat," Vilbi added. "Don't even think of swatting. You wouldn't dream of striking someone in your own family, would you?"

The children eyed the bees warily. Yellow missiles arced about them.

"You are the elven army," Lifu said, her voice like honey. "You are brave and unafraid, because everything in the forest is your ally. Follow me slowly, as if you were swimming in honey. No bee wants to sting you. If they do, they die. They want to be your friends. Come, meet your new family."

Lifu led them, a troop of nervous sleepwalkers, into a clearing ringed with thirty hives, each a humming straw dome. The bees were not happy. Lifu knew this from the tight curves of their flight. Two weeks had passed since she and Vilbi had smoked the hives. They had taken three quarters of the combs and cut the wax cells open with warm knives to steal their honey. Flowers were all but gone. The hives had barely enough food to last the winter. If even one child panicked the rest might run, and the bees would chase them down.

The elves paraded slowly to a firepit in the center of the clearing, where Lifu had set up a circle of benches and stumps. When everyone had found a seat without being stung, Lifu allowed herself a sigh of relief. Without being asked, Vilbi began lighting a fire. A little smoke always put the bees at ease. Enough smoke would put them to sleep.

Lifu took the lid off a bucket that held fragments of mostly drained honeycomb. "For your initiation into the hive, here is a gift from your new family. Take a small piece, each of you. Suck out the honey and chew the wax." As she passed the bucket around, eager hands reached for this rare treat. When everyone had taken a piece the bucket was still half full.

A small girl asked, "Can we have more?"

"The rest is for the others in our hive." Lifu walked to the edge of the clearing and dumped the bucket between hives. Within seconds scout bees had found the treasure. By the time Lifu returned to the firepit, bees were no longer circling the children. Instead they were whirling about the broken comb, cleaning out honey to complete their winter stores. Vilbi threw a handful of fallen leaves onto the fire. White smoke swirled up, leaving Lifu adrift in a cloud.

"King Harald has ordered us to play a war game with three armies — Norsemen, Christians, and elves." She swept her hand to the circle of young faces. They were uncertain, a bit frightened. What was Bluetooth thinking? Children who enlisted as elves were unlikely to grow up as warriors. The king had said the game was for his amusement, but Haakon had seen it as preparation for an actual war, and Brother Michael had accepted it as an opportunity to sway wayward souls. The elves, Lifu was beginning to realize, represented a third way. These children were an alternative to swords and hellfire.

"How does the game work?" The voice came from the same boy who had asked about bee stings.

Gunhild spoke up, unbidden. "If you touch someone with a wooden weapon, they're your captive. You tie their hands and bring them back to your base. The army that touches the king first wins."

"But that's not fair!" an older boy objected. "The Norse army has shields and axes. The Christians have swords and chain mail. All we've got are bees and sticks."

Lifu said, "I've seen warriors who would stand against swords, but run from a bee. To win we'll have to think like a hive."

"How do we do that?"

"Bees send out scouts to gather information secretly," Lifu said. "Who here has learned something about our rivals?"

After a pause, Gunhild raised her finger. "It's not much, but I've learned the Christian army is calling themselves the bishops. They've gathered all the chain mail they can from the older men. They say it will make them invulnerable."

"Who told you that?" a girl asked. "Palling?"

Another girl added, "What did you trade for his secrets?"

There were giggles. In response Gunhild merely held her head high.

Lifu asked her, "Have you learned anything from your brother? He is commanding the Norse army."

Gunhild shook her head. "Svein doesn't talk with me about such things."

Vilbi threw another piece of wood on the fire. "But he does with me."

"At sword practice?" Lifu asked.

"And afterwards." Vilbi sighed. "He follows me around."

"What has he said?" Gunhild asked.

Vilbi sighed again, as if most of the things the prince told her were not useful. "They're calling the Norse army the berserkers. They want to eat magic mushrooms before the game. Svein thinks it will make them strong. I'm afraid it will just make them crazy."

"Or very sick," Lifu said. "Even the right sort of spotted red mushrooms can kill. I'll arrange with Jarl Haakon to provide what they need. But I'll mix one part of mushroom with twenty parts of puffballs."

The princess smiled. She asked Vilbi, "What else did you learn from my brother?

"He says the only kind of leather that counts as armor is thick horsehide like this." Vilbi tapped the stiff cups protecting her shoulders. The leather clunked like wood. "Even then, he says it only counts for stopping swords, not axes. He thinks the leather army is doomed."

"Do you?"

Vilbi sighed. "Our chances are slim."

Lifu walked around the ring of children, studying their faces. They expected to lose. They had chosen to be elves because they knew they were not warriors. But they were also the brightest children in all of Hedeby. Most of them had no idea of their potential. She stopped in front of the older boy who had complained that the war game wasn't fair.

Lifu held out her right fist on the flat of her left palm. "Do you know the game Stone-Steel-Leather?"

He shrugged. "Sure,"

"Then play it with me now. Tap twice and the third time make your choice. Ready?"

"I guess." Grudgingly he held out his palm. He tapped it twice with his fist, matching Lifu's moves. When their hands came down for the third time, his stayed as a fist while Lifu flattened her palm with a clap.

"You chose stone," Lifu said. "I chose leather. Leather covers stone. I win." She covered his fist and squeezed. "Play again?"

In reply the boy held out his palm and tapped it twice. When his fist came down for the third time he held out two fingers like a knife. Lifu's fist remained a fist.

"You chose steel," Lifu said. "But my stone smashes steel." She hit his fingers with her fist — not too hard, but hard enough that it must have hurt.

"One more time?" Lifu could almost hear the boy's mind working through the possibilities.

He nodded. "Ready."

This time on the third tap Lifu flattened her hand to represent leather. But the boy had repeated himself, holding out two fingers like a knife.

"Steel cuts leather!" he exclaimed, sawing her palm with his fingers. "I win."

"What did you learn?" Lifu asked. "Remember that our armies are named for stone, steel, and leather."

The boy sat back on his stump, thinking. "Each army has a weakness. But each of them also has a strength."

The girl beside him was shaking her head. "I don't see our strength."

"Then let's look for it." Lifu walked to one side of the circle, where she kept beekeeping supplies. She set an empty straw beehive on a stump. "Let's pretend this is one of the bishops. According to our scout bee, what do they think makes them invulnerable?"

"Chain mail," Gunhild answered.

Lifu opened a wooden chest and took out a shirt of chain mail.

"Where did you get that?" a boy asked.

"My husband is a smith." She draped the suit of iron rings over the beehive. "Doesn't our bishop look tough? Vilbi, you're handy with a blade. Could you have at him with your dagger?"

"No point. He's got chain mail."

"Give it a try anyway."

Vilbi shrugged. She slid a dagger out from a hiding spot in her leather armor. Then she stabbed the beehive squarely in the chest. It fell off the stump but was otherwise undamaged.

"You see? No point."

"What if your blade *did* have the right kind of point?" Lifu reached into the trunk and took out a strange, thin sword — little more than a wire with a handle.

"What's that?" Vilbi asked.

"Something I asked my husband to forge. Spring steel without a flat blade, but with a very sharp point."

Vilbi hefted the skinny weapon in her hand. She slashed a few Z-shapes in the air. The wiry blade whipped about with a whoosh. She bent it back with her fingers and let go. The sword sprang straight, singing.

"Try it on our friend the bishop." Lifu set the beehive back on its stump.

Vilbi took aim at the beehive and lunged. The point sailed through the chain mail and came out the other side. She gasped, "It went right through steel!" She held up the beehive on her skewer, marveling. "If we use swords like this, the bishops are the ones who are doomed."

"We can't use steel," Lifu said. "But if we whittle wooden spears sharp enough, we can tag them successfully, even through chain mail."

As they considered this new weapon, the group was silent except for the buzzing of bees. At length a girl asked, "What about the berserkers? They have shields."

"Berserkers can't climb trees with shields," Lifu said. "Raise your hand if you like climbing trees." She looked around the circle. Half of the elven army had their hands in the air. To her surprise, Gunhild had raised her hand as well.

"Excellent. We'll divide our army into two forces. Gunhild will command the tree elves. Hidden by leaves, out of reach of axes and swords, you'll wait with spears in the trees above the paths that lead to the king. Vilbi, you'll command the other force, the warrior elves. Armed with pointy swords and horsehide armor you'll slip through the enemy's defenses to capture the king."

Lifu closed the wooden chest with a thump. "We have much to do. Weapons, camouflage, practice. Meet here tomorrow when the church bell rings ten. Until then, not a word."

* * *

A cold fog swathed the forest in mystery on the morning of game day. Lifu, Brother Michael, and Jarl Haakon each assembled their armies at their separate camps in the woods for final instructions. Then, by the rules of the game, the adults had to leave. Lifu, the monk, and the jarl each took up positions on platforms at the edge of the cemetery clearing. Michael's post overlooked the fjord to the north while Haakon was stationed inland to the south and Lifu was in in the middle to the east. Although the commanders were not allowed to leave their platforms, they could relay advice to their troops by shouting, using whistles, or sending messengers.

King Harald, dressed in chain mail, furs, and a crown, had made himself comfortable on a cushioned high seat at the top of the hill. Eight of his ablest warriors — all fathers of children in the game — stood guard in a ring about him. Although the men wore swords in scabbards on their belts, the only weapons they were allowed to use in the game were wooden staffs, which they held upright like pikes.

There had been frost and a full moon in the night. Fallen leaves had become brittle and crackly underfoot, making stealth difficult. Every hedgehog and thrush sounded like a vagrant cow. By the time the church bell rang twelve the fog had thinned enough that the sun was visible as a white ball halfway up the sky, chilly as steel.

King Harald asked one of his men to sound a lur-horn. The note trumpeted out across the forest.

"Let the games begin!" The king announced. Then he settled into the furs on his chair to watch.

No single spectator was able to follow the progress of the three armies. That was precisely what gave the game its thrill. But Lifu managed to learn quite a bit from her network of elven spies. The rest of the story she pieced together later.

The berserkers had drunk a mushroom soup. It made a dozen of the boys so queasy that they had to be left in camp to guard the base. Meanwhile Vilbi had led the warrior elves through the woods for an assault on the king. But as soon as they crept out into the cemetery clearing, thirty Christian bishops emerged from the other side, intent on the same goal. A few elves had managed to reach the king's defenders, where they were blocked by staffs, but mostly the two armies fell upon each other. The elves fared poorly, their careful camouflage useless in the open. Vilbi and a few others were forced to retreat to the woods with just four captives, while the bishops bound the hands of a dozen elves.

But as the jubilant Christians marched back to their base camp they ran directly into the shields of the advancing berserkers. In the chaos that followed, shouts and stumbling children seemed to be everywhere.

By the time the church bell rang once, each of the armies had retreated to their bases to regroup. The elves now numbered just fifteen, including Vilbi and Gunhild. Their twelve captives, taken primarily by tree elves with spears, sat on the benches whimpering about bees. The hives did not like this game. Angry worker bees, with no other work at hand, seemed intent on targeting captives who attempted to move too fast or complain too loud.

Gunhild took charge, summing up the situation. "We don't have enough warrior elves in armor to capture the king."

"Perhaps by stealth —" Vilbi began.

Gunhild cut her short. "No. We can't hope to win, so we want to force a draw. We'll all take to the trees at the edge of the clearing. Then we'll turn back anyone who comes for the king. That will leave the bishops and the berserkers in the woods, fighting each other until the church strikes two. Agreed?"

Vilbi nodded reluctant assent, and the others joined in.

"All right. Let's take up our positions." The princess led them off into the woods.

Lifu was surprised when she saw Vilbi climbing a tree near her platform. She called in a loud whisper, "Aren't you supposed to be attacking on foot?"

"There aren't enough warriors left," Vilbi whispered back. "I can't get close enough by myself."

"Maybe you could throw your sword like a spear?"

Vilbi wrinkled her nose. "Would that count?"

"If the wood touches him, yes."

Vilbi tried holding her sword like a spear. The problem was that it wasn't a sword at all. It was just a pointy wooden skewer. Even Lifu could see that it couldn't be thrown effectively for any distance.

Suddenly there was a shout of glee from a tree halfway to Brother Michael's platform. "Ha! Got you!"

Palling had crept up to the edge of the clearing and had been poked from above by Gunhild's wooden spear.

"Right through the chain mail. It counts!" The princess jumped down beside him. "Give me your sword."

The young man sagged his shoulders in defeat.

"The commander of the Christians," Gunhild taunted, examining his wooden sword. It had been painted white, with a red Maltese cross on either side. "What were you doing out here by yourself anyway?"

"Looking for the Norse army," he admitted glumly. He spoke Norse almost like a native Dane, but with an English accent like Lifu's. "I thought the priest might have news."

"Hands behind your back," Gunhild commanded. She tied his wrists with a cord, a little tighter than necessary. Then she gave him a shove. "Off we go to visit the bees."

"I adore bees." Palling whistled a tune as she pushed him down the trail.

"Stop that," she said.

"Stop what?" He whistled some more.

"Stop whistling."

"We English love music. I was told you know how to play an English lute." He whistled again.

"Stop it! You'll let everyone —"

Suddenly six large boys crashed out of the bushes on either hand. In a moment they had pinned Gunhild with the tips of their white wooden swords.

"What have we here?" One of them jabbed her on the side. "A princess! And without armor. You're our captive now."

She objected, "But I've taken Palling captive."

"She did get me first," Palling admitted.

"But now we've got *her*." The boys pulled her hands behind her back and began tying them.

"Wait," she cried. "First let me take Palling to my base."

"Hardly. We're taking you to *our* base."

Palling shook his head. "It wouldn't be fair to capture her and set me free. She killed me back at the clearing. She ran a spear through me from a tree."

"Then you're both dead." The boy who was tying her hands paused, puzzled.

"We can't let them go, and we can't take them to the beehive camp," another boy said. "Let's just tie all their hands together and leave them here. It's not long until the bell rings twice. Meanwhile, we've got berserkers to hunt."

The boys pushed Palling and Princess Gunhild back to back, tied their hands together with rope, and left them in the woods.

At first the young couple argued about what to do. They tried walking sideways, but stumbled so badly that they broke out laughing. Then they discovered that they both could invent jokes by mixing Norse and English words. Palling taught the princess a bawdy English song. She responded with a naughty Norse verse. Eventually Gunhild decided that holding hands with this English thane wasn't such an awful punishment, even if they were bound so tightly that their rears bumped together.

Meanwhile, although Gunhild herself was no longer defending the clearing, her strategy seemed to be working for the elves remaining in the trees. Berserkers and bishops were avoiding the cemetery hill, instead clashing in the woods and taking captives. Soon neither army had enough fighters left to mount an attack on the king.

When his mushroom fever faded, Svein found himself alone. Slowly he realized that he had spent most of the game battling Christians, which wasn't technically the point. The goal was to capture the king. As his head cleared he made his way toward the old cemetery, hoping to see how well the king was guarded, and whether there might be other berserkers on hand to help.

This brought Svein to the ring of camouflaged elves. More cautious than Palling, Svein crawled the final fifty feet to the clearing on his belly. As a result he was out of reach of Vilbi, who was lying on a tree branch above him with a sharp wooden skewer. She considered throwing her stick, but decided it would safer simply to drop on top of him. Unfortunately her horsehide armor made a slight scraping sound as she fell.

Svein rolled to one side, dropping his shield and clutching his ax. Vilbi hit the ground but then sprang on him like a cat. The two of them rolled down the slope, wrestling and kicking. Vilbi's cap came off, wrapping them both in long yellow hair. They had fought together in mock battles under the watchful eye of Jarl Haakon for years, and had always been evenly matched. Svein was larger, but Vilbi was nimbler. On and on they rolled, neither able to get the upper hand. Finally, when the sound of surf warned that they were nearing the bluff's edge, Vilbi hesitated, and Svein pinned her with his weight, his hands on her wrists. For a minute they lay locked together panting, their hearts racing.

"Should I kill you or kiss you?" Svein asked.

How about a third choice?" Vilbi squirmed, succeeding only in rubbing the stiff horsehide of her chest's armor against him.

"A kiss," he decided, lowering his head.

"No!" She conked her forehead against his, so hard that he momentarily lost his grip. In an instant she had wriggled free. She sat on her knees, breathing hard, watching him.

"Why not, Vilbi? I like you."

"Yes, but I like girls."

"Huh?" Svein crawled up on his knees to look at her. "You what?"

Vilbi lowered her eyes. "I admire you as a prince, Svein, but if I ever kiss someone, it's going to be another girl."

Svein ran his hands over his face. First he had been dizzied by mushrooms, then he'd been conked on the head, and now this. "By the gods, this game is making me crazy."

"Maybe we can capture the king by working together?"

Svein shook his head at her. "Now I know you're crazy. The berserkers are all in prison. It's just you and me, and we've captured each other."

"I've got an idea. Let's go back up the hill and get our weapons. You attack the king's men with your ax like a berserker while I sneak up from behind."

"With that little stick of yours? You'd never get close enough."

"I told you, I've got an idea."

"Throwing your stick at him?"

"Better than that." She took his hands earnestly. "If it works, we'll share the credit. Berserkers and elves will all feast with the king. What do you say?"

Svein lifted her hands to his lips and kissed her fingers. Then he looked longingly into her eyes.

Vilbi bit her lip. She gave her head a shake. "I'm sorry, Svein. I can't be your girl that way."

Hi sighed. "Then I would want you as my shield maiden."

"That I can do." She squeezed his hand and let go. "I'm going to need a huge distraction for this ploy to work. You have to promise to be as berserk as possible."

Svein got to his feet. "That's a promise I can keep."

They walked back up the hill together. While Svein collected his fallen shield and ax, Vilbi put on her camouflage cap. Then she took out her dagger, cut a two-foot length from an elderberry branch, and began reaming out the pithy core with her wooden skewer.

"What are you doing?" Svein asked.

"Never mind. Just give me a minute and then go berserk."

"All right. I'll attack from the far side of the clearing."

Vilbi didn't look up from her work. "Watch out for elves in the trees."

"Right." The prince made a show of swaggering across the field, waving his wooden ax.

King Harald taunted from his high seat. "Time's almost up, and the armies have been reduced to just one attacker?"

"Stone smashes steel," Svein called back.

"Steady, men. The young prince might go berserk."

Meanwhile Vilbi had broken off the sharp tip of her skewer and inserted it into the hollowed tube. Then she began squirming up through the grass, camouflaged by her green-and-brown-striped leather armor.

All at once Svein let loose a fearsome roar. He bit his wooden shield. Then he charged up the hill, swinging his ax wildly. He actually managed to bowl over the first of the king's men, although the others blocked him with poles. They didn't hit very hard — after all, he was the king's son. Svein flailed like a wounded bull, and seemed about to break through them after all.

The king stood up, alarmed. "Stop him!"

The men locked their poles sideways. Svein gave an insane growl, his eyes white, and bit one of the defenders' hands. The man howled, shaking blood. Another man walloped the boy in the knees, below his shield. Svein sank to the ground at the king's feet, groaning.

Harald reached down and took away the boy's wooden ax. "You'll never win like this."

A distant, tinny clank sounded from across the forest.

"The game is over," the king announced. "The church bell has — Ow! These cursed bees."

As the bell rang a second time the king swatted the bee that had stung him through the chain mail on his side.

"What is this?" the king wondered, plucking a small wooden dart from his skin. "Not a bee?"

"Not a bee, Your Highness." Vilbi stood up from the grass, holding the blowgun she had fashioned. "A girl."

"A girl? Who? Aren't you Haakon's daughter?"

"Yes. And I've touched you with a wooden weapon before the bell sounded twice. You are my captive."

Svein coughed, still on the ground, holding his knees with pain. "You lose after all, Father. You're dead, and I am the new king."

Harald looked at the dart, and his son, and the girl. "No. Apparently it was Haakon's daughter who struck me. That means the elven army are the victors."

Vilbi took off her cap. "Your son's diversion was part of our plot. We agreed that if it worked, both the elves and the berserkers would share in victory."

"I see." Harald frowned, considering how to judge the game's outcome. The ringing of the church bell had already brought many of the combatants out of the forest. "Sound the lur-horn," he commanded. "Summon the rest of the armies."

Some of the children emerging from the forest were bloodied or limping. Harald was surprised to see his daughter Gunhild walking hand-in-hand with Palling. Apparently the game had brought her together with the leader of the Christian army after all.

Harald raised his arms to the throng of children. "The king has been captured." He took a gold ring from his finger and held it up. "I had planned to give a ring to the commander of the winning army.

Because I was taken captive by a warrior elf, I must give this ring to Lifu, commander of the leather army."

A few of the children dressed as elves cheered. Most of them, however, were too astonished to say anything at all. The rest of the crowd murmured with a mixture of disapproval and disbelief.

Next Harald took a second, larger ring from his fingers and held it up.

"It seems that the elves did not act alone. They succeeded only because of a plot hatched with my son Svein. As a result of their agreement, I am obliged to give out a second ring, this time to Jarl Haakon. His Norse army will also feast with me tonight as victors."

A much greater cheer rose form the crowd. Shields and axes waved in the air. Only the children with white swords and red Maltese crosses looked downcast. Harald saw this, and spoke to them.

"I am sorry to say that although the third army, the steel army of bishops, also fought bravely, they have ended this day in defeat." Harald turned to the monk at his side. "Brother Michael, you were to be their inspiration. Are you now prepared to admit that your religion is no match for the gods of Denmark?"

The monk pressed his palms together and lifted his eyes to the sky. "There is but one God, and He never fails those who believe."

"Come now," Harald chided. "Your bell has struck twice. The judgment day you speak of has arrived."

"Yes." Michael held out his arm, extending the folds of his brown robe toward he sea. "Turn around, Harald Bluetooth, and behold the answer of the Church of God."

In the distance, emerging from the last wisps of the morning fog, three ships were sailing up Slesvig fjord toward the docks at Hedeby. Although they were still far away, they were obviously much larger than any longship in Harald's fleet. Each had three masts instead of one. Their white sails billowed with red Maltese crosses.

"What is this?" Harald demanded. "Who are these sailors?"

The monk bowed slightly, concealing his hands in the folds of his sleeves. "It is the answer you requested, King. The Bishop of Hamburg is sending you craftsmen, supplies, and a missionary priest named Poppo."

"Poppo? What kind of name is that? Are his men armed? Should I alert my troops?"

"Not if you welcome these new Christian guests as you welcomed my Benedictine monks."

Jarl Haakon said, "They're sailing against the wind! What sorcery allows these foreigners to defy the air itself?"

"Triangular sails," the monk replied. "The bishop sent word that he had some Arab caravels available for our mission."

"And what exactly is this mission of yours?" Harald asked.

"Peace and good will. The bishop asks permission to build a cathedral. It's a large church, built of stone."

"Stone? No one builds houses out of stone in Denmark." Everyone knew that Denmark had no bedrock. It was a land of sand and pebbles.

"I'm told the craftsmen include masons from Italy. They would cut stone in Norway and bring it by ship. They will need entire mountains to finish the task. The cathedral is intended to seat a thousand worshipers at once."

Even Lifu caught her breath at the scale of this project. The only structure in Norse legend capable of holding a thousand people was the hall of Vallhalla — and it was not of this world at all.

Jarl Haakon whispered to the king, "This monk is a spy. He has been in secret contact with the enemy."

"Is that against the rules?" Harald asked. "Even you used spies in your game."

"This is no game, Your Highness. We should fight the Christians. Their religion is not our way. We could overpower their crews and take their ships."

But by now Harald was deep in thought. Lifu saw him once again as a dreamy-eyed boy. He spoke as if to himself.

"The Pope must have laughed at the message I sent. To him our longships must have seemed a mere mosquito fleet. Our berserkers, just a crazed rabble."

"But the bishops lost today," Haakon said. "We can make them lose again."

Harald put his hand on the jarl's shoulder. "Tonight I think we should all feast together. All three armies and these Christian messengers."

Haakon narrowed his eyes. "You would let the Christians win?"

"My hope, old friend, is that no one has to lose."

CHAPTER 12
HEDEBY, 1940

Nothing had ever seemed lonelier than the long train trip back from Copenhagen to Hedeby. Mette was relieved when she was met at the tiny Gammeltorp railway station by her faithful assistant Henrik, complete with his usual bow tie, a winning smile, and two heavy black bicycles.

"Henrik! How thoughtful." She admired the bikes. "Have they got the old bicycle factory in production?" She had noticed that the once rusty rails to the Gammeltorp factory were now shiny from use.

He gave a short laugh. "Still not yet. I had to buy these in town." They both knew that despite the excavation's lavish funding, they were not allowed to buy motor vehicles. "Here, let me take your suitcase."

Henrik lifted her valise onto his bicycle's luggage rack. Mette watched him, marveling how little she really knew about her second in command. His features were pleasant but unremarkable, without any of Julius' debonair pretension. Henrik was stronger, more reliable, and older. How much older? Without his stodgy tie, no one would think him over the age of thirty-five. Why had he never married? Or had he? She knew he was originally from the city of Odense, where he had worked in the Hans Christian Andersen House. It was a museum for the famous fairy tale author who, like Henrik, had always worn a bow tie. H.C. Andersen had thought of himself as an overlooked misfit. His story "The Ugly Duckling" had been autobiographical, about an ungainly baby that later proved to be a beautiful swan. But the story was a fiction, because Andersen himself had actually grown up to be an awkward adult with a long nose. After Andersen became famous he had traveled to visit his contemporary Charles Dickens in London.

There he had outstayed his welcome. Dickens had been forced to resort to ruses and finally subtle threats to rid himself of the ugly Dane. Why, Mette wondered, had all of this come to mind at the thought of Henrik? Certainly he was much better looking than H.C. Andersen.

When Henrik began tying her valise onto the bicycle rack Mette helped by holding the knot in place with her finger.

"Oh!" Henrik said, pausing.

"What is it?"

He finished tying the rope, but his cheeks had flushed pink. "It's just that you seem to be missing your engagement ring. I imagine you left it at a jeweler's to have a matching band made for the wedding."

Now it was Mette's turn to redden. "Actually, Julius and I —" her words trailed off into a meaningful silence.

"I'm so sorry," Henrik said. But the earnest look in his eyes said the opposite. He was delighted that she was free. Had he been sweet on her all this time?

Mette got on her bicycle and set off toward Hedeby. She wasn't usually one to run away from confrontation, but her head was now as confused as her heart. She had heard of the danger of rebound love. The heart wants to fill a void and grasps at the first available candidate. Henrik was a perfectly nice Danish man, but he was no catch. And he was her colleague. Their relationship had always been professional.

Her heavy bike swerved on the uneven cobblestones. She almost ran into a mailbox before regaining control.

Henrik caught up with her when they reached the woods. Then he bicycled a length behind and to the left, like a goose flying off her wingtip.

She sighed. This would never do either. She backpedaled, tapping the brakes so the two of them rode side by side. She asked, "Did you discover anything at the excavation while I was gone? More coins?"

"Without you we don't seem to have much luck. We've just found more traces of wooden posts, wooden planks, a wooden chest, wooden everything. The whole town seems to have been made of wood. Virtually no glass, no pottery — and certainly no swords."

"The colonel wants a sword, doesn't he?" Mette latched onto this new topic. "What we need to find is an old burial ground. Where did Hedeby put their dead? Otherwise our best hope is a ship in the bay.

A man in armor could have sunk with one of them."

"I'm afraid we won't get at any sunken ships this season," Henrik said. "The pile drivers are having trouble with tidal currents. And it's getting harder to requisition steel for the coffer dam."

"What good is all our funding if the Germans only give us permission to buy bicycles?"

Henrik laughed as if Mette had told a much better joke than she actually had. Now she noticed that every time she pedaled, her skirt exposed a knee. Was Henrik noticing this too? She was riding a men's bike, so if she stopped to stand, the bar in the middle would hoist her hem to her thighs. Finally, when they bicycled through the gap in the old Danevirke wall, a sea breeze threatened to balloon the skirt into her face. She dismounted with a hop, swinging both legs to one side.

Henrik stopped, looking back with concern.

In that moment she pictured a life with Henrik, reading newspapers with coffee and pastries on a Sunday afternoon. Blond children were sailing toy boats out past swans on a sunny lake. It was a dilemma as old as Denmark itself — weighing the thrill of risk against the charm of *hygge*.

"Are you all right?" Henrik asked.

She nodded. "Go on ahead. I'll walk from here."

* * *

That fall, as the world tilted toward winter, time seemed to slow down, catching its breath after the frantic summer. Julius wrote to Mette less often, but still at least once a week. His letters passed the censors without a single black mark. He mentioned nothing about the occupation, the resistance, or marriage. Was he trying to earn her love back slowly? Or had he accepted that they would always be nothing more than friends? Somehow both possibilities left Mette unsettled.

Meanwhile, the radio reported that the Luftwaffe had ceased its bombing raids over London. Instead Hitler's troops were building concrete pillboxes along the Atlantic beaches. The Nazis were regrouping, seemingly unsure of their next move.

At Hedeby, the sunken ships remained in the bay's sand. With the coffer dam still only half finished, the pile driving barge had steamed back to Schleswig for the winter. The Polish prisoners of war had been given the parts for canteens and coffee pots to solder together. Colonel Wedel's soldiers stayed to oversee them, but the Danish archeologists were sent home in early December. For the three darkest, coldest months they would work in the National Museum's basement, sorting and cataloguing the summer's finds.

For Mette, it was a season of sorting and cataloguing her emotions. At work, Henrik cast her warm glances that she hesitantly returned. He had begun offering to take over some of her tasks, such as organizing the *Julefest*, the museum's Christmas party. Mette was no socialite. She suspected that she had only been assigned the party preparations because she was a woman. She was happy enough to leave the job to her assistant.

But Julius kept finding ways to show his devotion as well. Each day when Mette returned home from work a small gift would be waiting by the door of her garret apartment — a red carnation or a tiny box with a marzipan reindeer. How did Julius find such rarities in wartime? He had not left to fly for the RAF. His perseverance made her doubt her decision to end their engagement.

Her most fervent hope was that Julius and Henrik could be kept separate. Europe had enough rivalries already. But that hope dissolved when she arrived with her parents for the National Museum's *Julefest* and found the Gustmeyers already in the lobby, checking their overcoats at a table. Beside them, the statue of Harald Bluetooth held out a sword, as if to precipitate a confrontation or to serve as a hat rack.

Mette whispered to her mother, "Were you the one who invited the Gustmeyers?"

"Me?" Kirstin Andersen raised her eyebrows innocently. "All the major donors are invited. The Gustmeyers are friends of the museum — and of ours, I hope."

Julius wore a perfectly fitted white tuxedo that set off his black hair and mustache. He turned, caught sight of her, and gave a slight smile, bowing his head just enough that his brown eyes ran approvingly down her floor-length red dress. Before she could respond the double doors to the reception hall opened and Henrik strode in, grinning.

Mette had never seen her assistant quite this lively before. Instead of his trademark bow tie, he wore an open shirt and tails. His polished black shoes shone in the light of the chandeliers. "Welcome, one and all," he exclaimed, holding his arms wide. Where had he found this sudden courage, Mette wondered? Was it the gaiety of the evening, or had he bolstered himself with drink?

"Mette, you look radiant," he said. "Herre and Fru Andersen are the luckiest parents in Copenhagen." He went on with hardly a pause, "And the Gustmeyers, such an honor that you can join us. Julius! I don't believe I've seen you since that tragic day in April, out at Jelling. How are you?" He held out his hand.

Julius shook his hand. "My parents and I are well, thank you." He added quietly, "So far."

"What you need are refreshments." Henrik beckoned them to follow. "We've set up the whole Yule assortment in the next room. Stock up before the children start their performance. This way, everyone."

Mette marveled that tonight, for once, Julius had worn a bow tie while Henrik had not. It almost seemed as if they had switched roles. Henrik had suddenly become suave and outgoing while Julius appeared timid, as if the bow at his throat had tied him up with Henrik's inhibitions.

Garlands of fir boughs decorated the reception hall. Tables decked with white linen held punchbowls and silver trays of appetizers. A trio of fiddlers played carols beside a large fir tree on a stage.

What stopped Mette and the others short was the sight of German uniforms. Colonel Wedel and half a dozen officers were sitting at a table at the far end of the hall. Three of them had brought their wives.

Mette's father muttered, "I thought this was a Danish party."

Mette sighed. "I suppose if we're inviting museum donors, we have to invite them all."

"That's just it." Henrik lifted his shoulders apologetically. "Our party is only possible, despite rationing, because of the colonel."

"A dangerous choice," Julius said quietly.

"Yule is supposed to be a time of truce," Henrik replied. He went to greet other guests in the lobby.

CHAPTER 12 ~ 1940

Mette's father drifted toward the table with the drinks, followed by Julius and the elder Herre Gustemeyer. The largest punchbowl held *gløgg*, a sailors' grog traditionally mixed with red wine, rum, and whatever else was on hand. Hot spiced apple cider filled another bowl, but it had attracted less of a queue.

Mette and the women headed first to inspect the array of appetizers. Pickled herring, cheeses, meats, and sliced eggs had been arranged on little square slices of dark pumpernickel bread, each topped with a dollop of mayonnaise-like *remoulade* and a sprinkle of chives.

"I'm afraid it may not all be kosher," Mette's mother whispered.

"Oh, we Danes have to be a little flexible at Yule," Fru Gustmeyer replied. Mette noticed however, that Julius' mother passed over the *røllepølse*, a spiral Christmas sausage made primarily from pork.

Equipped with refreshments, the Gustmeyers and the Andersens sat down together at a table near the stage. Mette chose a chair on the opposite side from Julius. By unspoken agreement, the table conversation avoided both the war and the broken marriage engagement. As topics ran short, everyone was pleased when Henrik brought a dozen children onto the stage, clapping his hands for attention.

"Merry Yule, everyone!" Henrik called out. "Of course it wouldn't be Yule without *nisser*, our Danish elves. Fortunately, some of our staff's children have agreed to pitch in with a song." He opened a bag, took out some floppy red knit caps, and fitted these on the heads of the shy flock of boys and girls on stage. This made the children so unbearably cute that Mette was not the only one in the audience hiding a smile. When the fiddlers struck up a popular folk tune and the children began attempting to sing — a verse about Christmas elves arguing over a stolen rice pudding in an attic — it was very hard not to laugh out loud. At the end, heartfelt applause filled the room with good cheer.

Henrik plucked off the children's hats. "Now I feel there is magic in the air — Yuletide magic that children should not see. So everyone under the age of twelve will have to go outside to the lobby. Wait out there until you're called. And for heaven's sake, don't listen at the door."

Martina, the staff artist, ushered the children outside. As soon as the door was closed Henrik whispered, "Quick! Everyone on the staff, to the stage. You've got five minutes to decorate the tree. Everything you need is in the boxes."

Mette stood up and took her mother's hand. "You too, Mom."

"But I'm just a volunteer," Kirstin objected.

"We need every elf we can get." Mette led her up onto the stage. They began festooning the tree branches with glass balls and heart-shaped baskets. Woven from red-and-white strips of paper, the baskets were filled with nuts, raisins, and sweets. Claus used a ladder to tie a straw star at the top. Eskil and Asger set to work clipping metal pine-cone-shaped brackets onto the branches, fitting each with a candle.

Meanwhile Henrik had gone to stand by the closed door. In a voice loud enough that the children in the lobby could certainly hear, he said, "What is this? I don't believe it! A trap door is opening from the ceiling. Now a whole army of elves is climbing down into the room. Are they going to attack?"

Abruptly Henrik changed his voice to the gruff tone of an old elf. "No, we elves don't care about war. We're here to bring Yuletide magic. We wait all year for this kind of fun."

A slight thump at the door suggested that the children were almost falling over each other to listen.

"Look!" Henrik cried, his voice returning to normal. "There are grandmother elves, children elves — all kinds. They're bringing decorations for the tree."

He switched back to the gruff elf voice. "And presents too, even for the children. Everyone should know that Yule has come to Denmark."

Henrik whispered to the decorating crew on the stage, "Ready?"

Eskil and Asger were lighting the last of the candles. "Just a second. All right, ready."

Henrik flipped a light switch, plunging the hall into darkness. Only the stage remained dimly visible, lit by the tree's flickering candles.

"I almost forgot!" Henrik called out. "We've left the children outside, and now the elves are all climbing back up into the attic. Good bye! Thanks!"

In his elf voice Henrik grunted, "See you next year. Now open those doors." Then he grasped the two handles and swung the doors wide, stepping to one side.

A crowd of wide-eyed children's faces appeared in the faint candle-light, their mouths agape in wonder. A few peered up at the ceiling in search of elves. But most simply gawked at the miracle of the Yule tree. In the dark and cold of the Danish winter, a hundred tiny beacons of hope and love lit what seemed to be the most beautiful thing in the world — a promise that brighter times lay ahead, if only one dared to believe.

The children rushed to the stage, eager to find presents with their names. But the museum staff caught them, joined hands, and began circling the tree. The fiddlers launched into a Yule tune, and everyone danced around the tree, watching the candles from all sides as they sang.

> High atop the green fir tree
> Shines the glow of Yuletide.
> Fiddler, play a merry tune,
> Now it's time for dancing.
> Just put your hand in mine,
> Don't yet reach out for the sweets.
> First admire the Yule tree,
> Soon enough you'll get treats.

Only when they had sung four verses did Henrik turn on the hall's lights. Then the adults snuffed the candles and the children fell onto the presents like little wolves.

In the intermission that followed, children rushed about comparing their toys. Adults, meanwhile, headed back to the refreshment tables for resupply. The mood was festive enough that everyone mingled amiably, including the Germans.

At this point the tables nearest the stage were moved to make room for a dance floor. The musicians put away their violins and instead brought out a saxophone, a trumpet, and a clarinet.

"Find partners, everyone, for the Champagne Gallop." Henrik cued the band to play a few bars as an introduction. Then he walked over to Mette's table and held out his hand. "May I have the honor, Frøken Andersen?"

Mette was speechless. She didn't like being put on the spot, but he'd left her no polite way to refuse. Did Henrik even know how to dance, she wondered? Her assistant seemed to be revealing an entirely new side of his personality.

With a "why not?" shrug, Mette took his hand and positioned herself on the dance floor for a gallop — a speedy polka in four/four time.

A dozen other couples joined them, waiting for the *pop* of a champagne cork that served as the dance's starting gun. Henrik put his right hand firmly on her waist and held her hand out so far that their bodies nearly touched.

The musicians had no champagne, so the clarinetist simply stomped the stage with his wooden clog. Then they were off like a shot. Couples zoomed about, dancing in hurried triangular paths that occasionally collided. To Mette's amazement, Henrik steered them through the crowd like a soccer star through a field of defenders. When the clarinettist's wooden shoe banged the floor for the dance's final pop, she was out of breath.

But when she and Henrik returned to her table, Julius was already standing with his hand out. "May I?"

She fanned her face. "I hope the second piece is slower."

Julius took her hand. "I hope so too."

The music that started was "In the Mood," an American hit popularized that year by the bandleader Glenn Miller. Although Miller's big band had played it at a jazzy pace, the three Danish musicians had enough trouble with the syncopated arpeggios that they chose a somber tempo, as if the mood were wistful. For a while Mette danced stiffly, keeping her distance from the white bow tie. But Julius was so patient, never attempting to pull her close, that eventually she leaned against him and ended the dance with her eyes closed, wishing the mood would not end.

The click of boot heels woke Mette from her reverie.

"*Entschuldigung, Herr Gustmeyer,*" Colonel Wedel said. A Nazi eagle pin glinted from his uniform. He tapped the shoulder of Julius' white tuxedo. To Mette he said, "*Darf ich, Fräulein?*"

Mette looked up at the officer. How dare he cut in!

Julius answered with a nod. "*Natürlich, Herr Oberst. Das Fräulein gehört mir nicht.*"

The lady doesn't belong to me? At that moment Mette wished she did. But Julius released her hand and returned to his seat, leaving her with a man she didn't trust.

The colonel had paid for this party, so she could hardly refuse him a dance. The band played the introductory bars of a piece in three/three time. The melody seemed familiar, but Mette couldn't quite place it.

"Do you waltz?" the colonel asked.

"*Jawohl, Herr Wedel.*"

A brief shadow crossed his face. "We can speak English, Mette. And please, if I have to remind you one more time to call me Franz, I will soon forget my own name."

"I'm sorry, Franz." She took his hand. The first verse began, and soon they were stepping, dipping, and turning about the floor — one two three, one two three, at half an arm's length.

"Heine," the colonel said.

"I beg your pardon?"

"The song," Wedel explained. "It's a poem by Heinrich Heine, set to music by Friedrich Silcher. One of my favorites. Do you know *Die Lorelei?*"

"Yes," She recognized the melody now. "We had to learn it in German class at school." She could still remember the first verse:

Ich weiß nicht was soll es bedeuten,
Daß ich so traurig bin.
Ein Märchen aus alten Zeiten,
Das kommt mir nicht aus dem Sinn.

I don't know what it could mean,
But somehow it makes me sad.
There's an ancient fairy tale
That I can't get out of my head.

"Old legends. Elves," Wedel said. "Denmark is a candy store for a history professor. I'm so lucky to be working with you."

"I was afraid you would think our progress at Hedeby has been slow," Mette ventured, speaking to his shoulder.

"A few more showy artifacts would be good," the colonel admitted, "But the Reich has guaranteed our funding at least through next year."

"Really? Despite the —" She didn't want to say the word 'war' at the *Julefest.* "Despite everything?"

"Perhaps because of everything, my dear."

Mette missed a step, scuffing the side of his shiny boot. It was disturbing enough that he had called her "my dear," but how was she to interpret the rest of his remark? How could the excavation be linked to the war effort? The song was ending, and there was so much she didn't know.

"You are a bewitching dancer, Mette." Wedel cast a glance toward

Mette's table. "I hesitate to leave you with your previous partner."

She drew in her breath. "What do you know about the Gustmeyers?"

"Is there something I should know?"

Instantly she regretted her question. "They are friends of my family."

"Friends should be chosen with care." He lifted her hand. Then he nodded once and strode back to the German officers' table.

Mette sat down in a daze, her heart beating in her throat. There had been a warning in the colonel's words. Perhaps she had been foolish to follow Niels Bohr's advice and encourage Julius to stay in Denmark. Not only were the Gustmeyers Jewish, but their son really was involved with Holger Danske, the Danish resistance. Julius no longer spoke to her about the movement, so she didn't know the extent of his involvement. Now she wondered how much the Germans knew, and how much they suspected.

Mette sat out the next few dances. The thought that Julius was at risk made her realize how much she had come to admire his persistence. What she had feared most was that he would abandon her. She had broken off their engagement as a preemptive move, to avoid being hurt. But Julius was still here, as attentive as ever. Maybe she was the one who had lacked patience?

The German officers kept returning to the refreshment table for mugs of *gløgg*. One of them called out to the band, "*Spiel Lili Marleen!*"

When the musicians appeared not to understand this request, the officers were just drunk enough that they began singing the German military tune themselves:

> *Vor der Kaserne, vor dem großen Tor,*
> *Steht eine Laterne, und du stehst noch davor,*
> *Wie einst, Lili Marleen —*

> Outside the barracks, outside the camp's main gate
> There's a special streetlight where you would
>   always wait,
> My dear, Lili Marleen —

Mette knew that the last line was supposed to end with a repeat of the Nazi dream girl's name, "Lili Marleen." But a drunk German major sang his own variation:

> My dear, Lili *Jensen!*

The officers all roared.

The rest of the hall, however, fell silent. Giving the Nazi girl a Danish name was an act of arrogance. Colonel Wedel's dance with Mette had been tolerated, but this new affront was a step too far.

Julius stood up, as solemn as Rhett Butler in the posters for *Gone With the Wind*.

"Julius, don't!" Mette whispered, afraid he might do something that would get him arrested.

Julius turned away from the Germans. He faced the others in the hall, took a deep breath, and began to sing.

Der er et yndigt land —

For a moment everyone sat transfixed, listening to Julius' baritone voice singing the Danish national anthem. By the second line a few others had joined in. Soon the musicians picked it up as well. People began standing up in solidarity. By the last line the hall was on its feet, singing the anthem to the outraged, red-faced soldiers:

> There is a lovely land,
> Crowned with ancient beech trees,
> By the salty Baltic strand, the salty Baltic strand.
> With rolling hills and dales,
> Its age-old name is Denmark,
> And it is Freya's hall, and it is Freya's hall.
> As long as seas have waves,
> As long as beech trees grow,
> Our country shall stand fast, and it shall stand fast.

CHAPTER 13
JELLING, 986

"We'll have to mix more white," Lifu grumbled, using her horse-hair brush to dip up the last of the whitewash from a wooden pail. "Vilbi, bring me a double handful of chalk." Lifu watched her apprentice cross the churchyard to the sack of crumbly white rock. Such a strong young woman, always in the curvaceous leather armor that made men look twice — to no avail. Could Lifu even call her an apprentice anymore?

Nine winters had passed since they had played "Capture the King" at Hedeby. After Prince Svein turned eighteen he had been given command of the Trelleborg ring-fort on Zealand. Vilbi had followed him there, organizing an entire ship's crew of shield maidens. Each summer they sailed to the ends of the realm, but in the spring and autumn Vilbi still chose to return to Hedeby, learning herbal medicines and tending the beehives with Lifu. Lifu herself had advanced from being an English tutor. When Princess Gunhild married her Danish-English thane Palling, Lifu had become one of the princess's eight attendants. Some of the ladies-in-waiting served as nursemaids for the three babies that eventually arrived, while others helped prepare food or weave linen for the royal household.

Lifu's role was less well defined. Sometimes she helped her husband Grady design silver jewelry for the princess. This spring, after King Harald had announced that he was building a wooden church to rebury his father Gorm in Christian style at the old capital of Jelling, Lifu had been assigned to design and paint the third face of Harald's rune stone. Nearby, workers were nailing wooden shingles on the church's spire. Carved wooden dragons leaned out from the eaves.

"Is this too much?" Vilbi held out a scoop of white powder.

"No, dump it in." Lifu mixed in a big spoonful of lard. "Animal fat is what holds it all together." She gradually stirred in half a pitcher of milk until the mixture had the consistency of thick cream. Then the two women began painting the remainder of the freshly chiseled side of the haystack-sized granite stone.

"Have you and Grady ever thought of having children?" Vilbi asked.

Lifu paused, her brush in mid-air, wondering where this question had come from. Then she realized: Vilbi herself was now of the age when a woman wonders.

"No children have come for us," Lifu said, painting again. "My life seems fated for other assignments. And what about you, Vilbi? There are men enough who would like to help out."

The young woman frowned at the white rock. "I know. I've sometimes thought of bedding one just for that purpose. But it doesn't feel right either."

"You have your crew of women."

"Yes. As you say, we seem to be fated for other assignments. Still, it leaves a hollow."

"Each of us begins empty, like a rock that's been painted white." Lifu stood back, admiring their work. "The top part's still wet, but we could start decorating the bottom. Which color should we do first?"

"Which colors do you have?"

"Black, red, and brown. A little yellow."

"No blue?"

Lifu shook her head. "Blue is tricky. If you use the juice of blueberries it fades to nothing after a day in the sun. Let's start with the row of runes at the bottom. Black is easy enough to mix from soot."

While Lifu mixed up a pot of black paint, Vilbi washed their brushes in a pail of water. "You taught me to read runes and to tell the truth. I wonder if you are following your own advice."

Lifu looked up at her from the side. "Do you think this stone is lying?"

"Not the first two sides," Vilbi admitted. "Harald Bluetooth really did build this burial place for his father Gorm. And it's true enough that he won all of Denmark and conquered Norway. But look what you're writing now."

Lifu had begun inking in the runes on the newly carved, third side of the stone: AND MADE THE DANES CHRISTIAN.

"The king wanted it written this way," Lifu said. "I suppose he thinks it's true. Or that it will be." As Harald had aged and the power of the Holy Roman Empire had grown, the king had gradually shifted from tolerating Christianity to promoting it. As in England, the populace was slow to embrace the new religion. "You don't have to paint the runes if you don't like them. Paint the dragons' eyes instead."

Vilbi dipped her brush but stood back, surveying the whitewashed carving. "What is this, anyway? A life-size picture of a man covered with snakes. Is this supposed to be Jesus?"

"Or Odin?" Lifu suggested. "He hanged himself in a tree."

"But this man's arms are stretched out, as if on a cross. It's Christ."

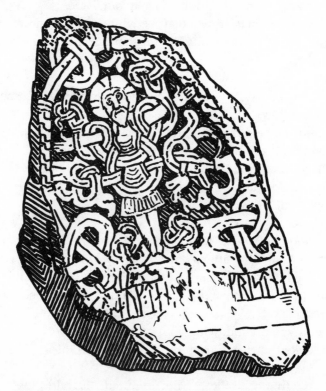

Lifu finished the runes and rinsed her brush. "You're right. Harald wanted a Jesus. I tried to make it a little vague. Odin hanged himself for knowledge, and Jesus for compassion. Both seem worthy goals. Shall we paint him red?"

"Jesus? Red?"

"No, I suppose he would be brown and yellow. The dragons should be red."

"I don't see the compassion in Jesus." Vilbi began dotting the snakes' eyes. "I know that's why they say Christianity is a religion for weak people. Slaves and women can dream about a happy land in the sky while they suffer. Meanwhile the bishops are laughing at them, getting richer and more powerful all the time. Where's the compassion? How can you support a religion like that?"

LIfu stirred up a pail of red paint, using pigs' blood, lard, and crimson mud from Swedish iron bogs. "I've learned to be more accepting. But I'm not hiding Christianity's flaws either. Take a look at our Jesus."

Vilbi stepped back. "He's covered with snakes."

"Exactly. The priests will look at this and say, 'Our mighty Lord is bringing order to the chaos of pagan gods.' Anyone else would look at it and wonder who's winning."

Vilbi tilted her brush back and forth. "Maybe. I've learned a lot about you over the years, Lifu. I think there's something else going on. Something deeper. I wish you'd tell me what it is."

Men began shouting from a hole they had dug near the top of Gorm's grassy burial mound. The men wore the black and brown robes of the Church. It was impossible to make out their words.

Lifu dipped her brush into the iron-red paint and began tracing a dragon tail. Her thoughts tumbled back to the night at Jelling when she had read the children's fortunes and won her freedom at Thyra's bonfire. Further back, she had saved her own life by becoming Harald's spy. Beyond that the memories dimmed.

Lifu spoke as if to herself, "There was a sword."

"A sword?" Vilbi asked encouragingly.

"Yes. A sword of power that Thyra thought was cursed. I sensed it too. The Norse gods had given it the power of victory, but at the cost of evil."

"Where is this sword now?" Vilbi's voice could have been Lifu's own. Her apprentice had learned everything from her.

Lifu looked up at the men arguing atop the mound. "With Gorm. But if there's a new religion, the curses of the old gods no longer count. When Gorm is buried in a church, we all should be safe."

* * *

Bluetooth had decreed that the service in Jelling would be a family gathering, and it was true — if you counted every jarl, helmsman, and priest in Denmark as family. Some wore armor, if that was the most elegant clothing they owned. Weapons, however, were forbidden on the sacred grounds of the stave church, between the old burial mounds of Gorm and Thyra.

Ships had been beaching on the shores of Vejle fjord for the past week, leaving men and families to walk the road up through the forest to the old wooden town of Jelling. Curious crowds examined the freshly painted rune stone. Others walked around the pillared breezeway of the stave church. As yet, only priests were allowed inside. Even Lifu, who had seen the inside of the one-room church in Hedeby, wondered what Christian secrets this monumental, cross-shaped tower might conceal.

On the morning of the service a bell began tolling from a window in the spire. Huge and slow, the great bell swung, the voice of a new god demanding its due. Priests had been inside the church since before dawn. Their muffled chanting was an eerie echo, as if from a world beyond the grave.

Lifu had been busy helping to ready the royal family. Everyone was to wear white linen. All the clothes had to be carefully starched and ironed with wooden rolling pins. Gunhild and Palling were draped with silver jewelry — braided chains, crosses, and a filigreed tiara for the princess. When the bell stopped, the procession set out from the royal hall, passing the rune stone on their way to the church doors. Leading the group was the missionary Poppo, wearing a red robe with gold-embroidered crosses. He was followed by the Danish bishops. So far, only four bishops had been permitted to build churches in Denmark — at Århus, Odense, Ribe, and Slesvig. Each of the bishops carried a staff with a curlicued top encrusted with jewels. Poppo, whose cathedral was still no more than a stone foundation at Roskilde, wore a tall, two-pointed white hat.

Behind the bishops came King Harald and Queen Tove, their golden crowns held high. Tove's hair, still black, cascaded over the shoulders of her trailing white gown. Age had left Harald's long beard nearly as white as his tunic. Years of weather wrinkled the skin about his eyes.

Next in the procession were Gunhild and Palling, trailed by Lifu, holding the hand of the couple's four-year-old son, and then the ladies-in-waiting who carried the two smaller children.

Finally came Prince Svein, leading a wary troop of hardened soldiers. Svein's beard had grown out a flaming red with two dagger-like points. It had already won him the nickname "Forkbeard." Because he had no wife to accompany him, Svein had brought two of the top lieutenants from each of Denmark's five ring-forts. They wore white tunics, as the king had commanded, but covered them defiantly with chain mail and black leather belts. Vilbi, at Svein's side, wore her usual leather armor over a white shift.

As the procession approached the church it occurred to Lifu that their marching order was a reflection of Denmark's spiritual progression. In the lead, the bishops were the most devout Christians of all, but their churches had so far been founded only in the south and west of the country, where the influence of Rome was strongest. At the back, Svein's warriors hailed from military outposts in the north and east of Denmark, where belief in the old Norse gods was still strong. Lifu herself was in the middle, having come to value both religions.

The massive arched doors of the church had been carved with a relief of long-limbed dragons wrestling themselves in knots to bite their own tails. As the doors creaked open on iron hinges the scent of fresh wood, wax, and tar wafted out from the darkness within. When it was Lifu's turn to step inside, she saw only a few shafts of light. Smoky sunbeams angled down from small window openings somewhere far above. Then she noticed the candles — hundreds of wax and tallow tapers. Some burned on giant iron rings suspended from the ceiling by chains. Rows of candles at the end of the church lit a sort of stage, with monks chanting on either side. Only gradually, as her eyes became accustomed to the gloom, did she notice the decorations. Every pillar, beam, and stave of the church's interior had been painted — a riot of color that rivaled her work on the rune stone. Red-and-white patterns of knots twisted up the walls, highlighted with shiny stripes of what could only be genuine gold leaf.

"Grandfather!" Gunhild gasped.

Lifu followed the princess's gaze to the stage at the far end. Now she could see that the candles there surrounded a skeleton on a table. Dark sockets in the skull stared up at a wooden cross. A shawl of gold embroidery cloaked the collarbone. The bony hands, crossed on the ribcage, clutched the gilt scabbard of a sword. Apparently Gorm the

Old had not endured the years as well as his two-named sword. Was it Fenris, Holger, or both?

When the king's entourage gathered around the table, the monks stopped chanting. One of them warned in a thick Irish accent, "Be careful, Your Highness!"

"Brother Michael," Harald said. "I should have known you would be here. And what should I fear in this church?"

"The hole in the floor behind you, Your Highness," the monk replied. "Your father's new Christian grave."

"A grave is indeed a thing to fear."

The missionary Poppo held up a hand with jeweled rings on every finger. "The interment comes after the service, Your Highness. Shall we begin?"

"What about the crowd outside?"

"This is sacred ground. They are not all Christian."

"They will be." Harald straightened his back as if to work out a kink. "Bring them inside."

"All of them?"

"Pack the hall, priest. This is your chance to show them the power of the Christian god."

Poppo sighed. "I hope they are ready." He signaled the Benedictine monks to open the doors and invite people in.

The first men to enter the church crouched in the doorway, peering about as if they suspected an ambush. After them came curious young people, then women, and then entire families. Because each newcomer had to pause in the bright light of the portal, taking in the strange smells, the darkness, and the colored woodwork, nearly an hour passed before the church was full.

"Move closer together!" the king commanded. "Make room for everyone."

Children perched on men's shoulders for a better view. Women complained that they could hardly see. The chilly air of the church grew warmer, redolent of earth, sweat, and candle smoke.

Finally the great doors closed with a thunk. In the darkness that followed, the crowd's murmuring ebbed.

"People of Denmark!" Harald called out to the crowd. He held his hand toward the skeleton at his side. "This is the church of your kings. It is the church of my realm. We are here for a Christian service by the missionary Poppo."

The red-robed holy man pressed his palms together. *"In spiritu sanctu —"*

"Not in Latin," Harald cut the priest short. "Explain what you're doing in Norse, so everyone can understand."

Poppo nodded slowly, tilting his pointed white hat. Then he raised his voice and spoke to the crowd, although his accent made his words hard to understand. "Today is the holy day of Easter."

"What?" A voice called out from the dark.

"Today is Easter," Poppo repeated louder. "The name may be new to many of you, but it is the oldest and most sacred of Christian holy days. Easter comes in the spring, a time of rebirth after the dark of winter. More than nine hundred winters ago Jesus Christ, the son of the one God, was hanged on a cross by Roman soldiers. When he was dead his mother Mary laid his body in a tomb in a cave. Men sealed the entrance with a large stone. Easter celebrates the morning three days later when Mary returned to find the stone rolled aside. Jesus had risen from the dead to share his message of love and forgiveness with mankind. Then he ascended to heaven to join his father in the sky."

Grumbles of mistrust spread through the crowd.

Poppo continued, "Easter, the holiest of days, is the perfect occasion to place King Gorm in this newly completed church."

A voice asked, "Is old Gorm coming back to life?"

Another man called out, "Are his bones gonna fly through the roof?"

Laughter rippled through the crowd.

Poppo held up his hands until quiet returned. "The bones of King Gorm will remain here in sacred ground. His soul, however — the part of him you cannot see — will rise up to heaven and live forever with God. This is the promise of the Church: eternal life for those who accept the faith."

Even Lifu found this part of the Chrstian doctrine mysterious. What part of a skeleton couldn't be seen? The promise of eternal life depended entirely on believing in invisible things. Much of the Norse gods' world was mysterious too, but you could always see the lightning, ravens, and tides that were evidence of the gods' work.

"Before we bury Gorm," Poppo said, "King Harald has asked that we give the souls of his family this same gift of eternal life through the rite of baptism. King Harald and Queen Tove, step forward, remove your crowns, and kneel before God."

When the royal pair knelt on the stage, the crowd gasped. What king would bow to a foreigner?

Poppo dipped his hand into a silver basin and splashed water onto their heads. "In the name of the Father, the Son, and the Holy Ghost, I baptize you as servants of the Lord."

Servants!

Next Poppo called on the princess to bring her family forward to accept the rite. Although her husband Palling had been baptized long ago in England, he knelt alongside Gunhild. Three ladies-in-waiting held their children. When Poppo splashed water on the heads of the children, the smallest baby began to cry.

A woman's voice from the audience asked in shock, "Babies too?"

Poppo appeared not to hear. "The next to accept the rite of baptism is Svein, the prince known as Forkbeard." He motioned for Svein to step forward and kneel.

The prince walked as far as the front of the stage. Then he stopped, face to face with the skull of Gorm the Old.

"No," he said quietly.

"Kneel, Svein!" the king commanded.

Svein turned to the crowd in the dark church. Backlit by the candles his silhouette loomed with broad shoulders. His two-pointed beard seemed to glow red. His ears stood out, the left one cut in battle.

Svein took a deep breath and began to recite: "This oath to Aesir all we swear —"

At first the crowd was silent, stunned to hear the prince's powerful voice declaiming the ancient Norse anthem. By the second verse, however, Vilbi and the lieutenants of the ring-forts had joined in. Soon the entire crowd was reciting the poem in unison, stamping their feet on the plank floor to the rhythm:

> This oath to Aesir all we swear —
> To Odin, Freya, Tyr, and Thor —
> Ice! Hail! Leek! Blood!
> All-knowing gods of earth and sky
> Till Bifrost breaks and Fenris bodes,
> Hear us, heal us, shield our homes.

We sail in wind and waves and weather,
Battle boldly, die by blade,
But never break our bond to these,
The gods of Denmark, gods of old.

Svein turned to Gorm's skeleton and withdrew the old king's sword from its scabbard.

Lifu covered her mouth in horror. The blade was still shiny, dripping a clear liquid. Harald must have buried the scabbard full of oil to keep the sword from rusting. Even he must have thought a time might come when the sword would need to swing again, cursed or not. Surely he had never imagined that his own son would be the next to hold it, in defiance of the king.

Svein lifted the sword to the crowd. "If you stand with me against these foreign priests, let me hear your answer!"

The roar that filled the church threatened to blow out the candles. Poppo and the monks retreated to pillars by the back wall. Harald Bluetooth stood his ground, but he looked old and weak in comparison to his son.

When the clamor died down Svein turned the tip of the sword toward Harald. "Jelling is neutral territory. You have allowed no weapons here but this one, the sword of Gorm the Old. My grandfather was the warrior who used this blade to win a kingdom. He was the one to conquer Denmark — not you, Father, despite what your rune stone says. Gorm believed in the old gods. Now we will see if there is power enough left within his steel to win the kingdom once again."

"What do you know about his sword?" the king asked.

Forkbeard smiled. "I too have spies." He exchanged a glance with Vilbi.

In that moment Lifu realized that Vilbi had learned too much as her apprentice. The shield maiden had been trained to win secrets as well as battles. But Vilbi had served a different master than Lifu all along. She had spied for her old sparring partner, Svein. Did they know the extent of the sword's curse? Did anyone?

"Jelling is no place for battle," Svein continued. "Go, Father. Gather your forces and I will gather mine. We will see who is finally forced to cede the realm."

"What kind of son would challenge his own father?" Harald replied. "I am still king."

Ignoring him, Svein turned the sword's tip toward Gunhild. "As for you, my sister, the only quarrel I have with you is your foreign faith."

"Would you attack me as well?" Gunhild asked, lifting her head so the blond hair below her crown swayed on her shoulders. "Are you such a brave man that you would slaughter my baptized children?"

"No, but you should leave Denmark. This fight is not about you. Go to England, the Christian land where your husband was born." He waved the sword toward Lifu. "And take your English tutor, the witch with one green eye. She never was a Dane."

Then Svein raised his voice to the crowd. "To the ships! To the ring-forts! Danes, join with me to set Denmark free!"

CHAPTER 14
HEDEBY, 1941

Mette worried about Julius throughout the war's second year, even when work at the Hedeby excavation seemed that it must demand all of her attention. His defiance of the German officers at the museum's *Julefest* had been thrilling, but it had marked him as a troublemaker. And although the Danish government was still run by Danes, the Gestapo had been increasing pressure to expose the underground movement and "do something" about Denmark's "Jewish problem." Mette reread each of Julius' weekly letters, trying to assure herself that he was safe. The replies she penned grew warmer, once again beginning with "Dearest Julius" and concluding, "Your Mette."

Almost every day the radio reported yet another victory for the Nazi military machine. Throughout 1941, there were no defeats. Partnered now with Italy and Japan in an "Axis" alliance, Germany's power circled the globe. When Italy's fumbling invasion of Greece came to a standstill in April, the German Wehrmacht marched to the rescue, capturing the entire Balkan peninsula in a single month. From Greece they crossed the Mediterranean and sent the British army reeling back across North Africa to Egypt.

In June Hitler surprised the world by launching "Operation Barbarossa" against his own treaty partner, Josef Stalin. The blitzkrieg of German panzers surged east as fast the tank treads could roll, across Ukraine and the Baltic states, deep into Russia to the doorstep of Moscow itself. Each month the Axis alliance swelled, adding Slovakia, Hungary, Rumania, Finland, and Bulgaria as partners.

Meanwhile, the ranks of the western Allies had grown thin. France was gone. Britain had managed to rally only its own Commonwealth — distant lands like Australia, New Zealand, and Canada. Although the

American president, Franklin Roosevelt, had convinced Congress to increase military spending as a precaution, the United States remained stubbornly neutral. This was not America's war. Mette's brother Lars, finishing a degree in journalism at the University of Oregon, wrote that he was earning some easy extra credits toward graduation by taking a class with ROTC, the reserve officers training corps.

When Mette visited Schleswig to check in with museum director Matthiasen, she marveled that exotic luxuries had begun filling the shelves of the town's shops — Greek olives, Sicilian sardines, Spanish oranges, and French wine. Her budget allowed her to order a few such novelties. When she did, the shopkeeper chuckled, "*Der Krieg scheint ja rentabel zu sein*" — It seems the war is paying off.

Steel, however, was not something she was allowed to order. When the pile-driving barge returned to Hedeby's bay in the spring, Mette instructed the engineers to pull up half of the steel plates that been placed the previous fall and to reposition them to build a smaller coffer dam. Instead of laying bare three sunken Viking ships in the bay, they would instead concentrate on just the largest wreck. It was a gamble, but excavations always were.

A different gamble led her to the sword.

When summer came and the archeologists were still waiting for pumps to drain the ship behind the steel dike, Henrik invited Mette to take a bicycle ride into the surrounding countryside. He had a loaf of French bread, an Italian salami, and two bottles of Danish beer. She happened to be wearing pants from the morning's work, so she was dressed for bicycling. She said yes.

They set out west along a dirt lane, following the bluff along the edge of Schleswig Fjord. Seagulls sailed behind them, following the bicycles like kites. Mette had tried to tame her hair with a cloth band, but the salt breeze made it frizz out over her ears nonetheless.

Most of the farm houses they passed had been converted to vacation rentals, taking advantage of the ocean view. Each cottage had a German name, either painted above the door or forged in old-fashioned cursive letters from wrought iron — *Seelust, Marienruh, Strandheim* — Joy of the Sea, Mary's Rest, Beach Home. Mette and Henrik joked about the lack of creativity.

But then they bicycled past a very old, crooked farm house with a Danish name, *Krigerhøj*.

"Warrior Hill?" Mette asked aloud. She stopped and looked back at the thatch-roofed building surrounded by pink hollyhocks. "I wonder why. Let's see if anyone's home."

"If you want." Henrik got off his bike and began walking back with her.

An old man was weeding a strawberry patch beside the house.

"*Guten Tag*," Mette called out in German. "We're from the excavation at Hedeby. I don't suppose we could ask a question about your house?"

The man squinted. Evidently he had been evaluating her accent. He responded, "*Joda!*"

They both laughed and continued the conversation in Danish.

"I see your house has an unusual name, Warrior Hill. Can you tell me why?"

"Well," the man replied, chewing for a moment on the inside of his cheek. "I reckon that would be because of the bones in my goat yard."

"Bones?" Mette didn't want to get her hopes up. Any bones would probably be from the farmer's own livestock.

"Come along, then," he sighed, setting aside his hoe. "Seems like everyone wants to take a look."

He led the way around the house and through a gate in a stone wall. Beyond was a grassy hill studded with boulders and goats. At the summit a black-and-white goat stood proudly atop a large granite boulder, chewing its cud sideways.

"That one up there I've named Forkbeard," the farmer said, pointing with his thumb to the goat.

"Like the old king, Svein Forkbeard?" Mette asked.

"Yeah, except she's a nanny."

Henrik was examining the boulders with growing enthusiasm. "Look at this, Mette. These stones were brought here on purpose. The hill's right by the fjord, overlooking the whole area. It's clearly a paleolithic site."

"It's the burial hill of Viking warriors," the farmer said.

"More likely from the Stone Age, two thousand years before Svein Forkbeard's time." Mette had seen similar paleolithic sites in Denmark. Virtually all of them had been looted for artifacts long ago. "This whole hill's been dug over like a potato patch. The jumbled bones here would be useless for scientific research."

"Maybe not all of them, *Fru* Scientist." The farmer sniffed. "Take a look over the edge of the cliff."

The hill ended at a bluff that had been eroded by the sea. Mette walked to the edge and cautiously peered over. Fifty feet below, waves broke on a sandless shore of cobbles and green slime.

"Here," the farmer said, pointing.

About three feet down, just out of arm's reach, a white stick was protruding from the cliff. Then Mette realized it wasn't a stick at all.

"Good God," she whispered to Henrik. "It's a femur."

"No, ma'am," the farmer said, "It's a bone."

Henrik knelt beside her. "This really could be an undisturbed Viking grave. It's about the right depth, and close enough to the cliff that looters might have overlooked it."

"Until now, when it's most at risk." Mette stood up and faced the farmer. "We'd like to excavate this site properly. We can pay you two hundred *Reichsmarks* in rent, but anything we find belongs to the museum in Schleswig."

"Two hundred?" The man held out his hand to shake. "You've got a deal."

Colonel Wedel soon became the most enthusiastic follower of the little excavation at Warrior Hill. The Viking-Age skeleton that emerged from the cliff edge had lost its lower legs and feet to erosion. The remaining bones lay face up with an acorn-shaped iron helmet on the head and the metal remains of a round wooden shield on the chest. There was no chain mail, but the torso was covered with a thick horsehide vest that might have served as armor. Twelve half-burned beeswax candles surrounded the skeleton. The candles were the best preserved of all the finds.

But what interested the colonel most were the dagger at the skeleton's hip and the strange, thin sword at its side.

"It looks like a skewer," Colonel Wedel complained, examining the sword on a table in the laboratory room in Hedeby.

"It's an epee," Mette said. "Epees became popular in the Middle Ages because they could pierce chain mail. This is the first one I've seen in a Viking tomb."

"What sort of Viking sissy would wade into battle with a fencing sword?"

Mette cleared her throat. "I should tell you, Colonel —"

"Franz."

She began again. "I should tell you, Franz, that I think we are looking at the grave of a woman."

"What? A woman warrior?"

"The pelvic structure, the ribs — it suggests the skeleton is female."

He shook his head. "That's inconclusive. The skeleton was damaged and incomplete. This is definitely a warrior. Look at the weapons."

"Shield maidens are known from the sagas. The historian Saxo was writing a century or two after the Vikings, and he had a strong Christian bias — he called Svein Forkbeard a patricidal pagan — but he said Svein was forced to rely on women to defeat his father. I'd like to have these bones analyzed at the University in Copenhagen."

"No, no, no." The colonel kept shaking his head. "The Reich wants to unearth a sword of power. They say they need something to back up their Germanic victories. Call it propaganda if you want, but Adolf Hitler believes it. And he does not want a sword that came from the grave of a woman."

Mette was quiet for a moment. "Then perhaps we should keep looking."

"Yes, by all means. The ship in the sand should be dry by autumn."

* * *

It rained so heavily in the fall of 1941 that Hitler's armies finally slowed in the mud of Russia. They dug trenches on the outskirts of Leningrad and Moscow, opting to besiege the two cities and starve the population out during the winter.

At the Hedeby excavation, the overworked pumps at the coffer dam in the bay failed during a November downpour. Mette decided to give up for the season and leave the shipwreck flooded, preserving it in saltwater until the pumps could try again in the spring.

On the first day of December Mette sent the Danish archeological team home to Copenhagen for the winter. There were no Christmas parties planned. This year Colonel Wedel had canceled funding for the National Museum's *Julefest*. The Germans were not interested in facing a hall full of Danes singing their national anthem, especially not if the anthem was led by a Jew.

Mette was desperately looking forward to seeing Julius again. And she was increasingly worried about their future.

* * *

Mette's fears mounted when Julius did not answer the door at his apartment. The woman next door told her the apartment appeared to have been vacant for weeks. Mette went straight to her parents, two floors down in the same waterfront building, to find out what was going on. Her mother was out, doing volunteer work at the National Museum, but her father welcomed her with a big hug.

"Mette, my darling girl," Magnus said, chuckling through his red beard. His eyes seemed more wrinkled than ever. "You are a bright star for a sailor on a dark night."

"What's happened?" Mette loved her father, but he could be so maddeningly short of words that she sometimes wanted to shake him. "I just went to Julius' apartment and the neighbor said he hasn't been there for weeks."

"Days, maybe." Magnus clapped her shoulder. "The boy's all right for now. Just cautious."

"Cautious? Doesn't he want to see me?"

"*Joda*. He was hoping you'd get here in time."

"In time for what?" Mette really was about to shake him.

"A little party. Tonight, at his parent's apartment by the Nyhayn dock. We've been invited to celebrate Hanukkah with the Gustmeyers."

"Hanukkah?"

Magnus sighed. "My girl, you are repeating everything I say as a question."

"Because you aren't giving me any answers! Why Hanukkah? We're not Jewish."

"Last year the Gustmeyers came to our Christmas party, so it's their turn to host. The festival is supposed to start at sundown, but we're

176

invited at midnight. Wear dark clothes. Try not be seen on the way."

A shiver of fear slowed Mette. "There's something you can't tell me, isn't there?"

Her father nodded. "And some things you should hear from Julius himself." He studied his daughter uncertainly. "You really haven't heard the news, have you?"

"What news?" She had rushed from the train station to Julius' apartment, ignoring the crowds at newsstands. Now she looked to the newspaper on the dining room table, where the headlines lay unfolded from breakfast. She sank into a straightback chair, reading.

The Japanese had destroyed the U.S. Navy with a surprise attack on America's main Pacific base. In Russia, Leningrad was about to fall. The Axis conquest of the world was nearly complete. The United States, the last great democracy, was crippled. Even if America joined the war, it was too late.

She looked at her father, her eyes damp. "What about Lars? He's training with the reserves in America."

"He's sure to be conscripted for the Air Force over there. But it's not just Lars. Without a navy, the United States will need every pilot they can get."

Mette covered her mouth with her hand. If the Americans needed pilots, Julius might be tempted to go.

* * *

That night Mette slipped out of her garret apartment just before midnight. She wore a brown beret and a black overcoat with padded shoulders. Copenhagen was as cold and dark as a crypt. Wet snowflakes blew through the streets' canyons. Fishing boats creaked against Nyhavn's tarred pier like restless dragons. It was hard to tell in the dark, but one of the bobbing silhouettes resembled her father's ship *Kong Knud* — the King Canute.

She hurried to the stone entryway of the Gustmeyers' townhouse. As instructed, she rang the buzzer three times, waited, and then buzzed again. A moment later the lock clicked open. The hall inside was black — the light bulb had evidently been removed for the blackout — so she felt her way along the wall, groping for the handle of the front door. When this portal creaked open she was met by the smell of cooking oil and the flicker of candles. Dozens of tapers lit the stairs as if for a chapel.

Julius came bounding down two steps at a time and caught her in his arms. "Mette! I've been so worried you wouldn't make it."

"Me? What about you?"

He grinned — a movie star smile with straight white teeth beneath a straight black mustache. "My dear, I will gladly risk a few hours to celebrate the festival of lights with you."

"Are you in trouble?"

"A little."

"What? Why won't anyone tell me?"

"Please, just wait a while. I'd rather not talk about it yet. Hanukkah is a time for celebration. Come on upstairs. Our parents are up there, eating everything as soon as it comes out of the kitchen."

His enthusiasm was hard to resist. As Mette followed him up the stairs, she couldn't help but remember her own childish anticipation on Christmas Eve, when the scent of candles and baked goods had similarly promised a happy time of presents and family and love.

They were greeted with cheers at the top of the stairs. To the right, in a kitchen with electric lights, Fru Gustmeyer and Mette's mother were stirring kettles on a gas range, apparently as happy as witches over a cauldron with a secret potion. To the left, candles in the dining room lit the elder husbands — Magnus tipping back in a chair amidst a cloud of pipe tobacco smoke, and Herre Gustmeyer at the table, raising a cut-glass goblet.

"At last, we're all here," Herre Gustmeyer exclaimed. "To the table, everyone. Tonight our candles burn for an old miracle — and for the friendship of two families."

"I'll be just one more minute, Jakob," Fru Gustmeyer called from the kitchen. "Meanwhile, you might pour wine for someone other than yourself."

Julius' father rolled his eyes, but he also stood up and began adding pink wineglasses from a cabinet to the Royal Copenhagen china on the table. "So, Frøken Andersen, what's this we hear about you discovering a Viking warrior with one rib too few?"

Mette told about the grave they had found on Warrior Hill, with its horsehide tunic and beeswax candles. Before she could explain about the epee, however, her mother and Fru Gustmeyer came in with two steaming platters of fried food, and everyone's attention turned to dinner.

Herre Gustmeyer stood solemnly before a menorah with nine candles. He recited a long verse — or was it a prayer? Mette couldn't tell because it was entirely in Hebrew. She noticed Julius mouthing the words, as if he knew the text by heart. Then Herre Gustmeyer offered a toast she could understand — *skål,* the Danish word for "cheers!"

After one sip of sweet red wine Julius turned straight to the food. "Do you know latkes?" He offered Mette what looked like a squashed brown fritter.

"No, but it smells good."

"They're to die for. Fried potato pancakes. And doughnuts filled with currant jelly, my absolute favorite."

"Is everything deep fried?" Mette asked.

Julius nodded. "That's the miracle of Hanukkah."

Herre Gustmeyer wiped his white goatee with a linen napkin. "The festival of lights celebrates the rededication of the Temple in Jerusalem in 165 BC. There was only enough sacred oil for one night, but it miraculously burned for eight. Hence the oil and the candles."

"It's not right to celebrate with blacked-out windows," Fru Gustmeyer complained. "The candles are supposed to be visible to everyone, to let the world know we're free."

The word "free" dimmed the festive mood. Julius said quietly, "Hanukkah is about rebellion. That's why the festival of lights comes in the dark of winter. It's about fighting back when all hope seems lost."

Magnus leaned forward. "What is this story of rebellion?"

Herre Gustmeyer set aside his fork. "One would think a family connected with a historical museum would know."

Mette's mother replied defensively, "Isn't Hanukkah about an uprising led by the Maccabees?"

"More or less," Herre Gustmeyer admitted, softening his reproachful tone. "Judea had been ruled by Egyptians for centuries. The pharaohs had allowed freedom of religion. But then the Syrians took over. The occupiers outlawed Judaism and defiled the Temple with sacrifices to their own gods. Among the Jews, a man named Judah started an underground movement to overthrow the Syrians. They called him Judah Maccabee."

"In Aramaic," Julius explained, "The word *maccabee* means 'hammer.'"

His father continued, "The Maccabees drove out the Syrians. For a hundred years Judea was free. Hanukkah celebrates the rebirth of our religion. The beginning of a Golden Age. Until, well, you know."

"Until what?" Mette asked.

"Until the Romans," Julius said.

His father explained, "Two Jewish brothers were arguing over which one should rule Judea. Each of them separately asked the Romans to intervene on his behalf. When the legions arrived they killed twelve thousand Jews and slaughtered the priests of the Temple. The Chosen People have pretty much been on the run ever since."

For a moment everyone at the table was silent. Then Julius slapped the table with his hand. "Enough! This is Hanukkah. Mourning is forbidden. Where are the presents?"

His mother clicked her tongue. "Honestly, Julius. How old are you? Seven?"

"Seven was a golden age, Mother. Let's all be seven for a while."

Everyone laughed. Fru Gustmeyer spoke in a mock sing-song voice. "All right, children. While the grown-ups clear the table, you can go look for your Hanukkah toys on the piano bench."

"Come on!" Julius pulled Mette to the piano. Two blue velvet bags were hidden behind a stack of music books on the bench. Julius and Mette sat on their knees, untied the bags' string closures, and dumped out the contents. Gold coins spilled across the bench — but they didn't clink like proper coins. Mette bent the foil cover off of one.

"They're chocolate," she marveled.

"Hanukkah gelt," Julius said. "Don't eat them all. You'll need some for the game." He reached his fingers into the bottom of his velvet bag and took out a square wooden top. Each of the four sides had been carved with a different Hebrew letter.

"Even I know that's a dreidel," Mette said. "But I don't know how to play."

"The four letters stand for the Hebrew words, 'Great Things Happened There,'" Julius explained. "That's a reminder of the miracle with the oil in the Jerusalem Temple. But the letters also stand for All, Half, None, and One. We start by each putting out two gelt coins as an ante. Then you spin the dreidel. Depending on what comes up, you either get the whole pot, half of it, none of it, or you have to ante one."

"Vikings had dice games like this," Mette said, pushing out two chocolate coins. "With these rules, wouldn't the pot keep emptying out?"

"Whenever the pot has fewer than two gelt, we both have to ante. Ready to play?"

"Sure."

For a while they spun the top, cheering or grumbling as their stacks of chocolate coins grew or shrank. It felt good to imagine they were seven years old, safe from the worries of the world.

Still, Mette was the one who broke the spell.

"I'm sorry about last year, when I got mad. I was thinking of myself. I didn't want you to leave. I thought it was too dangerous."

Julius spun the top and won the whole pot of four coins. They each had to ante a coin again. "It's been a dangerous year."

Mette bit her lip. "You are in trouble, aren't you?"

He nodded. "But it's been worse for others." He lowered his voice. "In Holger Danske we got word that the Germans have herded hundreds of thousands of Jews into ghettoes in Poland. They're dying of disease and hunger. Even more have been sent to work camps. But we're not sure they really are work camps. The Jews who go there are never heard from again." He handed her the dreidel. "Your turn."

Mette spun the top and had to ante another coin. "It almost sounds too horrible to be true. I mean, here in Scandinavia —" her voice trailed off when she saw his sharp gaze.

"Do you want to know what I've been doing this past year?" he asked.

Mette nodded.

"I've been forging Swedish passports for Norwegian Jews. I use my camera and a darkroom in my apartment. I did a pretty good job too. I had to carve copies of official rubber stamps and mimic signatures. Even the paper I used was a perfect match." He spun the top and came up with nothing. "But it didn't work. Last month the Nazis rounded up thirteen hundred Norwegians — just about every Jew in Norway. They've been shipped in cattle cars to Czechoslovakia. Our sources say at least half of them are already dead."

Mette drew in her breath. "What went wrong?"

Julius shook his head. "There must have been an informer."

"A spy?"

"It's the best explanation. We suspect there are a few Danes who secretly work for the Germans. One of them must have tipped off the Gestapo to raid my apartment. I wasn't home when they came, but they found my darkroom. I can't go back." Julius handed her the dreidel.

She just held it, looking at him. "Where can you go? They'll be looking for you. Even here —"

"I know. You spin and hope to win. Go ahead, it's your turn."

Mette spun the wooden top. It wobbled dangerously near the edge of the piano bench, circled back unsteadily, bumped against the music books, and tipped over. The Hebrew letter that faced up was one she had forgotten. "What does it mean?"

"You win half."

"Only half?" Instead of looking at the gelt, she was looking at him, reading the sadness in his eyes. "You're leaving, aren't you?"

Julius nodded.

Her heart was beating in her throat. "When?"

"Tonight."

"So soon!" They had hardly been together again for two hours. Now she realized how precious those hours had been. And unlike last year she could not ask him to stay. Instead, all she could ask was, "How?"

"On your father's fishing boat. He'll smuggle me aboard with a load of fishing nets."

"The German patrol boats could stop you. If they searched, both you and my father would be —"

Julius stopped her with a raised hand. "Tomorrow, in Sweden, we'll see if I've been clever enough at forging papers to get a flight to the United States. I hear they need pilots."

She clutched his hands. "Let's get married. Tonight. I've been a fool to keep putting you off."

"No, darling, you've been right. It's too dangerous."

She began to object, but he shook his head. "It wouldn't be fair to tie you down, not now. Nonetheless —" He reached into his suit jacket pocket and took out a ring — the same engagement ring she had angrily stuffed into the same suit pocket a year earlier. "I would be honored if you would wear this for me until I return."

Mette took the ring, blinking back tears. "Do you promise you'll come back?" She knew it was a stupid thing to ask — it was the sort of thing a seven-year-old girl with a crush might blurt. But at that moment she felt no wiser than a seven-year-old girl.

"I promise." He folded her into his arms in a desperate hug. Then he whispered something that she only later realized was a verse from an old English ballad.

"I'll come for you by moonlight, though hell should bar the way."

CHAPTER 15
OXFORD, ENGLAND, 994

She blinked in confusion, trying to focus on the ravens. Was this another dream? Only in the land of dreams would you expect to see Odin's birds Huginn and Muninn. But this time a white dove was circling with them. Were the ravens chasing it or being chased? And when she woke up, would she discover that she was somewhere else, in a different time?

There were children's voices behind her. Lifu turned and saw Gunhild's three small children hiding in the dark. Frightened, they pointed at a shaggy shape emerging from the gloom. Its claws were sharp. Its eyes were red.

Grendel, the monster from Beowulf's saga, continued toward them hungrily. Lifu stood, unable to move, as if her hands and feet had become iron weights.

"Grady!" she called.

Suddenly the smith was by her side. He charged forward with a sword, but the blade bounced off the monster. Grendel shambled toward them, undaunted.

"Let me try!" It was Sigi, Gunhild's young daughter. The little girl picked up the fallen sword, struggling with its weight. But instead of trying to stab the monster she used the tip of the blade to cut a cross in the palm of her own hand. Lifu tried to cry out, but could say nothing.

Sigi held up her hand to the monster. A bloody cross glared out defiantly from the child's white palm.

Howling in dismay, Grendel shrank back into the shadows. And Lifu opened her eyes.

* * *

"My lady? I've brought eggs and chamomile tea."

Lifu sat up in bed rubbing her eyes. A young serving woman was speaking to her in English. The room had plank walls and a thatched ceiling. Out the door a lawn sloped to a river. There were sheep by the bank. Nothing was familiar. It had happened again.

"I'm sorry if I woke my lady, but *oo!* It's not every day the lady is called to see the king." The English servant set a wooden platter and a ceramic cup on a table by the bed.

"I — I've overslept." How old was she this time? She seemed to be in England, but when, and how? She touched her face. There were more wrinkles than before, but not too many. Perhaps the gods had only made her sleep away a few years.

"Say my name," she told the serving girl.

"What on earth?"

"Just say it."

"Why, you're Lifu, the Lady of Oxford. What a peculiar mood my lady has this morning. Perhaps you'll feel more like yourself after you've had your chamomile with honey."

"Perhaps so." Lifu was hungry, and the scrambled eggs smelled good. She swung her legs out of the bed, a wooden compartment filled with pillow-like straw bags. Apparently the Lady of Oxford deserved this kind of luxury.

Lifu noticed that a pair of men's boots stood before an adjacent, empty bed compartment.

She sipped some of the honeyed tea and asked casually, "Have you seen the Lord of Oxford this morning?"

The girl laughed. "What a mood my lady is in! Your husband Grady is no lord. He's been at work in the smithy since dawn. Or did you mean Duke Palling?"

"Yes, of course, Duke Palling." Lifu ate a spoonful of eggs, thinking quickly. She was still married to Grady, the Irish silversmith. Was Palling still married to the Danish princess Gunhild? And what of Gunhild's three children? Lifu remembered casting Gunhild's fortune with rune staves long ago, turning up dark omens.

"I suppose the duke is with Gunhild," Lifu said, feeling her way through the uncertain territory of this new time. "They would be preparing for this business with the king."

"That's right." The serving girl smiled brightly. "See? I told you. All my lady needed was her honeyed tea. If you like I can stay and help you pack for your trip to London."

"London?" Lifu had not meant to repeat this word as a question. Her mind was full of question marks. She needed a plan.

"Oo, you'll be gone at least three days, what with sailing there and back." The girl sighed dreamily. "How I'd like to see it someday! Not as I'd get to see King Aethelred like you, but the market streets and the walls and the bridge!"

The servant's wistful tone gave Lifu an idea. "What would you say if I asked you to come along as my maid?"

"Oo!" The girl's already large eyes grew even rounder. "Is my lady joking?"

"No, but I want you to help me with a joke. A sort of game."

"What kind of game?" The girl sounded suspicious.

"I want to know what everyday English people think about things. I hear the opinions of Danes all the time. So here's our secret little game. For the next few days I'm going to ask you simple, basic questions, about things everyone knows, and I want you to answer in plain English, just as you see it."

"Would I really get to go to London?"

"If you play the game. Are you ready?"

"I suppose."

"Good. We'll start with an easy question." Lifu smiled to hide her own confusion. "What is your name?"

The girl rocked back on her heels, laughing. "Why, I'm Mildrid, my lady! I'm your Mildrid."

"Of course you are, Mildrid. Well done."

Mildrid used her apron to dry tears of laughter from her eyes. "Oo, my lady, I think I'm going to like this game."

* * *

As Lifu and Mildrid packed a bag with clothes, jewelry, blankets, and food for the trip to London, Lifu managed to learn quite a bit about why Mildrid thought she belonged in Oxford. To her dismay, Lifu found that she had lost nearly eight years of memories. But then she considered that she might have lost an equal number of years the last time, when she had "awakened" at the age of ten in the Danish court of King Gorm the Old. Back then she had nearly gotten herself killed before convincing Harald Bluetooth to spare her. She remembered the circumstances. As a young man Harald had been hired by an English duke to harry his rival, the duke of Oxford. Harald had brought Lifu back to Denmark as a hostage, and then a slave, and then a spy. Oxford had been a troublesome frontier village where the borders of Mercia, Wessex, and the Danelaw met. When Harald left England he had given control of the town to a Danish family. That family's son had apparently been Palling, the English Dane who had won Gunhild's heart during a game of "Capture the King" in the woods outside Hedeby.

Mildrid explained that Palling had been planning to stay in Denmark with Gunhild, but they were caught in some kind of battle between Viking kings and had to leave. When they arrived in Oxford to take over management of the Duchy, Lifu had been recognized by the English locals as the missing heiress.

As Mildrid retold this story, Lifu realized what an awkward position this must have put her in. The Danes viewed Lifu as a former slave, a mere handmaid to Gunhild. The English didn't know what to make of Gunhild, a foreigner who claimed to be a princess, but they were fairly sure that Lifu was the rightful duchess of Oxford.

The issue had been resolved by the expedient of creating a new title for Lifu: the Lady of Oxford. The poorly defined rank was vague enough that it gave Lifu a great deal of freedom.

"Lucky you," Mildrid said, hoisting the leather bag to her hip. "As the Lady of Oxford you can do whatever you like. Oo, crazy things."

Lifu was curious to find out what crazy things she had done for these past eight years. And what was behind her strange bouts of amnesia? The first time her memory lapsed she had been convinced that it was the work of the mischievous, all-knowing Norse god Odin. Her purpose, it had seemed, had been to prevent Harald Bluetooth from taking up his father's cursed sword, a weapon rumored to bring both victory and evil.

Just before her second loss of memory she had seen Harald's son, Svein Forkbeard, brandish that same sword in the Jelling church, threatening to drive out the priests of the new Christian religion. Where were the old gods now? Here in Oxford, Lifu's jewelry seemed to consist of crosses, not Thor's hammers.

Or perhaps her amnesia had an entirely different explanation. She might have inherited a weakness of the brain. That could explain why her parents had angered a neighboring duke and had been killed. Or the amnesia might just as easily have been caused by poison. She had an uncanny gift for using medicinal plants, but could she have experimented with the wrong mushrooms?

"My lady?" Mildrid stood in the doorway, looking concerned. "The duke and duchess are expecting us soon at the ship."

"Oh! Yes, of course." Lifu snapped from her reverie and followed Mildrid out into the sunlight of her new English world. After a few steps she stopped. Above the thatched rooftops of Oxford rose the spire of the largest building she had ever seen. The walls were stone. The wooden spire seemed to pierce the sky itself.

"Look at that tower!" She exclaimed. "What is it?"

Mildrid gave her a worried look. Then she broke into a smile. "Oh, I get it. We're playing the game."

"Yes, the game," Lifu said, clutching at this explanation. "What is this building?"

"It's St. Frideswide's Church, my lady. Where you've started your school."

"My school. Tell me about my school."

"Oo, this is fun," Mildrid chuckled. "The church is only busy on Sundays, so you convinced the priest to let you use it on other days for other things. You've got people who teach about reading, writing, languages, poems, songs — all kinds of things. Some folks like it and some don't."

"Do I teach about herbs?"

Mildrid wagged her finger. "Witchcraft isn't allowed in church.

Although there's some who whisper about what you do at that bee-hive place of yours in the woods."

"People will gossip about anything," Lifu said, in a lofty tone that she thought might befit the Lady of Oxford. Then she walked down the lawn toward the river dock. A group of men were loading a pointy-prowed craft that seemed too large to call a rowboat but too small to be considered a proper Viking longship. To her surprise none of the men wore beards. Although they were speaking Norse to each other and were as tall as Danes, they were clean shaven. Lifu decided she liked this change in fashion. It made them all look younger.

"Hello? What?" One of the brawnier men was speaking English to her. "So now I'm invisible?"

Lifu took a second look at the man. He wore the leather apron of a smith.

"Grady!" Although eight years had passed, he looked younger and decidedly better without his trademark red beard. "You're speaking English."

Grady scratched his thinning hair. "Well, yes. You're the one who said that's what we should do in England."

"Of course." Lifu couldn't help blushing — and not just because everything she said seemed awkward. The smith before her was her husband. Despite the scar by his eye, he was handsome. He had probably spent much of the night in her bed enclosure. And yet he now seemed a stranger.

"I know it's just a few days," the smith said, looking down and scraping his shoe with some embarrassment. "But I wanted to see you off. I'll miss you."

Lifu wondered how he was able to speak English so well. His Norse had been graveled with Irish gutturals. Could she have given him lessons?

"Can't you come with us to London?" she asked.

"No, not me." He scuffed his shoe again, as if to polish the pier's deck. "Too much noise and smoke."

"You'd rather stay here, banging iron by a forge fire?"

He grinned. "You know me too well. It's the crowds and kings I'm shy of."

The world needed more such honest men, with such honest love. Lifu put her arms around him and held her head against his chest. All else might be a muddle, but the slow hammer of Grady's heart was as steady as an anvil.

When she stepped back, Grady put his hand into a side pocket of his apron. "I brought you something."

"A present?"

"Well, yes. You said you needed something to give the king. So I thought to myself, What do you give a man who has everything? Kings don't need more jewelry."

Grady held out his hand and opened it to reveal a two-pronged dinner fork.

"A fork," Lifu said. "You want me to present the king of England with a fork."

"It's a good fork," Grady replied, his tone defensive. "Hardened steel so the tines are sharp. I plated it with silver so it won't rust."

"Yes. Very nice." Her voice was flat.

"And it sings."

"It sings? How?"

Grady tapped the tines against the boat's gunwale. The fork hummed faintly, the whine of a mosquito.

"It's louder if you stand the handle on wood." The smith held the end of the fork against a wooden oar. At once an eerie note sang through the air. The Danes who had been loading the ship stopped their work. The tone could have been a voice from another world. Slowly it faded away.

"A toy, really." Grady handed her the fork apologetically. "Come back soon."

Meanwhile Princess Gunhild and Duke Palling had been leading a procession of servants down across the lawn to the dock. Palling called out in Norse, "Are we set to sail?"

"Yes, my lord," a Dane replied.

Lifu was pleased to see that Gunhild's three children had grown up healthy, tall, and attractive. Sigi in particular was a beautiful teenager, with long blonde hair tied in a knot over her bare shoulder. Eric's jaw was square like a man's, but spotted with youthful pimples. Frida bounced on springy legs, asking in a high voice if she couldn't go along to London after all.

"No," Gunhild said firmly. "We've only room for eight oarsmen and two maids. Now be good and obey Sigi."

By this time Grady had taken the opportunity to slip away. He was lumbering up the slope toward his smithy.

When Princess Gunhild turned to board the ship she almost ran into Lifu. "Oh yes, Lifu. The king's messenger did ask that we bring you along, although I don't know why."

"I don't know either," Lifu replied. Then, still unsure of her position, she added, "My lady."

"And who is this?" Gunhild demanded, indicating Mildrid.

"It's Mildrid, my servant," Lifu said.

"She's English," Gunhild objected.

"Yes." Lifu marveled that the once carefree princess had become gruff and imperious. She wondered if that was a result of being a princess in a foreign land, where her royalty might not always be respected.

Lifu added, "Since we're going to see the English king, I thought an English servant might help."

"We won't have room for her in the prow. You may sit with her in the back." Gunhild stepped on board. The oarsmen on either side offered their arms as she made her way to the front.

When everyone was settled, Palling stood in the prow and gave the order to cast off. Soon the oars were dipping in unison, four on each side, and the people waving from the Oxford shore gradually became too small to distinguish. The calm river was no wider than a well-thrown stone might cross. Willows crowded the banks on either side. All Lifu could see of the village was the steeple of St. Frideswide's Church. She assumed Oxford would have a bridge of some sort — or at least a ford for oxen — but it must be out of sight upstream.

All day long the men rowed along the curving Thames River. Because the little ship had no rudder, Palling would order the men on one side to raise their oars while the others rowed to steer around bends. The river widened, with only an occasional farm creating a gap in the riverside woods. An easterly breeze and the current of the river helped them along. By the afternoon a muddy rim along the banks announced that they had reached tidewater. Then the ebb of the distant sea pulled them yet faster.

Alone in the back of the boat with Mildrid, overseen only by the oarsmen who spoke little English, Lifu had hours to play her game.

"Tell me," Lifu told Mildrid, watching the ripples of their wake spread out behind them. "Why do people think the king has called us to London?"

"Oo, you don't need a game for that answer," Mildrid said. "Gunhild's brother has been at it again."

"You mean Svein Forkbeard, the king of Denmark?"

"King of pirates, more likely. Almost every year he shows up on the south coast with his ships, raiding and robbing."

"Why the south coast?"

"The Danes are barbarians, that's why," Mildrid said, and then caught herself, her hand to her mouth. "Present company excepted."

Lifu found it troubling that the English thought so little of Danes. Svein's raids had clearly left the impression that the people of Denmark were violent thieves. Her own experience in Denmark had been quite different. There she had been told that the Danish settlers in England — those in the area known as the Danelaw — were the only peaceable folk in Britain.

"Has Svein attacked the Danelaw, in the east?" Lifu asked.

"His own people?" Mildrid scoffed. "No, it's Christians he's after. He plunders monasteries and robs churches. And he kills anyone who stands in the way."

"Where's the English army? Doesn't Aethelred have ring forts?"

"Ring forts?" Mildrid wrinkled her nose. "What would that be? Forts where the men wear rings?"

Lifu described the five great military compounds that Harald Bluetooth had built. Surrounded by a circular palisade, each fort had sixteen boat sheds and sixteen dormitory halls. At a moment's notice, a ring fort could launch a fleet with a thousand men.

"Oo!" Mildrid said, her eyes wide. "I'm sure as King Aethelred has nothing like that. There's hardly an army at all unless it's called for. Then each wapentake and hide has to deliver."

"Slow down, Mildrid." Lifu was having trouble following these foreign terms. "Remember the game? Explain in plain English about hides and wapentakes."

"Well, I don't know exactly. I suppose a hide must once have been a group of farms that had to contribute a hide, and a wapentake must have been an area that had to come up with a weapon. All of England's divided up that way, with acres and furlongs and ealdormen and such — probably since the days of King Alfred. It seems confusing, but that's how the king calls up the army. Each little area has to send a soldier and provide a weapon."

Lifu put her hand to her forehead, sensing the start of a headache. No wonder Aethelred was powerless to stop Svein's raids. The English had no standing army. Rival jurisdictions had little motive to send the king their best fighters. Even when a force was assembled it had to move slowly by land. The English system of cataloguing farms might be an efficient way to collect taxes, but it was a terrible way to field a unified defense.

"Doesn't King Aethelred have a navy?" Lifu asked.

"He spends endless amounts of silver building ships, but it's all wasted."

"Why is that?"

Mildrid gave her a knowing look and made a wiggling motion with her fingers, as if she were scooping coins off a table. "Sticky fingers. The people in charge pocket the money. When ships are delivered they're late, or built on the cheap."

Lifu sighed. The Thames had become a choppy arc of gray between wide flats of smelly mud. The setting sun lit a magenta pall in the sky ahead — presumably the smoke of London's evening dinner fires.

Svein Forkbeard didn't need a magic sword to rob the Christians in England. Corruption, incompetence, and petty rivalries had left the Anglo-Saxon side of the island as vulnerable as a bloated cow.

"My lady?" Mildrid asked quietly. "Are we still playing the game?"

Lifu bit her lip. The game with Mildrid was insignificant compared to the larger game she didn't understand. Why had she been made a player? Perhaps it didn't matter which gods were pushing her deeper and deeper into dangerous territory. The enemy was always the same — evil, violent, and stealthy.

* * *

Torches had been lit along London Bridge by the time they finally arrived in the capital. The flickering lights cast a dozen streaks of gold across the water. To the north the walls and steeples of London were mere silhouettes against the faint summer glow of the night sky.

"Who goes there?" A soldier's voice called out from a platform beneath a torch.

"Palling of Oxford!" the duke called back.

The weary oarsmen pulled up to a wooden bridge piling and tied the boat to a slimy ladder. They stowed their oars and stretched their

THE SHIP IN THE SAND

sore muscles.

The soldier leaned over the railing above. Torchlight outlined the curve of his metal cap. "You're expected, Palling. We can take our time bringing your baggage and servants to the Blackgate Inn, but we're to deliver the three of you straight to the king."

"The three of us?" Palling asked. With the creaking of the boat and the sloshing of the tide it might have been possible to mishear. "I'm here with Princess Gunhild."

"Yes, yes," the soldier called back. "The duke, the princess, and the witch."

Palling looked confused, but Mildrid merely nodded. In broken Norse she said, "I think, sir, he means the Lady of Oxford."

Gunhild put her hands on her hips. The boat rocked and she nearly fell over. When she regained her balance she said, "I still don't see why the king would want to see my old English tutor."

"And why would he call me a witch?' Lifu wondered out loud.

"The title of Lady of Oxford is strange for many people," Mildrid said, still using clumsy Norse. Then she gave a little hop and switched back to English. "Isn't it all too exciting? London! The king! Oo, I could die right now and be happy."

The soldier rapped his knuckles on the ladder. "Step lively now, the king is waiting."

Gunhild complained about climbing the ladder. Even Lifu had to admit it was a disgusting way to enter London, crawling up slippery slats that dripped with foul-smelling seaweed. A horse-drawn wagon with plank benches was waiting for them on top of the bridge. An escort of horsemen with lances and chain mail raised Lifu's suspicion. Were they being treated as royal guests or prisoners?

The ride was comfortable enough on the wooden bridge, but then the wagon rumbled beneath a stone arch in the city wall and began thumping violently on cobblestones. Half-timbered houses leaned out over them on either side of the narrow street, each story jutting out further than the last, so the gables nearly touched overhead. Candles glowed from windows that seemed to be made out of round pieces of glassware. Lifu had seen glass bottles in Denmark, of course, although they were considered rarities for the wealthy. In London, people apparently cut them up to fill entire windows with panes.

The wagon turned a corner and splashed into a muddy street with an overpowering stench of sewage. The houses were smaller here, with thatched roofs. Raucous voices and the wheezy whine of a strange musical instrument blared from a doorway. An old man with only one arm waved a stick at them. Children in rags peered out with dirty faces from gaps in a fence. A scrawny dog vomited in a gutter. Lifu wondered if this could really be the wonderful city that Mildrid had dreamed of visiting.

The wagon paused before another stone gateway while a drawbridge rattled down on heavy chains. Then they rode through a tunnel to a courtyard with a two-story stone building. Half a dozen soldiers, some with candle lanterns, came to help them down from the wagon.

"Where are our quarters?" Gunhild demanded. "I need my servants and my baggage."

The soldiers appeared not to understand her Norse. "Come," a captain said, practically pulling the duke by his elbow. At the top of a broad stone staircase he opened a wooden door that was studded with iron rivets.

Inside, hundreds of candles lit a large room with a parqueted floor and a carved wooden ceiling. Brightly colored tapestries on the stone walls depicted leaping deer and lions.

A gray-haired man with a pointy white beard approached them solemnly. He wore a scarlet robe that puffed out oddly at the shoulders and knees.

"I am Thomas, the king's reeve," he said in English. "Thank you for coming so quickly. This way, please."

"You can't just —" Gunhild began to object. But the reeve had already signaled for two footmen to open a double door. Beyond was a hallway with more candles, and at the far end, through another double door, they saw the king.

In the middle of a room nearly as large as the Jelling church, Aethelred was eating dinner by himself at a large table. Lifu judged him to be about thirty, although it was hard to tell because he had the pale features of a boy and the frail frame of an old man. Instead of a crown he wore a round cloth hat that reminded Lifu of a soup bowl. Below it, mouse-colored hair frizzed out over his ears. He took a bite from a chicken drumstick and made a disapproving face. Then he squinted at them questioningly.

The reeve took this as his cue. He bowed. "This is Palling, Your

Majesty, Duke of Oxford. With him is his wife Gunhild, Duchess of Oxford and Princess of Denmark."

"And her?" Aethelred asked, pointing his drumstick at Lifu.

The reeve faltered, uncertain.

Gunhild spoke in Norse. "She is Lifu, my former tutor. We now call her the Lady of Oxford."

Aethelred took a drink from a silver goblet. He set it down heavily and belched. "Speak in English, woman. And kneel."

"King! I am the princess of Denmark."

The king picked up a bunch of grapes. He began eating them slowly, one at a time. With his mouth full he said, "Kill her."

"What!" Gunhild almost shouted. Her face had gone red.

"Isn't that what your brother Svein would do, if our roles were reversed? Svein Forkbeard has no qualms about spilling English blood. Why should I hesitate to kill his Danish sister?"

The king scanned the platters on the table, picked up a sweetmeat, and examined it. "Or would you prefer to kneel?"

Gunhild, Palling, and Lifu lowered themselves to their knees. The princess's voice trembled with anger. "Is it therefore that you bring me to London?"

Lifu winced. Gunhild's clumsy English sounded like a bad translation.

"Yes, it is therefore." Aethelred smiled. He had mocked her in a way that she would not notice. But that was the end of his subtlety. "You Danes don't belong here. You speak differently. You think differently. You are heathens."

"My husband and I are Christian, King."

"So you say. Even Forkbeard has let himself be baptized a time or two, when it gives him an advantage. But we all know which devils he worships. No, all the bishops in England can't convince him to stop his looting." Aethelred leaned forward. "My question is, can you?"

"Can I what? Stop my brother from going Viking?"

"Exactly so. You are, you see, a hostage on this island."

The princess frowned. "Svein and I are of different minds. I was a — follower? No, a supporter — of our father, Harald Bluetooth. Harald was a good king. He did not go Viking. He brought peace to all the North. He became a man of Christ. My brother Svein is the opposite. They had a fight — a war."

Aethelred nodded. "You father lost that battle. If I recall, Harald was wounded by an arrow at sea. He died later in Pomerania."

Lifu caught her breath. This was the first she had heard of Harald Bluetooth's fate.

"Yes," Gunhild said. "My brother was generous enough to allow King Harald's body to be buried in the unfinished Danish cathedral at Roskilde. Palling and I, we came to England. But we are not friends to my brother."

The King nodded. "Then you are useless, even as hostages." He looked to Thomas, his reeve. "Take them away."

"To be executed, sire?"

"No, just take them away." Then he pointed to Lifu. "But leave this one here for me. Everyone else, out!"

As the reeve led Palling and Gunhild away he whispered to Lifu with a wink, "Our king fancies women of a certain age. But they rarely grow much older."

Lifu remained kneeling with her head bowed, quickly calculating her options. Running from the castle would be impossible. Submitting to the king sexually — if that was indeed what he wanted — would be unpleasant, but might conceivably buy time. Years ago she had out-maneuvered Harald Bluetooth by offering her services as a spy. Was Aethelred worthy of such a promise?

Lifu remembered that her husband had given her a sharp-tined fork. The castle guards hadn't bothered to search her for weapons. Would it placate the king if she presented him with such a mundane gift — perhaps in his back?

The double doors closed with a clunk that echoed from the stone walls. The king picked up his chicken drumstick and resumed eating. Lifu remained kneeling, although her knees were beginning to hurt. Minutes passed as the king dined, smacking his lips and drinking. Lifu waited, trying to calm her thoughts and steady her heart.

At length the king thumped his drumstick on the table. "Look at me!"

Lifu raised her head.

Aethelred grunted. "Then it's true, what they say. Your eyes are different colors. One green and one blue. What are you able to see, witch?"

She didn't blink. "I see many things." If he was going to address her as a witch, she was certainly not going to address him as "Your

Majesty." But then she never had addressed kings properly.

"Yes, I'm told it runs in your family." He pointed the drumstick at her warily. "They say the heiress of Oxford has come back from the land of the dead. That she has founded a school in a church. That she has dark knowledge from the other side."

Would she be safer, Lifu wondered, if the king thought she had supernatural insights? Would he fear her, or kill her?

She replied, "Knowledge comes in many shades."

"In shades." He studied her, chewing. "I hear what people say. They laugh when they call me 'Aethelred the Unready.'"

Lifu had to struggle not to smile. If this were truly the king's popular nickname, it was a wonderful joke. In the common tongue, *aethel red* meant "nobly advised." *Un ready*, however, meant the opposite — not advised at all.

The king lowered his voice "The advice I need is from the dead."

Lifu met his gaze. What could she say in response to this strange statement?

Aethelred nodded, as if she had actually spoken. "Bring a chair." He waved the drumstick at her.

She found a chair and brought it to the table opposite the king.

"Sit," he said.

Lifu sat. She was hungry, and at this close range the delicacies on the table smelled wonderful. But her heart was beating too fast to think of food. Slowly she closed her fingers around the handle of the fork in her pocket.

"My brother was killed when I was ten," Aethelred said. "Edward was only two years older than me. Our father had died by then, so my brother had already been crowned king. Edward wasn't much like me. We had different mothers, you know. He would fly into terrible rages. That's why the dukes and earls all favored me. And of course my mother. You know the rest."

Lifu loosened her grip on the fork. "Tell me anyway."

Aethelred looked at her, his eyebrows raised. "They killed him."

"They killed Edward? Who?"

"Not my mother," the king said. "A guard, I think, paid off by the earls. Everyone was glad. My brother was — well, he was unstable. But then the priests started saying how brilliant he had been. The archbishops of Canterbury and York told people that Edward would have been a better king. More nobly advised. They called him 'Edward the Martyr.' And now —" He lowered his voice. "Now in my dreams I see him silently calling to me from the other side."

The king pressed his eyes with his fingers, as if to push out a vision.

Lifu considered the man before her. The king was dangerously tormented. Anything she said might put her life at risk. But she suspected it was not mere chance that had brought her to the king's table. And that gave her the strength to take a gamble.

"Would you like to speak with Edward?" she asked. "Would you dare to learn your brother's advice?"

Aethelred was still pressing his eyes closed. His breathing was shallow. But his cloth crown tipped ever so slightly in a nod.

"Then call to him. The doorway to the dead is the table between us. Knock three times."

The king looked up at her. His eyes were bloodshot and damp. Once again Lifu was startled to see the round face of a boy — a small, frightened boy — on the shaky body of an old man. What gods did this man really trust?

Aethelred tapped the table with his knuckle. It was a small sound, but it seemed to fill the stone hall. He rapped again. Then he closed his eyes and tapped the table a third time.

Lifu counted silently to twelve before taking the fork out of her pocket. She tapped its tines lightly against her knee and touched the handle to the underside of the table.

The distant wail of an anguished spirit sang out, as if the table really were a portal that had opened onto another world. Even Lifu felt the hair on her neck standing on end.

The king swallowed. "Edward?"

The wail faded away. Lifu waited a moment and shook her head. "He's gone."

"Perhaps if I knocked again?"

Lifu shrugged.

This time the king rapped solidly on the table.

Lifu gave the fork a similarly solid whack against her knee. When she touched the handle to the underside of the table the resulting wail caused Aethelred to leap up in alarm, nearly tipping his heavy throne backwards.

"It would seem," Lifu said, "That you have your brother's attention."

Aethelred wiped his lips with the back of his hand.

Lifu closed her eyes half way, as if in a trance. "Sit down. Focus. What is it you want to ask Edward?"

The king sagged into his throne. "It's these Danes," he whispered, his look haunted. "What am I to do about Svein Forkbeard? He's back again this year, robbing silver, silver, and more silver. How can I make him leave?"

Lifu sat perfectly still, thinking fast. The Danish king had a standing army of five thousand men, and no easy way to pay them. Denmark was a land of small gravel islands. Its only mineral wealth was flint and amber. England had no army to pay, but seemed able to raise endless amounts of silver in taxes. The answer seemed simple.

She rapped the fork and made the table hum. Then she nodded, her eyes still half closed. "There you have your brother's answer."

"What? I hear only a whine."

Lifu opened her eyes. "Voices from the land beyond must pass through a narrow gate. The words are high and fast."

The king wrinkled his brow. "I can't make out anything. Can you, witch?"

She nodded.

"And what does my brother say?"

"Edward advises that you give the Danish king the silver he wants. Then he will go away."

Aethelred groaned, leaning back in his throne. "But that's extortion. And what if Forkbeard comes back the next year, demanding more?"

"If you bargain wisely, it will still be cheaper than building your own navy."

The king frowned. "That's probably true. Payments like that have worked in other cases, to buy time." He leaned forward. "But what if there were another way? I could win powerful allies through marriage. I grow weary of my wife, and Emma, the sister of the Norman duke, is coming of age."

Lifu tilted her head. "If you want to ask Edward, you'll have to call him back."

Aethelred rapped three times on the table, this time as peremptorily as if he were calling for another flagon of wine. "Edward! Should I marry Emma to win the allegiance of the Norman French?"

Once again the fork sang. Aethelred tilted his ear to the table, trying to make out the answer. Finally he shook his head. "What did he say?"

"Edward says the Normans are also Danes. Their grandparents are the same as those of the Danish kings. They will only betray you."

"Damn!" The king pounded the arm of his throne. "Then England stands alone. I'll give Svein Forkbeard his silver, but he'll mock me for it. This year, while robbing our churches, his troops carried a new banner — a blood-red flag with a white cross. The heathens were laughing at us with their own cross!"

Lifu almost dropped her fork in surprise. She had seen that banner in the dream of her eight-year sleep. Or no — it had been the opposite, a red cross cut into a child's pale white hand. An innocent child had turned back the monster Grendel. On an impulse, Lifu rapped the fork.

The singing table made Aethelred look up in puzzlement. "Edward speaks unbidden?"

Lifu nodded.

The king eyed her suspiciously. "And what does my brother say this time?"

Had she overplayed this game? If she hesitated, all would be lost.

"Speak, witch!"

"Your brother advises you to unite England under the opposite flag."

Aethelred folded his hands on the table. "And what would that mean, exactly?"

"I don't know." For the first time she looked uncertain. "But I think it would be a white flag with a red cross. A banner that could rally everyone in England — in Mercia, Wessex, Kent, and the Danelaw too. Something to show that all the people here are one."

The king touched his thumbs together with the slow rhythm of a candle dripping wax. "You are a strange one, Lifu of Oxford."

The thumbs kept tapping together. Lifu held her breath.

Suddenly the king bellowed, "Reeve!"

The double doors opened. The man in the scarlet outfit leaned in, his face a shadow above a ghostly white triangular beard. "Sire?"

"Take the witch away."

"Yes, Your Majesty."

Aethelred took a silver ring from his little finger and rolled it across the table to Lifu. Without another word, he returned to his dinner.

CHAPTER 16
EUGENE, OREGON, 1942

As the train rumbled out of the wheat fields of the Willamette Valley, blasting its discordant horn at a log truck by a crossing, Julius had time to wonder how he would recognize Mette's brother. Lars had always been the black sheep of the Andersen family, the boy who had turned his back on Denmark to draw cartoons in a forgotten corner of America. The only photograph Julius had seen, in the "rogues' gallery" of family portraits in the Andersens' Copenhagen hallway, had shown a gangly teenager smirking at the camera. And yet it was Lars who had finally won him permission to enter the United States.

Sweden had not welcomed Julius, a Jewish refugee who had shown up with wet clothes and false papers on a beach before dawn. Julius had spent a month arguing with authorities, gathering money from his family in Denmark, before he was allowed to buy passage on a freighter to Montreal. The Canadians had given him a six-month work visa, which he'd spent repairing small planes at rural airports until the permit expired, stranding him in Kamloops, British Columbia. The Canadians wouldn't let him enlist in their military, but a desperate final telegram to Mette's brother revealed that the Americans would.

The black sheep of the Andersen family, it turned out, had graduated with a journalism degree, won American citizenship, and enlisted in the U.S. Army all in the same month. With a few phone calls Lars had smoothed a path for Julius. The U.S. Army Air Force really did need pilots.

The ramshackle town that rattled by outside the train window didn't look like much of a city to Julius. The houses were far apart and built entirely of wood. The wide, straight streets had no people, but a surprising number of very large automobiles. The train rolled through

203

a switching yard large enough for half the trains in Denmark, and then past brick warehouses with broken windows. The steel wheels screeched to a stop beside a small wooden station amidst telephone poles. A sign on chains read "Eugene," but the place looked enough like the Wild West of Hollywood movies that it might as well have read "Dodge City."

None of the dozen people on the platform resembled Lars. Wearily Julius put on his fedora and his long black overcoat. It was a hot August day, but the coat was easier to wear than to pack. Then he lugged his leather satchel to the end of the car and down the steps to the United States of America.

An officer with a crewcut and a sunburn blocked his way. "Your papers, please?"

Julius fumbled for his passport — a real one this time, with a real visa. But would this gruff American official recognize it? Beside the officer stood a stunningly beautiful woman. Her blonde hair had long black roots. She had high, rouged cheekbones. She wore a fur collar, despite the heat. She too appeared to have stepped out of a Hollywood movie — a Chicago flick with gangster molls.

Now Julius took a second look at the officer. He wore a sharp, tailored uniform with the label "Andersen" above his breast pocket.

"Lars?" Julius asked.

The officer broke into a grin. "Julius, you dog. Come to fight for the Yanks instead of with my sister?" He clapped his arms around Julius and hugged him so tightly that the pins on his uniform left dents in Julius' overcoat.

Julius had been expecting Lars to speak Danish. He was still scavenging through his own somewhat limited English vocabulary for a response when Lars said, "Oh, and this is the dangerous Miss Svetlova. Sasha, allow me to introduce my almost-brother-in-law, Mr. Gustmeyer."

The starlet leaned over in a heady whiff of perfume and kissed Julius seductively on the cheek. Then she laughed, took out a handkerchief, and wiped off the red lipstick mark.

"Well?" Lars said. "You hungry yet?"

Julius was still struggling for words.

Sasha bit her lip. "Doesn't he talk?"

"*Joda!*" Julius finally blurted. "I mean yes, I do. Thank you."

"All right then," Lars said. "Take off your coat and stay a while, why dontcha? Let's get you a banana split."

With his coat over his arm, Julius followed Lars and Sasha three blocks down Willamette Street — a thoroughfare lined with gigantic signs for department stores, theaters, and drugstores, all shouting for attention. They stopped at Seymour's Café, where Lars ordered a mixing-bowl-sized ice cream concoction, three spoons, a large Coca-Cola, and three straws. They sat in a vinyl booth with a miniature jukebox on the table, sharing spoonfuls of dessert from the same dish as if they were children raised without manners by wolves.

Julius had assumed Lars would want to hear about Copenhagen and Julius' narrow escape to Sweden. This proved untrue.

"You're gonna love basic training," Lars said, scooping up a bit of banana with chocolate sauce. "Of course I'd done ROTC, but they put me through six weeks of hell anyway before giving me my commission. You know what they assigned me to?"

Julius shook his head. He was trying to see the similarity between Mette and her Americanized brother. If Mette had shaved off her frizzy blonde hair would it look as brutal as Lars' crewcut? Certainly her ears didn't stick out like the paddles on either side of Lars' head. Lars was also taller and much better muscled than anyone in his family. He did have Mette's tall forehead and steely blue eyes. Did Lars' father, Magnus, also have a cleft in his square jaw? Behind the elder

Andersen's beard, who could tell?

"Army Intelligence!" Lars said, laughing. "Now there's an oxymoron for you."

"A what?" Julius asked.

"A contradiction. Army — Intelligence. Get it?"

Julius didn't, but said, "That is your assignment?"

"Yup. Part propagandist, part spy. If I told you the truth, I'd have to kill you."

Julius set down his spoon, alarmed.

Sasha laid her hand on his. "It's all right. He's joking."

She spoke with a soft accent that Julius couldn't place. Definitely not Danish. Her name sounded foreign too. Now he wondered what her relationship was to Lars. The Andersens had never mentioned the existence of a Sasha.

"Hello?" Lars waved his hand in front of Julius' eyes. "I know it's hard not to stare, especially if she's holding your hand. But you've got your own fiancée, remember?"

"Oh! Sorry." Julius withdrew his hand. "I didn't know you were — how do you say? — on the road to marriage."

Lars took a sip of Coke with his straw. "I'm not sure it's what the folks in the Old Country want to hear — that I'm hitching up with a Russian doll."

Sasha turned her dark eyes on Julius, a sultry gaze that made him shiver.

She said, "I have Viking roots."

At first Julius thought she was talking about her blonde hair — but that made no sense, because the roots were black. Then he remembered something Mette had once said. "Weren't parts of Russia settled by Swedes?"

"Yes. Russia was founded by Vikings." She lowered her eyes. "But my grandmother was Jewish, and Russians treat Jews just as badly as the Germans."

Julius was about to object that this could hardly be true, but he hesitated. What did he know about Russia?

Lars filled the gap. "Sasha's family emigrated after the pogroms of the '30s. I met her in a linguistics class at the University of Oregon. She's helping with the war effort too."

"You work in a factory?" Julius asked.

"Not exactly. I'm a graduate student. I teach soldiers Russian so they can speak to our allies."

"With Sasha as prof, the poor saps never miss a class," Lars chuckled. But then his expression gradually darkened. He pitched his straw into the empty Coke glass. "The sergeant at the enlistment office wants to see you this afternoon."

"So soon?"

"Yeah, everything's moving fast." Lars took a pale blue envelope from his pocket and tossed it on the table. "But first I thought you'd want to see this."

Julius picked it up and gasped. "It's a letter from Mette! But — but it's addressed to you."

"Sure, she writes to me. No one knew where you were these past months."

"It is not possible to send letters to Nazi-occupied Europe," Julius said. He turned the envelope over. "This one has been postmarked in Sweden."

"Right, so here's the deal." Lars put his hands on the table as if he were measuring an imaginary box. "My Dad can smuggle mail out to Sweden once every few weeks. It's all uncensored, so it's the straight stuff. But we can't write back. We can't even give them our new address when we move. These letters are still coming to the university in my name, and Sasha picks them up."

"Does Mette even know if the letters are arriving? Can you tell her nothing?"

Lars patted the invisible box — a gesture that suggested Julius should calm down. Then he leaned forward, looked both ways, and whispered. "I'm with Army Intel, right?"

Julius didn't understand. "And that means?"

"It means we can get word through to Holger Danske, the Danish resistance. Short messages only. A few words at a time."

"Then she knows I'm with you? That I've come to America?"

"Yeah, she knows. She knows they want you for a replacement crew on a B-17 bomber. To fill the bunks of the guys who've been shot down." Lars shoved the envelope across the table. "Read it and weep. If more letters show up, Sasha here will send them to me, and I'll forward them to you, wherever you are."

"Thank you." Julius held the letter as if it were a wounded bird.

"How will I let you know my address?"

"Us guys in Intel, we know everything."

* * *

As soon as Julius had rented a room at the Eugene Hotel — and before going to see the recruiting sergeant — he spread out the tissue-thin paper of Mette's letter with shaking hands.

> Copenhagen
> June 20, 1942
>
> Dear Lars:
>
> How I wish I could receive news from you! Sometimes I feel like I'm stuffing these letters into bottles and throwing them in the ocean. I know it's foolish, but every day I walk the beach, as if I might find a bottle with your reply. By now you must have graduated from the university. Is Julius still out of touch in Canada? Please let me know, if you possibly can.
>
> The big news at the excavation is that the pumps have finally drained the site of the wreck in Schleswig Fjord. We're calling the ship Slesvig, using the Danish name. The upper half is gone — everything above the original water line seems to have burned. That's a puzzle. The rest of the wood has been preserved by a layer of sand that's muddy enough to keep out most oxygen. She's thirty meters from stem to stern, and clinker-built in the Viking style, with rust marks left from iron rivets. The wood is so soft it falls apart if it dries out completely. Preserving it will be a long, slow process. Colonel Wedel wants us to hurry up and find something more. Meanwhile he's kept the Polish POWs busy mounting a big, pointy antenna on top of our camp's water tower — something we truly don't need. Our two university interns, Eskil and Asger, have been using the tower's shadow as a sundial, pounding stakes into the field beside it to mark hours and months.
>
> At the start of June I had a week's vacation at home. Dad asked me to take the Gustmeyers out to visit the Bohrs again. Niels Bohr has been getting more worried since Julius had to leave. Apparently a former physics student, Werner

Heisenberg, came from Germany to visit. Heisenberg told him the physicists there have formed a "Uranium Club" to work on a secret project. Bohr was surprised that Heisenberg thought the Germans would win the war — although that is what most people seem to assume these days. Bohr wouldn't say, but I think Heisenberg asked him to join his "club," and Bohr refused. It would be a dangerous decision, either way.

Now I have to stop writing in order to work on an exhibit about our excavation for the little museum in Schleswig. It will be hard to celebrate another Midsummer's Night without you. And please, find a way to let me know if Julius and you are safe. I worry every minute of every day.

Your loving sister,
Mette

A week later, after a medical exam and crewcut at a Portland induction center, Julius found himself jammed into a cargo plane with a crowd of frightened, bald nineteen-year-old boys en route to basic training in Wichita Falls, Texas.

The Texas camp proved to be as bleak as anything Julius imagined the Nazis might devise — endless plywood shacks in a desert where they were told that "Oklahoma blows over in the morning and back at night." Everything about Army life seemed designed to strip the recruits of their humanity. Drawling Texas drill sergeants ordered them to polish the undersides of trucks. A captain yelled at Private Gustmeyer to step forward at inspection, just to demonstrate how ugly a crewcut could look.

Week after week, marching with full packs through the West Texas mesquite, Julius felt himself developing muscles he'd never known. His body hardened. Despite everything, he felt good. And yet every day he waited for a letter, and every day he was disappointed.

Until Santa Ana. After basic training Julius shipped out to the Cadet Staging Base in California. Each month twenty thousand men rotated through the program there to see if they qualified as air cadets, or if they would be "washed out." When the rows of recruits lined up at attention, a sergeant barked out, "Private Gustmeyer! The commanding officer wants to see you."

With his heart in his throat Julius broke ranks and made his way to the captain's office. Would he be rejected because he wasn't American, or because he was Jewish, or because he'd tied his shoelaces left-over-right by mistake?

The captain eyed him coldly. "Private, I hear you're from Copenhagen."

"Yes, sir."

"Last year some of your boys got an exhibition team together. My alma mater, UC Davis, whupped the bastards 112 to 6." He paused to let those numbers sink in. "The Dutch stink at basketball."

Julius nearly choked. Should he tell the captain that Copenhagen is in Denmark and not in Holland?

"Yes, sir. The Dutch stink, sir."

"I hope you know more about planes than basketball."

"Yes, sir. I am familiar with German Fokkers."

"Ha! It would be better if you were familiar with German aircraft." The captain shook his head. "Dismissed."

Confused, Julius saluted and turned to go.

"Wait a sec, Gustmeyer." The captain shoved a manila envelope across his desk. The packet was stamped SECRET. "I almost forgot. This came for you from Army Intel."

Julius' heart leapt. Could Lars have sent news from Mette? "Thank you, sir." He saluted and quickly left. Outside he sat under a palm tree and opened the packet to find another letter on blue, tissue-thin paper.

> Hedeby, via Copenhagen
> October 2, 1942
>
> Dear Lars:
>
> Amazing! After all those months of waiting for a message in a bottle to wash up on my little beach, one finally did! I have reread your seven words so often that they now seem like seven thousand. Of course I'm reading a lot between the lines. Still, you've given me hope that you and Julius really are all right, at least for now.
>
> Here at Hedeby our crew has been busy salvaging thousands of soggy wooden fragments from the Slesvig wreck — and we're only twenty centimeters deep. Gasoline is rationed so severely that we've been using three little sailboats to shuttle out to the excavation site in the bay. I've been in

town a lot, setting up a new exhibit at the Schleswig museum. The director there, Matthiasen, is a funny old bird. He's German, but of Danish descent. His pride and joy is an ancient two-piston steam locomotive that really ought to be moved for my new exhibit, but can't because it weighs ten tons. The city authorities keep threatening to dismantle it for scrap iron. Matthiasen insists the engine still works, and wants to demonstrate it by venting the smokestack through a pipe out a window, although everyone agrees this is more likely to burn down the museum than to prove his point. Thank heavens for this humorous relief!

The situation in Denmark is growing grimmer every day. The underground sabotaged a switch in the trainyard at the Århus docks. The damage was discovered before a trainload of German troops bound for Norway could be diverted into the bay. The Gestapo wants to shoot a dozen suspects, but Danish law has no death penalty. No one has been arrested yet for a bomb in the Fridtjof factory outside Copenhagen. It ruined machinery for manufacturing ball bearings. The factory is owned by Danes, and the Germans are threatening to "accidentally" blow up a theater in retaliation, so public sentiment is mixed.

I worry that the Danish government is losing control. It is getting harder for letters like this to get through. The mailman is cautious. The weather is worsening. I will write again when I can. Love to you both, and a big hug for Julius from

Your sister,

Mette

Julius aced the pre-cadet exams in math and physics. Although he ranked low in his class for the physical test, he was sent on to primary flight training in King City, California, in the heart of the Salinas Valley. There, with a flight instructor in the front seat, he flew a Ryan PT-13 low-wing monoplane — as pretty a little craft as Julius had ever seen take to the air. Cadets wore white tape on their helmets to indicate they had yet to solo. After just three hours of flight time, when Julius landed the plane as softly as a flying carpet, the instructor climbed out of the front seat of the open cockpit and waved him on.

"Hurray!" Julius exclaimed.

The instructor turned abruptly. "This is no 'Hurray'."

But when Julius landed again, by himself, the white tape came off. He loved to fly. Once, out of sheer exuberance, he did sixty-five consecutive barrel rolls down the length of the Salinas Valley.

And then came the loneliness of Hanukkah. Julius faced ten days of holiday leave with nowhere to go. Everyone else had homes with parents and girlfriends and Christmas presents.

At the last minute Lars invited him to Eugene. Together with Sasha, who had wrapped herself in furs like a model, they went to see *Holiday Inn*, a new Bing Crosby film at the Heilig Theater on Willamette Street.

The three of them walked back to Sasha's apartment in a cold drizzle. Neon signs reflected off the wet streets like soggy warning lights. Julius' thoughts were still far away, in the world they'd seen on the silver screen.

Lars must have been thinking of the movie too, because he mused aloud, "My sister said you remind her of Clark Gable. I don't see it."

"I do," Sasha said. "It was more obvious when he first arrived. His mustache was gorgeous."

Sasha gave Julius such a steady gaze that he reddened. For her part, Sasha seemed incapable of blushing.

They had to detour around a puddle where wet leaves had clogged a street drain. On the far side Lars said, "When you've got your officer's commission you should do the mustache thing again. It could help with our Gable project."

"You have a project with Clark Gable?" Julius asked, surprised.

"Yeah. He's training for a B-17 crew too. We're planning a promotional film with footage of him on actual missions."

"Isn't that dangerous?"

"Maybe. It turns out that Hitler's a big fan. He's offered a reward to shoot down Clark Gable and capture him alive. Army Intel would love it if we had a double."

Sasha shook her head. "It wouldn't work. Everyone knows Clark Gable doesn't have a Danish accent."

They walked the next few blocks in silence. At the apartment the three of them decorated a little Douglas fir tree with glass balls and tinsel. While the radio played carols they toasted Denmark and the Andersens and the Allies with mugs of Olympia beer.

CHAPTER 16 ~ 1942

When Sasha fell asleep on the arm of the sofa, Julius and Lars sat at the kitchen table, studying a wall map of Europe. The map had been perforated with colored pins like a voodoo doll.

"We lost a lot of B-17 crews bombing the U-boat yards at Rouen," Lars said, tapping a black pin in western France. "The Messerschmidts learned to attack from the front and shoot out the pilots."

Julius shivered. "What can be done?"

"The new bombers have guns in front, in addition to guns on the top, bottom, sides, and tail."

"A lot of guns," Julius said.

"That's why they're called 'Flying Fortresses'."

"Were the submarines worth the losses?"

"Oh, yeah." Lars ran his finger across the Atlantic to the Russian Arctic. "Now our convoys are getting through to Murmansk. We're shipping thousands of planes and tanks to the Russkies. All summer Hitler's been stuck, trying to take Leningrad or Moscow. Finally he struck off for the oil fields of the Caucasus instead." His finger traced a line of red pins southeast across Russia toward the Caspian Sea.

"Germany has coal, but no oil," Julius commented. "The Luftwaffe and the Wehrmacht run on gasoline."

"Exactly." Lars poked a new pin into a small dot on a river. "But along the way Hitler ordered one army to detour here to secure the Volga River. And now they're cut off, surrounded in Stalingrad."

"Hitler's armies don't lose battles," Julius said.

"They're freezing. They're starving." Lars glanced at his sleeping fiancée. "It's the Russian way."

Julius wasn't sure what to think. All three of them were refugees, including Sasha. But Lars already sounded like an American — blunt and pragmatic. He was also more complex than he seemed. When Lars' light-hearted manner cracked, Julius glimpsed an inner core hardened by adversity. Perhaps that was what the Army sought in a spy.

Sasha stretched, rolling her shoulders and stretching the knit of her tight black sweater until it revealed specks of white from the bra underneath. "Are you two still at it? I'm going to bed."

Julius couldn't help but watch her stretch and sway as she walked down the hall. He turned back to the map but had trouble focusing on the pins. He tried calling up a memory of Mette, and was frightened when her face was blurry, as if seen through frosted glass.

"Mette," Julius said, as if speaking her name aloud might bring her back.

"What?" Lars looked at him from the side.

"I was just wondering if you've heard from your sister."

Lars shook his head. "I think the mail route to Sweden is closed."

"They're cut off. Surrounded." Julius frowned.

"And Europe threw bums like us out," Lars said. He took a whisky bottle from the kitchen counter and filled two shot glasses. "Looks like we'll have to bomb our way back."

Julius tapped his glass with Lars', but his throat was too tight to say *skål*.

CHAPTER 17
LONDON, 1002

"We should kill the Danes," Aethelred said. The English king had felt haunted for years, and now he looked it too. His back was hunched with age and his bloodshot eyes had sunken into his miraculously unwrinkled face.

"Let's just kill them all."

Aelfric of Abingdon, the archbishop of Canterbury, frowned at these words. He was walking with the king alongside the moat of the London castle. It was the sort of foggy November morning when the cold mist from the Thames seemed to be struggling to rain, but couldn't. The king wore the ratty fur of a vagrant, while the archbishop beside him looked the personification of conscience, resplendent in his gold-brocaded white robes, tall miter hat, and shepherd's crook.

"I fear, sire, that an invasion of Denmark would be ill advised." Aelfric stressed the words *ill advised*, knowing they would needle a king whose own name meant the opposite. "Not only is winter an unpropitious season for sea travel, but our army is dispersed for the year."

The king scowled. "I wasn't suggesting we attack Denmark, you block-headed monk. That's where Danes belong. If only Svein Forkbeard would take them all back." He kicked a rock at a raven. It squawked and spread its great black wings, but did not fly away. In recent years the ominous black birds had replaced the seagulls that had once sheltered from storms on the castle lawns. The white gulls seemed angelic in comparison to these brooding black demons. Aethelred suspected the castle guards were secretly feeding them meat.

"Then what are you suggesting?" the archbishop asked. "Something must be done." The reason he had come to London was to protest that the Danegeld taxes had become intolerable. Eight years ago the king had persuaded Svein Forkbeard to leave England by buying him off with twelve thousand pounds of silver. That boatload of treasure had been levied by means of a painful tax on every manor, farm, and croft in England. The ransom had worked for a while. The Danish king had left England in peace for three years. When his raiders returned, however, they had demanded twenty thousand pounds of silver. This year their fee had risen to twenty-four thousand. When Aethelred was slow to deliver, the Danes had pillaged a monastery in Kent.

"Whose idea was it to start paying the pagan devils anyway?" Aelfric demanded. "Your brother, Edward the Martyr, would have had a bolder plan."

The king balled his fists. Edward himself had suggested paying the Danegeld! But Aethelred hesitated to reveal that his dead brother had spoken during a séance with a witch from Oxford. Instead he said, "I do have a bolder plan. Forkbeard could only have been this successful with the aid of spies here in Britain. We don't need ships to strike a blow that will cripple the Danish king. Our dispersed army is our strength."

The archbishop tilted his head, cocking the pointed miter at a precarious angle. "How so?"

"We'll call on my Anglo-Saxon soldiers to rise up and kill every Dane in England."

Aelfric raised his eyebrows. "You would slaughter tens of thousands of civilians?" After some reflection he said, "Yes, genocide might be the answer."

"What?"

"Genocide. It's a Latin term, from the Greek for —"

"Speak English, monk!"

The archbishop coughed lightly. "Genocide is the elimination of an entire race. In this case, the purification of the Anglo-Saxon people. In short, a holocaust."

"A what?' You're doing it again."

"A holy fire. A burnt offering to God. The eradication of a heretic race and their false religion." He paused. "I assume the pagans' property would fall to the Church as compensation for Forkbeard's raids."

"Their property would fall to the Crown," Aethelred corrected him sharply. Then in a milder tone he added, "I would, however, donate much of it to the Church in exchange for your prayers."

The archbishop smiled. "That scale of generosity would atone for any number of sins. When would this cleansing begin?"

Aethelred thought for a moment. "Next Saturday might be good. We take Sunday as a day of rest, but the Danes observe Saturday as some kind of wash day. They'll be in their baths."

Aelfric nodded. "That would be November 13, the name day of St. Brice."

"Brice? Who was he?"

"An early French bishop."

The two men continued strolling along the grassy verge of the castle moat. Aethelred asked, "Did this Brice fellow perform miracles?"

"Of course he did. When his washerwoman claimed that he'd fathered her child, he disproved it by carrying hot coals in his cloak without burning the fabric."

"Did that convince his parishioners?"

"Not completely. Brice had to flee to Rome for seven years. There the Pope exonerated him and made him a saint."

The king furrowed his brow. "I think I'll order my soldiers to march in the name of St. George instead. He slew a dragon."

"Good point. People will think of Beowulf. You know, heroes killing Danish monsters."

The king and the archbishop both chuckled, heading back now toward the castle.

* * *

In a brick shed in the ancient oak forest outside of Oxford, three women were chuckling as they stirred a cauldron of bubbling brew.

"It is wash day," Lifu said with a wink. Her ash-blonde hair had silvered with age, but she still allowed it to hang straight over the shoulders of her dark woolen dress.

The two other women, Egwina and Aelfu, were younger, prettier, and less confident. In the same way that women were not allowed to attend classes in Lifu's school in the Oxford church, men were forbidden from the forest center where Lifu taught about herbal medicines and bees. Attending these lessons generally required an alibi at home, and for wealthy wives with Danish servants, wash day was a suitable excuse to slip away.

Egwina lifted her wooden spoon and sniffed. "It feels strange to lie to my husband in order to malt barley. He loves ale."

Aelfu agreed. "My Egbert might as well be married to his ale cup. He'll fight for it when he won't for me."

"That's just it," Lifu said. "What makes men violent when women are not? What causes wars?"

"Other women," Egwina said.

"And ale," Aelfu added.

"Or maybe," Lifu said, "Some men are caught in a deeper curse. This is why we are here, to see if we can create a deeper cure."

Egwina and Aelfu exchanged an uncertain glance. Egwina asked, "What are we making, if not ale?"

"A medicine for angry souls." Lifu dipped her finger in the brew and tasted it. "Men do love ale. What can we add that will make the ale love them?"

Egwina asked, "You'd put medicine in ale?"

Aelfu shrugged. "Egbert would never suspect medicine there."

"Exactly." Lifu lowered her voice. "I propose that we add the two most soothing medicines we have — honey and flowers."

"Flowers in ale?" Egwina scoffed. "That truly does sound like witchery."

Lifu set aside her wooden spoon and took a pouch down from a nail on a rafter. She dipped in her hand and held out a palm full of dried green petals. "These are flowers from the hop vine I've been growing on the wall outside all summer. Smell them."

The two women leaned in. Aelfu closed her eyes. "It's the calm of a summer day!"

"No," Egwina said, squinting. "It's the sweet must of autumn when the harvest is in."

Lifu sprinkled the petals into the cauldron. "Let us see if it can turn angry souls to the sweetness of peace."

As she stirred in the flower petals, however, a strange distant cry came from the forest outside.

"Oo! Help! Oo!"

As the cries grew louder, Lifu recognized the voice of her handmaid Mildrid. But never had her English servant wailed in such distress. Lifu set aside her spoon and opened the shed's door.

"Oo, milady! Oo!" Mildrid's hair was in disarray. Her hands and her linen frock were splashed with strawberry jam. At first Lifu thought that the preserves must have exploded in a fireplace while Mildrid was cooking. Then she realized with a chill that the stains might be blood.

"It's the king's men, milady! The soldiers have gone mad!"

"Calm down and speak sense, Mildrid. What's happened, and why are your hands red?"

Mildrid collapsed on a stump inside the door. She buried her face in her hands, smearing blood amongst her tear streaks. "Milady! They're murdering everyone in Oxford."

"What! Everyone?" Egwina knelt beside her.

Aelfu fetched a damp rag. "If that were true, how did you escape?"

Between sobs Mildrid managed to say, "Not everyone, milady. Just the Danes. I saw it with my own eyes. Young Eric tried to stop them at the manor door. They — they —"

Lifu objected, "These men couldn't be from Aethelred."

Mildrid looked up, her eyes wide. "They announced the king's orders. They carried his new banner. They — they — ." She broke down in tears.

Lifu, Egwina, and Aelfu exchanged shocked glances. Lifu put her arm around Mildrid's shoulder. "Tell us what happened. What did you see?"

"A soldier tried to club Eric on the head. But the boy dodged the worst of the blow and stood his ground. Then it looked like another man punched him in the stomach. I thought Eric took it well, but then —" Mildrid's eyes glassed over.

Lifu shook her gently. "But then what?"

"Then I heard Eric say, in an amazed little voice, 'You've — killed — me.'" Mildrid looked open-mouthed at Lifu. "The tip of the man's sword was sticking out the back of Eric's shirt. And I thought to myself, 'Oo! It looks just like a little red fish leaping out of the linen.'"

The other women stood speechless with horror.

Mildrid cleaned her face with a rag as she continued her story. "The duke and duchess ran out the back with the other children. I just stood there like an idiot and said, 'What'd you go killing Eric for?' A captain in the doorway laughed. He said, 'Leave her. She's obviously English. Take what you want and move on to the next house.'"

"Great God in heaven," Egwina said. "Why is Aethelred killing Danes?"

Aelfu gasped. "My servants! I hope they don't get my cook Gudrun."

Lifu narrowed her eyes. "I've met Aethelred. He is a clumsy, ignorant man. Our king has neither the courage nor the skill to fight the Danes who sail here to raid England's churches in summer. So instead I suspect he's killing the Danes he can. He's sent his troops after the English Danes whose families have lived here a hundred years, paid his taxes, and fought his battles."

Egwina said, "This sounds like an evil that calls for more than flowery ale."

"You're right." Lifu took off her apron and brushed her hands. "Come on, Let's go stop them."

Aelfu gaped at her. "That's crazy! We should be running away. You can't stop an army with a wooden spoon."

"If we don't stand up against murder, who will?"

Egwina wiped beads of sweat from her forehead. "I don't know. I don't know."

Mildrid looked up at her mistress. "Are you really going back into town? Now? Just like that?"

Lifu nodded.

Mildrid sighed. She stood up and threw the rag aside. "Sometimes I wonder if you are crazy, milady. Still, I won't let you walk into hell alone. By God, I won't."

Egwina wrung her hands. "I'm afraid. But I'm even more afraid for my family. My husband is half Danish. I have to know if he and my daughter are safe." She glanced to Aelfu uncertainly.

Aelfu shook her head. "This is no battle for women. I'll stay here to see that the barley doesn't burn."

"Good," Lifu said. "If you like, bar the door behind us." She set off on the footpath through the woods toward town. Mildrid and Egwina followed behind her at a distance.

Even before Lifu reached the edge of the forest she smelled smoke. Twice she saw young people running through the woods, even faster than if they had been chased by bees. At the high road she stopped to let Mildrid and Egwina catch up. Families with carts, horses, and dogs were hurrying along the dirt track toward the English lands of Wessex.

"Doesn't your family live near the town square?" Lifu asked Egwina.

The Englishwoman nodded.

"Then we'll stop to see my husband's workshop first. It's on the way." Lifu worried about Grady. He wasn't Danish, and he spoke English well, but he lacked the accent of a native. Most of the craftsmen near his shop were Danes. Would the soldiers know the difference? And what would happen if they attacked a blacksmith in a shop filled with weapons?

Two plumes of smoke were billowing into the sky. Lifu's heart sank when she saw that one of them was coming from the craftsmen's quarter, just outside the town wall.

As they walked closer, however, Lifu recognized Grady's two English apprentice boys carrying pails of water. Then Grady himself peered out of his shop's door. When he saw Lifu he rushed to take her in his brawny arms.

"Thank the gods you're safe!" He squeezed her so tight she could hardly breath.

She gasped, "And you?"

"Oh, the soldiers killed Thorkell, the leather master, but then we turned them back."

"How did you manage it?" Egwina asked. "Weren't you frightened?"

The Irish smith studied the nervous Englishwoman. "The king's soldiers aren't after the likes of you. They're killing Danes."

"But they only killed one?" Lifu asked.

"That's what I saw. Just before midday hundreds of troops from London marched up and secured the gates to the city. Most of them went inside, but a few dozen came over here. They got Thorkell, looted his shop, and set it on fire. By then I'd managed to distribute some weapons and confront them. They ran pretty fast when they saw our halberds. Since then we've been putting out the fire."

The smith paused, noticing Mildrid. "I saw you running out of the city gate toward the woods. How did you get past the guards?"

"They let English people through, just not Danes."

Grady eyed her somberly. "Where are the duke and duchess?"

"I don't know!" Mildrid started to cry again. "Eric tried to stop the soldiers at the door. They killed him, but the rest of the family escaped out the back. Where do you think they are?"

Grady nodded toward the city gate. "In there. And there aren't enough of us to save them with halberds."

"No," Lifu agreed. "But perhaps if we attack with wooden spoons?"

Grady wrinkled his forehead.

"Follow me." Lifu set off toward the gate.

The smith held out his broad hands in disbelief. "Does anybody understand this woman?" Nonetheless he followed her, with Mildrid and Egwina close behind.

"Halt!" Guards on either side of the gate lowered their pikes. "State your names."

Lifu lifted her head. "I am Lifu, the Lady of Oxford. Stand aside."

Mildrid added, "I'm her handmaid Mildrid."

Egwina said, "And I am Egwina of Oxford. I need to see my family."

One of the guards pointed his pike at Grady. "Who are you?"

"Grady the silversmith."

"You don't sound English."

Grady unleashed an unintelligible torrent of guttural verbiage at the man.

The guard fell back, withdrawing his pike. "Sorry!"

Inside the gate Lifu asked, "What did you say to him?"

"The Lord's Prayer in Irish."

"And that worked?"

"God knows why."

Mildrid ventured, "Even I could hear it wasn't Danish."

Egwina peered anxiously down the empty streets. "Where is everybody?"

"Follow the blood." Grady pointed to a blurry red stripe on the cobblestones. "They must have dragged the bodies off to burn."

Soon other red tracks joined from side streets and broken doors. The bloody stripes were leading toward the largest plume of smoke in the sky. Lifu noticed a hum in the air, and realized it was the voice of a vast crowd somewhere before them.

"The town square!" Egwina cried, starting to run ahead.

Lifu caught her by the arm. "Let's go together."

A mob with torches filled Oxford's central square, chanting

"England! England!" and "Burn the foreigners!" For some reason, the only thing actually burning seemed to be St. Frideswide's Church. People were throwing rocks through the stained glass windows and then tossing torches inside. Already flames were licking the edges of the wooden roof.

Egwina shoved through the crowd, with Lifu and the others close behind. Egwina made her way to the open door of a half-timbered house and called out, "Frederik! Bilone?"

A woman leaned out the second-story window of the adjacent house. "They're not here, Egwina!"

Egwina raised her voice above the crowd. "Where'd they go?"

"To the church," the woman shouted back. "The Danes all fled to St. Frideswide's."

Grady bellowed, "What about the duke?"

"Him too," the woman said. "Palling and Gunhild led everyone there. They must have thought a church would be safe."

"Quick!" Lifu said. "Let's see if we can open the church doors."

She fought her way back across the square, but was stopped short of the church by a ring of soldiers restraining the crowd. Every few yards along the line an English soldier held a pole with the banner of St. George — a red cross on a white field, the opposite of the Danish flag.

"Stay back!" one of the solders told her. "We don't want anyone to get hurt."

"I am Lifu, the rightful duchess of Oxford. I command you to let me pass."

"Ha!" the soldier laughed. "The duchess is inside, saying her last prayers to the Danish gods. Go away."

"Wait," the soldier beside him objected. "I know this woman. She really is the duchess — the old English duchess. The one inside is a Danish impostor."

"Are you sure?" the first soldier asked, lowering his arm.

Lifu used the moment to squirm past him and climb the church steps. But then she stopped.

The wooden doors of the church had been barricaded with the bloody bodies of dead Danes. Soldiers were piling furniture and branches against them for a pyre.

"Stop!" Lifu commanded. "Remove all of this and open the doors."

The soldiers paused. Even the crowd in the square grew quiet, craning their necks to see the woman who had dared to climb the church steps.

An official with a trim white beard and a scarlet uniform stepped down from the portal to confront her.

"Well, look who's here," he said, smiling. "The witch of Oxford herself. It's been some years since we met. Do you remember?"

Lifu's memory had gaps, but she could not forget this arrogant official. "You were in the London castle. You're the king's lackey."

"The king's reeve," he corrected. "It may surprise you to learn that Aethelred also remembers you, and more fondly than you deserve. In fact, he has charged me to deliver you a message."

"And what is that?"

"The king acknowledges your claim to be a duchess. In exchange for eliminating competitors to your title, however, —" he paused, waving toward the burning church, "Aethelred is taking for himself the larger portion of the contested properties."

Lifu narrowed her eyes. "By what law does a king murder his own citizens and take their land?"

The reeve shook his head. "Laws are for Danes and weaklings. In England, the king is the law."

"And that allows Aethelred to burn a church full of people, something even the Danish king has never done?"

"This church was defiled," the reeve explained. "It has been used as a school."

"Since when is knowledge defilement?"

"Since heathen times. The Danes say that Wotan poked out his own eye for knowledge. How smart is that?" The reeve pointed up at the church. "Christ, the true God, calls instead for faith."

A gust of heat and smoke swirled down from the flaming roof, momentarily forcing everyone to cover their eyes. When Lifu looked up again, two soldiers were dragging a naked body by its arms through the crowd. Although the corpse was face down, the long blonde hair and white buttocks suggested the victim had been a girl.

"Here's one more, now that we're done with her." The first soldier laughed. He flipped her over onto the pile.

Lifu froze, her head spinning.

The girl was Sigi. Princess Gunhild's daughter had hardly made it to her fifteenth year. Now her wide eyes and bluish face spoke of abuse and strangulation.

The second soldier took out a dagger. He cut two quick perpendicular slashes across the girl's bare white chest. "There! It's the cross of St. George. Now she's English."

Lifu staggered back on the steps, the whole world whirling about her. Once, in a dream, she had seen that cross cut into this same girl's hand. In that vision, Sigi's sacrifice had turned back a monster. Long ago the fortune-telling runes in Jelling had boded an ill future for Danish princesses. But who could have imagined such a dark betrayal?

Dimly she heard the reeve command, "Light the pyre. Burn them all." More dimly yet, she heard the church's great wooden roof beams crack, collapsing into the stone nave. A wave of heat and sparks swept over the crowd, singing hair and banners.

Then all was black.

* * *

Lifu awoke with a chill, lying in damp grass by the river.

"She's coming to!" Grady called out. He knelt beside her. "My love, are you really back?"

She nodded. Behind his shoulders the sky was red. It was not the rosy hue of a natural sunset, but rather the color of flame.

Grady stroked her cheek. "Sometimes I wonder where you go, and what you see."

"Sometimes I wonder what I've missed." Lifu licked her lips. Her face was warm, as if sunburnt. "What happened to all the people in the church?"

Grady shook his head. He did not have to tell her that the Danes of Oxford were dead.

Mildrid appeared beside the smith, her hands to her face. "Milady! You were great, standing up to them like that. From now on I'll carry a wooden spoon into battle with you anywhere."

Another woman came to kneel on the other side of Grady. It took Lifu a moment to realize who she was.

"Aelfu? I thought you stayed behind to brew ale."

The young Englishwoman bit her lip in embarrassment. "When you marched off like that I changed my mind. Women might not be able to make things right, but we can't just sit by if they're wrong."

"Where's Egwina?"

Mildrid said, "We haven't seen her since the church collapsed, milady. I reckon her family was in there."

Lifu raised herself to her elbows. "We're at the manor house. You must have carried me all the way here."

Grady grinned. "You're not as heavy as you think."

"And you're the proper duchess now," Mildrid put in. "The king can claim all the land he wants but he'll have to leave you the cottages by the river."

"What do you plan to do?" Aelfu asked. She sounded anxious, as if she were already having second thoughts about righting wrongs.

"I'm not sure yet." Lifu stood up too quickly and had to bend over until the vertigo passed.

"Are you all right?" Grady asked.

"Just dizzy." She straightened and took Grady's arm. "Let's go see what's left of the manor."

Looters had already stolen most of the glass from the windows. The interior was similarly bare. Chairs and dishes were missing. Chests had been broken open and ransacked. Even the straw ticks of the beds had been ripped apart and strewn across the floor in search of valuables.

"Could the soldiers have done all of this?" Lifu wondered aloud.

"I can't imagine, milady," Mildrid said. "They might have grabbed some silver, but they were only here a few moments."

"It's the neighbors," Aelfu said, sighing. "The people in Oxford are no better than anywhere else."

Eric's blood by the front door had dried to a brown stain. As if drawn by ghosts, Lifu followed the route the rest of the family had taken through the house to the back door. Even the heavy kitchen table had been stolen.

Surveying the damage from the back yard, Lifu said, "At least they left the woodpile."

Grady stood beside her. "I suppose we should be grateful for small blessings, Lifu."

And then, like a tiny echo, the word "Lifu" came out of the twilight. It could have been a bird, or even a cricket. Lifu squeezed Grady's hand. "Did you hear that?"

"Hear what?"

The tiny voice repeated, higher now, "Lifu?"

Lifu gasped. "The woodpile! Quick."

Grady wrinkled his brow. "What?"

But Lifu was already at the woodpile, throwing pieces of firewood left and right. Soon she uncovered a gap between two stacks of wood — a cleft that had been hastily covered over.

A small white hand reached up from the darkness. "Lifu?"

Lifu shoved the stack of wood aside. Then she pulled a child out of the darkness. "Frida! You're alive."

The ten-year-old girl started to cry. "Mother told me not to come out, but it's been so long, and I'm hungry."

"Thank God, oh thank God." Lifu sat on the firewood, hugging the child and rocking.

"Oo!" Mildrid approached with wide eyes. "The duchess must have known the others might not make it. She hid our little Frida in the one place no one would look."

"What's happened to Mother?" Frida demanded. "Where are the others?"

The adults looked at each other tight-lipped. Grady muttered, "At least there's one Dane left in Oxford."

Mildrid added, "And a princess, at that."

Lifu brushed the blonde hair from the girl's face. "Your mother died saving you from the king's soldiers."

"What about my father and Sigi?"

Lifu shook her head.

Frida dried her eyes, taking this news with surprising calm. Perhaps she had guessed as much already from her hiding place in the woodpile.

"I saw the soldiers kill Eric. Why do they hate us?"

"They were sent here by the English king," Lifu explained. "Aethelred is a bad man. He's afraid of people who are different."

Frida frowned. "My uncle is a king. Is he a better one?"

Lifu weighed all that she knew about Svein Forkbeard. He had been an obstreperous boy, and had defeated his own father in battle. He had taken a cursed sword from his grandfather's grave. He had raided English churches for years. He certainly was not perfect.

"Well?" Frida asked. "Is my uncle better?"

"Yes," Lifu said. "He is a better king. And you know what? I'm told he has a son about your age. A boy named Knud."

"I've heard of Knud. His name means *knot*." Frida tilted her head. "Did they name him that because he's tricky, or tough?"

"I don't know," Lifu admitted. "Would you like to meet him?"

"By going to Denmark?" Frida looked out at the dark smoke above the city, at the anxious faces of the adults, and at the windowless manor house. Young though she was, she seemed to understand. "Yes. I think we'd better go."

Lifu nodded. Despite the girl's stoic response, Lifu herself was on the verge of tears.

Aelfu had not said much until now. "You can't be serious. You'd just leave everything in Oxford and take an orphan girl to Denmark?"

Grady put his big hand on Aelfu's shoulder. "I think this is one orphan that King Forkbeard would very much like to meet. Hers is a story that could launch a Viking fleet."

"I'm sorely afraid you might be right," Mildrid said, wringing her hands. "But I'm not one for sea travel, milady. Do you reckon I could stay here to keep an eye on the estate?"

Lifu didn't answer. Instead she was staring off into the dark distance.

Grady knew that look all too well. "My love? Where are you?"

"Or when?" Her voice was hollow.

Grady swallowed. "What have you seen this time?"

Lifu sighed. "There may come an age when a fleet from England is called upon to rescue Denmark. But in our own world, it seems the Danes have been called upon to rescue the English."

CHAPTER 18
COPENHAGEN, 1943

"They're going to kill the Danish Jews." Magnus Andersen kept his head down as he spoke to the thirteen leaders of the Holger Danske resistance movement in the gently rocking cabin of the *Kong Knud*. "Just like in every other Nazi-occupied country, the Gestapo plans to round up and deport the Jews to death camps."

With his big, gray-streaked beard, rimless spectacles, wrinkled eyes, and old-fashioned briar pipe, Mette's father looked like a Norwegian troll in comparison to the bright young faces of the other underground fighters. Many of them were still students at the university. All of them were uneasy in this new meeting place, on a smelly fishing boat in Nyhavn harbor, right in the middle of Copenhagen. But their previous hideout, in the basement of the National Museum, had been raided the week before and two men had been imprisoned by the Gestapo. There must have been an informer in their midst. No one was sure who the traitor might be.

A young man with bony features raised his slender hand before speaking — a sign that he really must be a student. "When is the round-up supposed to start?"

"Three nights from now, on the Jewish New Year. The Germans figure the Jews will be in synagogues for Rosh Hashanah on September 30, but the next night they'll all be at home, where they're easier to arrest."

A voice from a dark corner of the cramped cabin asked, "How do we know this is true?"

"How do we know anything is true?" Magnus sucked on his unlit pipe. "Our Swedish mailman says the Germans asked for confirmation that the Swedish government won't issue passports to Danish Jews without consulting the Reich. The Swedes agreed, but a date slipped out, and the Swedes have leaked word to us. In the meantime, the only Jewish Dane the Swedes are willing to accept is Niels Bohr."

The bony student pounded his knee. "Why is this our problem? None of the other resistance groups has stopped Jews from being deported. Maybe the Nazis are just holding them in camps until the war is over."

A bald middle-aged man stood up. Known only as "Hans," he had been the chief organizer of the Copenhagen cell. "Two million Jews have been deported in Europe so far. But the Nazi work camps only have room for about a hundred thousand of the healthiest. We can't stand by and let Danes be dumped in mass graves."

The voice from the dark corner added, "Besides, when they round up Jews, they usually take the Communists too."

The student flushed. Everyone knew he held a Communist party card.

"We should have done something a month ago, when Denmark still had laws," another voice added. Again there was a silence as the group considered the truth of these words. All summer the underground had been plaguing the Germans with sabotage and strikes, slowing the shipment of supplies from Denmark to the Nazi war machine. On

August 28 the Gestapo had issued an ultimatum, demanding that the Danish government ban strikes, impose a curfew, and punish sabotage with death. When the politicians of the Danish *Rigsdag* refused, the Gestapo had taken a hundred hostages — prominent politicians, Communist leaders, and the chief rabbi of Copenhagen. That same day the Danish government had resigned en masse. Since then the Gestapo had ruled Denmark with the iron fist of martial law.

The student shook his head. "I still don't see how we're supposed to save the Jews if Sweden won't take them. That's the only practical escape route."

"We'll have to work on that through diplomatic channels," Hans said. "In the meantime we need to find families willing to hide Jews from the Gestapo."

"That's quite a risk," the voice in the corner said. "How many refugees are we talking about anyway?"

"Over seven thousand. We have two days."

This time the silence was even longer and more ominous. Every Dane who opened his home to a Jew would risk being shot. If the Jews couldn't be transported to Sweden they might have to stay in hiding for years.

Magnus rapped his pipe on the ship's wheel. He was merely knocking out the ash so he could fill it with fresh tobacco, but he also got the attention of all thirteen men in the tiny cabin.

"Magnus?" Hans asked. "Do you have an idea, or are you just lighting your pipe?"

"Both, I suppose." He took a pouch from his pocket and began pressing pungent shag into the briar pipe bowl. "Seems to me the only leverage we have with Sweden is the physicist, Niels Bohr. I hear the Americans want him pretty badly, and the Swedes want to oblige, but the Nazis don't want to let him go. My daughter Mette has gotten to know the Bohrs. She's tried to talk him into leaving twice. So far he hasn't been interested in being smuggled out. But I'll call him tonight and drop by his house tomorrow. Maybe I can be more persuasive. Then I'll shuttle him over in the *Kong Knud*."

"You'd have to sail in daylight," Hans pointed out. "This wouldn't be like your previous trips. With the curfew the Germans are shooting anything that moves at night. By day, patrol boats will be watching for you."

The student objected, "And saving one Jew won't make a difference anyway."

"Depends on who it is, and how it's done." Magnus struck a match. He took a few quick puffs until the tobacco lit. "Meanwhile, I'm leaving the easy job to you boys. All you have to do is find hidey holes for seven thousand Jews."

* * *

That night the streets of Copenhagen were quiet, but the phone lines were buzzing. Anonymous callers from Holger Danske began alerting Jewish citizens — and in fact anyone in the telephone book with a Jewish-sounding name — that the Gestapo was planning a nationwide pogrom for the night of October 1. The resistance fighter known only as Hans woke the acting chief rabbi Max Friediger from his bed. Hans convinced the rabbi to launch his Rosh Hashanah services the next day by asking everyone in his congregation to leave their homes. A growing network of telephone callers began locating sympathetic families on farms and in villages where Jews might be concealed.

By dawn it had begun to seem possible that the Gestapo wouldn't find many Jews when they launched their raid. But unless there was a way to spirit the hidden thousands to neutral Sweden, the Reich would eventually track them down.

Sunrise had barely pinkened the steeples of Copenhagen when Magnus drove a rumbling fish delivery truck south toward the Carlsberg brewery. He had called ahead to the Danish physicist, and he had asked several other people to call the Bohrs as well. But he still wasn't sure Bohr had been convinced of the situation's urgency — until he saw the suitcases by the mansion's front door.

"Fresh fish!" Magnus called out, stepping down from the truck.

The front door opened to reveal a frowning Niels Bohr. He wore a dark suit, a blue tie, and a bowler hat — as if he were checking into the Hotel D'Angleterre instead of fleeing a Nazi pogrom. "Herre Andersen? A pleasure to meet you." He held out his hand to complete the formal introduction. Bohr attempted a smile. "I understand your daughter is marrying my young friend Julius Gustmeyer."

Magnus gripped the limp hand of the physicist in his hefty paw. "I'm afraid that's been put on hold while Julius learns to fly B-17 bombers in California."

"I had no idea."

"These are strange times. Are you ready to leave Denmark?"

"Actually, I am," Bohr said. "But it's my wife and my son Aage. They insist on either coming with me to Sweden or staying here at Carlsberg."

Magnus took a breath that filled his barrel chest. "Herre Bohr, if your family attempts to come with you to Sweden, they will be turned over to the Nazis, like every other Danish Jew without a visa. If they remain in this house, the Nazis will load them into cattle cars and ship them to a concentration camp in Czechoslovakia." Magnus leaned to one side, looking through the doorway to the figures in the foyer. "Would you like me to repeat those options louder, or did you get the message?"

Niels Bohr's wife Margrethe opened the door the rest of the way. "We heard, but we haven't wanted to believe."

Aage, a fit-looking man in his early thirties, asked, "Where would you take us?"

"Either to my daughter Mette's vacant apartment or to the guest room being prepared by my wife Kirstin." Magnus pretended to doff a nonexistent top hat. "You may have first choice. The other apartment will be taken by your friends Claudia and Jakob Gustmeyer."

"Oh! Are they having to move as well?"

"Fru Bohr, the resistance is currently relocating seven thousand Jews." Magnus' tone suggested he was done doffing hats. He aimed a thumb at the fish truck. "This is your ride."

Aage and Neils each took suitcases. When the younger man opened the back he complained, "It smells like fish in there."

"Better than cattle," Magnus replied.

Niels asked, "May I sit up front?"

"Sorry. Today you're a tub of mackerel."

"Then I guess I'll sit on a suitcase." He helped his wife up the step to the back.

Magnus latched the door behind them. A moment later the fish truck was rumbling back into town, continuing the day's deliveries.

It turned out that the elder Gustmeyers lived in a house with an alley for service vehicles. As a result it was fairly easy to load the elderly couple into a fish truck without being noticed. Similarly, the Andersens' apartment building had a gated parking garage that was perfect for concealing a smuggling operation. The whole group got out and carried the Bohrs' suitcases up an enclosed stairway. Kirstin met them at the apartment door with chicory coffee and biscuits. After half an hour's coffee klatsch Magnus walked the Gustmeyers four blocks over to Mette's garret apartment.

The real problem, Magnus knew, was getting Niels Bohr onto the fishing boat without being noticed. The physicist was one of the most recognizable people in all of Denmark. With his bowler hat and suit, he was hardly in disguise. Crowds of people strolled the Nyhavn docks during the day. Magnus opted again for the fish truck.

Niels said tearful goodbyes to his wife and son, and then followed Magnus back down the apartment stairs to the truck. A short drive later, Magnus parked at the Nyhavn dock next to his boat's gangplank. Søren, his first mate, was already on board, idling the diesel engine. The *Kong Knud* was small enough that it could be sailed with a crew of two, although more hands would be needed to accomplish much actual fishing.

Magnus unlatched the truck's back door and left it ajar. He whispered to Niels, "Sit tight until you hear a car horn that won't quit. Then walk onto the boat like you own the place and hide in the cabin." Magnus took out the suitcase, carried it down the gangplank, and handed it to Søren.

"Where's the rest of our cargo?" the mate asked.

"Coming soon," Magnus said. "Be ready to push off." Then he went back to the street. He strolled along the crowded sidewalk until he found a car with an unlocked door. He leaned in, depressed the horn with his left hand, and pointed across the roof with his other hand, shouting over the din, "Don't jump! Oh my God, there he goes!"

While the crowd stared up at the adjacent building, Magnus dodged back to the boat, pulled in the gangplank, and eased the throttle forward.

As the *Kong Knud* putted out past the dockyards of Copenhagen's harbor, Niels Bohr peered out cautiously at the camouflaged troop ships, the machine gun checkpoints, and the sandbagged anti-aircraft cannons. Between the armaments, a small bronze statue of a mermaid looked out wistfully toward the open sea.

"She gave up everything to live in what she thought would be a better world," Bohr mused.

"Who?" Magnus asked.

Bohr nodded to the window. "The Little Mermaid."

"Oh, her. She's surrounded by Nazis now."

"Why aren't they stopping us?"

"They might, if we strike off toward Swedish waters. But they have to let us fish. Every field kitchen in the Wehmacht serves Danish herring."

Beyond the Langelinie jetty the waves were choppier. Although the wind blew spray across the bow with each wave, Søren kept working on the back deck in his yellow slicker, moving the arm of a crane from a roll of nets to a dinghy with an outboard motor.

"You're risking a lot on this trip," Bohr said, watching the mate try to keep his balance. "If we're stopped, they'll probably send me to the university in Berlin. You wouldn't get off so lightly."

"Everyone's taking gambles," Magnus replied, his hand on the wheel. "The Germans are building rockets to target England. The Americans are messing around with your uranium theories. As for me, I just run a boat."

"How is it that your daughter became interested in archeology instead of fishing?"

"Mette gets that from her mother, I reckon."

Bohr tipped back his bowler hat. "I hear she's digging up a ship in Germany."

Magnus nodded proudly. "Aye, in the old Danish capital of Hedeby. The Germans want her to find the sword of the Viking king, Svein Forkbeard."

"A sword? Why?"

"Legends say it's a sword of empire. Hitler believes it might have the power to win his war."

Bohr laughed. "That's superstitious nonsense. A fairy tale."

Magnus eyed him levelly. "Sounds as believable to me as splitting atoms."

Suddenly there was a shout outside. Søren yanked open the cabin door. "Trouble dead ahead, captain."

Magnus squinted out the front window. "Damn! It's the *Walküre*. Right in front of Saltholm Island."

"A German patrol boat?" Bohr asked, alarmed. "Can we outrun them?"

"Not if she's between us and Sweden." Magnus turned to the physicist, sizing him up. "How much did that bowler hat of yours cost?"

"This?" Bohr took it off, puzzled. "Thirty crowns. Why?"

"I'll pay you back someday. Trade it for Søren's cap."

The first mate took off his knit cap and tried on Bohr's bowler. It fit snugly, and made the fisherman look a bit foppish.

"Now trade coats," Magnus told them. Bohr took off his black suit overcoat and put on Søren's yellow slicker.

"Still not good enough." Magnus stuck his briar pipe in Bohr's mouth.

"That's better." Magnus placed Bohr's hands on the ship's wheel. "Keep steering to the left of Saltholm and you'll hit the Swedish harbor in Landskrona."

"Wait!" Bohr cried. "I don't know how to steer a —"

But Magnus and the first mate were already going out the cabin door. Magnus shouted back, "Just keep going straight and you'll be fine." He closed the door behind him, muffling the physicist's complaints.

Out on the deck Søren asked, "Do we have a plan?"

"Sort of." Magnus switched on the crane's electric winch. "Get in the launch and race like hell around the right-hand side of Saltholm."

"Aye aye." Søren climbed into the whaleboat. Even before the winch had lowered the boat, Søren pulled the cord to start the outboard motor.

"*Halt!*" A German voice came across the water. "*Alle Schiffe werden kontrolliert!*"

"What?" Magnus shouted back in Danish. "We don't speak German. We're just setting eel traps."

The *Walküre* slowed to quarter speed. She was a relatively small patrol boat with a single machine gun mounted on the bow. Beside the gun Magnus could now make out a German officer with a pair of binoculars. The man scanned the deck of the *Kong Knud*. Then he jerked his binoculars to the side, noticing the motorboat that was speeding in the opposite direction around Saltholm. Both boats were still in range of the machine gun, but one of them looked like an ordinary Danish fishing boat and the other looked like it had an escaping physicist on board. The officer disappeared inside the cabin. A moment later the *Walküre* revved its motors and turned, following the speedboat.

When Magnus went back inside to take over the wheel, Bohr's hands were shaking. "How did you do that?"

Magnus took back his pipe. "My daughter told me about your uncertainty principle. I figured, maybe even a physicist can be in two places at once. And the closer you look, the less sure you are that he's there at all."

Bohr asked, "What will happen when they catch up with him?"

"They'll find a genuine Danish fisherman with a launch full of genuine eel nets."

"And a bowler hat?"

Magnus shrugged. "Anything's possible in fairy tales. Meanwhile, we're in Swedish waters."

The white church steeple of Landskrona shimmered ahead. Now that Sweden was in sight, Bohr seemed to grow thoughtful. "What happened to the Little Mermaid?"

Magnus scratched his beard, puzzled by this abrupt switch. "In the fairy tale?"

"That's right. I remember she traded her voice for legs, but then what happened?"

"She was in love with a human prince."

"Did that work out?" Bohr asked.

Magnus thought for a moment. "Not really. She couldn't talk, so the prince married someone else. She wound up throwing herself into the ocean to drown. I think she turned into sea foam or something."

Bohr nodded. "Hans Christian Andersen's stories never ended well."

"Want to know how your story will end?" Magnus asked.

"Do you know?"

Magnus nodded. "Things will work out fine for you, but everyone else will have hell to pay."

They were already slowing so their wake would not rock the boats in Landskrona's harbor. Bohr asked, "What do you mean?"

"You're a scientist. Figure it out. You've made it to Sweden, Meanwhile your family and every other Jew in Denmark will be sent to Nazi death camps. Are you OK with that?"

"Of course not. But what can I do?"

"You're the only one who can save them."

"I don't understand."

In the two minutes before they docked, Magnus helped him to understand.

When the harbormaster came rushing up, excited that a rogue fisherman from Denmark had brought the famous physicist for transport to England, Niels Bohr responded, "I am not leaving Sweden until I speak with King Gustav. I need to tell him to admit the rest of the Danish Jews."

The harbor official looked flustered. "But you can't talk to the king. You're not even Swedish. He doesn't talk to just anyone."

Magnus suggested, "Maybe he'd listen to the most popular Swede in the world. Who do you think that might be?"

The harbormaster didn't have to think long. "Greta Garbo, I suppose. The actress."

Bohr asked, "Do you have a phone?"

"Yes, of course."

"Good. I'd like to place a call to Hollywood."

* * *

After three days of watching the harbor with a telescope on the balcony, Kirstin was beginning to lose hope. Margrethe and Aage Bohr also took turns scanning the horizon beyond Langelinie for the twin masts of the *Kong Knud*. Of all the apartments Julius had built on the waterfront, Kirstin had chosen this one for its view, so she could keep track of Magnus' comings and goings. This time, however, it seemed her husband might not be returning at all.

They kept the wireless tuned to Radio Sweden, hoping for news. The Danish stations, now controlled by the Nazis, carried only propaganda, but surely the Swedes would have reported the arrival of the famous Danish physicist. Day after day the station in Malmö seemed to be broadcasting only polkas.

To make matters worse, the Gestapo had carried out its pogrom as planned during the night of the Jewish New Year. Kirstin, Margrethe, and Aage watched in angry frustration as trucks from the Waffen SS began delivering the first Jewish deportees to the Langelinie dock. The *Wartheland*, a troop transport ship capable of carrying thousands, lay alongside the quai with a gangway to a hellish black portal in its side.

Throughout the morning of October 2 the crowd of captured Jews slowly grew. Through the telescope Kirstin could see families sitting on their luggage, crying. German guards with guns strolled up and down the line, shouting and kicking. Some of the guards opened suitcases, stealing what they wanted and scattering the rest. One made a game of throwing people's hats into the water.

By noon the last of the trucks had left and the soldiers began shoving deportees onto the ship.

Kirstin did a quick count. "One hundred and eighty-seven," she said, musing. "Fewer than two hundred, out of more than seven thousand."

"Maybe the resistance managed to hide most of the Jews after all." Aage focused the telescope. "Hey! That's Marcus Melchior."

"Who?" Mette asked.

"The chief rabbi of Copenhagen," Margrethe explained. "He was one of the hostages they took last month when the Danish government resigned."

"Actually, it looks like a lot of the deportees are from that group of hostages." Aage stood back from the telescope. "That means the Gestapo's round-up last night only turned up about a hundred Jews."

Margrethe said, "Then the others really must be in hiding, like us."

The Swedish radio station bonged a familiar tune with chimes. "And now for the twelve o'clock news," a voice announced. Kirstin and the others cocked their ears.

"Last night forces of the German military conducted raids throughout Denmark in an effort to resolve what the German minister of propaganda, Joseph Goebbels, has referred to as Denmark's 'Jewish problem.' It is unclear at this point how many Danish citizens of Jewish descent have been gathered for deportation. Meanwhile, this morning at ten a.m. His Royal Majesty King Gustav issued a directive to all Swedish authorities. By order of the king, Danish Jews who reach Sweden's shores will be issued Swedish passports. I repeat, Danish citizens of Jewish descent and their spouses will be granted asylum in Sweden."

Margrethe covered her mouth with her hand. "Did Niels make it in time? Is it too late for us?"

Aage pointed to the crowd filing onto the German ship. "It's too late for them."

"But maybe —" Kirstin stopped in mid-sentence. The telephone on the parlor sideboard was ringing. She walked inside but then hesitated, her hand shaking.

On the fourth ring she lifted the heavy black receiver. "Hello?"

"Is this the fish shop on Strøget?"

Kirstin's heart leapt. Of course this wasn't a fish shop, but she would recognize that gruff Norwegian voice anywhere. "Magnus!"

"Captain Andersen here. I can't talk much right now, but I'm going to need a delivery."

"What?" Kirstin pressed the receiver closer. "What kind of delivery?"

"Four tubs of mackerel."

"Magnus, are you all right?"

"I'm going to need this shipment right away. I think you know which tubs I mean. There are two in the garret at Nyhavn and two right there in your shop. Could you bring them in your delivery truck?"

Kirstin's heart raced. Her husband was being watched. Someone was listening to their phone call.

"Where would you like these fish delivered, captain?" she asked.

"To the two o'clock ferry at Elsinore. Load them into a boxcar at the back of the ferry train. Check in with the brakeman there. Got it?"

"Of course. Two o'clock."

"And bring three thousand crowns in cash."

"What!" This was an enormous sum — as much as Magnus earned from his fishing in several months. Would it even be possible to get this much cash so quickly?

Magnus' voice explained calmly, "It turns out this kind of delivery has an export fee. Good luck."

The phone line clicked, and then there was a vacant buzz. Kirstin slowly set the receiver back onto its cradle.

Margrethe and Aage were watching her. "Was that your husband?" Margrethe asked.

"Yes, but I think the Germans are watching him."

"Where is Niels?"

"In Sweden, I suppose. Maybe he was even the one who convinced the Swedish king to help. Magnus seems to have a plan to smuggle you to Sweden too."

Aage asked, "When do we leave?"

"On the two o'clock ferry from Elsinore. But there's a catch."

"There's always a catch," Aage said.

Kirstin nodded. "The brakeman on the ferry train wants a fee of three thousand crowns."

Aage whistled.

Margrethe, however, merely walked over to the purse she'd left beside the sofa. She took out three bundles of bills.

"Let's go," she said.

* * *

Kirstin had trouble driving the fish truck. She hadn't learned to drive until she was forty. Now that she was seventy, manipulating the truck's giant steering wheel felt like wrestling a kangaroo. Worse, the gear system required double-clutching. Aage explained the process to her in principle but could not demonstrate it because he had to ride in back. Apparently the engine and the wheels needed to turn at the same speed in order for the gears to mesh properly. This worked when up-shifting, but downshifting proved to be such a shuddering grind that Kirstin wound up relying solely on the brakes to slow down.

After loading the back of the truck with the Bohrs and the Gustmeyers, Kirstin lurched into first gear, probably tipping everyone over in back. Then she set out in search of back roads toward Elsinore that might not have Gestapo checkpoints. This took her past straw-thatched farm houses and fields of black-and-white cows. She followed road signs to Hørsholm, Hillerød, and only then to Helsingør — the Danish name for Elsinore. Finally the red-chevron highway pointers began also showing a little black steamship — the ferry to Sweden.

This route took her down a steep, narrow brick street lined with sooty buildings. The truck's brakes screeched in protest when she reached the harbor yards.

Across an inlet of bobbing masts rose the Baroque spires of Elsinore Castle. In the play *Hamlet*, Shakespeare had filled that fortress with ghosts and madmen. In Napoleon's day the castle's guns had fought a British armada to a standstill. But every Dane knew that a statue of the Viking warrior Holger Danske was also in there, sleeping away the ages in a vaulted basement corridor, waiting to be awakened to save Denmark in her hour of need. Surely, Kirstin thought, it was time for the old hero to stand up, yawn, and raise his sword.

Car horns beeped impatiently behind her. Kirstin's fish truck was holding up traffic. The two o'clock ferry, a white behemoth idling black smoke at the end of the dock, would sail in less than fifteen minutes. Signs directed cars to the right, where SS soldiers with guns were conducting inspections. Trucks were supposed to go straight, into another area full of German uniforms.

Kirstin turned left into a railroad yard where a diesel train was waiting its turn to roll onto the ferry deck. The train's passenger cars were shiny red with black lettering that read *DSB — Danske Statsbane*. Behind the passenger cars were two black oil tankers and a wooden boxcar. A uniformed man on the back step had a whistle and a red cap. Kirstin leaned out of the truck window. "I've got four tubs of mackerel here for export. Is this where I unload?"

The brakeman glanced about warily. "Did you bring the paperwork?"

CHAPTER 18 ~ 1943

Kirstin fanned the bundles of banknotes in the window.

"All right, quick, back up to the door."

Reverse was not a gear Kirstin had used before on this truck. After some experimentation and a lot of grinding, she managed to nearly ram the side of the boxcar.

"Hold it! Stop!" The brakeman slid open the boxcar door and unlatched the back of the truck. The Bohrs and the Gustmeyers began moving their luggage to hiding spots behind what appeared to be giant electric transformers.

Meanwhile Kirstin handed over the cash and demanded, "Where's my husband?"

"Captain Andersen? He's gone fishing."

Kirstin grabbed the brakeman by his shoulders. "For three thousand crowns you owe me the truth."

The man shook himself free. "Lady, I don't owe you anything. I'm risking my job here. If the Gestapo finds out about this, I'll be shot." He let out a breath. "Besides, I told you the truth."

"My husband is fishing?"

He nodded. "The captain made a run to Sweden a couple days ago. Since then patrol boats have been watching him like hawks. So he's out there fishing. I guess it distracts the Germans from noticing everything else that's going on."

"Like what?"

"You want to know?" The brakeman looked her in the eye. "Get back in that truck of yours and drive to Hillerød. Ask in the church there about the Elsinore Sewing Club. Now get off my train."

He practically pushed Kirstin out of the boxcar. Then he slid the door closed and sealed the latch with a padlock.

When Kirstin hesitated he whispered through gritted teeth, "Get out of here!"

Kirstin climbed into the truck. Slowly she drove back from the docks the way she had come — a route that happened to take her through Hillerød. The scenic old town lay hunched beside a lake with a reflection of Frederiksborg Castle, the summer home of Danish royalty. The town's church had whitewashed stone walls and a steeple with a stair-stepped summit. It looked like any of hundreds of Danish village churches.

Kirstin parked the truck in front. She walked up the stone steps and tried the iron handle of the wooden door. It was unlocked, like all Danish churches. The great door swung open with a creak. The dark entrance hall smelled of candle wax and dust. An iron donation box had a sign with a picture of the smallest Danish coin and the words, "Every øre helps."

In the nave beyond, shafts of light from stained glass windows dimly lit the sails of a model ship hanging from the ceiling. So many sailors and fishermen had died over the years that every Danish church displayed a model ship, as if to console the widows.

"Can I help you?" A priest emerged from the shadows, his palms pressed together, a white collar above his black shirt.

"I'm not sure," Kirstin said, embarrassed and uncertain. "I'm driving the fish delivery truck outside. I came to ask about the Elsinore Sewing Club."

The priest slowly tapped his fingertips together, studying her. "This way, please."

He led her up a staircase to the organ loft. Then he unlocked a door in the stone wall and took her up two more flights on a narrow spiral staircase. The door he unlocked at the top of the stairs opened onto a vast dusty attic, apparently above the nave's ceiling.

Only as Kirstin's eyes gradually adjusted to the murk did she realize that the attic's floor was crowded with blankets and bags. Perhaps a hundred people lay there, waiting. Some of them stood up to get a better look at her. There were people of all ages, dressed in their best travel clothes.

"How many can you take?" the priest asked.

"Maybe fifteen?" Kirstin wanted more time to think. She hadn't expected to be smuggling yet more Danish Jews that day. How much room was there in her truck? Did she have enough gasoline?

"Where am I supposed to take them anyway?"

The priest turned to her with surprise. "Why, to the Elsinore Sewing Club. At the harbor in Gilleleje."

She nodded woodenly. "All right."

An old man with a long white beard stepped forward. "Children first. Please, take my Hebrew class."

A group of children assembled beside the Hebrew instructor. They ranged in age from about seven to fifteen. Instead of suitcases, they wore matching red knapsacks. They could have been kids from any village school in Denmark.

"Let's go," Kirstin said, a lump in her throat. What did she think she was doing? She had no way to guarantee the safety of these children. Their parents and their teacher had no reason to trust her, but no one was objecting.

At the bottom of the stairs the priest stopped to unlock the iron donation box. He withdrew a roll of banknotes the size of his fist, bound with a rubber band.

"The congregation has raised a donation for the sewing club," he said, handing the wad of cash to Kirstin. "It's only five thousand crowns, but I'm hoping the club will charge less for children."

Kirstin took the roll of money, her throat dry. "Thank you."

"Let me know if the sewing club needs more. They're the ones taking the biggest risks."

Kirstin helped the children into the back of the truck. Then she drove north toward Gilleleje. The village faced the Kattegat Sound toward Jutland rather than the Øresund Strait toward Sweden. Kirstin reasoned that the resistance must have chosen Gilleleje in the hopes that its harbor would be less closely watched.

When she reached the center of the village and turned downhill toward the port, however, she found the street blocked by a police car with flashing lights. A policeman waved her to a stop. Even if she had been confident about using reverse gear there was no room to turn around. The officer wore a sidearm at his hip. She was trapped.

"Out of the truck, please. May I see your papers?"

Until the policeman spoke it hadn't really struck Kirstin that the officer was Danish. Now she noticed that the car was labeled *Politi* instead of *Polizei*. The man's cap had a checkered band and his trousers had a red stripe. She climbed down from the driver's seat and held out her driver's license, hoping that she might yet be able to talk her way out of disaster.

The officer frowned at the license. "You were born in 1873, Fru Andersen. Do you often drive trucks?"

"I'm just filling in today."

"Filling in." He repeated the phrase skeptically. "The Gestapo reports that there's been an increase in suspicious activity near the ports recently."

"Really?"

"The Germans are short handed at the moment, so they've asked local authorities to check everyone approaching the harbor." He glanced past her. "What's in the truck?"

"A delivery." Kirstin tried to act casual, but couldn't help swallowing.

"Mind if I take a look?"

Should she say yes or no? Fear left her paralyzed. This was her worst nightmare. Why had she agreed to take this second load of refugees? She had already helped the Bohrs and the Gustmeyers escape. Now the children would be deported and she would go to prison.

The policeman unlatched the back of the truck. The door swung open, revealing a cowering crowd of terrified children.

The policeman sighed. "Who is this delivery supposed to be for?"

Kirstin almost choked on the answer. "The Elsinore Sewing Club."

The policeman closed the truck door. "Just checking. I was told to keep an eye out for anything suspicious."

Kirstin blinked at him. "You don't really mean I can go?"

He nodded. "*Joda.*"

She pulled the roll of banknotes out of her pocket. "Do you need to see some paperwork?"

He laughed and waved her on. "Save it for the sewing club."

CHAPTER 19
THE NORTH SEA, 1003

The sea was full of dragons.

Serpent prows with gaping maws bobbed on the waves as far as Lifu could see. Each of the ocean steeds lifted twenty-two oars at once. The rows of wooden blades resembled great brown wings, beating the water, flying against a fresh salt wind. Seagulls accompanied the dragons past the low sand islands of Frisia toward England.

Lifu rowed. Beside her Grady rowed. Nearly everyone rowed except the tillerman in the back and the helmsman in front. Even the Danish king pulled an oar, his broad back bending along with the rest.

Most of the two hundred and twelve ships in the Danish armada held fifty men. Those dragons rode low enough that the oarsmen pulled against pegs in the gunwales. Svein Forkbeard's longship, however, held sixty-four. Its flanks were so tall that the oars pierced a row of holes beneath the warriors' shields. Each oarsman sat on a wooden box, a sea chest with a few personal belongings — and room enough for the return voyage's silver.

Svein had named his flagship *Grendel's Grandmother* as an alliterative Viking joke. But now the verse-monster had been roused from its lair to avenge a murdered princess in Oxford. When they set sail from Hedeby the skalds had spoken of poetic justice. Lifu worried about what kind of justice they might really be bringing.

The king had emptied Denmark's ring-forts and put eleven thousand men to sea.

After the St. Brice's Day Massacre Lifu and Grady had smuggled Frida across the English Channel to Normandy by claiming that the ten-year-old girl was their daughter. Bribing the fishermen had required all of Lifu's tact and much of their silver. At Bayeaux they discovered that none of the Norman Vikings spoke English. Only a few of the oldest remembered Norse, having switched long ago to French. With difficulty they learned that King Aethelred had recently abandoned his English wife and married Emma, the sister of Richard II, Duke of Normandy. Aethelred evidently imagined this alliance would protect him against retaliation for the Danish massacre. Lifu suspected, however, that the Norman French were laughing at him behind his back. Why would they be interested in attacking their Danish cousins? Now that the Normans had a viable claim to the English throne they would be casting covetous glances at England itself, a far richer and closer prize than Denmark.

No Norman ships were sailing north that winter, so Lifu and Grady bought ponies for the dangerous overland trek to Denmark. A month later, on a snowy evening in the dark of Yule, they finally arrived at the Danevirke Gate to Hedeby.

They found Svein Forkbeard in the royal hall, so drunk on mead that it was his twelve-year-old son, Prince Knud, who ordered servants to take them in. Knud was taller than his cousin Frida and nearly as handsome, but with an oddly hooked nose that made him look much older.

The next day it was long past noon before the king felt fit enough to receive them. He listened with his head in his hands as Frida, Grady, and Lifu each told what they had seen in Oxford. The events were no less barbaric in the retelling. Svein's sister, Princess Gunhild, had been burned alive in a church along with her husband Palling and hundreds of unarmed Danes. Young Eric had been run through by one of Aethelred's swordsmen. Other soldiers had raped and strangled Svein's niece Sigi. Then they had defiled her corpse in front of an English mob by cutting a bloody cross into her naked breast.

Svein rose up, his face white. He paced around the hearth taking deep breaths. When he could finally speak, his words shook out like broken icicles. The English were monsters. Their king was a feckless coward. The slaughter of innocents called for more than retribution — it called for change. Aethelred had attempted to exterminate the people of the Danelaw. Now, Danish law would answer.

Forkbeard spent the next six months in preparation. He waited until June, when the crops were sown and new ships had been built. During that long spring Lifu fell back into her old role as tutor, teaching Frida,

Knud, and the other children of the royal household. Grady returned to his old smithy, forging weapons for the gathering army.

When the day came to sail from Hedeby's docks, Knud wanted to go, but was told by his father that he was too young. Surprisingly, Frida also wished she could return to England. The girl was homesick. But it was decided that Lifu would first need to establish herself as Duchess of Oxford. Then, because she and Grady had no children of their own, they agreed that they would foster Frida as the duchy's heir.

Now, as the longships cleared the tip of the last Frisian island, the headwind shifted to port. The helmsman Theowulf, a giant man with piercing blue eyes, scanned the horizon's clouds. He sniffed the air. Then he called out, "Oars up! Prepare to raise the mast!"

Theowulf lifted a coiled lur-horn to his lips and blew three rising notes to alert the other crews to the order. One after the other, horns on the other ships began answering the call.

Shipping all the oars at once was a dance the crew had practiced in calmer seas. Each pair of rowers had to pull their oar in across the ship without hitting their neighbors. There was so little room on the deck for storage that the oars had to be lifted to racks and lashed in place.

Lifu and Grady were the least experienced in this exercise. The sailors behind them lent a hand, swinging their oar up to the rack.

Shipping the oars was awkward, but it was nothing compared to the dangerous task of raising the mast. Half the crew lifted one end of the massive forty-foot tree trunk, dangling its tip overboard at the stern. Meanwhile the rest of the crew began pulling it upright with ropes. Until the ropes could be secured, the rolling of each wave threatened to wrench the log loose. If it fell to the deck it could crush a dozen men.

Finally the mast stood amidships, a red-and-white pennant at its top streaming in the brisk wind. The breeze would make for swift sailing, but it complicated the raising of the sail. Teams of men heaved on ropes through pulleys. Sailcloth flapped erratically below the rising boom. With each gust the ship tilted. Boxes slid across the deck. Sheets whipped loose. Lifu and the others scrambled up to the windward gunwale, trying to balance the ship before it could tilt too far and capsize.

When the sail was up, cocked at a slant to catch the wind, the slender dragon shot forward through the waves like a live fish. Leaning hard against the handle of the rudder the tillerman steered north, angling away from the Frisian coast. Splash after splash, the prow bucked ahead. Wind whipped Lifu's hair, but what took her breath away was the sight of the sails. Svein had ordered a new design woven for the assault — red as blood, with the white cross of Denmark across the middle. Everywhere the giant sail-banners strained against the wind.

The swarm of dragons split the waves.

The sea belonged to the Danes.

By day each of the eleven thousand men believed what Svein had told them, that England lay helpless before them. As night approached they all worried that it might be a trap.

The midsummer sun swung low to the northwest, as if to light distant Iceland, the stormy home of the North's most renowned skalds. The crew gathered near the mast, where the king had removed a floorboard. He brought up bundles of flatbread for dinner. Men dipped horns of fresh water from a cask and sat shoulder-to-shoulder along the gunwales, eating. Lifu was the only woman, but she joined them, sitting on a box beside Grady.

The king sat amongst the crew with his two-pronged beard and his gilded silver helmet. "Skalds!" he called out. "Sing us the saga of

Slesvig Fjord!"

Three men stood up. For the next hour they declaimed a series of verses about Svein's rise to power. The story interested Lifu because the crucial sea battle at Hedeby had fallen in the eight-year gap she had mysteriously lost. Although this version had obviously been composed to denigrate Harald Bluetooth and extol his rebellious son, many of the details sounded credible.

According to the saga, Harald's jarls had been waiting at Sliasthorp, the island base across the fjord from Hedeby. When Svein's fleet appeared, gathered from the ring-forts, he managed to block the mouth of the fjord, penning in Harald's ships. Rather than face a siege or flee inland, Harald chose to row out to meet the rebels. The priests of Hedeby tolled their church bell, praying for victory. But Harald's ships were outnumbered, thirty to fifty.

Harald had chosen Jarl Haakon as his helmsman. Haakon had insisted on bringing his warrior daughter Vilbi on board as an archer. All day as the battle raged, the fjord grew redder with blood. Emptied ships were set loose. When Harald was down to just ten ships he bent over to help a fallen comrade. In that moment an arrow caught him in the side where his chain mail exposed a gap. He cried out, pulling the arrow free with his own hands. But after that he no longer had the strength to wield his sword.

By evening Haakon advised the king that they should raise their sails and flee to Pomerania. There the queen had relatives and Harald might recover from his wound.

Harald agreed, but first he told Haakon, "I have been too generous, my old friend. I gave you my sword thinking that you, as my helmsman, would need it more."

Haakon looked at the bloody sword in his own hand. "Why is this so generous? Because it belonged to your grandfather, King Gorm?"

"No," Harald replied. "Because its power was granted by the gods. The man who wields Fenris is invulnerable to the steel of warriors."

Haakon frowned at the blade, considering the ancient runes that decorated it. If the legend was true, perhaps there was still hope. He commanded the crew, "Take the king to Pomerania. Vilbi and I will remain to win the battle." Then he jumped to another ship and continued the fight.

Lifu shivered in her woolen cloak. The skalds had stopped, as if their telling of the battle verse had run aground. The sun had sliced into the sea, bringing a chill breeze.

"Is that all?" Lifu asked.

Svein glared at her, switching his gaze from her blue eye to her green one and back. "That is the saga."

"But what happened next?"

Svein grumbled. "The curse didn't work. Haakon died. I set his ship on fire. He sank in his armor together with the sword."

"And Vilbi?"

"She managed to swim free but was hit by an arrow. We found her the next day on a beach. I buried her with honors on Warriors' Hill, overlooking the battle site."

It was Grady who spoke next. "That wouldn't seem to be proof, Your Highness. The sword might still have been charmed. Haakon died of fire and water, not steel."

The king was shaking his head. "No. I found out later that Gorm had the wrong sword all along." Svein pulled a blade from the scabbard at his side. The steel sang. The last light of the sun caught its blade, flashing off the damascened steel, the delicate etchings, and the runic name: FENRIS.

Lifu caught her breath. "How is this possible? Did you dive into the fjord to retrieve the sword?"

"No, Gorm's sword still rests beneath the waves at Hedeby. But what manner of magic did it really possess? My grandfather had originally received the sword as a wedding gift from the Caliphate of Cordoba."

Lifu nodded, remembering. "That is true. I recall Gorm talking about it on his death bed. He said the sword was a gift of the Arabs. But he also thought it must have been forged somewhere else, long ago. Despite the runes he called the sword Holger and said it had the power to save Denmark. His wife Thyra didn't like the sword. She said it wins victories, but at the cost of evil."

Lifu reached out to touch the blade. Then she drew her hand back. "This looks like Fenris. Is it really a different sword?"

Svein slid the sword back into its scabbard. "Gorm was deceived. Long ago, when the sultan of the Caliphate first found the sword, he had a copy made. The Arab smiths are cunning with such work. The sultan kept the original. When he was a very old man he heard the saga of my victory in Slesvig Fjord. He knew the false sword had been lost. The sultan sent me the real Fenris, the original, as a wedding gift when I married."

Lifu weighed these words. If there were indeed two swords, how could Svein be sure that the original was in his scabbard and not at the bottom of a fjord? The only way to test its power would be to let a warrior attempt to kill the king. She doubted that even Svein would submit to such a proof.

Aloud Lifu mused, "The Arabs worship Allah. They are fighting the Christian kingdoms from the south. A clever sultan would want to open a northern front in that war by arming a pagan king in Scandinavia. Especially if the Caliphate had come across a bit of dark magic."

Svein smiled, tapping the sword's hilt. "And with that gift our attack will be unstoppable."

"Sunset!" The helmsman Theowulf called from the ship's prow. "I'll start the night's count. Should we continue due west, Your Highness?"

"Stay the course," Svein replied.

The other crewmen looked at each other. One asked, "What is our course?" Another suggested, "We're too far north for the Isle of Wight."

Lifu asked, "Are we going up the Thames to Oxford?"

Svein waved these comments aside. "If we sail up the Thames we'll be stopped by the weirs at London Bridge. Then we'd lose half the army trying to storm London's walls. The Isle of Wight would be a better approach if we were attacking overland from the south. But we've landed at Wight so often they'll be expecting us there."

A crewman asked, "Then where are we going, Your Highness?"

"To the heart of the Danelaw. On the solstice all the thanes from England's east gather for the Thing Meet at Oundle. This year I think it's time that they be joined by the thanes of Denmark."

"Why?"

Svein looked about at the dark faces but could not determine who had spoken. "At the Meet we will learn exactly how much damage Aethelred has done. Then we'll ask the Law Speaker what we are entitled to demand as compensation."

Lifu nodded. "It is always best to let the law speak instead of a sword."

The king grunted. "Vikings are men of their word, but also men of the sword. Now get some sleep, all of you."

Crewmen spanned canvas tents above the deck. Men rolled themselves in blankets and curled up on the deck's planks. Lifu huddled with Grady in the prow near Theowulf. The giant helmsman stood there, mumbling to himself as he stared out at the stars.

Lifu couldn't sleep, listening to Theowulf's muttered chant, the slosh of the waves, and the shiver of the sails in the wind.

When the helmsman finally stopped mumbling to pick up a lurhorn, Lifu asked, "What on earth have you been chanting?"

"Me?" Theowulf stood there in the dark. "The *Heimskringla*."

"The saga of the Norwegian kings?" Lifu asked, bewildered. "Why?"

"It takes seven hours to recite. That's how much time we have until sunrise at this latitude."

Lifu marveled, "You recite a saga as a clock?"

"It works. After each chapter I sound the horn to keep the fleet together."

Theowulf lifted the spiral tubing to his lips and blew a long, mournful tone — two falling notes. Soon the same two notes began answering across the blackness of the sea from other helms.

In the dark the fleets' tillermen adjusted course, aiming their dragons as one toward the heart of the Danelaw.

* * *

There was no land in sight at dawn. Even the seagulls had turned back. A layer of clouds left the sea as gray as freshly honed steel. The endless wave-points could have been knives, stabbing at the dragons from the deep. For the younger soldiers in Forkbeard's army — those who had never awakened to the vastness of the World Ocean — this was a morning of fear. Older hands whittled spoons from scraps of wood or played dice on the floorboards.

When a faint purple line appeared on the horizon at midday, a cheer spread from ship to ship. Still heading west with a brisk wind, the red sails clipped past a low headland into The Wash, a broad bay that extended into the middle of the Danelaw. White surf rumbled along the shores of Norfolk to the left and Lincolnshire to the right. A herd of sheep startled across a pasture, clanking the tinny bells at their necks. The distant tolling of church bells carried across the water.

Lifu had never before seen this eastern shore of England. She marveled at how much it resembled Denmark. If it weren't for the occasional church spire the low green fields on either side of The Wash might have been Danish islands.

When the fleet reached the end of the bay in the afternoon, the helmsmen blew a lur-horn to signal that the crews should lower the sails and stow the masts. With the oars out once again, the king's flagship slipped over a shallow sand bar into a river channel, followed in single file by the rest of the fleet. The river was broad near its mouth, but it soon narrowed and twisted.

After a few hours they ran out of water. The oars on either hand had begun catching in the shore's brush. Keels scraped on the gravel of riffles. Svein ordered his army to pull the ships up onto the bank of a broad pasture.

Then, with an efficiency that Lifu found almost incredible, eleven thousand men turned the pasture into a Viking city. In less than two hours a gridiron pattern of muddy streets appeared between rows of tents. Armed patrols marched about the encampment's perimeter. By nightfall the ships' crews were cooking dinner on campfires.

The king ate no better than the rest, ladling up a bowl of fish stew made with dried cod and barley. When he was told that a local delegation was requesting an audience, Svein belched. "Send them in."

The two men who approached in the firelight were unarmed,

dressed in plain linen tunics and leggings. They introduced themselves as the Thane of Oundle and the Law Speaker's clerk. Speaking Norse with the quaint lilt of English Danes, the thane asked hesitantly, "Have you come in peace, Your Highness?"

Svein wiped his mouth with the back of his hand. "Isn't this the solstice?"

"That would be tomorrow, Your Highness."

"Aren't all free men invited to the Thing Meet in Oundle on the solstice?"

This time the law clerk answered. "Yes, of course, Your Highness. Nearly eight hundred people have gathered for the Meet. And you have brought — how many?"

"Eleven thousand."

The clerk cleared his throat. "We don't usually have so many visitors from the Old Country."

Svein stood up and crossed his arms. He was a head taller than the clerk, and his chest was twice as broad. "The Danes have come to answer King Aethelred's murders. We demand a verdict."

The clerk fell back half a step, his hands raised. "Very well, Your Highness. We'll call a jury tomorrow. But perhaps you could attend with a smaller group? Fifty or so? And just as a reminder, weapons are not allowed."

"Fifty?" Svein said. "Agreed. Now leave us."

The Thane of Oundle raised a trembling index finger. "Just one more thing, Your Highness. This is my pasture?"

The king took a thick ring from his hand and flipped it to the thane. The silver flashed over and over in the firelight.

* * *

In the morning the smoke of Viking campfires blended with the river mist to shroud Oundle's valley in wisps of white. Walking up the hillside with the king's entourage, Lifu felt as if she were climbing into the clouds — as if she might emerge into a higher heaven-world of the gods.

256

And then that was exactly what seemed to happen. The fog thinned overhead, revealing a startlingly blue sky and a low yellow sun. Behind them Oundle lay hidden in the valley's sinuous river of mist. Ahead a vast tableland of fields and forests truly seemed to belong to a brighter, better land.

The Danelaw parliament met in a naturally semicircular bowl at the tableland's rim. Soldiers there demanded that the visitors leave their weapons. Svein unbuckled the scabbard that held Fenris, adding it to a heap of swords and axes. But he also left five men to guard his sword.

"Your dagger?" a soldier asked Lifu, pointing to a crease in the linen at her hip. She withdrew the hidden knife and left it with the others.

The amphitheater was ringed with rock ledges that served as benches. A large crowd of men had already assembled, but room had been saved near the front for the Danish king and his retinue. Lifu — the only woman — drew curious looks as she took a seat between Grady and Theowulf. Before them on a rock outcrop an old man in a white robe was shouting with his eyes closed about the price of goats.

Lifu leaned to the helmsman. "Theowulf, do you have any idea what's going on?"

"That's Ottar, the Law Speaker," Theowulf whispered back. "For three days before the solstice the speaker recites the entire code of law. He was elected not just for his judgement, but also for his memory."

"Aren't the laws written down?"

"Written?" The helmsman eyed her suspiciously. "I've heard people say you dabble in witchcraft."

"Writing is not witchcraft," Lifu objected. "I had a monk teach the skill at my school in Oxford. Anyone can learn to write."

Theowulf grumbled. "Not me. And not Ottar either. He's blind."

Meanwhile the Law Speaker had finished his recitation. He lifted his head and opened his eyes. They were as white and deceptively empty as the fog concealing a Viking army in the valley behind him.

A younger man stepped up onto the rock. Lifu recognized him as the clerk who had visited their camp the night before. He spoke with a voice that filled the amphitheater. "Thanes! Danes! Men of the Danelaw and of Denmark! You have heard our laws. Later in the Thing any of you may propose changes to the law. Every man will be allowed a vote. This year we will also elect a new Law Speaker. Ottar has served us well, but his three-year term has come to an end.

Candidates must have the support of twenty sponsors. Nominations will begin tomorrow."

Murmurs spread through the crowd as people considered which man among them might deserve such a post. Their earnestness suggested to Lifu that the Law Speaker carried as much responsibility as an archbishop, if not a king.

"First, however," the law clerk shouted, raising his arms to quiet the crowd, "We are here to judge the claims of those who feel that laws have been broken this past year. In deference to our guests from Denmark, it has been decided that their case should be heard first."

Ottar, the white-bearded Law Speaker, held up a staff of twisted wood. "Svein Forkbeard, King of Denmark! Step forward and state your charge."

Svein stood up and faced the crowd. With his gilt helmet, chain mail tunic, and two-pronged beard, he looked every inch a Viking warrior. He raised a fist and bellowed to the crowd, "Hear my words, men of the English Danelaw! I charge your king Aethelred with the murder of my sister Gunhild and her family."

"Murder is the highest of crimes," Ottar said. "Do you have witnesses to support your charge?"

"I have two witnesses." Svein pointed to Lifu and Grady.

Ottar nodded. "Then I hereby call for a jury to hear your case." He considered for a moment with his eyes closed. Then he called out the names of twelve men. Most were jarls and prominent citizens, but a few were farmers and tradesmen. They came from all over the Danelaw, from Cambridge to York. One by one they made their way through the crowd and took their places in chairs to one side of the Law Speaker's rock. When the jurors had settled, Ottar said, "Call your witnesses, Svein Forkbeard."

Grady spoke first. He stammered and had to be told repeatedly to raise his voice. When it was Lifu's turn, however, her voice rang out clearly. In grim detail she described the blood, the mob, and the fire.

Everyone leaned forward, listening. People gasped in horror.

"Did you not see similar murder with your own eyes?" Lifu demanded of the jurors. "King Aethelred's order was to kill every Dane in England."

The jurors shook their heads. The Jarl of York stood to speak. "Soldiers in the Danelaw received the king's order, but chose to ignore it. Most of them are Danes themselves."

A murmur from the crowd acknowledged the logic of this. Soldiers could hardly be expected to kill their own families.

The jarl continued, "The massacres on St. Brice's Day took place in the borderlands outside the Danelaw. Although we did not witness these murders we have all heard of the violence. And this raises a question for the Law Speaker. Are crimes committed outside the Danelaw within our jurisdiction?"

Ottar stroked his beard. The veins in his white eyes rolled down and then rolled back up. "The alleged crimes deal with Danes, so the complainant is entitled to a verdict under our law. Enforcing a sentence, however, would be a different issue. For now, we ask only a verdict of the jury."

The twelve men moved their chairs together. After a few minutes' discussion the Jarl of York once again stood up.

"Do you have a decision?" Ottar asked.

"First we have another question of law," the jarl replied. "The charge is against King Aethelred but the actual killings were committed by his soldiers. Who is responsible, the man who gives the order or the ones who carry it out?"

Ottar's eyes once again rolled back into his head, as if searching within his brain for an answer. At length he said, "If the man who gives the order has sufficient power over his servants, he is responsible for the results of his orders. The servants themselves are accountable only if they exceed the order or benefit from it personally."

The Jarl of York nodded. "In that case our verdict is unanimous. We find Aethelred, our king, guilty of the murder of Princess Gunhild and her family."

Svein raised both fists and roared — a terrifying growl that made the hairs on Lifu's neck stand on end.

"Death to Aethelred!" Svein cried.

"No," Ottar objected. "That is not our way." He thumped the rock with his staff until he won the attention of the angry Danish king.

"What? Aethelred is guilty!" Svein shouted. "He deserves to die."

Ottar shook his head. "The English have no law, but they have a saying, 'An eye for an eye and a tooth for a tooth.' That creed of vengeance would make the whole of England blind. Sometimes I wonder if it has."

The white eyes of the Law Speaker stared out in defiance at the crowd. "The Danelaw knows no penalty of death. Crimes are punished with fines. Silver is paid to settle scores. Even repeat offenders do not face death, but rather are banished from the land as outlaws."

Svein scoffed, "I've found it is hard to banish a king without killing him."

The Jarl of York commented, "And I've heard that Svein Forkbeard loves silver. How much would he be entitled to collect for his losses?"

Ottar rolled back his eyes, as if to reread the wording of the law. "The *wergild* in compensation for killing a free man is one hundred pounds of silver. Payment for a free woman is fifty pounds. Slaves and children are ten. That would mean Svein is due one hundred and fifty pounds of silver for the loss of Gunhild and Palling. Their two children were of age, so that would double his payment. Altogether he is owed three hundred pounds of silver."

"That's all?" Svein demanded.

"That's all. Others who lost relatives on St. Brice's Day may press their own claims."

"And how am I to collect this fee?"

Ottar's eyes rolled down, staring straight through the Danish king. "That is up to you."

* * *

A different meeting took place that night in the Oundle pasture by the river. While the Viking army celebrated Midsummer's Night with drink and bonfires, Svein Forkbeard convened a summit of his top advisers in the king's spacious tent. Torchlight flickered from a circle of solemn faces. There was no table in the center, but rather a red woolen carpet spread on mats. At one end the king sat on a folding throne, his ring-clad fingers gripping the carved dragon heads of the armrests. His helmsman Theowulf, several captains, and half a dozen notables from the Danelaw sat on sea chests around the edge of the carpet. Lifu, Grady, and a score of others stood in a larger circle behind them.

"We have a verdict," Svein said. "The Thing has granted me the right to collect three hundred pounds of silver, but not to kill Aethelred."

"I think the verdict was broader, Your Highness," Theowulf commented. "You also have the right to claim compensation if any servants of the king went beyond his orders or benefitted from them. That could include the soldiers and townspeople in Oxford. I imagine many of them have taken over the property of your sister."

"Is this true?" The king looked to Lifu.

She nodded. "Most of the duchy has been confiscated. Aethelred gave some of it to the Church and distributed the rest to his supporters."

"Then this does justify a broader campaign," Svein mused. "I think the warriors celebrating outside tonight are eager to collect a bigger prize than a single bucket of silver."

"Perhaps, Your Highness, the English crown itself?" The Jarl of York sat on the edge of his box seat. "Anger runs deep in the Danelaw against Aethelred. I have five hundred men who would march with you tomorrow if your goal is London."

Svein raised an eyebrow. "You would have us kill Aethelred despite the verdict?"

"Our king doesn't fight, Your Highness. He sits in his London palace like a pig in a sty. If you defeat the English army you won't have to kill Aethelred. He will run away to France with his new Norman wife and leave the throne to you."

Svein leaned back, slowly stroking his beard. His fingers twirled the twin tips into points.

"Your words raise two questions, jarl. First, do I want to be king of England?"

"You would be a better leader than Aethelred, Your Highness."

"Or would I become like him, a pig in a sty? London is no place for a Viking. The heroes of the North fight their own battles, sail their own ships, and drink mead in the stave halls of their ancestors. The day I am crowned king in London will be the day I give up my seat in Valhalla."

Theowulf said, "Most of the men who sail with you aren't ready to settle in England either, Your Highness. We can teach Aethelred a lesson with our summer raids and then return with our silver to winter feasts in Denmark."

"That would be my choice as well," Svein agreed.

"A pity," the jarl said. Then he turned again to the king. "You said my words raised two questions, Your Highness. What was the other?"

Svein frowned, thinking back. "Oh yes. You suggested that you might help me defeat the English army. Where in the name of Thor's thunder are they? Does anyone know?"

The men on sea chests looked at each other, shrugging.

"I do, Your Majesty." A voice from the back had spoken in English.

Svein switched to English. "Who speaks? Step forward."

A small man with dark hair and an underbite made his way to the center of the carpet. "I am Edowic, chamberlain of the Earl of Southampton, Your Majesty." He paused and then added, "You speak English, Your Majesty?"

"I was taught by the Duchess of Oxford." Svein switched back to Norse. "Apparently you understand our language but don't like to speak it yourself. Are you a spy?"

"Yes."

Svein blinked. "I like men with the courage to speak honestly. Tell me, English spy, what is a chamberlain?"

"I serve the Earl of Southampton, Your Majesty."

"You've told us that already. I asked you what a chamberlain is."

"I am —" The little man groped for words, even in English. "A chamberlain is like one of your helmsmen, but for an earl with no ships."

Theowulf ran a hand over his face. "Sounds like a useless twit. Do you really know the location of the English army?"

"They're in Sussex. Aethelred expected that you would land at the Isle of Wight, as usual."

"This is too much honesty," Svein said. "Apparently you are a traitor as well as a spy."

"No, Your Majesty." The chamberlain lifted his head. "I was sent by the earl to study your laws at the Thing Meet. Many of Aethelred's nobles are unhappy with him. He uses Roman law. In that system, all authority and judgements come from the king. The Danish method seems to work the other way, with authority coming from the bottom up. Juries decide guilt. People have a say in the creation of new laws. Dukes and earls can overrule the king."

"Not often," Svein said. He frowned. "Are you suggesting that the English nobles want to join the Danelaw? That they would crown a Danish king?"

"No, Your Majesty," the chamberlain said quickly. "They would prefer an English king. But they would like the rights of Danes."

Svein tapped the dragon head of his armrest, thinking. "You have just heard me say that I do not wish to be the king of England. You know that I would rather sail back to Denmark each fall. Is this why you are willing to betray your own army?"

The man jutted out his jaw even further. "Aethelred has sent five thousand soldiers to Southampton, Your Majesty, but they are running wild. They attack our women and loot our homes. They plunder food from the farms without compensation. In all respects but one, they are a worse plague than your Danish raiders."

"And in what respect are these English brigands better?"

The chamberlain cocked his head as if the answer were obvious. "They are Christians, Your Majesty. They would never attack a church."

The Jarl of York added, "This is a problem, Your Highness. We in the Danelaw are also mostly Christian. We too would prefer that you left the churches in peace."

"But that's where the treasure is," Svein objected, thumping the armrest. "Churches are where priests hoard the silver they steal from you."

"They do not steal, Your Majesty," the jarl said. "We donate silver to the Church because we believe."

"You believe the priests, even when it's obvious they are lying?" Svein eyed him levelly. "Not long ago, when exactly one thousand years had passed since the birth of Jesus, priests announced that he was coming back to judge us. In this apocalypse, as they called it, all of the world's nonbelievers would be ravaged by plagues, volcanoes, horsemen, and other tortures, while the Christians would be lifted to a happy place above the clouds. With this threat they managed to convince the Icelanders to convert. Poppo, the same priest who had baptized my father Harald Bluetooth, fled to Italy to prepare for the second coming of Jesus. He dismantled the ruins of the Roman city of Aquilea and used the stones to build himself a mighty tower. From its height he planned to watch the suffering crowds below while he rose to heaven. But there was no apocalypse. The Icelanders were tricked. Poppo is still in his tower. The priests have lied to all of you."

"They may have merely misread the scriptures, Your Highness," the jarl replied. "Apparently the apocalypse will arrive after one *more* millennium, in the year two thousand."

The Danish king rolled his eyes. "I am not going to wait another thousand years. Churches have the silver I need. If anyone has a better idea for paying my troops, I'd like to hear it."

"I do, Your Majesty," This time a different English voice had spoken up from the back of the tent.

"How many English spies do we have in here?" Svein shook his head in disbelief. "Step forward, whoever you are. You can take the place of the Sussex chamberpot."

"Chamber*lain*, Your Majesty."

"Get out. Make room for the next English backstabber."

The chamberlain hurried away. The man who strode out onto the carpet in his place was so lanky that it looked as if someone had propped up a farmer's tunic with cow bones. A mop of red hair topped his skeletal head. He fell to his knees like a collapsing scarecrow and unrolled a jingling gray cloth before the king, revealing six silver soup spoons and a slender silver bracelet.

"Who are you?" the king demanded, "And what is this?"

"Well, you see, I'm Alfred of Nottinghamshire, Your Majesty. I brung the silver you want."

Even Lifu had trouble understanding the man's English, both because of his odd northern dialect and because every third or fourth word was Norse. Evidently he used this pidgin glossary when negotiating with Danes.

"Six spoons," Svein said with bemused disdain.

"Well, you see, there used to be nine, Your Majesty," the man apologized. "But it cost me three to buy my way in here."

Svein cast a dark glance to the guards at the tent entrance. "Is an audience with the king as dear as that?"

The farmer nodded, his eyes wide. "You Danes drive hard bargains, Your Majesty."

"And what do you propose to bargain for with the rest of this —" the king waved a hand deprecatingly at the spoons "— this massive hoard?"

"Well, we was hoping as how you might come to Nottingham, you see? To free us from the shire reeve."

"Who is this reeve?"

"Ulfcetel, he calls himself. He came out of nowhere six winters ago with two hundred men. They took over the shire and doubled the taxes. Anyone who complains is locked in stocks. Then he takes their farm, you see?"

The farmer caught his breath. He glanced about the faces in the tent with a hunted look, as if one of them might turn him in. "I daren't go back without an army, you see?" He looked to the king, his lips trembling. "I mean Your Majesty, sire."

"Isn't Nottingham within the Danelaw?" Svein asked.

The Jarl of York cleared his throat. "Yes, Your Highness, but this Ulfcetel has chosen to secede. Actually, I don't think he's paying tax to Aethelred either."

"Another brigand." The king sighed. "What are Nottingham's defenses?"

"The best, Your Majesty," the farmer said, shaking his bony head. "There's a stone wall six feet high topped with a twenty-foot palisade of sharpened staves. Guards patrol a catwalk along the top, at the ready to sound the alarm. Then there's three soldiers in chain mail standing watch at every gate, you see?"

Still kneeling, the farmer pushed the spoons closer to the king. "We knows as how it's dangerous, Your Majesty. But we're willing to pay, you see?"

"Keep your spoons, Alfred. If the Danes come to Nottingham we'll take our payment directly from the reeve."

Svein Forkbeard rose from his throne. At once everyone in the tent also stood up. "I came here to avenge my sister's murder in Oxford. As usual, it seems that England is awash with calamities. Do we have any other spies with advice for my campaign?"

When no one dared to speak the king waved his hand. "Then leave me to plan my strategy. Theowulf and the Duchess of Oxford may stay. The rest of you, return for instructions at dawn."

As the tent began to empty, Lifu stopped Grady by his arm. She pulled him to the carpet and told the king, "My husband will join us for this council."

"A smith?" Theowulf scoffed.

Lifu turned her eyes on the helmsman. "Yes, Grady is a smith. And I'm a witch, remember?"

The king sat on a sea chest. "There's no use arguing with her. Sit down, all three of you."

Lifu, Theowulf, and Grady pulled up wooden boxes opposite the king. When the last of the other retainers had left the tent, Svein leaned forward and whispered, "Our goal is Oxford. Lifu here is the rightful English duchess. She and her husband are the keys that can open that city's gate."

"Perhaps, Your Highness," the helmsman admitted. "But Oxford lies halfway between us and the English army at Southampton. If they get there first, they'll fortify the city."

"Our army would have a head start," Lifu suggested.

"But roads in the south are in better condition than the roads we will have to travel," Theowulf countered. "And our force is not swift by land. We have always relied on ships for speed."

The king nodded. "We'll have to trick them with a diversion. I'll leave a thousand men here in Oundle to guard the ships. Then I'll lead the rest away from Oxford, north to Nottingham. By the time the English chase us up there they'll be tired and confused. Meanwhile, Lifu can ride to Oxford with her husband."

Grady objected, "This plan seems a little unfair, Your Highness. You're taking ten thousand men to capture Nottingham, but you're asking that Lifu and I capture Oxford by ourselves."

"You're not capturing the city, you're returning home. Oh, I'll find you a few dozen English-speaking soldiers to take along. But to make this work, you can't be coming from Denmark. You're returning from half a year visiting family in Mercia, or Ireland, or something." The king winked. "I'm giving you the easier job. I have to figure out how to open a heavily fortified gate at Nottingham."

"With the help of ten thousand men," Lifu said.

"No, our king needs only one," Theowulf said. "I can open that gate single handed."

"Alone?" Svein sat back. "Were you thinking of borrowing my cursed sword for protection?"

"You can keep Fenris, Your Highness. All I need are nine spears and three arrows."

Svein chuckled, obviously delighted that his helmsman would invent this scale of Viking challenge. "This is the stuff of sagas, Theowulf. Tell me, how would you use so few tools to capture Nottingham?"

Theowulf spread his hands to lay out his plan. "The guards will be watching for a larger attack. At night, one man should be able to slip up to the palisade unseen. Then I'll insert the spear tips between the staves and climb up the spear-shafts like a ladder."

The king clapped his hands. "Excellent! And how would you deal with the guards in chain mail at the gate?"

"Remember Vilbi, the shield maiden with a sting?"

The king and Lifu both nodded.

"I saved some of her thin metal arrows," the helmsman said. "They fly as silently as owls and pierce chain mail like wasps. Once the guards are stung, I'll open the gate and wave you in."

Svein laughed. "If this works, I promise you first choice of the reeve's treasures."

Lifu asked, "But isn't Oxford your real target?"

The king nodded. "Nottingham is merely a ploy. The plan is to lure the English army as far as Mercia. Once Oxford is behind them, we'll circled around to the west and pillage the city."

"Pillage?" Lifu frowned. "I thought you were only collecting three hundred pounds of silver."

"Yes, of course. But we also want to reclaim any property that has been confiscated from the Danes. Your job, Lifu, is not merely to open the gate. I want you to mark the doors of the houses that were stolen by the English. Perhaps you could use one of your runes."

"The S-rune, for Svein," Lifu said. "I'll put a charcoal thunderbolt on doors that once belonged to Danes. But I don't want another slaughter."

"I understand what you want. Still, you might find an excuse to lure the friendly civilians out of town. You know, the people who were not part of the mob."

Lifu considered this. "I suppose I could invite people to a home-coming celebration at my workshop in the woods. It's usually only for women, but I could say it's a gathering for families."

Grady added, "We should invite everyone who was part of the school too. You can say you're planning to start classes again."

The king nodded agreement. "It would be best if such people were not underfoot on the day my army comes to town."

Grady asked, "And what day will that be, Your Highness?"

"Three weeks?" Svein looked to his helmsman for advice.

"Twenty days should do it, Your Highness," Theowulf replied.

Lifu counted the days in her mind. "That would be July 10, a Saturday."

"Wash day for the Danes," Grady commented.

Svein Forkbeard drew his sword and held it upright in their midst. Torchlight flickered from its damascened steel.

"This time it will be wash day for the English."

CHAPTER 20
OUNDLE, ENGLAND, 1944

The sky was full of dragons.

As the first streaks of dawn lit the east, silver B-17s glinted overhead like morning stars. The dragons that roared loudest were still on the ground, preparing for takeoff from the Polebrook Airfield.

First Lieutenant Julius Gustmeyer ran through the preflight procedures with his co-pilot Randy Kowalsky, checking all one hundred and fifty instruments on the panels of the crowded cockpit. That morning the twenty-five crews of the 351st Heavy Bombardment Group at Polebrook had been roused from their bunks at three a.m. for a breakfast of real eggs — a treat reserved for men facing combat.

Julius' stomach churned nonetheless. This was his fifth mission over the Continent, and their target was Hamburg. Heavily defended, the Reich's biggest port had once been one of his favorite destinations, just a fifteen-minute flight from the Danish border in his Fokker monoplane.

Today their bombing run would take them within sight of Schleswig Fjord. He hadn't heard from Mette in nearly a year. Was she still excavating a ship there? Would she look up and see the contrails of the Eighth Air Force? Was she still wearing his ring?

"*Lucky Lady,* you're cleared for takeoff." The voice in his headphones sounded almost cheerful. But every pilot knew this was one of the most dangerous parts of the mission. The week before, two B-17s fully loaded with bombs and fuel had touched wingtips while turning onto the runway. The resulting explosion had rattled windows four miles away in Oundle.

Julius glanced to his co-pilot. "All clear, Ski?"

Second Lieutenant Kowalski, also wearing a leather flight jacket and officer's cap, gave him a thumbs up. "Let's go, Gable."

Kowalski was a freckled kid from Pittsburg, eight years younger than Julius. None of the eight other crew members was older than twenty. Lately "Ski" had begun trying to grow a mustache, inspired by the pencil-thin Clark Gable mustache Julius had allowed himself to regrow. From the first, Julius'

nickname at the base had been Gable. Everyone remembered the Hollywood star who had flown five missions from Polebrook the previous year. Major Gable had joined a crew as an observer, but had been awarded the Distinguished Flying Cross nonetheless.

Julius pushed the throttles forward, maddening the propeller roar of four giant engines. The plane shivered and pressed them back into their seats. Hangars and trees began racing past. Within feet of the end of the runway the bomber finally lifted its tires, lumbering up over dark farm fields. Then the ground fell away and they were sailing along the valley of the winding River Nene, eastward into the gray of dawn.

Above The Wash — a dark inlet of the North Sea — hundreds of colored flares were slowly falling in streamers through the sky, calling the aerial armada together. To make bases less vulnerable to German attack, bomber groups had been dispersed among more than a hundred airfields throughout the east of England. From Anglia to Yorkshire, more than a thousand crews assembled here, searching for the color combination of their lead plane's flares. When Julius spotted their group's red-green signal he steered into a pattern nearby. Then Ski fired their own red and green flares out the window, adding to the increasingly spectacular display. Once all the groups were accounted for, a vast aerial ballet commenced, grouping formations of thirty-six planes one minute apart in a line that stretched from England to the Continent.

Eleven thousand men were sailing to avenge the Nazis' wrongs.

Over the void of the North Sea, as the plane climbed to cruising altitude, ice crystals began forming on the inside of the cockpit window. The air became too thin to breathe. The plane's aluminum skin was flimsier than the metal of a soda can. Pressurizing or heating the interior was impossible. Instead Julius pulled on an oxygen mask and plugged in a socket to warm the electrical wires in his flight suit.

As the engines droned, Julius had time to think about his parents. At the end of his pilot's training he had been shipped to Ardmore, Oklahoma for assignment to a crew. There they had gone through final B-17 training. Before flying one of the fortresses to England, however, they had all been given a week's leave to say final farewells to family. By then Jakob and Claudia Gustmeyer had made their way to Toronto, Canada. They desperately wanted to see their only son before he went to war, but they couldn't get visas to the United States. Julius sent them a telegram, telling them to meet him at the international bridge in Windsor. Then he hitchhiked a day and a half to Detroit and walked across the border with his own brand-new American passport. For the next three days they strolled in lakefront parks and dined at sidewalk cafes, laughing and talking as if the war had never been.

But then news had come of the D-Day invasion. Waves of dead men were washing onto the beaches of Normandy. The Luftwaffe was throwing everything it had at the western front to regain control of the skies. Fru Gustmeyer clutched her son, dampening his neatly pressed officer's shirt with her tears.

His father had shaken his head. No, he hadn't seen or heard from Mette Andersen in more than a year. But her parents had saved their lives. He and Claudia had hidden out in the Andersens' apartment while Magnus sailed to Sweden with Niels Bohr. Even Jakob had no idea how Bohr had managed to convince the Swedish king to accept Danish Jews. But as soon as they had heard the news, Mette's mother had driven them to the Elsinore ferry in a fish delivery truck. When they arrived in the Swedish port of Helsingborg, railway workers had opened their boxcar expecting to find a load of transformers.

"From there, all it took was money to get to Canada," Jakob Gustmeyer said. "But even money won't get us across the next bridge."

Julius held up his new passport. "I'll see to it that you make it into the States."

"Can you really do that?" his mother asked.

"Lars Andersen did it for me."

His mother sighed. "I'd love to live in New York." Then she took his hand earnestly. "You'll join us there?"

Julius nodded. "If I can."

"Can't you promise?"

He had looked aside. "I've already made a different promise, Mother."

"You have? To do what?"

"To find Mette first."

* * *

Now his eyes were damp as he looked out the side window of the cockpit. He wiped his face with his gloved fist and looked again. A faint white stripe stood against the blue. He pressed the intercom button of his headset to call the navigator.

"Hack, what's that land off to the right? Germany?"

A voice squawked in his headphones. "It's a Frisian island, sir. Still part of Holland, I think."

Now Julius noticed that the contrails before them had thinned. "Are all the squadrons heading to Hamburg today?"

"Just ten, sir. The rest are going to bomb the hell out of the Germans in France."

Co-pilot Kowalski put in, "Pray for bad weather over England tonight, boys. Then they'll have to divert us to French airfields. Gay Paree, here we come!"

This had happened once, on a day when the *Lucky Lady's* crew had not flown. Seventeen other crews from Polebrook had spent a day in the newly liberated portion of France. One overzealous pilot had celebrated by flying his B-17 beneath the arch of the Eiffel Tower. The returning crews had reported that liquor was everywhere, but so were booby traps left by the Germans. Two airmen had died after triggering grenades. What France lacked, apparently, was soap. Even now the *Lucky Lady* was carrying two dozen bars of Ivory as trade goods, just in case.

"Twenty minutes to the bombing run," the navigator announced.

"What's our target in Hamburg, Gene?" Julius asked the bombardier. "The submarine docks?"

"No, sir," the bombardier replied. "We got them last year. This time it's housing for the shipyard repair crews. We're carrying incendiary bombs, sir."

Julius tightened his lips. It seemed less heroic to be targeting workers instead of machinery. He had seen the mock-ups at the airbase in Oklahoma. The Army had forced captured German architects to build exact replicas of the barracks used by the Reich's wartime workers. The buildings had been accurate right down to the red tile roofs and beaverboard bedroom walls. Then B-17 crews had trained by blasting the models with different kinds of bombs to see which did the most damage.

Those buildings had been empty. From twenty thousand feet even the real ones in Hamburg would look like dots on a map. It didn't pay to think about the people inside.

"Here comes the welcoming committee," Kowalski said over the intercom. "Messerschmidts at one o'clock high. All right, gunners, let's show them how grateful we are."

The fleet tightened formation, as close as turbulence would allow. Triangles of bombers, nearly touching wingtips, were stacked in all directions like chain mail. But this metal lattice bristled on all side with machine guns.

The German fighter planes dove through them like needles. Engines whining and cannons blazing, the Messerschmidts targeted wing tanks and cockpits. In ten minutes of mayhem, three of the fighter planes spun out of control, trailing black smoke. The deputy lead B-17 dropped out of formation, one of its engines on fire. Julius and

Kowalski counted out loud as the white puffs of parachutes bloomed. Eight. Nine. Ten. All of the crew made it out. But they were over the mouth of the Elbe. It was better not to think what would happen when they landed in water.

"Flak time," Kowalski announced.

"I'm afraid we need to start our bombing run, sir," the bombardier replied.

"Wouldn't you know it." Julius threw the switch that transferred control from the cockpit to the bomb bay. "The ship's yours, Gene." Then Julius dropped his hands and sat back. For the final minutes of the run, as the bombardier sighted in on the target, there would be no evasive maneuvers. All Julius could do was watch as the white puffs of exploding anti-aircraft shells gradually came closer, finding their range. Far below, the German flak gunners would be watching the puffs as well, recalculating distance and elevation. Red rings on their cannons' barrels recorded how often they had found their mark.

A blast shook the *Lucky Lady*.

"It's just my arm," the radioman cried out on the intercom. "The ship took most of it."

"Bombs away," the bombardier announced. A stack of 250-pound bombs began rumbling off a ramp. A moment later he said, "She's yours again, Lieutenant."

Julius pulled the wheel hard to left, banking to match the plane in front of him. As the squadron droned in a giant arc above Hamburg, a plane at the back spiraled downward, missing half a wing. Julius waited for the count. But no chutes opened.

He looked at the ground below. Suddenly he recognized the proud Hansa city laid out like a map — St. Pauli on the Elbe waterfront and the gigantic, gutted spire of the Sankt Nikolai Church on the Alster.

Fires were everywhere. They had not merely destroyed the shipyard barracks. They had ignited a firestorm that would engulf the whole of Hamburg's old downtown.

Tens of thousands of civilians might die in that holocaust.

Was this truly the solution, he wondered — to answer one unholy fire with another?

A voice in his headphones said, "That'll clean out those Nazis."

Like a distant echo, another voice added, "It's wash day for the Germans."

* * *

The next morning most of the *Lucky Lady's* crew went for a two-day leave to London. After a breakfast of bluish powdered eggs Kowalski and the others got on an Army bus that would take them to the train station in Peterborough. From there Piccadilly Circus, the center of the world, was just an hour away.

Julius wished he could go, but this was the solstice. Captain Lars Andersen had suggested they meet in Polebrook to share a pint in celebration of Denmark's Midsummer's Night.

After breakfast Julius dragged himself back to his tarpaper barracks and fell asleep on his bunk with his clothes on. He did not wake up when the bus clattered back on its return trip from the Peterborough station, nor when knuckles rapped on the barracks door.

Finally a hand shook the polished toe of Julius' shoe. "It's Holger Danske himself, sleeping away the ages."

Julius groaned, afraid to open his eyes. The worst moments of his life had been waking up to the garish light of the bright yellow bulb that roused the crew on mission mornings.

Julius squinted and groaned again. The uniform before him had an oak leaf cluster at the collar. "Good God, Lars. You're a major now. Do I have to salute?"

"Let's not and say you did." Lars sat on the end of the cot, creaking the springs. "Besides, I hear you're in line for a promotion too."

"I am? Where did you hear that?" Julius swung his legs to the plank floor.

"I'm with Army Intel, remember? We have our ways." Lars winked. "Just imagine: Captain Gable. You'll have the girls lining up."

Julius was finally awake. "Have you heard from your sister?"

"Maybe. Let's talk about it later."

"Why? Is something wrong? Is Mette OK?"

"I think so, but —" Lars looked out the window.

"But what?"

"It's complicated." Suddenly he changed topics. "Say, I called ahead and booked you a room in Oundle for the party. Let's hike down there and paint the town red."

"Shouldn't a major have a Jeep?"

"Naw, we spies have to sneak everywhere. Grab your AWOL bag, Gable. We're going to see the bright city lights."

When they carried their bags out the base's gate, the sentry snapped to attention and saluted.

Julius said, "Tell me now, Lars. Did Mette get another letter through to you?"

Lars looked back at the airfield's camouflaged hangars as if he had heard a different question. "You know, the Brits built a hundred airfields like this at the start of the war. But they also built a dozen fakes."

Julius responded with a frustrated grumble. His future brother-in-law obviously knew more about the situation in Denmark than he was willing to admit.

"The decoys look more real from the air," Lars continued. "Shiny tin planes. Tidy cardboard buildings. You've probably seen them from the air without knowing the difference."

"Too bad the Luftwaffe gave up trying to attack England."

"From the Nazi point of view you're right. Back in 1940 the RAF was two weeks away from buckling. If Hitler hadn't sent his forces to Russia, we'd be speaking German here."

"Instead England's become a big aircraft carrier for schmucks like me." Julius only used Yiddish words when he was feeling low. The old Jewish language seemed to have so many terms for suffering. He pointed to a rambling manor house at the end of a tree-lined side lane. "Know who lives up there? The Rothschild family. England's Jews donated land for our aircraft carrier's runways."

The paved road to Oundle was empty save for the two men in American officer's uniforms. The track tipped over the edge of the tableland and arced around a broad natural amphitheater. Without a word Julius left the road and followed a sheep path across the grassy bowl to a rock outcropping that overlooked the valley below. A small river — hardly more than a sluggish creek — meandered through green grain fields toward the village's strip of small stone buildings.

Behind him Lars asked, "Do you come here often?"

Julius nodded. "When I get tired of speaking English I sit out here and think like a Dane. I guess because we're in the middle of the old Danelaw here."

"The Danelaw? What's that?"

"A thousand years ago this whole part of England was settled by Danish Vikings. Sometimes I can even picture their ships struggling up that creek. Red sails with white crosses. Voyagers from the Old Country."

"I don't miss Denmark. I'm certainly not looking forward to going back." Lars turned to walk back to the road.

Suddenly angry, Julius walked quickly to catch up. "Then why the hell did you come out here for Midsummer's Night? We could have been in London. There they have dance clubs and theaters. Noel Coward has a new play, *Blythe Spirit*, that's supposed to be a riot. The Red Cross is offering free tours of the city to American servicemen. Gorgeous British girls take you to see the Tower of London and then home to meet Daddy and Mummy for tea. I thought that was the sort of thing you like."

Lars stopped on the sheep path. "London's not safe."

"It's not?"

"Not now. Hitler has developed a new kind of rocket to repay us for your bombing raids."

"His V weapons aren't so dangerous." Julius knew that the *V* in the rockets' name stood for *Vergeltungswaffe* — payback weapon. But the missiles were clumsy, badly aimed, and slow enough to shoot down easily.

"The V-2 rockets are different," Lars said. "They're powered by jet engines. They're too fast to intercept. The warheads are bigger. And they've perfected the guidance system. Now they're able to pinpoint downtown London. Even the clubs and theaters where servicemen hang out. We've got nothing to stop them. Nothing."

"That's why you're in Oundle?" Julius asked, dumbfounded.

"Partly. We need to talk, but we're not supposed to. Loose lips sink ships. We're both going to need a pint or two first."

A lorry crested the road's downslope and threw on its air brakes, snorting like a drowning bull. Julius ran to the road's shoulder and stuck out his thumb. "Come on. I'm buying at the Oundle pub."

The truck pulled over. "Throw your bags in back."

The back of the lorry was full of carrots. Lars and Julius tossed their bags on top and climbed in front beside the driver. Soon they were careening down the left-hand side of the narrow road.

"Are carrots rationed?" Julius asked.

The driver laughed so hard he had to pound the steering wheel. "They're too healthy. Haven't you seen the posters for Doctor Carrot?"

Julius shook his head.

"They're trying to get everyone to eat carrots now instead of stuff we import." The driver aimed his thumb to the load in back. "This lot's going to the brewery."

"Good Lord," Lars said. "Don't tell me they're making beer out of carrots."

"I wish. The carrotade they bottle is so vile you have to choke it down. Why, they even freeze it to make ice lollies for the kids."

"Carrot popsicles?" Julius couldn't help smiling.

"On a bloody stick." The driver shifted down as they approached the first of the stone cottages lining the road in Oundle. He shifted his voice to a lower gear as well. "Just between you and me, carrots is our secret weapon. Eating carrots lets you see in the dark. That's why our Poms have night vision and the Krauts don't."

The driver pulled to a stop at a small triangular roundabout — Oundle's modest version of Piccadilly Circus. Lars and Julius got out, fetched their bags, and thanked the driver for the ride.

The driver pulled his cap lower over squinty eyes. "It's not just you Yanks. Carrots is why we'll win the war."

When the truck had left Julius said, "Welcome to the bright city lights. What you see of Oundle is what you get."

Lars turned slowly around, sizing up the village. Everything was made of gray sandstone. Around the central plaza the buildings formed a two-story wall, with slate roofs interrupted by dormers. There was a Barclay's bank, a post office, a shabby tea shop, and a store with a window displaying toy boats and school supplies. A small street up-hill from the plaza led to a church with Gothic window tracery and a tall steeple, all made from the same gray stone. Crooked tombstones crowded the lumpy lawn of its churchyard.

Lars turned his attention to a memorial in the middle of the town plaza. A ten-foot sandstone pedestal topped with a small rusty cross had been dedicated to the young men of Oundle who had fallen in the "Great War 1914-1919." He ran his hand over an inscription from the Bible about the greatest gift that a man can offer, to "lay down his life for his friends."

Lars mused, "Interesting that they don't mention dying for your country, or for democracy, or for a better world."

"The First World War was pointless," Julius said. "Millions died for nothing."

"And now we're doing it all again, but with better equipment."

Lars picked up his bag. "Which way is the Ship Inn?"

"We're staying there? That place is ancient." Julius led the way along the narrow sidewalk of the town's main cobblestone street. After a hundred yards the sidewalk widened in front of a clock repair shop. Among the pendulum clocks ticking in the window was a timepiece he hadn't seen before. A ball bearing rolled slowly past a series of metal baffles until it tilted a brass plate and began rolling back the other way. The effect was mesmerizing.

Lars stopped beside him to watch. "You know, it isn't true about the carrots."

"Hmm?" Julius' thoughts were elsewhere. He wondered if the rolling-ball clock was powered by a spring.

"Vitamin A may be good for the eyes, but it doesn't give you night vision. That's a wives' tale dreamed up by my colleagues in British intel."

Julius turned to Lars. "Why would the Brits invent a story like that?"

"Because the Germans still don't know we have radar."

279

When Julius gave him a blank look Lars whispered, "Radar stands for Radio Detecting and Ranging. We send out radio pulses and pick up the echoes with antennas. The Luftwaffe couldn't figure out how RAF fighter pilots kept finding German bomber squadrons in the dark. So the Brits made a big deal about their pilots eating carrots."

"And the German High Command believed that?"

"They still do. If you're captured and tortured, will you tell?"

"When the Gestapo demands the secret of the carrots, I shall laugh in his face. Meanwhile, I'm about to torture you for a few more secrets about your sister."

"If this torture involves ale, I'm your man." Lars glanced down the street. A sign hanging above the sidewalk had a painting of a three-masted sailing ship. "Ahoy! I think I've found our harbor."

A chalkboard outside the pub bore two messages: "Fish & Chips 50p" and "Manchester Vs Arsenal 11:30." Red geraniums bloomed in boxes above bay windows on either side of a low black door. Inside, Lars nearly stumbled down two steps to a dim hallway lined with photographs of cricket teams. Another low doorway to the left opened onto a smoky dining room beneath sagging wooden ceiling beams painted a shiny black. One entire wall was taken up by an alcove that must once have been a gigantic fireplace. Now it housed a radio with a glowing dial. Half a dozen old men with pipes sat on stools around it, listening intently to an announcer's excited chatter.

At the other end of the room Lars and Julius found a barman wiping glasses. "Oh yes," the man exclaimed. "Our American guests." Then he stopped. "Major Gable? This is a surprise."

"Actually, my name's Gustmeyer," Julius admitted. "The mustache confuses people. I'm Danish. The truth is, we're both Danes."

"Danes, is it? We don't see many of them here." The barman opened a registry for them to sign. "A pound each for the rooms. The kitchen's open till eight."

As Julius took out his money he couldn't help commenting, "I was told everyone is Danish here. Wasn't this whole area settled by Danes?"

The barman puzzled a moment. Then he laughed, "Oh, you mean the Vikings! We did have our share of raiders come through. Bloody brutal, I'm told." He held his fingers up beside his head like horns. Then he led the way upstairs. Their rooms faced the street, with thick down comforters on lovely soft beds. A washstand in each room had a ceramic basin and a pitcher, but no soap. A bath with a claw-foot tub was down the hall.

Later, after they had settled in, Lars and Julius met again downstairs. They ordered lunch at the bar and found a quiet table by a window. The courtyard outside was full of barrels and potato plants.

"Why," Julius asked, "Do the Brits think the Vikings had horns on their helmets?"

"Didn't they?"

Julius looked at him and laughed. "You've been away from home too long. Either that, or I've been around your sister too much. No swordsman would put horns on his helmet. The horns would catch every blow."

"But they'd make him look fierce, like a devil."

Julius nodded. "That must have been it. The Anglo-Saxon historians were all Christian clerics writing hundreds of years later. They probably invented the horns so people would remember the Danes as pagan devils."

"Propaganda's half the battle," Lars replied.

The barman brought two amber pints, each with an inch of foam. "Your chips will be up in a tick."

When they were alone again Lars clicked his glass against Julius' and surprised him by switching from English to Danish. "*Skål. Til propaganda.*"

Julius switched to Danish as well. "We don't really need to speak in our secret code, do we?"

"*Joda.* That's why the Army assigned me to deal with the Danish resistance. You were in the Holger Danske group for a time yourself."

Julius ran his finger idly along the rim of his glass. "I tried to forge Swedish passports for Jews. I even tried to convince Niels Bohr to work for the Allies. Your family had better luck on both counts. All I managed to smuggle out of Denmark was myself." He looked up. "Has the underground been more successful lately?"

"More and more. After D-Day they sabotaged the train lines in Jutland. That delayed the transport of German troops from Norway to France long enough for us to get to Paris."

"Did the resistance lose many men?"

"A few. But the Gestapo also took two dozen captives. And they got the names of a lot more. Maybe even my father."

"They got Magnus?" Julius spoke so loudly that the barman turned to look.

Lars put his finger to his lips. "So far we think the Gestapo only has his name."

"He should escape by sailing to Sweden."

Lars shook his head. "Risky. And we need men like him in Denmark. Se we came up with a plan to destroy the Gestapo's records. The files are kept in their Copenhagen headquarters. You know, in the old Shell building across from City Hall? The problem was, the Gestapo imprisoned the captured resistance fighters on the top floor of the building as human shields."

"Fresh cod and chips," the barman interrupted, sliding two steaming baskets onto the table between them. Each basket was lined with newspaper that had become translucent from the fried food's grease. "And a big bottle of malt vinegar. Eat hearty, lads."

As soon as the barman was gone Julius whispered in Danish, "What did you do?"

Lars ate a fried spear of potato. "While you were diverting the Luftwaffe's attention yesterday, the RAF sent twenty Mosquito bombers and thirty Mustang fighters to Copenhagen. They had special bombs, designed to take out the lower floors of a building without starting a fire."

"Good God. Did it work?"

Lars tilted his head. "We destroyed the Gestapo's records. Eighteen of the captured resistance fighters escaped. But a few of the bombs went astray, hitting a boarding school. That killed a hundred and twenty-five civilians, including eighty-six children."

Julius covered his face with his hands. "Is it all worth it?"

"We think it is, or we wouldn't be here. Look at the bright side. Denmark was the only Nazi-occupied country that rescued its Jews. Even the ones that were sent to Czechoslovakia are being monitered by the Red Cross. They're all right. You and your parents made it to America. Our families are OK."

"And Mette?" Julius asked.

Lars unbuttoned his shirt pocket, took out a blue envelope, and tossed it on the table. "It's been censored and redacted by Army Intel four times. I'm still breaking the regs by showing you what's left."

Julius tore open the envelope, his dinner forgotten. The sheet inside was not in Mette's handwriting, but instead in the block letters of a telegram. Gaps marked the many places where text had been deleted.

DEAR LARS DEAREST JULIUS
BEHOLD ANOTHER MESSAGE IN A BOTTLE. THE
MAILMAN HAS...
I MISS YOU BOTH AND HOPE...
THIS SPRING WE ARE BACK AT HEDEBY, MAKING
PROGRESS DESPITE...
THE SLESVIG SHIP IS NOW MOSTLY IN WATER TANKS.
THE WOOD WAS 90 PERCENT WATER. IT TAKES 9 MONTHS
TO REPLACE THE WATER WITH WAX. NEW BUILDINGS ARE
BEING CONSTRUCTED BY ...
MUCH EXCITEMENT HERE WHEN WE FOUND A GRAVE IN
THE WRECK. A MAN IN HIS FIFTIES, TALL FOR A VIKING. HIS
CHAIN MAIL IS RUSTED, BUT THE SWORD...
WE...
IF ONLY...
DO NOT...
KEEP YOURSELVES SAFE. LOVE TO YOU BOTH.
METTE.

"Are you going to eat your cod?" Lars asked. His own basket was empty.

Julius shoved his fish and chips across the table. "They found the damned sword."

"One damned sword, at least." Lars sprinkled vinegar on the fish. "Although you're right, the colonel in charge of the excavation seems to think it's pretty special."

"What else do you know that's been deleted from this letter?"

Lars wagged his finger. "I've already told too much."

Julius grabbed him by the upper arm, almost knocking over the ale glasses. "Damn it, Lars. Your job is to share intelligence with the Danish resistance. That means me too, brother."

Lars patted Julius' hand and smiled to the barman to let him know that all was well at their table.

"Well?" Julius demanded.

Lars sighed. Then he whispered, "All right. We don't have good intelligence from Germany because it's hard to recruit Germans. So we've recruited some of the Danes on the Hedeby project. They think Hitler's working on a V-3 rocket. Something far bigger and more dangerous than we've seen. Something that could change the war."

Julius swallowed, his mouth dry. "Niels Bohr said the German physicists had formed a Uranium Club. He said a uranium bomb was possible. Where is Bohr now?"

"The Danish newspapers say he's in Moscow."

"Is he?"

"No. That's misdirection from our side. He's in New Mexico with his son, working on an American version of the Uranium Club. We don't know how far the German physicists have gotten. But we think they're moving the rocket base to a part of Germany that's closer to England. That way they could launch a huge payload. With their new guidance system, they could wipe London off the map. For all we know, they could even threaten New York and force us to sue for peace."

Julius had grown pale. "How reliable is this information?"

"Not very." Lars wrinkled his brow. "Mette thinks there's a double agent at the excavation. She doesn't know who to trust. And we don't know what to believe."

Lars picked up his nearly empty glass of ale. He tapped Julius' glass with a clink. "Aren't you glad you asked?" Then he drank the rest of the ale in one go.

Julius stared at him. "What happens now?

"We order two more pints."

"No, I mean to Mette? To us? To the war?"

Lars burped. "You get a promotion and keep flying until you're shot down. I'm being reassigned to the front in France. Now that the Germans have reinforcements from Norway they'll probably launch a counteroffensive."

"Can they still win a ground war?"

"Probably not. The Allies have already decided how to carve up the spoils. The French get the part near France, the Americans get the middle, and the Soviets get the east. I'll be marching with General Montgomery to northern Germany. If rockets don't blow up London first, the Brits are supposed to retake Denmark. Then they'll need a guy like me who speaks the secret code."

"No wonder you're not looking forward to the trip home." Julius poured the rest of his ale into Lars' glass. "Sometimes I think we Danes are doomed to wander the world, always searching."

"Mistaken for horned devils," Lars put in.

"Or worse yet, for the Dutch."

"What do you have against the Dutch?"

"Nothing. It's just humiliating to be confused with people from a different small country. It makes you feel so anonymous. So lost." Julius frowned. "Danes are like ghost ships, forever adrift."

Lars shook his head. "That's the *Flying Dutchman*. Now you're doing it yourself."

"Damn."

Lars leaned back and called out in English, "Barman, bring Captain Gable here another pint. You can't expect thirsty men to save the world."

CHAPTER 21
WINCHESTER, 1013

On the winter solstice, in a frosty English field, it seemed the dawn might never come. The bonfires of the evening's celebration still smoldered, but no one had drunk a drop of mead and few had slept. Five thousand Danes sat inside their tents, fully armored, intoxicated only with the thrill of coming battle.

Aethelred, the English king, was coming to slaughter them in their sleep.

Anticipation was a powerful enough tonic to silence the painful worm that had been growing within Svein Forkbeard all fall. This was his sixth campaign in England in the decade since Aethelred had murdered thousands of Danes on St. Brice's Day. Svein's tormented dreams had already warned him it might be his last.

The Danish fleet had sailed late that year, during a rainy summer that promised only crop failure and hunger at home. Trondejarl, Svein's vassal in Norway, had joined them at sea with forty ships — and news that cold rains were bringing famine to Norway as well. Together they landed at Oundle under sunny skies to discover warm fields of waving wheat. The storms of Scandinavia had missed the British isles. Pigs were fat. Granaries were full. Why go home to starve this winter? When autumn arrived, and with it enormous shipments of French wine to English monasteries, the Norwegians announced they were wintering here, and Svein agreed.

Was he still avenging the murder of his sister Gunhild? Yes, Svein's anger still burned. But the campaigns had gradually become a goal in their own right. Now the burn that hurt worst was the worm. Eaten from within by that nameless monster, he had shrunk to an old man. His two-pointed beard had blanched white, his back had bent, and his muscles had withered. Only the call of battle could fill him again with the strength of a man in his prime.

"They're coming, Father." Knud peered out a slit in the tent's flap. The prince had grown to become a capable and intelligent warrior of twenty-two winters. Although Svein worried that inexperience left his heir too easily guiled, he envied the boy's keen eyesight in what seemed the dark of night.

"Hundreds of shields in the first row," Knud continued, tipping his hooked nose from side to side as he squinted out with one eye or the other. "They've crested the hill and are coming down the field beside the forest, as you predicted."

Svein's heart pumped stronger. He flexed his hand on the hilt of Fenris. "We must wait." He closed his eyes and whispered a command to someone he could not see. "Wait, Trondejarl, until the English are fully committed. Until there is no turning back."

Svein could almost hear the hearts of his men in the tents about him. The sky slowly grayed enough that even Svein could see the top of the hill, now emptied of men. The field above their camp, however, seethed like a silent sea of English shields. Aethelred, he knew, would not be among them. The cowardly king who planned this attack would be safely back in Winchester, protected by a cadre of his best men. Instead the English troops would be led by Edmund, a crown prince no older and no more experienced than Knud. Let Edmund call for the attack! Why was the boy waiting so long? Was he afraid? Did he have a different plan? Already the dawn was near enough that Svein could recognize the dark crosses of St. George on the English shields.

"Charge!" The voice seemed too small and high for a commander, but it was immediately followed by the bellow of an English captain, "Kill the Danes!"

Svein threw the tent flap aside and stood forward with his sword raised. At the same time a shadow passed through the dark blue sky, as if a flock of starlings had taken wing. The feathered arrows of a thousand hidden archers arced out of the edge of the forest and into the flank of the English attackers, felling a hundred in one blow. Their battle cry broke into screams. A second volley flew. The English army faltered, raising their shields over their heads. When they lowered their shields to continue their charge, they were dumbfounded to see that the sleepy tent encampment had vanished behind a solid wall of Danish shields. A white-bearded king at the front raised his sword and roared. As a third volley of arrows launched from the forest, the wall of five thousand Danes began to march forward.

Half of the English force turned — only to discover that the crest of the hills behind them was now picketed with the spears of two thousand Norwegians. Trondejarl's men lowered their spears and ran down the hill, the teeth of a rapidly closing upper jaw.

The slaughter was brief. The Norse had few losses, but within an hour the bodies of two thousand Englishmen littered the field. An equal number had thrown down their weapons and run, scattering to escape as best they could. A circle of English shields had protected Prince Edmund, allowing him and a few score of his men to battle their way out toward Winchester to bring news of the defeat to Aethelred.

Let them go," Svein said, suddenly weary. "England no longer has an army."

And it was only then, when the worm inside him writhed in victory, that the Viking king began to realize what he had done.

* * *

Three days later, on a morning when half of Svein's troops were celebrating Christmas, the delegation Svein had been dreading finally arrived.

A caravan of fifty finely dressed nobles with elegant wagons and proud horses stopped at the top of the hill, where the good road ended. They were quickly confronted by Danish guards, who accompanied them down the length of the battlefield, between rows of stacked English corpses. The frozen grass crunched underfoot, brown with blood. All of the dead soldiers' weapons and gilt decorations were gone. Most of their clothing had been stripped as well. Danish workers were chipping through the frosty ground to dig two long burial trenches. The weather was cold enough that they seemed in no hurry. Svein ached from his shoulders to his groin, but he tried to stand straight to meet the visitors. Beside him his son Knud looked puzzled by the arrival of the delegation. The helmsman Theowulf, however, seemed to understand. A crowd of curious Danes soon gathered behind them.

When the Englishmen stopped before the king, a trim-bearded man in a scarlet outfit spoke, "Hail Svein, King of Denmark and Norway."

"Hail yourself," Svein grumbled. "I suppose you'll have to tell me all your names."

"Yes, Your Majesty, if you wish. I am Cedric, Lord Mayor of London. This is Aelfric, Archbishop of Canterbury. And here is Edward, Earl of Southampton, whose chamberlain claims to have met you at a Danelaw parliament some years ago."

Svein nodded, recalling the confessed spy. Meanwhile the London mayor continued, introducing a score of earls, dukes, and prominent London citizens. When he finished, there was an awkward pause. By now half the Viking encampment had assembled behind the king, craning their necks to see what was happening.

Svein held out his hand to the army and raised his voice so that all could hear. "I would introduce my seven thousand warriors, but I believe that most of our guests have already met them."

The army of Danes and Norwegians laughed, a sound like the roar of cobbles on an ocean shore.

Svein lowered his voice and switched from Norse to English. "What do you want?"

"We have brought gifts, Your Majesty." Cedric held out a jeweled box. "It is a Christmas tradition to follow new stars." He opened the lid, revealing gold coins.

"I asked what the hell you want."

The mayor cleared his throat awkwardly. "The English nobility and the citizens of London would like assurance, Your Majesty, that we might henceforth have a say in the law."

"The Danelaw?" Svein asked. "You want to be ruled by the code of the Vikings?"

"Not exactly, Your Majesty," the mayor quickly countered. "But we would like juries, a law speaker, and —" he hesitated "— checks on the power of the king."

Theowulf, the helmsman, called out loudly, "Which king? Where's Aethelred?"

The Earl of Southampton stepped forward. "King Aethelred has disappointed us. Despite his name he kept no counsel. He let others lead in battle. He became king only by murdering his own brother, Edward the Martyr. Now he has abandoned England."

"Oh?" Theowulf said. "And where is this despised king of yours?"

"Aethelred has sailed with his family to Normandy."

"Then England has no king," Theowulf replied. "And no army but ours."

A grinding pain in Svein's stomach made him wince. He put his hand on Theowulf's arm and whispered, "Has it really come to this, my old friend?"

"I'm sorry, Your Highness." The helmsman climbed atop a nearby barrel and shouted to the thousands that had now gathered. "Men of Denmark, Norway, and the Danelaw! The coward Aethelred has fled the country. His army is no more. You are now the rulers of England!"

A cheer rose from the vast crowd. Men waved weapons in the air. The delegation of English nobles shrank back a few steps.

When the roar subsided Theowulf continued, "Svein Forkbeard, King of Denmark and Norway, has already won the allegiance of the Danelaw, York, Northumberland, East Anglia, Oxford, and the Five Boroughs. He has conquered all of Mercia and Wessex. Today the remaining nobles of England and the mayor of London have come to pay him tribute. Raise your voices if you would elect Svein Forkbeard as king of England!"

The roar that followed shook the birds from the trees. Men stamped their feet in unison until the ground shook. "Hail Svein! Hail Svein! Hail Svein!"

The worm inside the king tightened its grip. Svein covered his face with his hands to hide the pain.

In their poetry, skalds later would ascribe the tears of England's first Danish king to revenge, joy, justice, or pride — but never to the emotion that wracked him on that Christmas morning — regret.

* * *

The new king of England did not go to London to parade victoriously to a coronation in a cathedral. Instead he marched his army north to a field outside the walls of Oxford. There, doubled over with pain, he ordered a small troop to carry him on a stretcher that night to the manor of his childhood English teacher, the duchess of Oxford. Lifu took the king to her study and closed the door. Then she ordered Svein to lie on a table. She examined him by candlelight. Svein shivered but said nothing as she removed his tunic and inspected the wrinkled flesh of his upper body. He had lost half of his former weight. Stringy muscles twitched at her touch. Most worrisome of all, small lumps had grown in the hollows of his armpits.

Lifu sighed. "You have the sign of the crab."

"A crab?" Svein asked. "I thought it must be a worm, devouring me from the inside."

"Call it a worm if you like." Lifu covered him with the tunic. "This is a sickness known by the Latin name for crab — *cancer.*"

"Why a crab?"

"The spidery red mark on your chest is still small, but it will grow to resemble a crab."

"And then?" Svein sat up.

Lifu said nothing. She turned her back and began warming a tin cup over the candle.

Svein lowered his eyebrows. "How much time do I have?"

"A month. Maybe two."

"But you are wise in the use of herbs. What are you preparing?"

Lifu tested the liquid she was warming. Then she handed the cup to the king. "This is ale, brewed with honey and the flowers of hops. My student Egwina has made it her specialty. It calms the spirit and relieves pain."

Svein tasted the brew suspiciously. It was both bitter and sweet. "But this is no cure. Among all your herbs, is there no remedy for the crab?"

"Certainly. No sickness can withstand the juice of the hemlock weed." She reached to a shelf and took down a small vial with a greenish liquid.

"No!" Svein pounded the table. "Poison is for cowards. A Viking dies with his sword in his hand." He turned aside and lowered his voice. "I tried to slay the worm in battle. At Winchester I led the charge into the thick of the English army without a shield. But it seems that my worm, like Grendel, is not so easily slain."

"Or perhaps you were wielding a treacherous sword?"

The king's hand felt for the scabbard at his side. "I scoffed when you warned me about this blade."

"It won you an empire that spans the North Sea," Lifu said. "Long ago I read your fortune in runes. Odin promised you would be king of Danes everywhere. Even as a boy, that was what you wanted."

"But now it seems the wolf god has doomed me to a straw death. No Viking would choose to be barred from the ranks of the battle-dead celebrating in Valhalla."

"Perhaps the gates to that hall are already closed."

Svein sighed. "You may be right. The age of the Norse gods is passing. My son Knud is a Christian. I may be the last of the Vikings."

"Will you go to London?" Lifu asked. "You would be more comfortable in a palace."

"To wallow in Aethelred's sty?" Svein shook his head. "No, I'll stay here in Oxford, in the old home of my sister. But one day I would like to go to London in proper Viking style. Promise me that."

"What would you have me promise?"

The king gritted his teeth in a strange grin. "When I die, sail my coffin down the Thames. Then burn the ship in the shadow of London Bridge."

Before Lifu could respond the king gasped. He clutched his stomach and fell back onto the table groaning.

Lifu sat beside him, stroking his brow until the pain passed. When he opened his eyes again he looked at her as if at a stranger. "Who — who are you?"

"I'm Lifu, your old teacher."

"You're not as old as you ought to be."

"What do you mean?" Lifu asked, alarmed.

"You were my teacher when I was a child. Before that you were a spy for my father. You knew my grandfather, Gorm the Old. Now you say I am dying, and I fear that it's true. But you — you seem beyond age. How is that?"

She turned away, her thoughts in turmoil. The flickering candle cast dancing shadows — fearful shapes from the gaps in her memory.

* * *

By the time Svein Forkbeard died in February, word of his illness had traveled so far that few were surprised. For weeks Knud had already served as king, setting up a temporary court in Oxford to receive visitors and issue rulings. Twice a day he walked to St. Frideswide's Church to oversee the stone building's reconstruction and to pray in its completed chapel. His Scandinavian troops, worried that their families might be starving, asked permission to return to Norway and Denmark with supplies of English grain. Knud agreed to pay their Danegeld with food as well as silver. Most of the ships at Oundle sailed that winter with the ballast rocks below their decks replaced by sacks of wheat.

Plans for Svein's funeral and Knud's coronation were combined, promising a single day of spectacle in London. The same delegation of clerics and nobles that had submitted to Svein at Winchester now met with Knud in Oxford to arrange the details. A flotilla of fifty ships would sail with Svein's body down the Thames while Knud marched overland with a thousand soldiers of the Danelaw. After Knud had been crowned by the archbishop of Canterbury in St. Paul's Cathedral everyone would proceed to a torchlit evening feast on the banks of the Thames. There they would watch Svein's ship burn in all its Viking glory.

Lifu, as duchess of Oxford, had been invited to bring her entire entourage for the festivities. None of them was more excited than Lifu's foster daughter Frida. The orphaned girl had grown to become a beautiful twenty year old with wide blue eyes, noble high cheekbones, and a mane of golden hair that she often tied up into a knot.

"Everyone will be watching, Lifu," she said as they sorted through their clothes in her bedroom's chest. "Let's wear red, but with white sashes for Denmark. Would it be too much if I had a tiara in my hair?"

"You are twice a princess now," Lifu said, nodding assent. She was worried about this coronation, but not because their choice of clothing would be on display. The English who had rioted on St. Brice's Day a dozen years earlier now seemed a little too eager to crown a young Danish king. Much was being made of Knud's popular concessions, weakening the power of the king according to Danish law. But had English sentiments about "foreigners" really changed so quickly?

Suddenly Frida set down her tiara and gave Lifu a solemn look, as if she had overheard every one of Lifu's thoughts.

"I keep wishing that it was only Aethelred," Frida said.

"Aethelred?"

"You know, that he was the only one who hated us. The English will never accept a princess who speaks Norse."

Lifu picked up the tiara and adjusted it on Frida's hair. "You are beautiful in any language, my dear. If anyone can win their hearts, it will be you."

Frida looked at her, switching her gaze back and forth from Lifu's green eye to her blue one. It was the same probing look that Lifu recalled from the girl's great-uncle, Harald Bluetooth. Frida was young enough that she was capable of frivolity, but she had also inherited the caution and wisdom of that legendary king.

"In the long run," Frida said, "The ones who will win them over will be teachers like you."

* * *

The morning of their departure from Oxford dawned clear, with the bare branches of wintry trees stark against a blue sky. Droplets of dew sparkled from green shoots of new grass, a promise of the coming spring.

Lifu oversaw the closing of Svein's wooden casket, reassuring herself that his sword Fenris was inside, gripped in the king's dead hands.

Once the fifty ships had set out — lightly manned but with a favorable breeze in their sails — Lifu returned to the manor house to make sure her retinue was ready for the three-day overland procession.

Frida, resplendent in her red dress and gilt tiara, exclaimed, "We can't find Grady anywhere!"

Lifu sighed. "He'll be hiding in his smithy." She walked to the workshop and dragged her husband back, practically by her ear.

"But I hate ceremonies," he objected, "And I'm not that keen on

London either."

"We'll need you nonetheless," Lifu said.

When the procession set off the Irish silversmith refused to ride with the others, instead trudging sullenly behind them like a condemned slave.

At Oxford's central square Lifu's entourage joined the elaborate wagons of Prince Knud's retinue. Waiting for them outside the city's east gate was the army of the Danelaw — a quarter mile of soldiers with shields and weapons, setting out in formation to march five abreast on the road to London.

The three days of the triumphal procession became one long festival of victory. To Lifu's surprise, cheering crowds lined the road in each village, waving Danish flags and craning to see the royals. Small children came shyly forward to present Knud with wreaths of greenery. Each night the soldiers built bonfires, recited verses, laughed, and drank. The loudest party of all was on the third night, when Londoners joined them with lyres, flutes, drums, and dancers outside the city's Westminster gate.

Only a small glitch marred the morning of the coronation itself. The soldiers manning the Westminster gate announced that the city had been declared a sanctuary by the Lord Mayor.

"Weapons need to be left outside," a captain of the guard called out from the watchtower.

Knud called back, "Today I think we can make an exception to this rule."

The captain crossed his arms. "Until you are crowned, I take my orders from the mayor."

Knud's face flushed red. "Your mayor takes his orders from me." He tipped his head toward the army he had brought.

Even the English captain must have realized how dangerous his defiance had been. He uncrossed his arms and explained, "Our streets are narrow, Your Majesty. We have no room for spears and shields. The townspeople are afraid your soldiers might do damage."

Lifu could see that Knud was still angry, but he was also considering his options. Killing these English guards would be a poor way to begin his coronation. The townspeople might really fear that he had come to loot their city. A token of peace would prove his good intentions.

"We will leave our spears and shields," Knud announced, "But we will keep our other blades."

"Very well, Your Majesty." The captain called to his men, "Open the gate for King Canute!"

Suddenly the celebratory mood resumed. As the Danelaw soldiers marched through the streets people waved and cheered from every window. The plaza before St. Paul's Cathedral was even more festive. Red banners with the white cross of Denmark hung from windowsills on either hand. Musicians and dancers performed before the cathedral. At the top of the steps the Archbishop of Canterbury smiled, holding out his hands in blessing.

When the last of the Danelaw soldiers had squeezed into the crowded square, the musicians suddenly retreated to one side, banging their drums in unison for attention.

The archbishop called out, "This is a momentous day for England! Today we celebrate a coronation that will at last bring us peace, unity, and law!"

The crowd responded with a roar. People in the windows threw snippets of paper and feathers that floated across the crowd like snow.

"And now —" the archbishop's voice sounded strangely uncertain "— and now I call for the king of England to step forward."

Knud stepped down from his carriage. He adjusted his sable cloak for the walk up the cathedral steps. But no one was looking at him.

Instead all eyes were on the archbishop, who had pulled open the cathedral doors to reveal the newly recrowned king.

Aethelred, with the hunched back of an old man and the weirdly smooth face of a boy, stepped out into the sunlight. Jewels glinted from his gold crown. He held the gold scepter of England in his withered hands. He gave the crowd a crooked smile and said, "God save England from the heathen horde!"

A gasp swept across the plaza.

Lifu looked about in alarm. She had seen this nightmare before. The cheering townsfolk had vanished. The Danish banners hanging from the windows were all being turned around, revealing their opposite colors — white fields with the red cross of St. George. Each of the windows facing the square was now occupied by an English archer with a drawn bow.

Knud demanded, "What is the meaning of this betrayal?"

Aethelred laughed. "No one wants a Danish king. When Svein died the nobles called me back from Normandy. Oh, I had to promise some changes about the law, but it was easy enough to gather loyal troops to lay a trap for you."

"There is no honor in this deception," Knud replied. "We came in peace."

"Victory is its own justice. You sent home most of your troops. Let's see how brave the rest of them are without their shields."

Knud stood there dumbfounded by the scale of this treachery. Lifu could almost see his thoughts. Should he attempt to burn the cathedral to kill Aethelred? Should he have his soldiers storm the houses to take out the archers? Should they scatter into the streets to slaughter the duplicitous civilians? With each of these options, thousands would die. And without shields his army's losses would be horrific.

Aethelred called out to the archers in the windows, "Kill the Danes! Kill them all!"

In the terrifying moment when the first volley of arrows arced over the square, Knud shouted his decision:

"To the ships! To the river!"

Then the flight of arrows landed, a rainstorm of death. The crowd surged toward the narrow streets that led down to the river, trampling the bodies of the fallen. A score of armored English guards with halberds had appeared as if by magic to flank the old king. Aethelred cackled, "Run, you foreign bastards. Run and die."

Knud glared defiantly up at Aethelred. "I shall be back."

Then Theowulf and a dozen Danes surrounded Knud like a wall. Together they hustled the king toward the Thames.

Half a dozen arrows had targeted Lifu's retinue. Most of the volley had fallen on cobblestones, but one feathered shaft protruded from the shoulder of Lifu's handmaid Mildrid.

"Oo!" she managed to exclaim before collapsing in a heap.

Grady hoisted her over his shoulder like a sack of grain. "Everyone to the river!" His broad back and arms served as a shield as he herded Lifu, the princess, and the others out of the plaza.

The crooked alleyway they followed toward the river was a gauntlet of death. Aethelred must have foreseen that the Danes would head for their ships. Archers in the windows above the street left the route clogged with bodies.

Grady grunted and huffed, driving the Oxford entourage before him like an angry shepherd. It was only at the riverbank, when Frida and the others sprinted for the safety of the ships, that Lifu realized how badly her husband had been hit.

Half a dozen arrows protruded from his brawny back, and two more waved from the dangling legs of the unconscious Mildrid.

Lifu clapped her hand to her mouth in horror.

The giant silversmith swayed, his speech slurred. "Let the ships go. We'll —"

He staggered to the nearest house and smashed open the door with his shoulder. Then he teetered forward like a felled tree, thumping face first onto the floorboards. Mildrid was thrown to one side. She hit a wall and groaned.

Lifu dashed in after her husband. She fell to her knees, too frantic to think clearly. All of her knowledge of herbs and healing seemed useless. "Oh, Grady! This is all my fault."

His breath rattled. He turned his head to one side, spat blood, and muttered, "No. You tried to stop them. You are the love —" His body shook as he struggled to draw a breath "— the love of my life."

She stroked the hair on his head and kissed him on the temple. Her tears fell into his stubbly red beard. "You are the love of my life too, Grady. I can —" she looked at the arrows in his back and despaired.

He rocked his head slightly. "You dream but cannot die."

"What?" She wiped her tears and knelt closer.

Grady's gray eyes caught hers, and he gave her a weak smile. "I will know more than you. I will find out if we meet Jesus, Gotama, or Odin."

It could have been a laugh that wracked his body. But by the time the spasm ended, his gray eyes had fixed forever, unblinking, into a realm beyond the living.

Lifu clutched his tunic and shook him. "Come back, damn it!" When his eyes didn't move she threw back her head and howled in anguish. Then she collapsed against his shoulder, sobbing.

"Oo, milady," a familiar voice said. "Grady saved our lives."

Lifu blinked back her tears. Mildrid was sitting up against the wall, seemingly unaware that she had two arrows in her leg and a third in her shoulder.

"Mildrid! Aren't you —?"

"It hurts something fierce milady, but I'll mend. Unlike your poor, brave Grady. Where are the others?"

Lifu looked out through the splintered doorway. Beyond the range of the archers, Danish soldiers had secured the beach. They were busy loading survivors onto Knud's fleet. The first of the ships had already hoisted its sail and was heading down the ever-widening Thames to the sea.

"They're going to Denmark," Lifu said.

"Oo! With the princess and everyone? Then we'll just have to keep the home fires burning, like last time." Mildrid shifted and winced.

Lifu let out a long, weary breath. Slowly she unclenched her fingers from the tunic of her dead husband. Then she went to Mildrid. Arrow wounds were not easy to treat. She would have to mix a salve of garlic and leeks. At least that might prevent the rot of death from taking hold.

As Lifu examined the damage, Mildrid asked, "Do you reckon they'll burn Svein's ship like you wanted, milady?"

Lifu paused. No, of course they wouldn't. The soldiers would need every ship to rescue the living.

"I'm afraid it looks like Fenris is going back to Denmark too."

CHAPTER 22
SCHLESWIG, 1945

"We need that sword! The Americans are coming." Colonel Wedel strode into the museum hall where Mette, Herr Matthiasen, and Henrik were updating the display of the Hedeby excavation's finds.

Mette looked up in surprise. "American troops? I thought they were still back at the Rhine."

"Not troops, bombers. There's an air raid alert. They'll be here in two hours." He propped open a glass display case and ran his fingers admiringly along the rusty runes on the flat of the ancient blade.

Matthiasen, the old museum curator, pushed back his conductor's cap and scratched his white hair in puzzlement. "Surely, Herr Oberst, you don't believe a sword can turn back the American Air Force."

The colonel shot him a cold glance. "Of course not. But there are those who believe Fenris has power. It will boost morale in the Gestapo's bunker. And it will be safer there, too." He loosened the display's clasps and lifted the sword free. Then, as an afterthought, he added, "The three of you should join me. Americans are sloppy. Most of their bombs seem to miss their intended target."

"And what is their intended target?" Mette asked. "A museum in a provincial border town?"

"No, no," Colonel Wedel laughed. "They're chasing a chimera that's shiftier even than Fenris. Our spies have convinced them there's a secret missile base."

Mette made a show of reacting with surprise. In fact, rumors had swirled about the hidden rockets for months. Several members of the Danish team had quietly been in contact with the resistance movement. And her brother Lars, in the American Army, had managed to relay a one-sentence warning about a German V3 project, possibly with uranium weapons.

Suddenly Colonel Wedel turned aside, held his stomach with one hand, and winced.

"Are you all right?" Mette asked.

"It's this damn ulcer. Every year it gets worse, like a worm eating me from the inside out." He looked to Mette, his eyes damp. "Please, for your own safety. Come with me to the Gestapo's safe room below City Hall."

"Thank you, Colonel, but no."

"Can't you call me Franz?"

Mette sighed, "No, Franz."

He turned away in frustration and walked angrily out of the museum with the Viking sword.

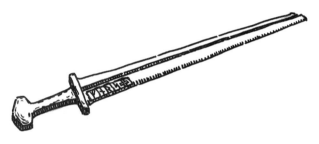

Henrik stood up nervously. "We really ought to go while there's still time. The target is dangerously close to the city."

Mette studied her assistant. Henrik was at least ten years older than her. Middle age might have made him cautious. And he had always been meticulous. Even now, labeling artifacts for a display case, he was wearing a bow tie. But the nervousness of his suggestion made her wonder.

"How is it," she mused aloud, "That the Gestapo knows American bombers are two hours away? They've never been able to predict air raids that far in advance."

Henrik blinked. "You heard the colonel. The Gestapo intercepted messages from the Danish resistance. Holger Danske must have called in the air strike."

"But how did the Gestapo intercept the message? There must be a leak. A double agent." She fixed her gaze on Henrik. "And how do you seem to know the location of the Americans' target?"

"I don't. I just assumed the target must be nearby."

Mette shook her head. "That isn't what you said. You said the target *is* dangerously close. It's you, isn't it? It's been you all along. You're the Nazis' pawn."

Henrik was not a tall man, but he drew himself up to his full five foot six. "Not a pawn, Mette. A knight. After today, the excavation at Hedeby will focus only on the ship in the bay. And our roles will assume a more natural order. I will be in charge, and you will be my assistant."

Mette stared at him open-mouthed.

The old museum curator beside her merely nodded.

Mette turned to Matthiasen. "What? Don't tell me you were part of this conspiracy?"

"No, but I saw it coming." Matthiasen waved a hand at Henrik. "The jealous subordinate, unlucky in love, pins his bow tie on a bigger fish."

Henrik shook his head emphatically. "That's not it at all. Don't you see? Denmark is a small country. We need the protection of a nation that shares the Germanic purity of our Viking past."

"That's crazy," Mette objected. "Nonsense like that has killed millions. And now the Nazis are losing. The war is all but over."

Henrik chuckled. "If only you knew. Tomorrow the Allies will think they have crushed us, but instead we will crush them. Their bombers are already out of radio contact with England, headed to the wrong target. There's nothing anyone can do to stop them."

He held out his hand to her. "Come with me, Mette. Let me keep you safe."

Her eyes had always been just slightly out of alignment, but when she was angry Mette saw double. Now her gaze sliced both of the Henriks before her like scissors. "I would rather be blown to pieces than share a bunker with a Danish traitor."

Henrik straightened his bow tie. "I hope you survive to change your mind. Then you will see that I am right." He gave her a curt military nod, turned on his heel, and left.

The slam of the font door echoed from the brick walls of the cavernous main hall. In the silence that followed Mette asked, "Now what?"

Herr Matthiasen shrugged, lifting the gold epaulets on the shoulders of his antiquated train conductor's uniform. "Now we stop the bombers."

Mette didn't know whether to laugh or cry. The shrunken Danish-speaking German curator was as much a relic as anything in his museum. It was hard to tell if his solemn expression wasn't a sign of senility.

"How do you propose we do that?" she asked.

"Well," he said, pointing to a garbage can. "You can start by cutting the bottom out of that thing. Meanwhile I'll hook up the window vents."

She looked at him dubiously.

He sighed. "Do I have to do everything myself?" He walked to the metal trash barrel, dumped it upside down on the floor, and traced an imaginary square on the bottom with his finger. "Right here. Chop the hole big enough for my arm."

"Chop a hole? With what? A halberd?"

Matthiasen seemed not to notice her irony. "A halberd would work. But use one of the reproductions. The originals are fragile." Then, ignoring her for the moment, he shuffled off toward a back storage room muttering, "Never did like ladders."

Left alone, Mette decided she might as well vent her frustration by attacking a garbage can with a halberd. It was harder than she thought. The weapon on the pole was not only heavy, but it was spiked with three different blades. Even when she managed to puncture the garbage can she realized it would take dozens of blows before she created a substantial hole. Meanwhile Matthiasen had leaned a ladder against the wall and climbed to a high window. He was connecting a metal duct from the smokestack of the Iron Dane to the open window. He had jerry-rigged this vent system two years ago, but had been ridiculed so severely that he never actually used it to test the clunky old locomotive.

"I suppose," he said over his shoulder, "You've figured out where the rocket base really is."

Mette whacked the can with her halberd. Then she wiped her brow. "Is it in the old bicycle factory in Gammeltorp?"

"That's the cover." He climbed down the ladder.

"I'd wondered," she said. "They've been taking workers and supplies in there for years. I've yet to see a bicycle come out."

He shook his head at the hole she had hacked. "These jagged edges are going to hurt. Take some tongs from the blacksmith display and bend them back."

"But why —?"

"We don't have much time." He stepped up into the locomotive cabin and began working on something she couldn't see. His voice sounded hollow from within that iron cave. "For the past month the train traffic to Gammeltorp has mostly been tank cars, probably full of rocket fuel. Hundreds of them. Now they're hidden on tracks under camouflage nets. That whole area behind the factory is disguised to look like a potato farm."

"How do you know all this?" Mette asked.

Matthiasen poked his head out the engineer's window, his face streaked with soot. "Huh?"

"I said, how do you know about the tank cars?"

"Connections." He winked and ducked back out of sight. "When you've worked for the railroad as long as I have, you hear all the dirt."

By now the smell of smoke was unmistakable. Mette set aside the tongs and climbed onto the locomotive to confront him. "What the hell are you doing? Trying to burn down the museum?"

He stopped shoveling coal. Sweat glistened on his forehead. He frowned as if seriously considering her accusation. "No, but that might work too. To turn the bombers you've got to give them a target other than the one they got at their morning briefing."

This stopped Mette. Both Henrik and Colonel Wedel had suggested that the bombers had been given the wrong target. "Do you know what the Americans are targeting?"

The curator rolled his eyes. "What do you think? A decoy."

"A decoy." She repeated the word slowly.

"A fake. A sham. Something that resembles a rocket base from the air, with a runway, lots of barracks, and what looks like a great big rocket ship right in the middle."

"Our water tower!" Mette might as well have been hit in the head with his coal shovel.

"Why else do you think the Reich has been funding your project for five years? Sure, some Nazi big shot might have wanted an old sword, but your real job has been to lead the bombers astray."

"Good God. But Hedeby is an archeological site."

"Tomorrow it'll be a crater."

"More than a hundred people are there!"

"Poles, Danes, a few naive Austrian soldiers." Matthiasen shrugged. "Nothing the Gestapo isn't willing to sacrifice."

"We've got to warn them." Mette jumped from the locomotive and ran to the telephone in the curator's office.

A minute later she was back, frowning.

"I already tried that when I got the ladder," Matthiasen said. "They must have cut the lines this morning."

"Then I'll have to go there myself."

"Now you're thinking." Matthiasen slapped the iron sill of the engineer's window. "And here's your ride."

"A train without tracks?"

"Have you looked?" Matthiasen climbed down and pointed to a short section of rail beneath the giant iron drive wheels. "How do you think they got this thing in here? A hundred years ago this building was a train station. The old tracks are still there." He flipped a ceramic floor tile aside, revealing that the rails really did continue. In a minute he had uncovered a rusty track that led straight into a brick wall. Beyond the wall, Mette knew, was a park with lawns and flower beds and benches. Could rails really still be hidden there as well?

Steam had filled the upper half of the hall with a hot, damp cloud. Somewhere a valve jittered and began to whistle. Matthiasen hefted the garbage can to the locomotive's coal hopper and climbed aboard. "You coming? Might be bumpy."

She climbed up behind him and braced herself against the engine room's doorway.

"Here goes nothing." Matthiasen shoved the throttle forward.

Hot steam shot out from the two big cylindrical piston boxes on either side of the boiler. The iron floor began to shudder. Then the great drive wheels jerked, waking up from their long sleep. The vent on the smokestack ripped loose, showering them with soot and sparks. The engine snorted a blast of steam and paused, as if preparing to draw a second breath. Machinery clanked and hissed.

Matthiasen pushed the throttle all the way forward. The iron monster shivered, rolling faster across the hall.

The metal prow of the cow catcher hit the wall first. Then the front of the boiler crashed into the bricks, buckling the building outward.

In the park outside, an elderly German woman with a dachshund had just stopped feeding pigeons, having decided that she really ought to report the fire in the city museum. Black smoke had been drifting from an upper window for several minutes. Where were the authorities when you needed them? With a humph she stood up from her bench and picked up her dog.

In that same moment the museum wall suddenly erupted, hurling bricks to all sides. With a colossal roar a metal elephant burst through a cloud of smoke and steam. The iron plow at its front began peeling two strips of lawn to either side. Pigeons scattered into the air. The old woman barely had time to escape before her bench flipped aside.

On the far side of the lawn the locomotive plowed up a sidewalk and lurched onto the tracks of Schleswig's main train station.

Matthiasen waved his red conductor's cap out the window, shouting to the startled bystanders, "Make way for the Iron Cow!"

"What if we meet another train?" Mette asked.

He pulled a pocket watch from his uniform. "Should be clear until the 12:14 from Flensburg. The problem is the switching yard. Keep your head down. This place is guarded."

Ahead the tracks fanned out in three directions. A German voice called out something. It was hard for Mette to understand over the noise of the engine, but she could make out the command, "*Halt!*"

"Prepare to halt!" Matthiasen pulled back the throttle and cranked up the brake lever. The drive wheels locked up, screeching metal against metal. The locomotive shuddered to a stop, hissing.

"I've got to go throw a switch or we'll end up in Kiel." Matthiasen took the trash can from the coal hopper, lifted it over his head, and clambered awkwardly down to the tracks. Through the hole in the top he told Mette, "As soon as I'm back, release the brake and push the throttle all the way forward."

The old curator had hardly waddled beyond the front of the locomotive when the first bullets began pinging off his garbage can. Some of the shots ricocheted with an angry whine.

Mette peered out fearfully, watching. The garbage can settled beside a switch that looked like a stick figure with a disk head and a lever hand. Martthias' arm reached out of the hole and grabbed the lever. But the angle of the hole prevented him from moving the lever very far. He backed up, tilted the can, and tried again. He managed to move the switch farther, but not far enough. Next he pushed off the garbage can, stood up, and pulled the switch with both hands.

In that moment a gunshot cracked. The old conductor doubled over, clutching his stomach.

"Matthiasen!" Mette cried, aghast. She was about to run out after him when she saw him crawling into the barrel. Then, slowly, the barrel began to roll back across the gravel. Bullets zinged, but the barrel kept on rolling. When it reached the shelter of the locomotive Mette pulled the curator out and carried him up to the floor of the engineer's cabin.

Blood dampened the shiny black belt of his uniform. He pinched his eyes closed with pain. But his wrinkled lips formed the word, "Throttle."

Mette pushed the lever. Instead of lurching forward the locomotive began shuddering. Steam hissed louder and louder, as if the boiler itself might explode.

Matthiasen winced, raising himself to an elbow. He grabbed the brake lever and released it.

At once the huge machine jolted forward. The drive wheels clanked past the switch, spinning faster and faster. As they chugged past the waterfront docks and headed out across the farm fields toward Gammeltorp, Mette knelt beside Matthiasen. She began unbuttoning his uniform. "We need to get you to a doctor."

"There's no cure for a Nazi bullet in the gut." He pushed her hand aside. Then he asked, "Do you hear them yet?"

"Hear what?"

"The planes."

Mette looked up. The sky was still empty — a cloudless blue. And the machinery was making such a racket that she could hardly have heard planes anyway.

When she turned back she was startled to see the old curator on his feet, staggering and dripping blood, his hands on the throttle. "Herr Matthiasen!" She exclaimed. Where did this withered old man find such strength? She stepped forward to support him but he held out his hand to stop her.

"There isn't much time left. I have to do this alone, Mette."

All these years she had called him Herr Matthiasen, and he had called her Mette. She admitted, "I don't even know your first name."

"Holger is a sorry name. Germans laugh at it."

Mette shook her head. "It's a name for a hero."

He sagged against the iron wall, looking out the window. "Next stop, Hedeby junction. This is where you get out."

"I can't leave you like this, Holger."

"No, I suppose not." He gritted his teeth and pulled back the throttle, slowing down. Suddenly he pointed behind them. "Good God! Look!"

But when Mette turned he placed his foot squarely on her rear end and pushed. She flailed in the air with disbelief. Then she landed hard on her shoulder and rolled down the grassy verge. By the time she got to her knees, her shoulder striped with blood, the Iron Dane was picking up speed again. Great puffs of soot belched from the smokestack. The locomotive stormed past the Gammeltorp platform and barreled around a curve toward the locked gates of the old factory. Machine guns began rattling on either hand, pinging bullets off the runaway engine. The gate held for half a second, stretching the chain link fence into a taut V. Then the broken wires whipped back, nearly slashing one of the guards in half.

Mette managed to scramble off the track. Holding her shoulder with one hand she began jogging along the dirt track toward Hedeby. Holger had chosen his own way to say goodbye. Now she had to focus on reaching the excavation in time to evacuate the others.

She had only run a few hundred meters when the sky to the east glowed orange. A moment later the leaves on the trees bent back with the force of a monumental blast. A black cloud began billowing up from the horizon where Holger had steamed the Iron Dane.

She stopped short, her eyes wet with tears.

Then she heard a distant drone. The American Air Force! Already she could see the glint of tiny silver crosses low in the western sky. She began running again toward Hedeby. The airfield she passed along the way was a joke — dotted with weeds — but no one would notice that from the air. She looked over her shoulder at the sky. Like an arrow made of clouds, contrails streamed behind the wedge of B-17s. Now there could be no mistake. They were targeting Hedeby.

Mette ran faster. Tiny black puffs of antiaircraft shells began dotting the sky at the front of the bombers' triangle. The lead plane peeled off to one side, streaming smoke. In another minute the squadron would be overhead, releasing their bombs.

It was too late to warn her colleagues. It was too late for any of them. She climbed to the top of the ancient Danevirke wall. The water tower beyond really did look like a missile. The Polish POWs, playing soccer in the assembly grounds, had stopped to point at the silver stars in the noonday sky. Mette's shouts were lost under the drone of aircraft engines.

She closed her eyes, wishing with all her might that she could send a message to the American crews:

"Turn!"

* * *

Major Julius Gustmeyer had had doubts about this bombing run since early that morning, when their navigator Hack showed up at the *Lucky Lady* with a big grin. "A milk run," he announced to the waiting crew. "Not Berlin. Not even Hamburg. Just a missile site on the Baltic."

This was Julius' forty-eighth mission. Everyone else had returned stateside as soon as they could, after thirty-five runs. Seniority had won Julius two promotions. The *Lucky Lady* now flew as the squadron's deputy lead. But he seemed to have no more authority than before.

Once they were over the North Sea Julius left the controls with co-pilot Kowalski and crawled down into the plane's Plexiglas nose to check in with Hack.

"Major Gable!" The navigator snapped to attention as best he could, strapped into a canvas chair between a fifty-caliber machine gun and a metal table. He saluted, but even this seemed clumsy with his oxygen mask and headphones.

"At ease, Hack. Could I take a look at the charts for our target? Let's get Gene over here too." Julius motioned for the bombardier to leave his station and join them.

Soon the three of them were hunched awkwardly around a map that was covered with a confusion of colored symbols and arrows.

"Here, sir," Hack said, pointing to a red circle. "On a bay near a town called Schleswig. Easy street. No flak for miles."

Julius' heart sank. "That's Hedeby."

"You know the place, sir?"

"Yes. It's near my home in Denmark. And it's not a rocket base. It's an archeological site."

The bombardier tilted his head. "Are you sure, sir?' At my briefing this morning they showed us recon photos of the bomb run. There's a rocket at ground zero, ready to launch."

"You saw a rocket?"

"It looked like one, sir," Gene sketched it in the air with a gloved finger. "Three legs, a warhead, and a point on top."

Julius slapped his forehead. "That's their water tower." He got up, crawled back through the cockpit, and squeezed past the racks of bombs to the radio man's station in the plane's waist.

"Major Gable, sir!"

"Sparks, can you get me a private, secure channel to Lieutenant Colonel Roberts?"

"It'll take a minute, sir." The radio man began contacting the lead plane.

Before long the colonel's voice was growling in Julius' headphones. "What the hell is it, Gable?' We're almost over enemy territory."

"I'm sorry sir, but this is important. I've looked at the charts with my navigator, and I believe we're bombing the wrong target. I'm from Denmark and know the area. What we're targeting is actually an archeological site called Hedeby."

The colonel grunted. "Sounds like a Nazi trick, building a missile base where they think we wouldn't bomb."

"Actually sir, I'm convinced it's a decoy. My fiancé is leading the excavation there."

For a moment the colonel was silent. "Is this channel secure, Gable?"

"My radio man says it is."

"All right. You don't know the whole story here. Our recon tells us that the Nazis have one last plan to win the war. They've built a base with a V3 rocket we can't shoot down. We've confirmed the location with informants on the ground."

"I still believe it's a fake, sir."

"Then where's the real missile base?"

Julius had no answer. "I don't know, sir."

There was another pause. "I'm sorry about your girlfriend, Gable. War is hell. Over and out."

Glumly Julius made his way back past the racks of 250-pound bombs to the cockpit. The shore of Jutland was already a pale strip beyond the blue sea. Maybe Mette was safely home in Copenhagen. Maybe the colonel was right about Hedeby. And yet a sick feeling in his stomach told him that a hidden evil was loose, and that no hero had awakened to confront it.

Below him the North Sea began dissolving into the sand flats and meandering inlets of southern Jutland. Once Danish Vikings had sailed up those rivers for an easy portage to their capital at Hedeby. Germans had occupied this lower part of the peninsula for eighty years. And now it might conceal the war's most horrible weapon.

"Bombing run in five minutes, sir," the bombardier said in the headphones.

"A milk run," co-pilot Kowalski put in cheerily. "No welcoming committee, no flak."

"Target coming up," the bombardier warned. "With binoculars I can already make out the airfield by the bay. Prepare to turn over the controls, sir."

Sick at heart, Julius held his gloved hand over the switch. But then a small yellow flower bloomed on the horizon to the right. The strange ball flashed orange and began billowing up black. "What's that to starboard, Hack?"

"Dunno, sir. Farm fields, I think."

"With a fireball that size? Looks more like a fuel depot to me."

Boom! Flak shells began puffing the sky ahead with brown clouds.

Kowalski shook his head. "This wasn't on the menu. Something's wrong."

All at once the sky before them disappeared in a wall of explosions.

Shrapnel pinged off the windshield.

"A box barrage!" Kowalski shouted.

"I can't see a damned thing," the bombardier cried.

A second later, when the plane flew out of the smoke, Julius realized that the antiaircraft gunners had targeted the lead plane. Two of the engines on the lieutenant colonel's B-17 were trailing smoke. He had dropped out of formation and was turning back.

"Major Gable?" A voice Julius didn't recognize squawked in his headset. "This is Smitters, Colonel Roberts' co-pilot. He's hit. We're heading home. Good luck."

Julius hit the throttle, steering the *Lucky Lady* to the front of the squadron. "Sparks, put me on all channels."

"To everyone, sir?"

"Friend and foe alike."

"You got it."

Julius took a deep breath. He was about to risk his career, probably a court martial, and possibly his life.

"Crews of the 351st squadron! The colonel has been hit. This is your commanding officer, Major Gustmeyer. We are diverting our bombing run. The airfield we've been targeting is a decoy. Repeat: A decoy. We are shifting our target to the fuel depot burning to starboard. On my mark, prepare to bank twenty degrees to starboard. Three, two, one, mark!"

He turned the wheel, tipping the huge plane sharply to the right. A quick glance behind him revealed ninety-six bombers slowly tilting their wings, curving the vast white path of contrails.

"Lock in on that fireball in the fields! Prepare to —"

Julius' words were cut short by an explosion that blew out the windshield, shattering glass into his face. A roar of wind pressed him back, drowning out everything. A familiar vibration in the floor, however, told him that their payload had started rolling off the racks through the bomb bay. He gripped the wheel, holding course. Then two more blasts shook the plane. Half the instruments went dead. The super chargers on the engines were running away. The right wing was on fire.

"The bomb bay's jammed!" the bombardier cried. "Half our load is still live on board."

"Abandon ship!" Julius called out. "Crew of the *Lucky Lady*, jump!"

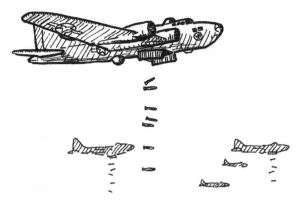

Kowalski nodded and headed back to the gun ports at the waist. Julius crouched down, signaling frantically for the navigator and bombardier to get out of the nose. They started crawling out, but at the same time the plane started to tilt to the left — the beginning of a deadly spin that would prevent the crew from jumping free.

Julius pulled the wheel hard to the right, turning the ship's massive rudder to compensate for the tilt. When that wasn't enough he jammed the ailerons down. The wings slowly leveled, but now the rudder and flaps were dragging down their air speed. The elevation needle began winding down, dropping thousands of feet.

He leaned into the blast of wind to count the parachutes: Three, four, five.

"Come on, guys! Get out!"

Six Seven. Eight.

The ground was coming up fast.

"Go! Jump!"

Nine. Everyone had made it. Julius took one last look out the broken windshield. The *Lucky Lady* was headed straight into a German village. With two thousand pounds of munitions on board, the B-17 would leave a crater half the size of the town. Hundreds of civilians would die. He yanked back the ailerons, allowing the plane to cant to the left toward a forest. Then he locked the controls.

Too late!

By the time he was stumbling back toward the bomb bay, the B-17 had rolled upside down, beginning its death spiral.

CHAPTER 23
OXFORD, 1015

Torches lit the forest path to the brewery where Lifu had asked the witches of Oxford to gather. At midnight they would call down the moon.

After a year and a half of preparation Knud had returned to England to avenge the treachery of his "coronation." But even with an invasion force of ten thousand he had been unable to capture London. Old King Aethelred had barricaded himself behind the city's walls. There he had reneged on his promise to share power with the English nobles. Twice Knud had besieged the city, and twice Aethelred had sent his son Edmund to drive back the Danes. The luck of the young English prince had won him the name "Edmund Ironside." Frustrated by London, Knud had instead marched his army on a spiral path through every other part of England, from Wessex to Northumberland, a parade of victories that should have proven his claim to the throne. But without the capital, he could never be king.

"Oo!" Mildrid flapped her arms, examining the silver runes on her black robe. "I don't feel like a proper witch, milady."

"Me either," Aelfu complained.

Egwina, who ran the brewery by day, yawned. "And we don't make much of a coven, just the four of us."

Lifu peered out the window of the brewery's thatched hut. "We're awaiting an important guest. And there she is."

The four women crowded by the glassless opening. A dark shape was shifting behind the torchlit tree trunks, flitting among the shadows as silently as a bat.

Lifu went to open the hut's door. "Hail to our mistress, the queen of the night."

The others stood to either side, their eyes wide. Suddenly the apparition filled the doorway, her face a ghastly, impossible red. Blonde hair blew about her head, catching on her crooked black nose.

Mildrid shrieked. Aelfu fell back.

But Lifu put her hands on the visitor's shoulders and hugged her tight. "Oh, my dear, my dear." A tear ran down Lifu's cheek. "You are safe here among friends, my daughter."

When Lifu stepped back the visitor pulled off the leather mask she had worn.

Mildrid gasped. "Princess Frida!"

The Danish princess put her arms around Mildrid. "It's a relief to see you well, Mildrid. I should have known that Aethelred's arrows couldn't stop you."

"It's my job to keep the home fires of the duchy burning for you, Your Highness," Mildrid said proudly. "But what of you, these past two years?"

Frida pulled back her blonde hair. "I've become a captain in Knud's army. We've won allegiance almost everywhere, except in London and Oxford, where the Danes were massacred. To answer Lifu's call I came in disguise. Although I admit the urgency of this meeting remains a mystery to me."

"Yes," Aelfu said, "Why us, and why now?"

The flicker of torches gleamed in Lifu's mismatched eyes, green and blue. "We are going to call down the moon to conquer England."

Aelfu bit her lip. "Five women? In a hut in the woods? We're going to overthrow the kingdom?"

Lifu lifted her head. "Once I trained an elven army to bring down a king."

Frida scoffed. "That was a game. You played Capture the King with my Uncle Svein."

"What I taught then is still true. Every army has a weakness. And each of us has a hidden strength. Egwina, for example."

"Me?" The Englishwoman scoffed. "My only skill is brewing ale. And that's only because you taught me to add medicinal herbs."

"Is that really why? Let's go out to the spring and see." Lifu led them through a back doorway. In an opening in the oak forest a stream was spilling out of a small pool. A reflection of the full moon floated on the water like a slippery disk.

"The moon is your secret strength," Lifu said. "Each month when she is full I call her down to bless the spring. If she is willing, she allows you to see the shimmer of hidden things — sometimes far away and sometimes in the future."

Lifu held out her hands, encouraging the others to join her in a ring. "Our task is to defeat Aethelred. The moon may choose to help us if our cause is just."

Staring into the water, Egwina tightened her lips. "Truly, our cause is just. Aethelred murdered my husband and my daughter. They burned in Oxford's church."

Frida added bitterly. "All of my family died at Aethelred's hands."

"And Grady," Lifu said quietly. "My brave husband."

"The archers only shot me three times," Mildrid piped in, "But oo! It hurt."

A wind rippled the pond into bars of light. For a moment as the darkness coalesced around the moon, Lifu glimpsed a shape beyond the surface.

The shadow of Niflheim. A fetch was waiting to take one of them to the land of the dead. Why was the price always so dear, and the chosen one so innocent?

"Did you see something, Lifu?" Egwina asked.

She nodded. "I saw a question." This was also true, and less cruel. "Where is Fenris, the sword of the Vikings? Was it buried with Svein Forkbeard in Denmark?"

"No," Frida said. "My uncle was laid to rest at Roskilde Cathedral in the Christian manner, without weapons. Knud kept the sword."

Lifu mused, "If Knud were wielding that sword, London should have fallen."

"But that's not my cousin's way," Frida explained. "Knud is pious. To show Christ's victory over the old gods, he had his father's sword encased within a gold cross. At every church on our campaign through England he sets the cross on the altar and prays to God for justice."

Mildrid's eyes widened. "Could someone pull the sword out of the cross? Then he'd prove himself to be the true king, like Arthur."

"It's welded inside for all time, Mildrid. And Knud's army already knows he is the true king."

"Where is his army?" Egwina asked.

"In Mercia. We just sent Edmund running back to London. He's claiming victory, but that's nonsense. All of Mercia has submitted to the Danes. I've even sealed that promise myself."

Frida's mysterious smile made Lifu suggest, "You have a secret, my foster daughter?"

Even in the moonlight it was obvious that the heiress of Oxford was blushing. "Eadric, the Ealdorman of Mercia, has pledged forty ships and two thousand men in support of Knud. He's very influential."

"And the most handsome Englishman in the Midlands," Aelfu put in.

Lifu lifted her foster daughter's chin with a finger. "Has Eadric influenced you as well?"

Frida broke into a broad grin. "It's a secret, but yes. I've promised myself to him."

The others laughed. They hugged Frida and offered congratulations. Egwina fetched mugs of ale for a toast. Then they drifted back inside, where Mildrid built a fire in the hearth.

When Egwina was refilling the cups she stopped in front of Lifu. "We're celebrating a betrothal. Why are you so solemn?"

Frida's smile dimmed. "Don't tell me the moon gave you a plan after all?"

"Maybe she did." Lifu looked about the group. "We need an invitation to Edmund's victory feast in London."

"That's easy," Aelfu said, lifting her cup merrily. "My family's always invited. No Danes in our lineage."

"Good. Bring Egwina. Offer to provide her famous ale to everyone in the court." Lifu glanced to Egwina and saw a flicker of fear. Had she glimpsed the shadow in the pool as well?

"What about me?" Frida asked.

"Ride back to Mercia as fast you can. Convince Eadric to betray Knud."

"What!"

"The English are always changing sides. Tell Eadric to go to London, throw himself at Edmund's feet, and promise to help rid England of the Danes."

"Lifu! Eadric has agreed to marry me!"

"Yes, but for the sake of all you hold dear, don't let anyone know."

* * *

In the dream Lifu flew to London as Odin's raven Huginn, dressed

317

in the black feathers of a witch. Torches lit the watchtowers of the city walls — an impregnable ring of fire, backed by the moat of the Thames. Fire, water, earth, and air. For once, soaring above the darkness that was England, Lifu saw the four elements of the world as a single whole. As Odin's raven, she knew everything.

She was even starting to remember an earlier life, before she had awakened as Lifu. Yes! Her name had been Groa then. She had lived in Norway, and of course she had been married to a smith. But that husband had worked with iron, rather than silver. Together they had forged a sword that had launched the Viking age. The gods had been guiding her ever since, trying to undo what had been wrought. How much would she remember this time?

Flying through the night she recognized the dots of light below as the fires of Eadric's army. The Mercians had camped in the same Westminster field where Knud had awaited the treachery of his coronation two years before. Her raven eyes spotted a wagonload of ale barrels bumping down the cobblestones of High Street toward a heavily guarded gate. Atop the wagon Aelfu and Egwina laughed lightly, trying to mask their fear.

Lifu sailed over the palace wall. More torches! The crowds at Edmund's victory feast strolled the castle grounds. Musicians in brightly colored clothes played lutes and pipes. Plank tables sagged with platters of beef, fowl, and delicacies. Naked blue women danced with dogs in a mock performance of Celtic lust. And beneath a blue-and-white-striped canopy, clapping his hands to the gyrations of the painted women, was the old king.

No one noticed when Lifu beat her wings twice, stretched out her thin black legs, and perched on a rock. All about the grounds the half-tame palace ravens were stalking the shadows, fighting over scraps of dropped meat. A withered gnome with a strangely boyish face, Aethelred hunched on his throne. A mixture of grease and drool dribbled from his lips. His bloodshot eye twitched. "More!" he croaked, clapping his hands. "More ale!"

Archbishop Aelfric, clad in immaculate white and gold, leaned to the king. "A delivery of ale has just arrived, Your Majesty. It is the new herbed variety, from Oxford."

"Oxford?" Aethelred's white eyebrows rose. "We must be careful."

KRAAAK! Lifu gave a deep throaty squawk. Then she cocked her black, beady eyes toward the palace gate. A troop of two dozen soldiers had pushed past the brewery wagon and were advancing rapidly. In front of the king's table the men suddenly stopped, fell to their knees, and pulled off their helmets.

The king frowned at this disruption of the dancing girls' performance. He squinted at the tousled red hair of the kneeling man in front.

"Edmund? What does my victorious son want now?"

"A greater victory, Father. There is a way."

Aethelred grunted. "Get up, boy. What is this way, and how much of my treasure will it cost?"

Edmund stood. He held out his hand to the man kneeling beside him "This is Eadric, Father, the ealdorman of Mercia."

"I know who Eadric is," Aethelred grumbled. "Look up at me, ealdorman. Let me see the face that makes women weak."

Eadric lifted his head. In her dream-form as a raven Lifu found that she was not an adequate judge of human beauty. The man's beak was too short and his eyes too blue. Could Frida really have fallen for such a pale bird?

"I've heard you are a traitor," Aethelred said. "That you have sided with the invader, Canute."

"No, Your Majesty!" Eadric protested. "How could I? Canute is ravaging Mercia, pillaging our farms and raping our women. I've come to you with a plea for help."

"Everyone wants something."

"But Father," Edmund said, "Eadric has a matching gift. He has brought an army of two thousand well-trained men."

Aethelred grunted. "Is that all you've brought, Eadric of Mercia?"

The ealdorman lifted his head. "No, Your Majesty. I have also brought information. My spies have learned that Canute has left his ships at Assandun, on the River Orwell. He is two days' march away, and the ships are lightly guarded."

"Don't you see, Father?" Edmund put in eagerly, "I can reach the ships before him. Without ships, the Vikings are cowards. When Canute returns to Assandun, we'll lay a trap. He'll march up to challenge my force, unaware that Eadric is waiting to attack him from behind."

Aethelred nodded slowly. "The same trick he used on us at Winchester. That was a day deserving of revenge."

The old king cast a cold eye on Eadric. "Are you loyal to England?"

"Yes, Your Majesty. With all my soul."

Aethelred held out his wrinkled hand. "Kiss my ring. It is the sacred seal of St. George."

Eadric kissed the ring.

"Now put your hand on your heart," Aethelred commanded. "Do you swear before God, the archbishop, and your king that you hate the Danes?"

Eadric held his hand to his chest. "I swear, Your Majesty, before all that is holy, that I hate the Danes."

KRAAAK! Lifu couldn't help crying out in alarm. Eadric's pledge sounded sincere! What if Frida was the one who had been deceived? Even Odin, with his all-seeing raven eyes, could not peer into the heart of a man.

"A toast to our English alliance!" Aethelred held up his empty glass. "More ale!"

Lifu fidgeted on her rock, ruffling her wings. This was the moment that mattered most.

Egwina nearly tripped as she hurried forward with a gigantic ox horn. "Ale, Your Majesty."

Aethelred stopped her with a glare. "What is your name, woman?"

"Egwina, Your Majesty."

"I've heard of your medicinal ale. What do you add to it?"

"Hops, Your Majesty."

"Hops," Aethelred repeated disparagingly. "A weedy flower. Is that all?"

"And honey, Your Majesty." She held out the horn to him, smiling stiffly.

"Nothing else?"

"No, Your Majesty."

"Then drink it yourself."

Lifu's bird eyes were quick enough to catch a shadow flash in Egwina's face. But no one else noticed the hesitation.

"Gladly, Your Majesty." Egwina put the horn to her lips and drank.

"All of it," Aethelred said.

Without taking a breath, Egwina tipped the horn further and further back.

"Now stop," Aethelred commanded. "Give the horn to Aelfric."

"To me, sire?" the archbishop asked, surprised.

"You have praised Oxford ale. Tell me how this batch compares."

The archbishop took the half-full horn. He sniffed it. He sampled it with his tongue. Then he took a draught. Finally he handed the horn to Aethelred.

"The hops are bitter, Your Majesty. The honey is sweet. I rather like it."

Aethelred chuckled, looking from Aelfric to Egwina. Then he put the horn to his lips and drank the rest in one go. Ale spilled out either side of his mouth onto the furs of his cloak. He belched and called out, "More ale!"

Lifu hopped from one claw foot to the other. Something was wrong! Egwina was standing like a soldier at attention. She had drunk half the horn. If the ale had contained an entire vial of hemlock juice as planned, her limbs should be numb by now. Her breath should fail. She should be staggering to the ground. Instead she was smiling!

Egwina waited until Aethelred had finished. Then she took the empty horn and walked back across the lawn — proud, tall, and as steady as the rock beneath Lifu's claws.

Lifu flew up in such haste that she lost a feather. She flapped across the palace grounds, squawking. She landed atop a barrel on the brewery wagon. Aelfu was peering around the corner of the wagon, wringing her hands as she watched Egwina slowly walk back. "Egwina! Did he —? Are you —?"

Egwina managed to keep her head high until she had handed the horn to Aelfu. Then she collapsed as if her body had melted and her clothes were empty rags. The shadow of the dead began closing over Egwina's eyes. But Lifu could see her lips forming the words, "My — family — is — avenged."

* * *

Edmund allowed but little time for those at the palace feast to mourn — and the truth was, few were sorry to see Aethelred the Unready dead. His reign had been the longest of any Anglo-Saxon king, and the least popular. Even Archbishop Aelfric, who convulsed for several minutes before stiffening, did not appear to be greatly missed. The pompous cleric had been a greedy lackey to the old king. When the two corpses were laid out on tables, servants made only a half-hearted attempt to shoo away ravens. Skalds later noted that the big black birds seemed unusually eager to peck this particular carrion.

Edmund's investigation into the deaths was swift and brief. Obviously the horn of ale had been poisoned. Egwina, the brewer who had prepared it, was found dead beside her wagon. The woman who had been seen with her had vanished into the crowd.

"Enough! We're wasting time." Edmund grabbed the Bishop of Winchester by the sleeve and dragged him to the dead king's table. "Mumble your Latin. Save his soul if you can."

The prince turned to the crowd. "Silence!" Then he bowed his head as the bishop prayed aloud. At length the bishop made the sign of the cross over Aethelred's crumpled body. "*Requiescat in pace.*"

"Rest in peace," Edmund said.

The crowd repeated, "Rest in peace."

"Now the coronation." Edmund pried loosed the crown that Aethelred had worn jammed almost to his ears. He handed the crown to the bishop. "Go ahead."

The bishop objected, "But that's the duty of the archbishop, Your Majesty."

"He's dead. How long does it take to get another?"

"Another Archbishop of Canterbury? Months, Your Majesty. The appointment would have to come from the Pope in Rome."

"There's no time. Do it."

"Me, Your Majesty? Now? There may be other —"

Edmund put his hand on the hilt of his sword. "You. Now."

The bishop nearly fumbled the crown in his haste to set it on Edmund's head. "For the glory of God and the sake of the country, I declare Edmund Ironside to be King of England. May the —"

"That's enough." Edmund cut him short. He raised his voice to the crowd. "Our country is under attack. At dawn tomorrow our army marches to defeat the invader. I want every able-bodied fighter to assemble at the Westminster gate. Empty the watchtowers. This is our one great chance to end the war." He narrowed his eyes. "In me, Canute will finally find a king who is ready."

* * *

After two days' march across Essex to the River Orwell, Edmund was pleased to find the situation at Assandun exactly as promised. The two hundred ships of the Viking fleet were so poorly guarded that his army had to kill only a few dozen defenders before the rest fled. The

Earl of Southampton wanted to burn the ships, but Edmund chose to leave them as bait.

Meanwhile Eadric positioned his two thousand Mercians out of sight behind a hill to the south. Edmund couldn't help but chuckle at the ealdorman, the only noble in England who insisted on riding a horse to battle. His white pony was so short that Eadric's feet nearly dragged on the ground. But unlike most horses, this one seemed stout enough to carry an armored man and still trot.

Knud's army arrived from the east early the next day. Edmund first noticed a haze of dust. Then there was the glint of sun on metal. The narrowness of Knud's column showed that the Danes had not expected trouble. The column paused, obviously assessing the English army blocking their path to the ships. Then Knud spread his forces to match the English line — exposing his entire south flank to the unseen Mercians.

Edmund strode along the front of his English troops, clanging his shield with his sword. The men roared their allegiance, "Ironside! Ironside!" The white banner of St. George flapped in the breeze. For once, it was the Danes who were unprepared.

"Archers, forward!" Edmund commanded.

A row of bowmen jogged into the field between the armies. They set their stance and sent a volley into the thick of the Danish force.

"Again!" Edmund cried. A second wave of feathered shafts took flight.

"Archers, fall back!" The bowmen jogged back behind the English line, where they quickly traded their bows for heavier steel.

"Men of England!" Edmund called out. "Charge!" He lifted his sword toward the enemy line. But then he held his ground until the English troops had run past him. From a vantage point safely at the rear, surrounded by a score of warriors, Edmund saw that the Viking line had also begun to advance — but not nearly so fast, nor with such angry roars. The two walls of men collided with a crash of metal as loud as the crack of a lightning storm.

Then the hacking began. Axes, halberds, and swords swung as if thousands of men were chopping wood, and not just each other. The two forces were so evenly matched that the line of battle hardly shifted. Edmund judged that the Danes might be willing to fight to a bloody draw. What they wanted most was to reach their ships. But

Edmund had other plans. He closed his eyes and wished a command to someone they could not see. "Wait, Eadric! Wait until the Danes grow weary. Wait until Canute can no longer turn back."

The Earl of Southampton called from the front line, "Where are the Mercians?"

Edmund held up his hand to urge patience. Then he spoke as if to himself, "Let the bodies pile a little higher."

A half dozen berserkers broke through the English line and ran toward Edmund, screaming in their alien tongue. The king didn't flinch, even as his bodyguard cut the attackers down.

"Now, Eadric!" he whispered.

When Edmund looked at the hill to the south the first spear-tips were just beginning to flash above the grassy crest. A small figure on a white English pony trotted out onto the top of the hill.

Edmund couldn't help but laugh. The ealdorman's little horse wouldn't frighten anyone. But his two thousand troops would soon put the Vikings to rout.

When Edmund looked again he had to blink. Was he seeing double? A second white horse had appeared atop the hill. A sheen of blonde hair fell from the helmet of this rider, covering her shoulders in gold. She raised a red banner with the white cross of Denmark. Then she called out in a high voice, "Attack!"

The Mercian army poured over the crest of the hill as planned, spears bristling at the front.

But to Edmund's horror the Mercians did not seem to be angling toward the Viking flank. Instead they were charging directly into the unguarded flank of Edmund's own line.

Treason! Eadric had lied! And who was this shield maiden by his side?

The Mercian spears cut through Edmund's Wessex fighters like a scythe through wheat. When the Earl of Southampton fell Edmund's entire southern flank collapsed, stumbling backwards into the chaos of the English center. The confused battlers there didn't know which way to turn their shields.

A frightened London captain called out, "To the ships, Your Majesty?"

Edmund Ironside quickly weighed his options. Staying to fight two armies at once would be suicide. His usual strategy would have been to retreat to London. But the Mercians now blocked that escape route. Canute's line had no gaps either. That left only the river to the north or the ships to the east.

Could his army make it to the ships in time? Perhaps they would be able to launch a few before they were overrun, but where would they sail? With Wessex and Mercia lost, the only part of England still loyal to the crown was London. His men weren't sailors. Rowing there around Anglia would take a week — and by then Canute would easily have marched overland to capture the city.

Where else could Edmund sail? To Denmark? If he struck off blindly across the North Sea he might not find Denmark at all — and he certainly wouldn't find a welcome.

Normandy ought to have been a safe destination — Edmund's father had always retreated there in times of need. Emma, Aethelred's widow, had powerful family connections among the Normans. But Emma was Edmund's stepmother. When Aethelred abandoned Edmund's English mother, he had promised his new Norman wife that her children would be first in line to the throne. As a result, Edmund's young half-bother in France had a better claim to the crown than he did. If Edmund landed in Normandy, he would be executed. The ships at Assandun offered no route of escape.

"To the river!" Edmund called out, pointing his sword to the north.

"The river, Your Majesty?' the London captain asked doubtfully. The Orwell might be only a stone's throw in width, but it looked deep in the middle. "Few men are strong enough to swim with weapons and armor."

"Then row some ships up as a shuttle. To the river!"

The slaughter that followed on the bank of the River Orwell left Edmund with fewer than four hundred men. Edmund himself had been caught in the leg with an ax as he was climbing a ship's gunwale.

A soldier had crudely bound the wound, but the king was hardly able to walk.

Edmund looked back across the river at the armies that had united against him. London lay helpless, beyond his reach. He needed to raise troops, but how?

"Where next, Your Majesty?" The London captain asked.

"Wales," Edmund said bitterly. "The last retreat of British kings. At least the Welsh will still honor their allegiance."

* * *

A month later Princess Frida arrived in Oxford with thirty men to escort Lifu to peace negotiations in Wales. Edmund had retreated to a fortress by the sea at Deerhurst. The Earl of Southampton was dead, but his chamberlain had managed to conscript two hundred men in Wessex and march them to Wales to aid in the king's defense. Meanwhile Knud, rather than split his army, had ignored London and instead fortified the Welsh border to prevent Edmund from returning. The stalemate had left neither Knud nor Edmund able to rule as king.

"Why do they need me?" Lifu asked as they rode out of Oxford.

"You can write," Frida said.

"Priests can write."

"Not in Norse and English."

The journey to Wales lasted three days. On the final morning they climbed through barren hills to a rock-lined arm of the sea. Knud's army had camped along the east side of the bay, guarding the route to England. Across the choppy gray water the stone walls of Deerhurst Castle rose into a shroud of mist. The white banner of St. George could have been a ghost hovering above a lonely tower.

Eadric met them at the edge of the Danish encampment. He embraced Frida so eagerly that he lifted her off the ground and spun her around. When he finally set Frida down and turned to Lifu, his smile dimmed. "They say your eyes see more than most, Duchess."

"My eyes are are just different colors," Lifu replied. "Is it true that Knud and Edmund are ready to negotiate peace?"

"King Edmund is wounded. He has no army to match the Danes. As for Canute, I think he's simply tired of battle. He suggested you as an intermediary, and Edmund agreed."

"When will they meet?"

"This afternoon, if you're ready." Eadric pointed to a small rocky island in the middle of the bay. "At the chapel of St. Agnes. I'll bring you there by boat. When you ring the chapel's bell Knud and Edmund will row out, unarmed and alone, from either side."

Lifu squinted across the choppy water. Small waves broke on the island's shore. The chapel itself was little more than a square outcrop of the native rock. It was as bleak a spot as the world could offer for a peace treaty.

After a meal of fish and gruel at Eadric's campfire Lifu gathered her writing supplies in a leather satchel. She and Eadric walked down to a cobble beach and untied a two-oar dinghy. Then he rowed her out to the island, helped her ashore, and set back off across the bay.

The air smelled of salt and seaweed. Seagulls cried, circling overhead. Lifu climbed steps that had been chiseled into the granite. The chapel itself was a single stone room with a bedrock floor and two arched windows. There were no benches. A slate slab served as an altar. A rope hung from a hole in the whitewashed ceiling. She pulled the rope, tolling a tinny peal. Then she waited, shivering against the cold.

Knud set out first, rowing the same dinghy Eadric had used. Edmund's boat was larger and slower, bucking the wind. Lifu had heard of the leg wound the king had suffered at Assandun. She wondered how much it had weakened him.

"Hail Lifu, teacher of kings." Knud dragged his rowboat up onto the rock. His white cloak flapped in the wind. He leaned back into the boat and lifted out a gold cross that was nearly as tall as Lifu.

"Fenris," she said, shaking her head. "You were supposed to come alone, Knud."

"Would you have me leave God behind?" He set the cross on the ground. "I've brought no weapon but my faith. Go ahead, see for yourself." He raised his arms.

Lifu hesitated, but then ran her hands along his muscled limbs and body. She stood back and nodded.

Knud picked up his cross. "Today more than ever is a time for prayer." He walked into the chapel, set the cross on the altar, and knelt before it.

Meanwhile Edmund's boat had begun thumping against the rocks. The English king stood stiffly in long chain mail, grimacing as the waves jolted him from side to side. His boat was too heavy to pull up, so Lifu tied it to the back of Knud's dinghy. Edmund swung a stiff leg onto the shore. Saltwater splashed, and he grimaced again. "Is Canute armed?"

"You weren't supposed to wear armor," Lifu admonished.

"I asked if the Dane is armed."

"No, and you must allow me to inspect you as well. Raise your arms."

"I will not."

Lifu scorched him with the glare of her mismatched eyes. "Raise your arms."

Edmund glared back, but he lifted his hands as instructed. His long mail made it difficult for Lifu to check him as thoroughly as she had Knud. When she touched his leg he cried out in pain.

"You wear a splint on your leg," she noted.

"Otherwise I can't walk, you fool. Come, let's get this over with. He limped up to the church but stopped in the doorway. "The heathen is attempting to pray! You Danes change religions as lightly as the Mercians change sides."

Knud stood to face him. "At least I have never broken my word."

"A pirate's word has no worth." Edmund balled his fists.

Lifu stepped between them. "Are we here to fight or make peace?"

Knud sighed. "To make peace, I hope. I have come to offer terms of a truce."

Edmund unclenched his fists. "Let me hear your terms."

"This is better," Lifu said. "Let's get started." She unrolled parchment on the altar. Then she pulled the stopper from a vial of charcoal ink, dipped a quill, and spoke as she wrote, "A treaty between Edmund Ironside of England and Canute of Denmark."

She paused "Should I write it in Norse as well?"

Edmund ignored her, looking instead to Knud. "Your terms?"

Knud laid his hands on the slate of the altar. "Let us be honest. I control the country. You have the crown. I propose that we share them."

"Share my throne? With a Viking? Impossible."

Knud commented, "Danes have shared this island with Saxons for eight generations. Each side has had its own law. If you and I cannot share, perhaps we could divide."

Edmund grumbled, considering this. "It is true that Danes have had their own law since Alfred. Watling Street has long served as a kind of border. I might be willing to grant you sovereignty over the old Danelaw if you would swear never again to trouble my Kingdom of England — Mercia and Wessex."

Knud shook his head. "Mercia is not yours. My cousin Frida is betrothed to Eadric. The Mercians have joined with me. If you and I are to divide the country, it would have to be along the Thames, not Watling Street."

"The Thames! That would give you London!"

"There is no other way. I've seen what you do when you rule London. You use it as a base to raid the countryside. Then you go cower behind the city walls. No, London must be mine. You can choose a new capital in Wessex. Or you can stay here, besieged in a castle in Wales. The choice is yours."

Edmund's fist pounded the altar so hard that the cross jumped. "Damn you! England should never be divided at all!"

"I agree. The island ought to remain whole."

Edmund narrowed his eyes. "In that case, add this to the treaty. As King of England I will rule in Wessex. For the time being you can rule the rest. But whichever of us lives the longest will reunite England and become king of all."

Knud nodded slowly. Then he turned to Lifu. "Write that out. Make a copy in Norse. When we have both affixed our signatures to this treaty it shall be our sacred bond."

Edmund nodded his assent. Then he crossed his arms, standing over Lifu as she wrote out the terms of the agreement on two separate sheets. Knud paced the chapel, peering out one window and then the other as if he feared that a fleet of ships might arrive to catch him off guard.

When Lifu was finished she read both versions aloud. Then she dipped the quill and held it out.

Knud took the feather and signed his name — ᚴᚾᚢᛒ on the Norse version and CANUTE on the English.

"You've studied sorcery?" Edmund asked.

"I have studied writing. I had an able tutor." Knud dipped the quill and handed it to the English king.

Edmund marked a large X on each document, explaining, "It means 'king' in Latin."

"Good enough," Lifu said. "Now, to show that your intentions are honest, shake each other's hands."

"Shake our hands?" Knud asked.

"It's an English custom," Lifu explained. "An open hand shows that you carry no weapon. It proves that you have met in good faith."

Knud held out his right hand. "I think I will like this custom."

"I know I do," Edmund said. But instead of holding out his hand he lifted the edge of his chain mail. He slid a thin knife up from the splint on his leg.

"A hidden blade!" Lifu drew back against the chapel wall. "You are as much a liar as your father."

"But more clever." The sword in Edmund's hand was short, with a flat handle and no pommel. It had fit neatly within the brace of his stiffened leg. "I have just tricked a Danish pirate into signing a contract for his own death."

Knud lifted his chin. "Killing me will bring you no honor."

"Let's try it and see." Edmund swung the sword at Knud's neck. The Dane ducked and lunged against the king's wounded leg. Edmund staggered back in pain. But he kept a firm grip on his sword. With his next swing he managed to slash Knud's shoulder. The Dane writhed backwards, blood welling from a slice in his white cloak.

Edmund prepared to swing his blade two-handed for a death blow.

In that moment Knud grabbed the cross from the altar. Edmund's blade clanged against the gold, inches from Knud's face. The Dane scrambled backward, parrying blow after blow with the heavy cross. He left a bloody trail to the doorway.

Outside Knud managed to stand up, but there was no place to run. Edmund had moved to block the steps to the boats. In all other directions the barren rock ended in cliffs.

Now Edmund advanced, slashing high and low, pounding Knud back toward a granite brink with such ferocity that Knud could scarcely move the cross fast enough to block the blows. At the cliff's edge Edmund raised his blade for a mighty final blow. Knud used the moment to swing his cross low, catching the king's wounded shin with a gold crossbar.

Edmund screamed — a cry of pain that echoed across the bay to the armies waiting on either shore. But still he gripped the sword, completing his swing with angry strength.

Knud rolled aside just in time, leaving the blade to strike sparks from the rock. Then Knud spun to his feet, using his momentum to swing the cross in a broad arc. When the golden crossbar circled back it caught Edmund's sword, wrenching it from his hand.

The blade sailed free, flashing end over end until it sliced into the waves below.

Knud bashed the cross into Edmund's ruined leg, crumpling him to the ground. With the splint torn free, the old gash in his flesh oozed pus and blood. Edmund rocked like a child, tears streaming down his face. "Kill me, you bastard. Steal my crown. The one who dies last wins."

Knud raised the cross for a blow that would batter the king over the edge.

"Wait," Lifu said behind him. "Is this to be the manner of your reign? Lay Fenris aside."

Knud paused, breathing hard. He looked at the dented cross in his hands as if he were seeing it for the first time. Then he stood it on the rock beside him. "My old teacher is right. The true God knows mercy, not vengeance." To Edmund he said, "Go back to your troops. Take

them home as the King of Wessex."

"You —" Edmund wiped his tears with his fist. "You would still honor our treaty?"

"I think the two of us have shaken hands in the customary manner of the English." He turned and walked back into the chapel. When he reappeared in the doorway with one of the parchment scrolls, Lifu held out the golden cross.

"Take Fenris. Destroy it."

Knud accepted the cross, frowning. "I'm not sure evil can ever be destroyed."

"Then what would you do?"

"When I'm crowned in St Paul's I'll have the cross mounted atop the cathedral's spire."

"To prove to the world that you've conquered an empire?" Lifu asked, her voice tinged with sarcasm.

"To prove to the world that evil can be contained." He held out his hand. "Come, I'll row you back to our camp."

Lifu glanced to the cliff edge where Edmund sat clutching his leg. "No. Edmund's wound needs more care than yours. I'll stay to see him to Deerhurst Castle."

Knud shook his head in wonder. "There's always more left to learn from you." Then he took his cross, stowed it in the larger boat, and set off across the bay, rowing through waves.

As soon as Lifu knelt beside Edmund she realized that he was beyond her care. The wound in his lower leg had never been treated properly. Purple streaks from the unclean gash showed that the rot of death had begun spreading toward his heart. Behind the tears in his eyes was a shadow. He had not been battling Knud at all, but rather the fetch that had come to lead him across the darkness to Niflheim.

"Let's go," Lifu said. "I'll row you to the far shore."

Soon, she knew, all of England would be ruled by a Danish king.

CHAPTER 24
NORTHERN GERMANY, 1945

"Two hectares of prime pine forest, reduced to charred stumps." The forester of Niederhausen shook his head, wagging the feather of his green cap.

Walking beside him through the woods was the town's part-time mayor and full-time watch repairman. "Did you find any bodies in the wreckage?"

"After an explosion like that? I couldn't even tell it used to be an airplane. Do you know how much that timber was worth? Where's my compensation?"

"Take it easy, Manfred," the mayor replied. "That plane was headed for City Hall. The pilot turned into the woods at the last minute. Your compensation is that I'm still alive."

"Worse luck. I've been angry ever since you let the Wehrmacht confiscate my truck."

"I didn't —" The mayor cut his own words short. Arguing with a constituent never helped. "Where did you find him?"

"Hanging in a tree. I don't think the parachute had time to open all the way. Branches might have broken his fall a bit, but he's pretty banged up."

"Unconscious?"

"Even after a day. I would have left him in the tree, but Martha insisted I cut him down. Now what are we supposed to do? Shoot him? Put him in prison?"

"I dont know. All our policemen were conscripted." The last thing Niederhausen needed was a prisoner.

They came to a small log cabin where the forester stored equipment. "Marthe?" The forester called out, "I've brought company."

A middle-aged woman with a pretty face and a kerchief over her brown hair opened the door. "Oh! Mayor Wandelhut. And here I've worn my old smock."

"You're a vision." The mayor gave her the warm smile that had won him so many votes. "I've come to see what you've found in the woods."

"Oh yes, the airman." She led them to a cot where a pilot in a leather flight jacket lay as if for a nap. His pants were torn and his jacket was scratched, but the forester's wife had carefully washed his face and combed his hair.

"He looks so familiar," she said, blushing slightly. "So nice."

"Yes, I see." The mayor studied the man's pencil mustache, high cheekbones, and slicked-back black hair. He too felt that he had seen that strikingly handsome face somewhere before. The he noticed a torn label above the pilot's pocket: MAJOR G—

"*Gott im Himmel,*" the mayor breathed. "This is Clark Gable, the American actor."

The forester's wife clapped a hand to her mouth. "Wasn't he the one in that movie about the American Civil War?"

The forester frowned. "What's an actor doing hanging in my pines?"

"It was in the newsreels," the mayor said. "Clark Gable joined the American Air Force to fly a bomber. The whole thing was a propaganda stunt. But Hitler's offering a reward."

"A reward?" The forester examined the pilot with renewed interest.

"That's what I heard." The mayor leaned to the pilot's ear. "Major Gable? Is that you?"

When the pilot didn't respond the forester slapped the American in the face. "Hey! Gable! Wake up!"

Julius rolled his head, mumbling with his eyes closed.

"He's talking in American." Marthe looked to the mayor. "Can you understand him?"

The mayor shook his head. He decided it might help if he shouted in German. "Is that you, Major Gable!?"

Julius groaned. A loud German voice was drifting through the fog. Somehow he managed to pull a German reply out of the clouds in his head. "That's what they call me."

Marthe gasped. "It's really him!"

"And he speaks German," the mayor marveled.

The forester leaned closer and shouted, "Is it true that Hitler is offering a reward for you?"

The fog cleared enough that dark memories were starting to return. Julius groaned again. "Hitler's short of cash these days."

The forester exchanged a knowing glance with the mayor. The news from Berlin had gotten worse day by day.

Julius opened his eyes. He was in a log cabin. He must have been thrown free from the *Lucky Lady*. Three German civilians were leaning over him with worried faces.

"Hollywood," he said.

"Yes?" the mayor asked.

"My director will pay you double whatever Hitler offers."

"Double!" The forester narrowed his eyes. "How can we be sure?"

Julius hurt all over. "Word of honor. *Reichsmarks* or dollars, your choice."

"When?"

Julius knew he would somehow have to keep even this promise. "Give me thirty days, OK?"

The forester's wife said, "He saved our town."

While the mayor and the forester argued about what to do, Julius gave the forester's wife a Clark Gable wink that made her blush.

* * *

Heinrich Müller was the Nazi no one noticed. Flying to Hedeby he imagined that he was one of Odin's ravens, the birds that noticed everything.

For years Müller had been the secret eyes and ears of the Reich. An aircraft mechanic and Munich policeman, he had worked his way up the ranks of the National Socialist German Workers' Party to become Himmler's right-hand general, in charge of the entire Gestapo. But Heinrich Müller was such a common name, and he was so nearly invisible, that he might as well have been a black bird peering out from behind Adolf Hitler's shoulder.

Below his fighter plane the last innocent remnant of the Reich rolled past like a green map — fields, forests, and little villages where life went on as it had for centuries. Behind him, the commander of Berlin's defenses was surrendering to the Red Army. Soviet tanks were rolling toward the Brandenburg Gate to hoist the hammer and sickle over the ruins of the Reichstag. Russian troops had already met American forces on the Elbe, pinching Germany in half. Everyone knew what the Russians did with prisoners. And yet it seemed that no one else on Hitler's senior staff had thought out a plan of escape.

Through the propeller blur Müller could see the blue of the Baltic. He banked left, following the white stripe of coast until he found what he was looking for — a ludicrously rocket-shaped water tower and a lonely little airstrip. He circled it twice, pleased to see that the people there had assembled in formation as instructed. Then he swung in low, bumped the tires with a screech of rubber, and taxied through the weeds in the pavement.

As soon as Müller opened the cowling he saw a colonel stumbling forward, his hat blown off by the prop wash, attempting to give a Hitler salute as he jogged along.

"*Willkommen*, Herr General!" the colonel shouted.

The engine coughed and died, allowing the propeller to stutter to a stop. Müller stepped out onto the wing and jumped to the ground. Then he brushed the dust from his long black coat. "Everything ready, Colonel?"

"Yes sir." Franz Wedel glanced about for his hat, smiling awkwardly. "We're all packed. The staff car is waiting. Do you have much luggage of your own, sir?"

"Two small boxes at the back of the cockpit."

"No problem, sir." Wedel motioned for two young Austrian guards to start loading the cases from the plane onto the truck. "We've prepared a little presentation in honor of your visit to our excavation."

"I don't like presentations."

Wedel reddened. "It's the sword, sir."

"The Viking sword?" Müller narrowed his eyes. When he interrogated people, his piercing gray-blue gaze was often all they remembered.

Wedel waved for Henrik to step forward with a black case. "This is our excavation director, Henrik Rasmussen. He'll be coming with us today."

Henrik opened the lid, revealing a pock-marked sword with a broken tip.

The general lifted out the relic. He turned it admiringly in his hands. "Yes. The etchings are eroded, but the runes are clear. If only we'd had this with us from the start. The wolf god is said to win empires."

Mette spoke quietly from the front row of onlookers. "At a cost."

The Gestapo general appeared not to have heard. He tucked the ancient blade under his arm and looked to the staff car, a black Mercedes convertible. Soldiers were struggling to lift the wooden boxes into the trunk. Although the boxes were small, they seemed astonishingly heavy.

"Good, then let's go," Müller said.

"What should I tell the workers, sir?" Wedel asked.

The general surveyed the rows of people. "Who are they?"

"We have eighty Polish prisoners, sir. And seven Danish archeologists."

"Tell the Danes to go home." Müller waved his hand as if to shoo them away. "As for the Poles, they can go to hell."

Wedel asked, nonplussed, "You'd shoot the prisoners, sir?"

"Worse. Send them back through the Russian lines." The Gestapo general climbed into the passenger side of the open-topped Mercedes. "Who's driving?"

Mette volunteered. If her suspicion was correct, she would be driving back alone. And sure enough, when Henrik and the colonel got into the back seat, they told her to drive to the Schleswig docks.

Colonel Wedel stood in the back seat to give the Austrian sergeant his orders. "Set the Polish prisoners free, Sergeant. You're in charge now. Heil Hitler!"

Mette jolted the car into first gear. Wedel caught himself by grabbing the backrest with the outstretched arm of his Hitler salute.

As soon as they were on the road to Schleswig, General Müller leaned back and said, "Rest your arm, Colonel. The Austrian house painter is dead."

Wedel frowned, obviously confused.

"The unemployed draft dodger," the general said. "I was in the Berlin bunker two days ago when he married Eva Braun. The next morning she bit a cyanide capsule. He shot himself in the head."

"Hitler is dead?"

"The Red Army was so close you could smell the borscht. Göring and I burned the bodies in a crater in the chancellery garden. When Göring went back to poison his own kids I figured it was time to go."

"Then who is leading the Reich?"

The general laughed. "Admiral Dönitz, a dimwit in Flensburg. What's left under his control is here on the Danish border. Fortunately, I've requisitioned the best remaining submarine. Anyone who's clever will be there."

Henrik straightened his bow tie. "Where are we going? To Brazil?"

"It's tricky getting through the Kattegat," the general admitted. "Sweden's neutral, but not all that friendly. We may have to head for Finland. The Russians wanted to annex them. Their country's a boggy icebox, but they owe us for saving it."

Nothing more was said until they reached the waterfront. Half a dozen other black Mercedes had parked by the gangplank to U-271, a submarine with a swastika banner. General Müller insisted they carry his boxes out first. Wedel tried and failed to lift one, so Henrik had to make two trips.

"What's in there, gold?" Wedel asked.

The general looked at him coolly. "What is your name, Colonel?"

"Wedel, sir. Franz Wedel."

"You're a professor, am I right?"

"Yes, sir. I teach history at the University of Vienna. That's why you chose me for the excavation."

"No, Wedel. I chose you because you are an idiot. And that was my mistake."

"I found you the sword of the Vikings!"

"Yes, but you failed at your primary task."

"I'm sorry, sir. I don't understand how the Allies discovered the V3 rocket site."

"There is no such thing as a V3 rocket. We had a fuel depot at

Gammeltorp and manufactured rocket parts there." The Gestapo smiled with half of his mouth. "In a way it was a decoy too, like your excavation."

"A decoy?"

"Yes. A distraction for today, so that the Reich will survive to rise again."

Wedel brightened. "I'll fetch my baggage."

"Don't bother. It's a small ship." Müller pulled out his service pistol and fired a shot into Wedel's chest. The colonel buckled backwards. His eyes glazed and he collapsed onto the ground.

"Would anyone else like to join the colonel?" Müller asked, waving his pistol toward Henrik and Mette. "I thought not." He turned to walk up the gangplank.

As soon as the general was gone Henrik rushed to Wedel's side. "My God, he's dead." Henrik hugged the body for a moment. Then he unlatched the holster at Wedel's hip and took out the Luger. "Mette! You've got to help me."

Mette sounded more tired than scared. "Why, Henrik? Why would I want to help?"

"The Germans have left me high and dry. Now I'll be marked for liquidation by the Danish underground. They'll kill me."

"Right. And what would you have me do about it?

"Give me a chance," Henrik said. "The same chance as the Danish Jews. Just a chance."

Mette weighed the Mercedes keys in her hand.

*　*　*

Julius traveled at night, mostly through the woods. The forester's wife had given him a loaf of bread, but it had only lasted for the first few days. Every noise gave him a shot of fear — the snap of a branch, the crunch of leaves. Often it was nothing more than a hedgehog rooting for insects in the duff. But on the ninth day, when a full moon filtered silver shadows among the tree trunks, he heard the tramp of an army.

Julius pressed himself behind a tree, scarcely daring to breathe. The sound grew louder — hundreds of footfalls and the mumbles of men. Who would be marching through the woods at night? A search party would have lights. He'd come so far from Niederhausen that he must be close!

Suprisingly the voices weren't German. They weren't English either. Were they Russian? Julius couldn't help but shiver. And then they were all around him, trudging past with ragtag backpacks and frightened eyes. A man cried out. They retreated, crouching. For a moment Julius considered trying to run. Then someone struck a match.

A beardless man with a worker's cap advanced toward him cautiously. The man examined Julius' flight uniform in amazement. "*Amerykański?*"

Julius swallowed hard, but managed to nod.

The beardless man held up his hands. "We surrender."

* * *

They were Poles, Julius learned as they sat together in the dark forest, sharing food and water. They had spent five years as prisoners of war, working at Hedeby. That afternoon a fighter plane had arrived with a general from Berlin, and everything had changed. The Austrian soldiers had buried their Nazi uniforms in an excavation pit. Before bicycling away to the south, the Austrians had told the prisoners that they were free. They could take whatever supplies they wanted and walk home to Poland. Meanwhile, the six remaining Danish archeologists had packed a few things into two of the excavation's sailboats. But instead of shuttling out to the Viking shipwreck as usual, they had continued past it, apparently intending to cross twenty kilometers of sea to the nearest Danish island.

"Was the director of the excavation with them?" Julius asked. "Mette Andersen?"

No, apparently Fru Andersen had been replaced as director a week earlier, after the air raid. The new leader was Henrik Rasmussen, a Dane who had secretly been serving the Gestapo for years. Rasmussen, Colonel Wedel, and the Berlin general had left in a staff car with Fru Andersen. No one knew where they had gone. The Polish men had been the last to leave Hedeby. The place was a ghost town.

* * *

The moon was high when Julius emerged from the forest at the Danevirke wall. He was thinking about the ghosts of Hedeby. Moonlight plated the fields with silver. The abandoned barracks looked like models in a diorama display. Mette had worked here for the duration of the war, trying to bring life back to a dead Viking city. He had promised to find her, and he had failed. Along the way he had been through hell. He no longer knew where to turn.

And then a light flickered in the distance near the bay. Just a small light, moving erratically. Julius wondered: Could there already be looters? The archeologists had left all of Hedeby unguarded.

Julius limped down from the earthen wall and made his way past excavation pits on a dirt track toward the sound of waves. This wasn't his job. He was an unarmed foreign pilot, as likely to be arrested himself as to frighten a thief. But the thought of Mette, and her years of dedicated work, kept him walking.

And sure enough, as he got closer he could make out two figures on a dock, loading something onto a small sailboat. Or no — only one of the figures was actually loading the boat. The other was supervising, with a flashlight in one hand and something else in the other. A gun?

Obviously they were looters. But there was something familiar about the man with the flashlight. Julius crept up behind a stack of planks. The man was wearing a bow tie. When he stooped to untie the boat's mooring rope the moonlight caught the man's face.

Julius nearly gasped aloud. Henrik! Julius remembered him as the assistant who had overseen the National Museum's Christmas party. If what the Polish prisoners said was true, Henrik had been a Gestapo collaborator all along. And now he'd returned as a looter?

"That's all of it." A woman's voice made Julius' heart leap. Mette! Henrik must have forced her to load the boat.

Without thinking Julius grabbed a plank and ran forward, using the board as a shield. A shot blazed wild in the dark. Julius swung the plank, catching Henrik's arm. Julius tripped and both men went down, sprawling on the dock. Something splashed into the water. Henrik was the first to his feet. He kicked Julius in the ribs. When Julius looked up Henrik kicked him hard in the face. Julius's head flopped backwards against the dock. He lay on his side, groaning.

"Julius Gustmeyer," Henrik said, standing over him. "You've always been in my way, turning up when you're least wanted. For years I've wished for the chance to kill you. Now, finally, I —"

An oar whacked Henrik in the side of the head, cutting his words short.

Behind him on the dock, Mette prepared to swing the oar even harder.

The first blow had staggered Henrik to one knee. He looked about at the crazed woman wielding an oar and sprang off the dock onto the prow of the boat. The oar whistled through the air above him. It twanged off the cable securing the mast to the prow.

Mette dropped the oar. "Julius! Is it really you? You're hurt! How —"

Julius raised himself to one elbow. Blood dripped from his nose. "You've got — to stop him —"

Henrik had already pushed the boat far enough away from the dock that it could only be reached by jumping. She shook her head. "No. Let him go."

"Let him go? He betrayed us all — the Jews, the Danes. He even betrayed your excavation."

"I know. He's a traitor. There's really nowhere for him now."

"Then why — ?" Julius didn't know how to finish the question. The sailboat with Henrik was drifting away on the night's breeze.

Mette let out a tired breath. "Even when wars end, the hating never completely disappears. All we can do is try to contain it."

Julius stared at her. "Amazing."

"Do you mean that in a good way?"

"I hurt too much to decide."

She took a handkerchief from the pocket of her dress. "Let me just clean you up a bit so I can kiss you properly. Then you can make up your mind."

* * *

Two days later a khaki Land Rover roared up to the front of Hedeby's main building in a cloud of dust. A British sergeant stepped out on the driver's side, eyeing the two people on the building's front step suspiciously. Major Lars Andersen got out on the other side, put his hands on his hips, and laughed.

"Gable! When I heard your plane went down I should have known I'd find you here, shacked up with my sister."

For a moment Mette and Julius just stood there open-mouthed. Then she rushed up and threw her arms around her brother. "Lars! How on earth did you —?"

"Take it easy, sis. I'm on loan to the Brits." He stroked her hair and looked up at Julius. "Hey, don't get jealous. I met her first."

Julius tipped back his officer's cap. "So it's true? The war's over?"

"In Europe anyway. General Montgomery's leading a parade into Copenhagen today. Danes are going nuts. Germans are walking home

CHAPTER 24 ~ 1945

with their tails between their legs. I asked if I could slip out to check on my sister's pet project. When the hell did you get here, Gable?"

"Just recently. I was —" he hesitated, "— hung up for a while."

"I thought you had a big operation here, sis. Where's everybody else?"

Mette's smile faded. She told him what had happened after the general had arrived from Berlin.

"Sounds like Gestapo Müller," Lars said. "Clever and deadly. One of the top dogs we haven't tracked down. Bombers with depth charges are scouting for subs, though, so we might nail him yet."

"What about Henrik Rasmussen?" Julius asked.

"Finding one guy in a little sailboat? Tricky. It'd take him days to get to Sweden, and weeks to reach Finland. What about you two? Why are you still hanging around?"

"We've been closing up the excavation," Mette explained. "I've locked up most finds in the laboratory. The wooden fragments of the Viking ship are soaking in tubs. It will all have to be guarded until I can get another team back here."

Lars chewed as if on a tough piece of meat while he considered this. "You need a rest, sis. I'll assign a few guys to watch the place. Go home. Tell our parents we're OK."

"How? In a Nazi staff car?" She pointed to the black Mercedes beside the building.

"Naw, we can use that here." Then, seemingly without reason, Lars started to laugh.

"What?"

"Well, what we really need is a pilot who can fly a Fokker to an airport that isn't shot up. Hamburg's toast, but Copenhagen would do." He raised an eyebrow. "Any volunteers?"

* * *

Denmark is a small country, especially when seen from the air. The Jutland peninsula resembles an elf with a pointy cap and a sly grin. Zealand looks like an elvish girl with kissy lips. With a little imagination, the archipelago of green islands between them becomes a wide-eyed child, surrounded by toys for Yule. From that height the country is a happy, quirky family full of *hygge*. It seems impossible that this minuscule elven home could have launched a Viking invasion to conquer England. Or that, a thousand years later, the little country could have defied the Nazi Reich, sidestepping the Holocaust.

Julius banked the fighter plane above the spires of Copenhagen. The streets below were full of crowds. People pointed to the sky in wild delight.

Mette smiled. She had always had an artistic bent. All it had taken was a little paint, adding red rectangles to the corners of the white swastikas, to turn each of the Fokker's insignias into a *Dannebrog*.

The first fighter of the Danish Air Force was coming home.

EPILOGUE
LONDON, 1947

The old woman wore dark glasses, even on a day of low gray clouds, so as not to alarm the tourists. People could be disconcerted that one of her eyes was dark green and the other bright blue.

A chipper young guide with bobbed red hair and a tartan skirt waved her hands, gathering the group on the church steps. "Welcome to St. Paul's Cathedral, everyone! Stay close please, if you're with the 10:30 tour."

A baby fussed. Mette bobbed in place, a little dance that made the infant at her shoulder burp. "Maybe this wasn't such a good idea."

"Nonsense. You've been wanting to see where Knud was crowned." Julius held a baby bottle under his arm to keep it warm. "I'll escape with Helen if need be."

"This is thought to be the fifth St. Paul's built here, on the tallest hill in London," the tour guide said, almost shouting to be heard over traffic noise. "The third cathedral, which saw the coronation of both of Aethelred the Unready and Canute, was destroyed by fire in 1087 and rebuilt by the Normans."

"Canute?" A man asked. "Wasn't he the crazy king who put his throne on the beach, imagining he could defy the rising tide?"

"That's right," the tour guide laughed.

"No it's not!" Mette objected, unable to stop herself. "That's a story invented later by jealous English clerics. Canute the Great ruled in peace for nineteen years, uniting England with Scandinavia. He brought law and democracy to Britain."

"Well!" The tour guide held up her palms like a traffic cop. "Apologies if you know better. As I was saying, Canute donated a gold cross, the only part of the third church to survive the 1087 fire.

When Christopher Wren designed the current building after the Great Fire of London in 1666 he mounted the cross atop the west facade." She pointed up. All heads turned to look at a small gold cross on a stone gable.

"When the German Blitz left London in ruins, the cross and the dome rose shining above the smoke unscathed, as if protected by a greater power. The one bomb that struck the church failed to explode. Throughout the recent war, St. Paul's stood as a symbol of English defiance."

This time the voice that spoke up was quieter, and wavering. "A symbol of evil, I suspect."

Not everyone heard the remark, but Mette studied the old woman with dark glasses. "Why would you say that?"

"Fakes were forged," the woman muttered. "The sword in that cross is nothing. Where is yours?"

"I'm sorry?"

The old woman shook her head. "I'm tired. But how can I rest?" She took off her glasses, revealing strangely mismatched eyes of blue and green. "You and your damned work are going to make me start all over again."

AUTHOR'S NOTE

While it would be inappropriate to include footnotes in any historical novel, readers may be interested to know which portions of *The Ship in the Sand* are historical and which are novel.

In the Viking-age chapters, I have tried to describe the Danish and English kings, their families, and their exploits accurately. Lifu and most other characters from that era are fictional.

Throughout the book, Karen Sullivan's pen-and-ink illustrations depict actual Viking artifacts, many of them discovered in Jelling or Hedeby.

I have attempted to portray the role of Denmark in World War II, the rescue of the Danish Jews, and the escape of Niels Bohr with reasonable historical authenticity, although I admit to inventing many characters and situations along the way. The Gustmeyers described in the book are fictional, for example, although the Gustmeyer house and the Carlsberg mansion are real. The Carlsberg mansion had a beer tap in the dining room, Niels Bohr dissolved his gold medals to hide them from the Nazis, and Greta Garbo telephoned the King of Sweden to help Niels Bohr.

On the day of Denmark's occupation by the Nazis, April 9, 1940, a German warship docked in Copenhagen at 4:20 a.m. as described. Troops captured key points of the city within minutes. For dramatic purposes I have King Christian X announce Denmark's surrender at the Amalienborg palace, when in fact his statement was read in a Danish radio broadcast at 6:05 a.m. that morning. The latter half of the statement is a translation of the king's words. The first portion is based on an accompanying statement by the Danish prime minister.

During the occupation, the Danish king often rode his horse through the city streets to bolster citizens' spirits. But Mette was right to question whether the king would also wear a Jewish star to frustrate the Nazis' pogroms. That was a fiction invented by Leon Uris in his 1958 novel *Exodus*. The Danish resistance movement remained small and disorganized until the Danish government resigned in August 1943.

Liberties have been taken with the archeological work at Jelling and Hedeby in order to align those stories with the book's timeline. Jelling was excavated in 1704, 1820, 1861, and 1941, when Danish archeologist Ejnar Dyggve dissected Gorm's mound and P.V. Glob proposed that the entire monument area had been laid out in the shape of a gigantic ship. An excavation of the north mound in 1976 supported this supposition, and measurements in 1992 confirmed it. The rune stones at Jelling were protected by glass enclosures in 2012. The remains of Gorm the Old have been reburied in the stone church beneath a runic symbol in the floor tiles. The runic alphabet described in the text is the one used in Jelling's famous inscriptions.

The chess pieces Lifu designs resemble the Lewis Chessmen, a cache of seventy-eight pieces found on the Isle of Lewis in Scotland in 1831. Manufactured in Scandinavia between 1050 and 1150 AD, the pieces are on display on the Isle of Lewis, in the National Museum in Edinburgh, and in the British Museum in London.

Lifu adds hops to ale for medicinal purposes. The earliest documentation of this innovation is by Hildegard von Bingen, a German abbess in the 1100s who also used prophetic visions to become influential. In one of Lifu's visions she imagines the original Danish flag, *Dannebrog*, with a white cross on a red background. Later she suggests its opposite, St. George's cross, for the English flag. According to legend the Dannebrog fell from the sky during a Danish battle in Estonia in 1219. However, both crosses were used in 1189 to identify English and Norman French Crusaders, so the banners must be older.

Knud (Canute the Great) reigned as King of England from 1016 to 1035. To simplify the chronology, I do not mention that Knud's older brother Harald became King of Denmark on Svein's death in 1014. When Knud was driven out of England in 1014 he suggested that Harald share the Danish throne with him. Harald refused, but he did help Knud raise troops to invade England in 1016. After Harald died in 1018 Knud became King of Denmark as well as England. Knud soon added Norway and part of Sweden to his realm. His Empire of the North Sea fell apart after his death. England succumbed to a violent invasion by the Norman French in 1066, ending Anglo-Saxon and Danish rule.

Bluetooth is known today as a standardized technology for the wireless linkage of computer devices. The name was chosen in 1996 by leaders of Intel, the Swedish company Ericsson, and the Finnish company Nokia because Harald Bluetooth had united much of Scandinavia—an earlier linkage. The Bluetooth symbol is a combination of the H and B runes in his name.

Hedeby, known today as Haithabu in Germany, was abandoned after its destruction by a Slavic army in 1066. Its rediscovery in 1900 aroused interest because the site had been relatively undisturbed. Excavations in 1900-1915 and 1930-1939 revealed the layout of the Viking town with its harbor and semicircular Danevirke wall.

In 1959, archaeological work at Hedeby led to the discovery of the largest known Viking warship in the muddy sand of the bay. In 2005 the museum at Hedeby began constructing replicas of Viking houses, walkways, and docks. To date, only five percent of the settlement has been excavated. Recent research has revealed the existence of Sliasthorp, a Viking military base on an island across the fjord from Hedeby.

Details about the training and service of B-17 pilots are from *To Elsie With Love*, a book by my father, J. Wesley Sullivan, a B-17 co-pilot. As for Clark Gable, the actor did serve on a B-17 crew at the Polebrook airfield near Oundle, England during World War II, and Hitler did offer a reward for his capture. The bombing raid on a supposed missile site near Hedeby, however, is fictional. Some Nazi leaders successfully escaped by submarine. "Gestapo" Heinrich Müller is the most senior Nazi whose fate remains unknown.

Today twenty thousand ethnic Danes live in Schleswig, Germany's northernmost region, maintaining their culture, language, and schools, and supporting the museum at Hedeby/Haithabu.

Archeologists do not know where the English Danelaw's Thing parliament met, but it could have been near Oundle. Excavations in Oxford have uncovered the skeletons of Danes slaughtered in the St. Brice's Day Massacre. Svein Forkbeard's sister Gunhild was reported to be among the slain, but the body of the murdered Danish princess has never been positively identified.

WILLIAM L. SULLIVAN

The author of six novels and more than a dozen nonfiction books, Sullivan grew up in Salem, Oregon. He completed his B.A. degree in English at Cornell University under Alison Lurie, studied linguistics at Germany's Heidelberg University, and earned an M.A. in German at the University of Oregon. He reads in a dozen languages, including Danish, Norwegian, and Old Norse. He undertook nine voyages to Scandinavia while researching Nordic sagas and Viking history for *The Ship in the Hill* and its sequel, *The Ship in the Sand*.

Listening for Coyote, Sullivan's journal of a thousand-mile hike across Oregon's wilderness, was chosen by the Oregon Cultural Heritage Commission as one of Oregon's "100 Books," the most significant books in Oregon history. Summers he writes at the log cabin that he and his wife Janell Sorensen built by hand in the wilds of Oregon's Coast Range, more than a mile from roads, electricity, and telephones. The rest of the year they live in Eugene, Oregon, where he volunteers to promote libraries and literature.

A list of Sullivan's books, speaking engagements, audio books, and favorite adventures is at *www.oregonhiking.com*.

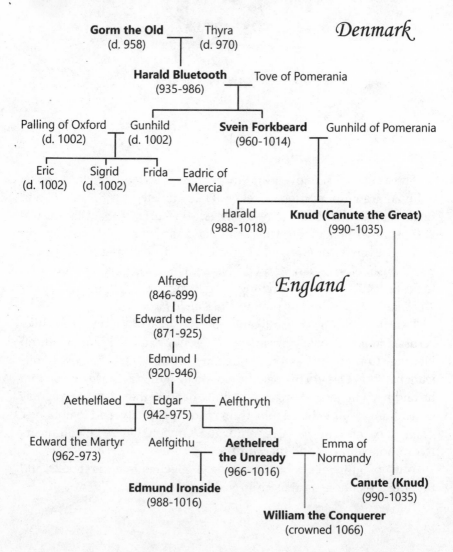

The Royal Lines of Denmark and England
in the Viking Age

Denmark

Gorm the Old (d. 958) — Thyra (d. 970)

Harald Bluetooth (935-986) — Tove of Pomerania

Palling of Oxford (d. 1002) — Gunhild (d. 1002)

Svein Forkbeard (960-1014) — Gunhild of Pomerania

Eric (d. 1002)

Sigrid (d. 1002)

Frida — Eadric of Mercia

Harald (988-1018)

Knud (Canute the Great) (990-1035)

England

Alfred (846-899)

Edward the Elder (871-925)

Edmund I (920-946)

Aethelflaed — Edgar (942-975) — Aelfthryth

Edward the Martyr (962-973)

Aelfgithu

Aethelred the Unready (966-1016) — Emma of Normandy

Edmund Ironside (988-1016)

William the Conquerer (crowned 1066)

Canute (Knud) (990-1035)